EX LEBRES

The Walpins

No Time
For Tears

Also by CYNTHIA FREEMAN:

A World Full of Strangers
Fairytales
The Days of Winter
Portraits
Come Pour the Wine

No Time For

ARBOR HOUSE

NEW YORK

Tears

A NOVEL BY
CYNTHIA FREEMAN

*To my publisher and dear friend, Don Fine, whom
I wish to thank for making Arbor House home to me, and
may the light in the window always burn brightly.*

Russia
1905

Chapter One

WINTER WAS A time to be feared. It meant hunger and idleness. It came upon them like a plague, a punishment meted out for all their sins of five thousand years. Would God ever forgive them? In time—in time, even if man never would.

The torrential rain that had persisted for the past five days left deep crevices in the earth, leaving in its wake a river of mud that would not dry till spring. Soon the snows of winter would come and freeze the mud to ice. But finally and mercifully, the elements had given them a reprieve. The heavens now rested, the rain had stopped. And now the small village which lay south of Odessa slept.

Huddled together, they lay on floor mats, this human fodder, close to the tile oven. What could not comfort their empty stomachs, they found in the closeness of one another. Silhouetted against the threatening sky, billows of black smoke arose from the chimneys and spiraled upward. The village lay in darkness except for the kerosene lamp that burned dimly inside the Rabinsky house.

It had been this way since the rains had come and gone. But sixteen-year-old Chavala, the eldest of five children, had little time to concern herself with what happened beyond the confines of the three rooms that were home to them. The past days and nights had been lived in torment as she watched her mother lay in the agony of childbirth. She spent her time between the small bedroom and kitchen where the cauldron of water boiled constantly. As she tore the sheets apart, she railed at the elements that caused Leah, the midwife, to lay in her cold bed with pleurisy and a hacking cold so violent that now she was coughing up blood.

13

It was a terrifying scream that made her forget Leah and hurry back to the side of her mother.

"Chavala," her mother said, barely able to form the words, "how are the others?"

Chavala took her mother's hand in hers and held it gently. She had not seen nor heard from her brother, Moishe, nor her three sisters, Sheine, Raizel and Dvora, since she had sent them along with papa to Mrs. Greenblatt's, who lived at the furthest end of the village. Chavala wanted to spare them the sight she now witnessed. "The children are fine. For them you needn't worry."

Her mother screamed again and lay back prostrate, drenched with perspiration.

Chavala's own breathing was labored with fear, the silent voice within her whispered, "God, dear God, help us, I beg you. I plead with you." And God must have heard. After five agonizing days, Chavala's mother emptied her womb of a child she had conceived in her fiftieth year.

Quickly, Chavala cut the cord, took the tiny infant out of the veil of placenta, held it upside down and spanked it into life. But no cry was heard. Again, she spanked it. This time harder, still not a murmur. Almost frantically, Chavala called out, "Cry . . . CRY!" But not a sound was heard, although Chavala felt the faint heartbeat and heard the shallow, slow breathing. It sounded as though any moment it might stop. "Live, do you hear . . . LIVE!" Putting her mouth to the child's, she tried breathing life into it. Still there was no sound. Chavala looked from the child to the mother and saw that the eyes were closed and the head lay lifelessly to one side. She stood in utter disbelief, but her mother was gone. She should have wailed and beat her breast and berated God and wept, but there was no time for tears, as she felt the near-lifeless body of the new babe in her arms.

Quickly, she ran to the kitchen and immersed the infant, first in a tub of water just hot enough for the child to endure, and then in cold . . . until at last, at long last, a new cry was heard in the world. Holding the red, scrawny babe in her hands, she looked down at the wrinkled face, then brought the emaciated body to her breast. "You are mine . . . you were given unto my keeping . . . little Chia . . . mama's life will be lived through you." As she wrapped the child in a warm blanket, Chavala looked up to see her father framed in the doorway. His eyes were red and swollen. She had not heard him enter the house, but from the look of agony on his face he must have seen mama.

Heavily, he sat down at the kitchen table. "I should not have listened to you, Chavala. It was my place to be here."

Her heart went out to him. He had lived through so much pain and joy with his beloved . . . He had married Rivka when both were seventeen. They had been childless for so long and then a miracle came into their lives when Chavala was born. Afterward, two years apart, each of the other children had come—a succession of miracles. Papa was such a good man, kind, pious. His great concern was that he could not provide a better living for them . . . that burned deep in him. But what he could not give them in worldly goods he made up for in his love for them. After all, did miracles deserve less?

Now, in her hope to spare him, Chavala had sent him away. And the decision fell heavily on her. "I know, papa . . . but I thought the others needed you."

"Oh, Chavala . . . my place was here."

Swallowing hard, she looked at her father in this moment of bereavement and anguish. "The sin, if any, is mine, papa."

"No, it is mine . . . I should have stayed. I should have been stronger than you and not allowed you to send me away. She was my wife . . . my *life*. May God forgive me, I could at least have held her hand as she passed into the valley of . . ." He could not finish the rest of the prayer. Instead he recited it silently as the tears came from his eyes. Chavala wept too, silently, but at this moment she was afraid of her emotions. Should she for one moment allow herself to let go, it would become impossible to rise above her bereavement. She had to be the strong one. So much and so many depended upon her. Let her father have the blessed release of grief. It was the only solace left for him. All the failures of his life were descending upon him. From his earliest beginnings, his one longing had been to be a rabbi, to devote his life to the service of God and to live in peace in the land of his forefathers, Eretz Yisroel. Each time a *landsman* went to Palestine he pleaded with him to send back a handful of earth. They were his greatest possessions, these tiny bags of ancient dirt from Eretz Yisroel. But life had denied him, deprived him of his dreams. Instead he became the village *shochet,* a job he did not enjoy, but one was not meant to enjoy his labor nor to question the will of God. Avrum Rabinsky was obliged to accept his lot in life. He set aside his longings and made a meager living for his family. Now, his Rivka had been taken from him and *that* was too much for him to bear. Yet even now in his grief he did not ask God why, but something inside him was broken beyond repair. Somehow, when he needed the strength of his faith he could not call upon the Almighty to bind his wounds. He admonished himself, his head bowed in shame and guilt. The confusions in his mind were written on his face, so it was not difficult for Chavala to read what was in his heart. He cried from the depths. She placed the newborn in his arms, hoping that she would help, but for a moment he was reluctant to take the child. She was too painful a reminder of his loss. Then, slowly, he took the infant and held it close while swallowing the tears that ran into his mouth.

"Papa," Chavala said softly, "the baby must be fed. I'll go and bring back Manya."

He sat looking down at the small motherless creature. She would be nurtured on the milk of another's breast. She would never know the love and comfort of a mother's lullaby sung while the child suckled in quiet contentment. This one would be fed and Manya would receive her few *kopeks.* Love was not what she was being paid for—quickly he berated himself. God was all-knowing and not to be questioned. God knew all and man's life was predestined from the cradle to the grave. Avrum Rabinsky should have praised God that he had been provided such as Manya. Without her the child would also die . . .

Putting on the shawl Chavala passed the open door to where her mother's lifeless body lay. The still body was now covered from head to toe with a stained sheet. Chavala swallowed hard to fight back the tears, closed the door and quickly rushed out into the cold early morning. For a moment she steadied herself against the wooden porch rail, breathing hard so as not to faint. Regaining her composure, she stepped down into the mud.

From across the road Dovid Landau sat at his cobbler's bench and watched through the window as Chavala tried to move forward, laboriously lifting one foot, then the other. Why did he love her so? She'd always been so distant, so aloof. He would have imagined Chavala would have shown some gratitude after he had added the small room where she could do her sewing, but not Chavala. There were no thanks, nothing. All she had said after his labors of half a summer was, "A palace it's not, but it'll do." Some favor she'd done him—giving him the great honor of providing a space for her to make a living. Still, as he watched her trying to lift her feet out of the mire, he felt ashamed of his anger. Why was he berating her this way? Chavala had never been a child. From his earliest recollections it was Chavala who had taken on the responsibilities of the family. He could never remember her without holding a sister or having one tugging at her skirts. It was as though Chavala's mother gave birth to them, then Chavala fell heir to their raising. He could also never remember her sailing nor going with the other children in summer to the meadow. She had no time for such frivolity. Poor Chavala, beautiful Chavala, with the thick chestnut hair that would have fallen to her slim waist if she'd not worn it braided and twisted around her head, making her look older than sixteen. Beautiful Chavala. With the lips that he so longed to kiss. Quickly he spewed the nails from his mouth, put down the small hammer and went to the door, opening it. He called out, "Chavala?"

She turned her head toward the voice. Tonelessly she answered, "Yes?"

"It's so cold. What are you doing out this early?"

Swallowing hard she answered, "I have to bring Manya back."

His eyes narrowed in shock. Manya? . . . Manya was the wet nurse. She was always used when . . . he quickly rejected the thought. Still . . . "Why Manya?"

For a long moment Chavala stood silent. To speak at this moment would risk tears, and she could not risk *that* . . . She bit her lower lip hard, then, "My mother died early this morning." Flat, matter-of-fact, to camouflage the awful hurt . . .

A gasp lay in Dovid's throat, as though the loss were his. The pain of what Chavala felt seared through him like a knife. Mrs. Rabinsky had been like a mother to him when his own had died of tuberculosis. Then shortly after, he witnessed the burial of his father. That was before Chavala was born and he was only six. He remembered so well how Rivka had taken him to her home. She held him close to her for comfort, sang him to sleep with her soothing lullabies, fixed a bed on a board between two chairs, put down a straw mat and covered him with Avrum's winter coat. She sat by his side until finally he fell into blessed slumber. In the morning she prepared a special treat of Chanukah *latkes* and sprinkled them with salt and pepper. But he could scarcely eat. "Why did she die?" he had asked. Her soft brown eyes looked at him. "Because, Dovid, it was God's will. We are only mortals and God must not be questioned. He knows what is best. We must trust in His decisions."

But why had God made such a decision? Who was God to take his mother from him? He did not like God. No, he would never like God. But he would always love Rivka Rabinsky . . . But this was not the moment for such painful memories. Grabbing his coat from the hook on the door, he slipped into it and joined Chavala. "I'll go to Manya's with you."

"Thank you, but I can go alone."

"Don't try to show how strong you are. You're only human, Chavala. You're not an oak."

"I want to do this alone," she answered, without rancor.

He knew it wasn't her stubbornness but her courage that spoke. To argue with her would be pointless. Picking her up in his arms, he walked awkwardly in the mud that came up to his ankles.

Chavala did not resist. She was too weary. In fact, there was a measure of gratitude while she rested in his arms, although she would not tell him so.

When they reached Manya's hut Dovid walked up the broken wooden steps and put Chavala down. He looked at her eyes, which were not red and swollen from crying, but he knew the grief that lay hidden. If only she would show a sign of her despair, release herself from the torment she held in silence. What comfort that could bring to her! But to do that would also show her weakness, and Chavala would never permit herself that luxury. Not Chavala. She would suffer alone. She did not thank him for his help and concern, instead she turned from him and knocked on Manya's door.

When Manya finally opened the door and saw the two standing there she knew at once the reason Chavala had come. Her large bulk trembled for a moment, then she invited them in, but Dovid said, "I have to go to the Chevra Kadisha."

Manya shook her head. Poor Dovid was the one the task had fallen to of notifying the department of burials that his beloved Rivka Rabinsky was gone. Manya also knew that with Rivka's passing all the understanding of a mother who nurtured Dovid's soul and fed his body would be buried. He had loved her so. It was to her that he had been able to confide his great love for Chavala, the frustrations of manhood as well as his disillusionment with God. Not once had she taken him to task nor forbidden him to speak such blasphemy in her house. Instead she tried in her gentle manner to explain, "Where is there to go, Dovid, for help and solace if you forsake God? No mortal's door is open for you to enter. You see, my darling boy, without the love of God we are lost. He is there when our courage has faltered, if only we call on Him."

He did not dispute her words, though they did not change him. He'd felt he didn't need the love of God so long as Rivka's door was open. And now it was shut, forever.

Manya put on her shawl, told her husband to attend to their child and with Chavala descended the steps into the water-filled rut.

Chavala slipped and fell face down in the mud.

Quickly Dovid helped her up. "Are you all right, Chavala?"

Throwing back her head, she answered quickly, "I'm all right, please let go of my arm."

Releasing it, he knew her anger was not directed at him. It was the same anger he'd felt when his mother died and he wanted to break the world into a thousand pieces. But for them there had been the gift of Rivka to guide him through the troubled nights. Now he desperately wanted to hold Chavala close to him so that she too would know the healing power of love. Perhaps then the fire of her anger and grief would dissipate like smoke. But it was useless to try . . . Chavala would hug and nurture her pain . . . it was how Chavala protected her wounded soul from feeling too much. He watched as the two women walked clumsily down the road, and when they'd entered Chavala's house and closed the door behind them he made his way to the Chevra Kadisha at the furthest end of the village, shaking his head in sympathy for her loss, which was also his.

MANYA took the infant from Avrum. Without a word he got up unsteadily and walked to the bedroom, closing the door behind him.

Chavala watched as the new one sucked greedily to get Manya's milk. When the frail infant was satisfied and asleep Manya handed the baby to Chavala, and then the two sat in silence, each with her own separate thoughts.

Not so much out of curiosity but from a feeling that Chavala needed to talk, Manya asked, "What's happened?"

The words seemed to stick in Chavala's throat, then almost inaudibly she said, "Leah was sick . . . by now, who knows, she could be dead too. Why are we so cursed? Why, Manya? What have we done to offend God so much that He allows us to suffer this way?"

Manya swallowed hard. "I don't know answers to life's riddles. I only know God's not to blame. Your mother, may she rest in peace, would have told you that—"

"My mother was a saint. I'm not. I think I hate the world, Manya. When I go into Odessa and see the way the rich Jews and the *goyim* live, I spit out. Why has God been so good to *them?* Why are they so privileged to have so much and we not a crust of bread? And my dear sainted mother died from neglect . . . where was God?"

"God was here, Chavala. It's not God's revenge."

"Then whose? What does it all mean when those rich pious Jews run to *shul* and pray so loud that God should hear them? It's very easy for them to pray on a full stomach, then go home to a warm house where their Russian servants serve them tea and upon us they look down. They don't have to wait for a Leah to bring their children to life. The rich doctors of Odessa provide their survival. Their warehouses bulge with grain, and we starve. Where is justice, Manya? Where? We live out our few years in misery and who comes to help? Our good, rich brethren in Odessa ignore us. Wouldn't you think, Manya, that God would look down from heaven and cry a little when the pogroms come? Isn't it strange how God passes over the houses of those privileged ones in Odessa? No, Manya, for us there seems no help."

"Please, Chavala, don't say such things. It's sinful to speak this way."

"The truth is never a sin. At least it shouldn't be. My mother is dead because of the sins of others . . . because we are forced to live like vermin. Where was God this morning when I asked Him for help? Was my voice so weak it couldn't be heard? No, Manya, my mother died because God's ears were elsewhere."

Manya got up and looked at Chavala. Her enormous bulk actually trembled. She would listen to no more. It was enough. "Get the baby ready so I can take her home . . . I'll be back," she said, and left, her feelings a mixture of outrage and pity.

Chavala stared down now at the child in her arms. "I swear to you, my little Chia, your life will be different than mine. I swear, I *promise.*" Chavala was so deep in her own thoughts she'd not heard Dovid come into the house, nor noticed as he stood framed in the doorway. When she looked up and saw him, she knew the death wagon had arrived to take her mother away. She did not move from her chair as she heard the muted voices and footsteps go in and out of the bedroom. She also heard the sound of her heart beating like a drum. Handing the little Chia to Dovid, she rushed to the pail and was sick. For a moment she stood weakly against the drainboard, breathing hard. Then, grabbing up her heavy shawl and wrapping it around her, she ran from the house to follow the wagon as it made its mournful way to the Chevra Kadisha. When it stopped she stood rooted in the mud as she watched the body of her mother being taken inside. Soon the women would be preparing the body, putting it into the white burial shroud. The sight of it in her mind was almost more than even she could stand. How long Chavala remained outside she did not know, but something deep inside her was brought up sharply as she remembered the other children.

She turned slowly and walked away. When she arrived at Mrs.

Greenblatt's, the door was opened and the woman's eyes looked into Chavala's grief-stricken face. There was no need for words.

IT had taken little time for the small village to learn of Rivka Rabinsky's passing. Mrs. Greenblatt held out her arms and brought the girl close to her. Stroking the girl's lovely hair, she finally said, "It's life, Chavala. We must learn to accept that we are all only mortal. The years of our lives are arranged and we must understand that . . ."

Chavala found little comfort in such well-intentioned words. Jews for centuries had accepted their fates with passive resignation. Not Chavala. Who devised such a plan, she cried out inside herself. God? What had the pious soul of her mother done to offend anyone, much less God? Why should she have been taken away so quickly? She should have been allowed to live, to have seen her children grow up to maturity. No, there was no justice. How could Chavala be comforted in a deity so cruel, or so indifferent? She separated herself from the embrace. "Thank you for your kindness, and now I want to take the children home." She followed Mrs. Greenblatt into the kitchen, where her brother and sisters sat in absolute silence at the table. Looking at their stunned expressions, she was furious at what had deprived them of so much. And so damned unfairly.

They got up all at once and embraced Chavala as the tears fell from their eyes. They spoke together, the words tumbling from their frightened lips . . . "Mama's dead, Chavala," said Moishe. . . ."What will happen to us?" asked twelve-year-old Sheine. Ten-year-old Dvora looked at Chavala as though she could find the answers to chase her fears, and the youngest, eight-year-old Raizel, who could not fathom what dying was . . . "Why did mama go away from us, Chavala?"

In spite of her effort to console them there was still a bitterness showing. "Because God decided He needed mama more than we do . . . now dry your tears. I've come to take you home. You must be strong. Papa needs us." As she adjusted Raizel's babushka she added, "You have a sister. Yes, children, rejoice. Little Chia is the gift mama gave us . . . now, come."

How quickly God wanted back what belonged to him, Chavala thought. What had come from the earth was returned to the earth . . . According to Jewish law the burial took place as soon as possible. It denied any display of ostentation, insisted on the starkness of burial rights. It was a tradition of thousands of years that a Jew was to be buried in an unadorned pine box, and the body laid to rest in a white linen shroud. It was not only a *mitzvah* but the duty of the entire village to attend the funeral as one family. It was almost a commandment. For Rivka Rabinsky the *landsmen* not only paid their respects but mourned her passing. They stood in the rain and watched the coffin being lowered into the cold ground and in that moment sobs reverberated through the morning air. In the minds of many was the thought that what they were now witnessing one day would be theirs, that their days too were numbered and that eventually all roads led to the grave. How important it was for mortal men to walk humbly with God . . . Don't forget it . . .

Avrum bent down and placed a tiny bag of ancient holy dirt on top of the coffin as the tears fell from his wrinkled face. "Sleep in peace, my beautiful Rivka . . . my days will be lived in grief until I lay side by side with you."

The children clustered close to Chavala as they watched. The eeriness in the small cemetery, the solemnity of the rabbi intoning the eulogy would trouble their dreams through the long, long nights to come.

All was silent now as each mourner threw a handful of soggy earth over the grave.

Dovid caught Chavala's arm as she faltered for a moment, then with Avrum and the children they walked slowly away from the cemetery.

The next seven days were spent in mourning as the men sat on the floor and prayed the ancient psalms for the dead while the women of the village paid homage to the bereaved Rabinskys by sharing the little food they had. . . .

A month had passed and now Avrum spent his every waking moment in the room he had shared with his beloved wife. Behind the closed door he stood in silent prayer. His grief was so consuming that Chavala could barely watch as he sat, mute, with the children at supper. He had eaten so little that his clothes clung to his emaciated body and the furrows of his face had deepened so that he was almost unrecognizable. It seemed that almost overnight his hair had turned completely white. His shoulders were bent. His eyes were vague, and the little he said was mostly beyond comprehension.

IT was difficult for Chavala to work at her sewing this particular morning. Her mind was a confusion. She stopped pedaling and stared out of the window. The first snow had fallen during the night, and the sight depressed her, as did her thoughts. Papa, it seemed, would never recover from his loss, never again would be a father the children could look to for protection and to provide even the meager living he had made for them before. His only comfort seemed to be the time he spent praying in his lonely room. His days were passed in the synagogue—praying to atone for all his sins—and when he returned at night he seemed oblivious to everything. Nothing Chavala could say helped. But they needed a father, not a shadowy figure who lived in grief.

Chavala knew what had to be done. Without further thought she got up and went to the kitchen.

The children were studying. Moishe looked up from his book as he saw Chavala putting on her shawl. "Where are you going?"

"I have to attend to something," she answered quietly and left without another word. Slowly she made her way across the road to Dovid's house. Shivering in the cold, she stood until he opened the door. For a moment he could not speak, then recovered enough to say, "Come *in*, sit down, I'll get you a hot cup of tea."

"No, thank you," she answered between chattering teeth. "I didn't come to visit."

"What then?"

Taking a deep breath, she said, "This Saturday after *Shabbes* we're getting married." That having been said, she turned and started toward the door. With her hand poised on the knob she turned again and faced Dovid, who stood, not surprisingly, in a state of shock.

"Be ready. I'll make all the arrangements."

He merely shook his head as he watched the door close behind her.

As she made her way through the snow she cursed the Russian winter. It wasn't enough, the way they suffered. God even subjected them to this kind of white hell. Out of breath, she knocked at Manya's door. She needed so badly to see the baby.

"Come in, come in. You'll freeze to death out there," Manya said.

Chavala blew her warm breath on her freezing-cold hands, then rubbed them together.

"Sit down, Chavala, I'll get some tea."

As she did so Chavala's stomach turned over. The house was so silent. Since her mother had died everything seemed to take on a sense of foreboding. "Where are your children, Manya?"

"I sent them to my sister's. Mendel is sick with a very bad cold and the children get on his nerves with all the shouting and fighting."

"If the Russians don't kill us, the winter will."

Manya sighed. "What can we do? They say we were born to suffer."

Again, the acceptance, the stoicism, the capitulation. We were born to suffer. *Why?* Chavala asked herself. By what divine rule? "Could I see the baby?"

"Yes, I'll go." Manya walked into the disheveled bedroom. In one corner were two makeshift cribs made from wooden crates, in the other corner Manya's husband lay on a mattress of straw. Going to her husband's side she bent down and felt his forehead. It was like fire to the touch. She wiped his forehead with a damp cloth and then lay another coat over him. "Rest," she told him, "rest. I'll bring you some chicken soup in a while. You'll see, the nourishment will make you strong in no time at all."

The man's eyes were glassy, he scarcely heard. Shaking her head, she got up from her knees and walked to where the cribs stood. First she looked down at her own sleeping child, then picked up little Chia. Soon she was back handing the infant to Chavala, and as Chavala looked down at the tiny creature, she again questioned—why, in God's name, did they bring children into the world? In God's name, indeed. Poor Manya could barely make the food go around, yet she could still speak about her eight blessings, her jewels, her life.

Chavala admired her, but she also felt a renewed determination . . . she would never allow herself to have more children than she could provide for . . . How this would be accomplished she had no idea, but she was going to *direct*, she was going to *plan* her life. Somehow she would do the impossible . . .

Manya looked across the table, knowing she had read the longings for motherhood in Chavala's eyes. "I know how you feel holding a baby in your arms. How good it is. If we never have anything else, He has provided us with the joys of a family. How barren our lives would be without it. It is what a woman was put on this earth for . . ."

But Manya had misread the look in Chavala's eyes. To explain would be futile . . . "Manya, I'm going to marry Dovid," she said flatly as she took the hard sugar cube and placed it between her teeth, then sipped from the glass of tea.

Excitedly Manya said, *"Mazel tov,* when did your father speak to him?"

"He didn't. I asked him."

For a moment Manya thought she'd heard wrongly. "You asked him?"

"Yes."

"How could you be so brazen? I'm almost afraid to ask, but does your father know?"

"No."

Manya shook her head. "You mean to say you actually went to Dovid *without* your father's consent?"

"I don't need anyone's consent . . . after all, I don't have a dowry."

"What has that got to do with it? You've offended your father. It's his place to arrange the marriage, his right as the head of the family. You know that, Chavala."

"Yes, I know. But I also know my father's no longer the head of the family. He doesn't, I'm sorry to tell you, even understand when I speak to him. He stopped caring about anything when he lost my mother, seemed to give up on life. Tell me, how long has it been since he saw the baby? You know, I doubt if he even remembers her."

Manya lowered her eyes and toyed with the crumbs on the table. "You shouldn't say that. He's a brokenhearted man, seeing the child hurts him—"

"I *know*, but I need a strong man, someone to be a real father to them."

"Well . . . I can't say you're wrong. I know this is a terrible time for all of you. And besides, it's wonderful to be able to marry someone for love. But Chavala, at least allow your father to have the honor of letting Dovid ask for your hand."

"I don't think he'd understand me if I asked. And besides, I'm *not* marrying Dovid because I love him. I wish I did but . . . well, I chose Dovid because it's right, he's like a member of the family. I know he'll be good to the children and protect them. And that's what I need, and what they need."

"You make it sound like you're buying a horse."

"Perhaps. And is that so different from most marriages? How well, Manya, did you know Mendel before you two were married?"

"What? Oh, one month."

"How many times had you seen him before?"

"Once. What else did I have to see him for?"

"I'm not criticizing, Manya. Mendel is a very nice man. But what if he had turned out not to be so nice, so kind, what then? At least I know Dovid. Better a man of my choice than to be traded off to some old man with nine children to take care of."

"All right. Fine. What's the use of talking? Nobody can reason with you, Chavala. But it's against our tradition—"

"Tradition won't protect us from the pogroms. It never has . . ."

Nothing she said seemed right, Manya decided. "I don't know, maybe your father won't be offended . . . Dovid is like a son, true enough. Anyway, we'll all make you a nice wedding." She smiled at her and hugged her.

Chavala was genuinely touched. "I would love that, Manya. And thank you, dear, but we're getting married this Saturday, after *Shabbes.*"

Manya's mouth was open but no words came out. When they did they were in anger. "You can't *do* that. You mother is only gone a month. You're still in mourning for eleven months. Everyone will criticize. No one will even come."

"I know. But I can't afford to worry about what people think. *I have to do what I have to do.*"

"You know what you're doing is a sin, a sin against your mother's memory—"

"I think my mother will forgive me, she will know I'm doing what I must. I wouldn't be getting married if things had been different. I wouldn't have had to be disrespectful. Well, for once God will have to understand. They say He knows everything. I am going to count on that . . ."

CHAVALA'S hasty trip to the altar led her to the *shul* of Rabbi Gottlieb. His arguments were much the same as Manya's, only with long, long passages read from the Bible to prove that Chavala's breaking with the old ways was against everything that was holy in the Jewish tradition. After he had finished all of his arguments Chavala stood quietly, looking him directly in the eye, and with arms folded against her chest she told him that he should ask himself if tradition was not also opposed to her living in sin with Dovid, which he would be responsible for if he refused to marry them. At last the bearded rabbi threw up his hands and told her the marriage documents would be drawn up for all to sign. He turned and left her standing alone in the cold little *shul.*

AVRUM was deep in prayer when Chavala returned home. She stood at his closed door for a moment, then finally summoned up the courage to knock. The response was so soft it was almost inaudible. As she entered the room he looked at her vaguely, then as though a veil had lifted he said, "Chavala?"

"Yes, papa. Come sit down. I want to talk with you."

He closed the holy book and sat next to her as docile as a child. Taking his hand in hers she said softly, "Papa, Dovid and I are getting married after *Shabbes.*"

He frowned, as though he had difficulty trying to understand. "You and Dovid?"

"Yes, papa."

The old man spoke now as though testing his own memory. "I spoke to him?"

"No."

"I don't understand—"

"Papa, dear, you must listen to me. If things had been different I would have done all the things that are expected of me as a good daughter. You must know that I love you and respect you. But we need Dovid. He's very important to us all, papa."

The old man shook his head, knowing more of his inadequacies than she suspected. At this moment he did not think of tradition as the past came rushing back to him . . . how often he and Rivka had dreamed of the day they would stand under the *chuppah,* the bridal canopy, with Chavala dressed as a bride should be. They had prayed that Chavala would take Dovid as a husband. The whole village would have rejoiced and sung, but now all the sounds of joy were gone from their lives, and in their place were the sounds of mourning. His sounds. The world of Avrum Rabinsky lay buried in the snows that covered the earth where his beloved Rivka lay. Poor Chavala would be deprived of her supreme moment. There would be no merriment and no memories to look back on, no mother to fuss over her as she prepared to join her betrothed in glorious union. Tears filled his eyes. "I give you my blessings, dear child. I hope you will have as your greatest gift the joys I knew with your mama."

Chavala put her arms around her father and held him close. "Thank you, papa. That is the greatest gift you could have given me. Will you stand under the *chuppah* beside me?"

"No, Chavala. I cannot. Not even for you. For me it would be wrong to go against my beliefs. My pain will not be over, even after mourning."

God help him, Chavala thought. And it was as much a request as a prayer. If anyone deserved it, her papa did.

ON Friday Chavala and the children scrubbed the house until it sparkled with cleanliness. Then she and Moishe stretched a rope from one corner to the other, hung a side blanket over it separating the sleeping area. She put down the floor mat that she and Dovid would share in their nuptial space, then prepared the *Shabbes* food for two days. That night she would light her candles. Placing the silver candlesticks on the table she realized that tomorrow she would truly become the matriarch, the head of her family, and Dovid would sit at the head of the table.

At three o'clock she went to the ritual baths to prepare for marriage. She would go to her husband in cleanliness and purity.

AFTER a near-sleepless night Saturday had finally come, but the day seemed to drag on endlessly. Finally, thank God, the sabbath was over and Dovid was knocking on her door. Without a word she placed the heavy shawl around her head and shoulders, and the two of them walked to *shul.*

Shivering in the freezing cold of the sanctuary they stood together as the rabbi intoned his blessings on them. Indeed, Chavala's hand shook as Dovid placed his mother's wide gold band on her finger. They did not embrace, only looked at each other. Dovid's eyes unmistakably expressed love, Chavala's determination. Dovid had not expected it to be otherwise, but he was convinced that with patience and understanding, in time she would be able to show the affection he knew she felt for him. As they were leaving the sanctuary the *minyan* of men reciting their evening prayers offered their greeting of *"mazel tov."* A beginning.

THAT night, after the others were asleep, they undressed in the dark and lay down side-by-side. Dovid moved close to Chavala. Reaching out to embrace her he whispered, "You've made me very happy, my darling."

She looked up at the dark ceiling. What could she say to him? That she'd married him out of necessity? He was her husband, with all the rights she had pledged herself to . . . still, she couldn't submit to his desires. Not tonight. Not yet. She was simply unprepared to do that, never mind her determination. Her answer was, "Thank you," and it embarrassed her as much as it disappointed him.

Dovid's uneven breathing frightened her. "Come to me," he said, pulling her closer.

She moved away. "No, Dovid. I'm sorry, not tonight . . . the children will hear . . ." A fine excuse. Tradition should have had her hoping to make a child . . .

He took his arms away and with understandable anger said, "Then they'll hear tomorrow night too. I'm your husband, Chavala. I won't ask you again. This is wrong . . ."

Abruptly he turned over onto his side, moving as far away as he could.

And in that moment Dovid greatly endeared himself to Chavala. He was not the submissive boy she had always thought he would be. As children he had given in to her every whim, but how little she knew of the man. How little one knew of anyone until she shared an intimacy with him . . . She would have bet that he would have been passive, she had counted on it, but Dovid, it seemed, was a *husband,* and she found herself liking him . . . no, more than that. In her fashion, she felt that she loved him. Now she *wanted* to be held close in the long winter night. But to ask would be an admission that she had wronged him, and her pride wouldn't quite allow her to do that. Not yet. Well, in the morning she suspected Dovid's anger would be nearly gone. She would please him by preparing a very special breakfast as a sign of her apology, and tomorrow night she would be his wife. . . .

But when she awoke after an unexpectedly peaceful sleep she found in the early dawn that the place next to her was empty, as empty as she now felt. And suddenly she was consumed with a different kind of fear . . . perhaps Dovid would never come back. What she had done by denying him gave him every right to have their marriage annulled. It was a sin for a wife to deny what rightfully belonged to her husband. All he would need do was submit his case to the rabbi, and according to Jewish law the marriage would cease to be. Quickly she dressed and nervously began the preparation for breakfast. As she rekindled the fire Moishe's voice startled her.

"Where's Dovid?" he asked.

"He . . . he had to repair a pair of boots for . . . for . . . Reb Bernstein. Now, no more questions. Get dressed and wash behind your ears."

"Why didn't he stay and eat?"

"I just told you. And I said no more questions. Do as I say."

"Why are you angry?"

"I'm not angry. Go wake up papa."

Moishe shrugged. When Chavala was upset there was no use trying to speak to her.

She sewed furiously all day long, and as she pedaled she listened for the front door to open, praying that Dovid would come back and say how sorry he was for not understanding, at least give her a second chance. But even as she thought it she knew he would not. Day became dusk, and her stomach turned over and over. After feeding the family she filled a lunch pail of hot soup, put on her shawl and walked across the road to Dovid's hovel. As she waited for him to open the door her warm breath steamed against the terribly cold air, but he did not answer her knock. Finally she called out, "Dovid, I'm freezing, open the door."

Still no response.

Frustrated, she pounded on the door, then kicked with her foot so hard that it throbbed. Finally the door opened. When she entered she found Dovid at his workbench, continuing to repair a boot without looking up. Well, at least she'd been honest with Moishe.

Trying to control her anger and frustration, now that she was here she didn't know quite what to say. Dovid's silence didn't help. If only he'd say *something*. Trembling in the cold, somehow she found the courage to set aside her pride and say haltingly, "Dovid . . . I want . . . I've come to—" She had intended to say she was sorry, to apologize, but the words would not come. "Supper's waiting for you."

He continued to work, which wasn't too surprising. She wanted to take his hammer and toss it out the window. "Dovid, I'm speaking to you."

He ignored her.

"Come home, Dovid, I have supper—"

"I am home."

"This is not your home anymore. We're married and your place is with me."

For the first time he looked up at her. "You should have remembered that last night. I'm not your husband."

"You're acting like a stupid child—"

"Like a stupid child, you think? Well, I'll show you how wrong you are." In one swoop he lifted her up into his arms and went to his room. Dumping her on the wooden cot, he ripped the dress from her body, hurried out of his own clothes and pinned her against the thin straw mattress. "Now I'll show you what a man is like." Without another word he spread his long, strong legs over her.

After a muffled cry of pain Chavala lay quietly as Dovid thrust deeply. The intensity of her own passion came shockingly to her. All the desires of womanhood rushed through her. Now that he had made her aware of them, she wanted Dovid to hold her, love her as a woman ought to be loved, but instead he dressed and without a word went out of the room, then through the front door, which he slammed behind him.

She shook her head, and in spite of some annoyance lay back in a kind of languor. It was not so bad being a woman after all. Not so bad

. . . Dovid leaving her side couldn't take away from her what she was feeling. Besides, maybe he'd only done it as a gesture of consideration, leaving her alone with her new thoughts. Yes, she was happy she had chosen Dovid to be her husband. She knew he would come to her again. Such pleasures were not likely to be denied, to himself as well as her. And with such thoughts, she fell into a deep, sweet sleep. . . .

She was startled when she woke up to find it was dark, and more disappointed than startled that Dovid was not at her side. Her former fantasies turned to misgivings. In her naiveté she had thought that Dovid would be consumed with the memory of what they had shared—which, naturally, would make it impossible for him to resist her. Dovid would be at her side, watching her sleep, waiting for her to wake up as he stroked her hair and kissed her lips. She wondered what his kisses would taste like . . . in the abrupt moments of discovery he hadn't kissed her. . . . Feeling frustrated and incomplete, she dressed quickly . . . and noticing the missing buttons from her bodice she smiled in spite of herself, then blushed, remembering the way Dovid had undressed her. Covering her garment with her shawl, she left and crossed the road. . . .

As the evening wore on and Dovid still did not come to her, all the fantasies slowly dimmed. Apparently making her a woman was a sign of his masculinity, not his ardor. Men and women were, no question, complicated. She really didn't know Dovid at all. She would have sworn that what had happened between them would have brought them closer together, but she'd been wrong. All the affection he had shown her as they were growing up was the love that existed between children, not the love of a man and a woman. In fact the more she thought on it, the more she was convinced he'd agreed to marry her mostly out of the love he felt for her mother. Yes, that must be it. Otherwise he wouldn't have left her as he had. No, Dovid did not love her, and down deep she silently wept. . . .

CHAVALA'S reasoning, of course, could not have been more mistaken. When Dovid left her he walked in the deep snow until he could not go on. Full of guilt, he berated himself for violating Chavala—what a terrible thing to inflict on his wife. If Chavala went to the rabbi and told him she'd been raped, there would be no question that she could obtain a divorce. He hated himself for what he'd done. Now he lay on his cot in the dark room and he too had tears in his eyes. The only comfort he found was in a bottle of vodka, which he drank until he reached a state of oblivion. . . .

AFTER two days he woke up in a besotted state of confusion. The stubble of two days' growth irritated his face, but his discomfort was slight compared to his deeper misery . . . Chavala would never forgive him, of that he was certain. Still, he loved her so, and the thought that he'd committed such an act was more than he could come to grips with. He got up unsteadily, put his head in a basin of cold water to try to wash away the remains of his stupor. Well, there was no debate any longer, he knew what had to be done. Pride was too expensive. He would beg, plead, do anything it took to try to redeem himself in Chavala's eyes, to persuade her to forgive him. He slipped into his clothes and crossed the road.

Standing in front of Chavala's door he paused before knocking. Then, finally, after taking a deep breath, he knocked. Too loud.

Chavala's heart almost stopped beating when she heard the knock. Moishe was about to answer when Chavala stopped him.

"I'll go," she said nervously. Trying to control her breathing, she opened the door only a crack.

For a moment neither of them spoke. Their hopes were both the same, but nothing of them was revealed by the expressions on their faces.

Finally Dovid said, "Chavala, please come to my place. I want to talk to you."

Her heart pounded. He was going to tell her they were through. Why else had he stayed away for two days? Divorce was a disgraceful thing and not to be taken lightly, but Dovid must have ultimately come to a decision.

Dovid waited outside in the freezing night as Chavala went to get her shawl.

When they got to his house she sat rigidly while he added the wooden sticks to the fire. He did not light the kerosene lamp. All the light in the room came from the fire glow.

After an intolerable silence they both spoke at the same time. "Dovid . . ." "Chavala . . ." Silence again.

Now Dovid tried again. "Chavala . . . don't talk, let me finish . . . I know you don't care for me . . . I guess I've always known, but for the sake of your dear mother, may she rest in peace, I ask for your forgiveness."

Chavala was grateful for the dark. At least it kept Dovid from seeing the tiny crystal tears that had formed in the corners of her eyes. Words simply would not come.

Her silence was the answer Dovid had expected. He had lost her, no question about it. "I can't blame you, Chavala, for how you feel. I won't stand in your way. You're free to do whatever you wish." He wanted to die.

Almost too softly to be heard, she now said, "I want to be your wife, Dovid." It took a moment for him to hear, to receive what she had said. And then with a kind of reverence he took her in arms and held her close. Slowly, her arms went around him, and together they went once again to his room, where at last they found the beauty of their honestly acknowledged feelings . . .

CHAVALA sat in the dimly lit kitchen with a darning basket in her lap. From time to time she would glance up and see the children surrounding Dovid as they sat at the kitchen table. More than once she pinched herself to see if it were real that he was her husband. She marveled at how blind she'd been about Dovid . . . how once she'd taken him for granted. Well, she now not only loved him, she was nearly in awe of him. Dovid was not only handsome, but his spirit and knowledge came like a shock to her. In spite of the fact she'd known him all her life, she'd really not known him at all. He had always been the young boy her mother protected . . . a cobbler, a neighbor. If not for the painful events that put them together, she would never have known how much she had missed. He had brought so much to them all. Even her father, Avrum, seemed more at peace. Since Dovid now provided for the family he could devote his time poring over his beloved books. Avrum felt God had sent Dovid, and he adored him as though he were his own son.

For the children, Dovid had opened up a world whose boundaries extended far beyond their small village. He excited and enchanted them. Until now their lives had been spent in the narrowness of learning psalms and commandments. Dovid explored the magnificent tapestry of their ancient heritage. He imbued them with a pride in who they were that went beyond tradition.

Moishe hung on every word as Dovid retold the stories of great and fierce warriors of ancient times, of how they had fought off every adversary, although they were outnumbered. The greatest of all stories was Masada, and the children sat in rapt silence, wide-eyed, listening to Dovid as he retold for them those heroic moments in history . . . After Jerusalem had fallen to the Romans, he began, a battle that cost them thousands and thousands of their legionnaires, a band of zealots formed. Ele'azar became their leader, a man made heroic by a cause he would die for. It was to Masada that the small band of Jews retreated to make their stand for liberty, for the faith. Masada, he went on, was a huge mountain that stood in the wilderness of the Judean hills, an immense rock built by King Herod the Great, who could not have foreseen at the time of his death that Masada had been created as a monument to God's will. The zealots climbed thirteen hundred feet above the Dead Sea, and at the summit found a refuge. Below stood poised the mighty Roman legions. Imagine, defying the strength that was mighty, Imperial Rome . . . For three years and against the greatest odds they were able to hold off the Romans. When they finally realized the end was near and they could no longer hold out against their enemies, the leader Ele'azar brought all his tribes together and spoke to them. It was for them, each and every one, to decide whether they should live as slaves or die as free men. They chose to die. Ele'azar spoke to all who had fought so valiantly. Standing in the center he studied each face. For a long moment he searched his heart, and then without hesitation he said, "My loyal friends, you have followed me to this forsaken place knowing what would happen. That one day all this would end. That day is now. But we resolved that neither the Romans nor anyone else would we serve, that we would serve no man, only God. Once before we were spared and continued to exist until our shackles were taken from us. It was then that we made our exodus from Egypt. We have lived according to the laws of Moses, and now the time has come that bids us to reaffirm our love of God by the determination of our deeds. We have never willingly submitted to slavery even though we were cast into it. We were the first of all men to revolt, and shall be the last to break off the struggle. I believe it is God who has given us this privilege, this choice. Life without freedom is darkness. Daybreak will bring an end to our existence, but we are still free to choose an honorable death with our loved ones. Our enemies cannot prevent that, no matter how much they try to take us alive." Ele'azar paused, and once again looked at the faces he'd come to know and to love. "Let our wives die unabused, our children without the knowledge of slavery. After that, we shall do for each other. But first, let our possessions, and the whole fortress, go up in flames. It will be a bitter blow to the Romans to find our dear ones beyond their reach, and nothing left for them to loot or plunder. Let us leave our store of food, to bear witness that we did not perish because of famine but because we resolved as one voice to choose death rather than slavery."

When the inner wall had burned, Ele'azar gathered the ten men the community had chosen to decide. It was a signal for all to return to their homes, where they were to lie down. Of their free will husbands embraced wives and children, then offered their necks to the stroke from those whose lot it was to perform the task. When the ten had carried out their mission, they in turn lay down their lives, until the last remaining man thrust his sword deeply and fell with the rest of his brethren. The legend of Masada became a beacon of courage, Dovid concluded, an inspiration handed down through the ages to Jews everywhere.

In the dimly lit kitchen in Odessa, that small assembly kept unusually silent. Finally Dovid spoke again, looking at each of the children and finally at Chavala. "We must always remember this story. The watchword is, *Never again Masada.* It is our pledge."

Moishe sat there perplexed, trying to understand the meaning of Dovid's words, repeating to himself, *Never again Masada . . .* except how did this apply to him? To his family? The stories of brave warriors were great, but Odessa wasn't Masada . . .

Seeing the confusion on Moishe's face, Dovid asked him what was the matter.

"What do we do, Dovid? The same thing that Ele'azar asked the zealots of Masada to do? Lie down and die when the pogroms start?"

"No. In fact, just the opposite. The story I've just told has a simple message for us . . . we must survive until we can redeem our land. The message of Masada is courage. It is burned into our souls, so that in spite of the pogroms no one will ever defeat our determination to become free. It is difficult to understand, I know, because we live as the oppressed, the downtrodden, but one day Eretz Yisroel will rise up, and on that day we will have our revenge for all the tyranny and injustice perpetrated against us."

Moishe still looked at Dovid in confusion. "How will we do that, Dovid?"

"Through Zionism."

"Zionism? What is that?"

"It's getting late, but tomorrow night I'll tell you about a man named Theodore Herzl. He dedicated his life to that one dream. There's so much I want to tell you about. How soon there will come from Eretz Yisroel a teacher, a *Bilu,* who like Moses will help us find the promised land once again."

"When will he come?" Moishe asked.

"Soon, very soon."

Chavala had been listening with some irritation. Believing that there was no hope that they would go anywhere, she felt it served no purpose to remind Dovid of those who had gone to Eretz Yisroel only to come back disillusioned. It wasn't the land of milk and honey. She remembered well the stories of those who had died from malaria and hunger, and the swamps. If there was any chance to change their lives, it was, she was convinced, in America. That was a new land. There was real equality and freedom there. And people lived decently, not in squalor. She'd literally dreamed about America, about arriving there and seeing the famous golden land of opportunity. *That* was where hope had reality, she passionately believed. But she kept silent, for now. Let papa have his dreams, and Dovid his hopes . . .

Moishe interrupted her thoughts with, "Will you take me to hear more about this?"

"Yes," Dovid said. "But no one must know about this, it would be very dangerous for all of us if we were found out. The Lovers of Zion is a secret society—"

"I'll never tell, Dovid. Never."

Nor would the others, they solemnly assured him. Chavala then scooted them off to bed, saying there had been enough stories for one night.

Moishe fell asleep thinking about what Dovid had said, conjuring up images in the dark, imagining the heroic figure of *Dovid* standing in the footsteps of . . . what was his name? . . . Ele'azar . . .

Sitting at the table drinking tea, Chavala said, "Dovid, please *don't* take Moishe to your meeting."

"Why? He's old enough."

"But he's also impressionable and romanticizes everything—"

"That may be, but it's also important for Jews to know who they are, where they came from. And besides, what's wrong with having dreams, hopes . . . ?"

"That's fine, if dreams can become reality—"

"And where is it written, dear Chavala, that they can't? You had a dream, as I recall, that if I built a shed to house a goat, it would give milk and you would be able to bring your baby sister home. Am I right?"

"You're right." She smiled at him.

"Well, your dream is now a reality. Tomorrow we can go to Manya's and bring back little Chia where she belongs."

In spite of all that was against it, Dovid *had* completed the shed. First there was the lumber, which he managed to acquire, then the snows . . . day after day he'd come into the house so frozen that not even a basin of hot water would thaw him.

"Oh, Dovid, no wonder my mother loved you."

"Your mother? About her, I knew. What about you?"

"Me too, Dovid. Oh yes, me too."

WINTER no longer seemed so terrible. Little Chia had brought a light and joy that leavened all their miseries. She was a ray of sun that no cloud could dull. The children took turns feeding her from a small wine bottle that Chavala had saved since Chanukah. Dovid had formed a nipple from the finger of a rubber glove and fastened it to the bottle with some of Chavala's elastic. . . .

At four months Chia had changed from an emaciated, tiny bundle of bones to a chubby infant who cooed and kicked vigorously. At night she slept alongside them in the tiny crib Dovid had made and Chavala had padded with down. How Dovid managed as he did was a thing of wonder to Chavala . . . even coming home with a bundle of coal and a few *eggs*.

Chavala sewed with the baby always at her side, and Dovid worked across the road with more enthusiasm than he'd ever felt before, turning out one pair of boots after another. This summer he and Chavala would take their wares into Odessa, and their combined efforts would secure their needs for the following winter. How good it was, he thought, to have a wife like his . . . as he worked away his thoughts drifted to the house across the road, to the woman inside it, to how she'd changed from the difficult girl he had once known to the understanding wife who gave herself so willingly. What more could he want?

Out of his love and admiration for Dovid, Moishe decided that if bootmaking was the noble profession his mentor had chosen, then it was only fitting he should follow in his footsteps. He worked alongside Dovid, whom he thought of as the finest bootmaker in Odessa. Maybe, thought Moishe, in all of Russia. He sold to the rich people in the city, refusing to accept less than he asked. When a man was a master at his craft he could command his price. He knew what he was worth. Working with Dovid gave Moishe an even greater pleasure . . . he could put a thousand questions to Dovid . . . his desire to know the world was insatiable. In fact, he'd thought of little else since he'd attended his first meeting of the Lovers of Zion. He'd been so impressed, sitting with the men in Reb Kaufman's darkened back room, and even though his voice was not heard, just to be a part of the great debates gave him stature. He hung onto every word as the huge red-bearded *chalutz* from Palestine spoke. The arguments flew, and Dovid always took up the one for the cause of Zionism. It seemed so clear to him that Herzl's dreams were their salvation, and yet there were those among them that strongly disagreed and stood in the way of every new proposal. Dovid, though, continued to hammer away, and Moishe was especially proud when Dovid stood in front of the small assembly and boomed out, "You fools. You disparage and debate whether Zionism is our salvation, while our enemies plot to destroy us. If we don't cling to our birthright of Eretz Yisroel, then where *can* we be free men that can direct our own destiny? For thousands of years we've suffered in the lands of the Diaspora. Our children die of starvation and we live out our lives without hope. Even our Russian overlords have freed their serfs. But our Jews still live without hope, in spite of the fact that a Russian revolution is being made right now . . . in every hamlet, every village the rumblings of hatred for the Czarists is rising and spreading. But you who feel that your salvation lies with *their* revolution are wrong. No matter how you try, in the end even the revolutionists will turn on you. Mark me well, *chevra,* our only hope for redemption lies in the land that was taken from us. And it is not God, nor the teachings of the Torah, nor the Talmud that will save us from the sword, as many of you religious fanatics believe, but a *land* that is ours and that we must claim. *No Jew, no matter where, will be safe until we have a country that belongs to us.* Then and only then will the world stand up and respect us. Leave us in peace. We are pawns to be used in any way our oppressors wish. I ask how you can be so blind, all of you who have lived in such misery. You who are so religious should remember, 'If I forget thee, oh Jerusalem, let my right hand forget its cunning . . . let my tongue cleave to the roof of my mouth; if I prefer not Jerusalem above my chief joy.'

"Can you forget? The white stones of the Judean hills are mixed with the blood of five thousand years. Are the lives of those who fought for generations to become meaningless? Can you forget? I say go up, or surely we shall perish, as we deserve to, because we have not learned the lesson of Masada."

Dovid sat down and wiped the perspiration from his forehead. Could a Maccabee have stood and spoken more forcefully than Dovid? He had stood tonight like the biblical David, the warrior. Yes, Moishe thought, his idol had been rightly named.

ALTHOUGH the long winter seemed reluctant to give way to spring, the snows finally melted, and once more the village came alive.

The grinding wheels of Yankel's rickety milk cart could be heard as he made his morning rounds, the sound replaced by his curses as he tried to lift the rear wagon wheel out of the mud.

Itzik, the butter and egg vendor, laughed as he cautiously walked past Yankel, thanking God that what he sold could be carried by the yoke on his back. His smugness soon turned to regret as he slipped in the slime. God was everywhere, Itzik thought, and this was his punishment as he lay facedown, covered from head to toe, and all his eggs broken.

"That'll teach you to laugh," Yankel called out.

Dovid looked from the window as he sat at his cobbler's bench with Moishe beside him, and counted his blessings . . . at least he'd been able to make his living indoors all winter.

Chavala felt a great joy this morning as she saw and smelled the first signs of spring. The cherry tree that stood alone in the small backyard was ready to burst out with blossoms. God, how she loved spring, the promised renewal of life! Feeling the awesomeness of nature's wonder, the remembrance of another time came happily back to warm her as though it were yesterday, and she remembered how mama picked the fine plump fruit and took the gallon jug, filling it more than half with sugar, then with pure, white alcohol. It was Chavala's honor to drop the cherries into the jug, one by one. Then the jug was stored away in the cellar and at Chanukah the jug was taken from its resting place. It was a time of gladness, as mama served the potato *latkes* and papa gave each one a very small glass of mama's wine. But it was the brandied cherries that Chavala enjoyed the best. She laughed now, recalling how she'd gone to the cellar one day and quietly uncorked the jug . . . she must have eaten two dozen before she felt light-headed and giddy. Realizing mama would find the cherries gone she replenished the jug with alcohol. Her guilt made her confess her great sin on the eve of Chanukah, and to her surprise her mother only laughed. "If you don't tell papa, I won't. Besides, after a few drops of my slivovitz, no one will tell the difference."

NOW the weeks turned to days, and that enchanted time of the year was once more on them . . . excitement permeated the air in the little village as the women began preparing for Passover.

Chavala took down the Passover dishes to be washed. The children scrubbed the walls and floors as though exorcising the miseries of winter memories.

Chavala polished the silver candlesticks until they shone. They were mama's cherished possessions, dearest mama . . . her presence would be felt.

Dovid, miracle man that he was, came home with a crate of eggs and a sack of onions, then accompanied his wife to the marketplace. The women of the village looked at one another as Dovid put the bundles of food into his handcart, stared at one another in disbelief. What husband did *that?*

At Reb Levi's stall they heard Manya arguing that the chickens were good for the *goyim* but not fit to be eaten by pigs.

Reb Levi endured this abuse from Manya every *Shabbes,* so why should this be any different, but he was wise to her. It was her way of trying to intimidate him by demeaning his poultry so she could buy cheaper. Manya, he already knew. She was famous for bargaining. "I wouldn't give you off a penny," he called back.

"Did I ask? I only want pound for pound for what I pay."

"Do me a favor, madam, go elsewhere. Aggravation from you I don't need."

"Aggravation I'm giving you? If your chickens were as big as your mouth, I wouldn't be complaining."

"*Oy vay,* a heart attack I'll get from her . . . all right already, here, take a capon for the same price."

Manya felt beneath the thick white feathers. This one was pleasingly fat. "So, for this great favor, what do you want?"

"Make it two *kopeks* and it's yours."

"One."

Some *chutzpah,* but Manya would outtalk him. In desperation he finally said, "I'll give your charity to the *shul.* "

On the way out she saw Chavala and Dovid. No wonder Chavala couldn't wait to marry him. He was so tall and handsome, *and* virile. Thick black hair, deep blue eyes, and those lips that must have tasted like sweet wine. But why was he here with her in the middle of the morning, he looked so out of place. There could be only one reason. Manya's eyes wandered to Chavala's middle. It had been after all, six whole months. Well, maybe being thin like Chavala was, she didn't show. Not like her, she was only in her third month and already she looked like six.

After their usual amenities they wished one another the happiest of Passovers and that they should all be blessed with good health above all . . . still, "A little prosperity wouldn't hurt," Manya added. . . .

At home Chavala's eyes and nose ran as she grated the horseradish root, then mixed the beet pulp, sugar and wine vinegar. Screwing on the top of the jar she laughed, it was so strong that if anything could ward off the evil eye it would surely be the horseradish. Then she began to chop the fish mixture in a large wooden bowl, and as she did so her mother came to mind . . . among mama's legacies was the recipe she'd left Chavala, but in mind only. Not written down. Yes, mama's gefilte fish was the envy of the village.

Sheine made the matzoh balls, while Chavala basted the chickens, and then together the two sisters put themselves to the task of making the sponge cakes. Sheine beat the egg whites and Chavala the yolks.

When all the cooking was finally completed, and since Passover had fallen on Friday, at three in the afternoon Chavala went to the *mikvah*. . . .

At the precise moment of the setting sun the family was seated. At the head of the table papa sat in his armchair, surrounded by eiderdown pillows. To his right sat Dovid, Sheine next to him. The closeness to Dovid made Sheine's pulse beat fast, this was a place she would rather not be. Sheine still lived with her dreadful secret . . . she was so much in love with Dovid that most of the time she could not even bear to be in his presence, and it was at those times, when he was near, that she was sullen and withdrawn. At nights she would lay awake and listen to the sounds of love beyond the hanging blanket, and out of fear that her sobs would be heard she buried her face in the pillow. To be so in love with her sister's husband brought pain and shame to her heart. If only she could exchange her place at the table with Dvora, who sat next to her. But this was the way they had always been seated, with Moishe across the table near papa. Chavala stood at the other end of the table dressed in mama's black silk with the white lace collar and the shawl over her head as she began the ritual of lighting the candles. But, despite herself, instead of listening to the inspired message of *Shabbes*, Sheine's thoughts were displaced by envy. Mama had left Chavala the small diamond earrings because she had the good fortune of being the eldest. She also wore the pair of wide gold bracelets that had been Dovid's mother's. Seeing how brightly they shone in the candlelight, Sheine thought Chavala looked like a queen tonight. *She* looked like the peasant she was. She bowed her head, not in reverence, but because the sight of Chavala with Dovid was too much for her.

The *seder* went on for hours, not a passage was deleted, not a song left unsung.

Avrum Rabinsky could have told the story of Passover without the aid of a Haggadah. It was a story burned into his mind, so that if he were blind it could still have come from his lips. Uncovering the matzohs and lifting up the plate for all to see, he recited, "This is the bread of affliction which our forefathers ate in the land of Egypt. All who are hungry come and celebrate the Passover with us. Now we are here, next year may we be in the land of Israel. Now we are slaves, next year may we be free men."

Moishe looked across the table, where Dovid's eyes met his and in both the message was clearly understood.

The plate was then put down and covered with a special fringed napkin and a second cup of wine was filled. It was Raizel's privilege, being the youngest at the table, to ask the ancient four questions beginning with: "Why is this night different from all other nights?"

Although Avrum answered, Dovid added silently, *Because of Chavala, the blessing and joy she has brought to my existence is why tonight is different . . .*

When the reaffirmation was proudly intoned by Avrum, "Next year in Jerusalem," again Moishe and Dovid nodded.

Chavala, though, prayed that next year they would be in the land of the free and the home of the brave . . . America. The Jews of that great land of opportunity had no need to return to Russia, broken in body and many in spirit from the malaria-infested swamps of Palestine. For the sake of her father and her husband, and apparently now her brother Moishe too, she was thankful, her thoughts could not be read.

She and Sheine removed the plates, then the cakes were brought to the table and Dvora served small bowls of fruit compote.

Avrum looked around the table at his children, especially the little one, and spoke silently to his Rivka. My dearest, you left me with so much, I weep that you cannot share this with me. Yet you are not far away. I know your spirit abides and is over us, and all the days of my life it will be so . . .

On Sunday Chavala prepared a platter of matzoh brei and when the sumptuous breakfast was over she left the kitchen chores to be done by the girls and returned to sewing while Dovid went back to his workbench.

The small village hummed with the excitement of market day. Sundays were always special. The women not only replenished their larders, but the square became a meeting place to exchange bits of gossip while their husbands attended to the affairs of earning a living.

The young yeshiva boys sat hunched over their Torah portions as their elders, dressed in their long black coats and wide beaver hats, debated the interpretation of the Law and Prophets.

In the stalls mothers visited while buying their briskets and beets to make borscht. Outside the children amused themselves with a stick and a ball. Nursing mothers with their babies at their breasts sat on a bench. The scene of this Sunday's Passover afternoon was the same as it had been for a century past. It was a good day, a happy day for the Jews in their small village.

But for the Christians in the city of Odessa, there was quite a different drama being enacted. As the church bells pealed out, calling the faithful to worship, their religious fervor was forgotten as they sat in their pews. Dressed in his robes, the bearded priest looked out to his flock in a moment of silence, then began: "This is a tragic day. A terrible act has been perpetrated upon one of our beloved children. At dawn this morning an innocent child was found murdered at the very door of this holy place. We are civilized people who live for the brotherhood of man and the kingdom of heaven. We preach and teach love, but our words go un-heeded. Who in this land could be so vile as to violate this angel? Who could be so perverse as to want the blood of this precious lamb? In the name of our Savior, the life of this maiden must be avenged."

Before the priest had finished a hue and cry rang throughout the sanctuary. As one voice they called out, "KILL THE JEWS, KILL THE JEWS . . . DEATH TO THE JEWS!" The parishioners ran from the church, the women and children told to return home, the men gone to saddle their horses . . .

Moishe was returning home flushed with excitement as he felt the *kopeks* in his pocket. He had sold three pairs of boots today. He would keep only a small part for himself and the rest he would give to Dovid. Going up to the front door, he paused, then looked into the far distance. Coming down over the hills he saw the smoking torches and the galloping horses. An army of students had joined in the crusade. Although the shouting was still not distinct, he knew. He'd seen this and heard the words before. Quickly he went into the house and stood in front of Chavala . . . "Pogrom, pogrom . . ."

Chavala clutched her heart but told herself she mustn't panic. If ever she needed her wits, it was now. She had Moishe come with her to the kitchen to open the trapdoor to the cellar, which was hidden beneath a heavy movable cupboard. After the two had managed to swing it open, she then went to summon her father. Without preamble—"They're start-ing, papa . . . they have come to kill us."

Taking his holy books, he obeyed.

When all the children were assembled, she sent them down. Dvora carried the canister of water, Sheine the matzohs, and Raizel the bottle of goat's milk. They were back in Egypt. But here there was no Moses to lead them across the parted sea and drown their oppressors. Handing Moishe little Chia, Chavala said, "There, safety is in your hands, light the candles." Then she paused and handed him the death pellets.

Moishe could only look at her, stunned.

"Remember Masada," she told him.

"What about you, Chavala?" Moishe said.

"I'm going to Dovid. With God's help we'll join you."

After she pushed back the cupboard with all her strength she started toward the front door but retreated back against the wall as the door crashed forward. And then her courage left her and in its place was terrible, stark fear. These, she knew, would be the last moments of her life. She stayed rooted to the floor, barely breathing. Her fears became even greater at the sounds of furniture being thrown against the wall. The most shattering sound of all was the crashing glass. They must have been in papa's room and had evidently found nothing, because the footsteps of heavy boots were heard going into her sewing room. Mama's diamond earrings, the gold bracelets Dovid had given her on their wedding day, the small diamond-and-amethyst brooch which had belonged to his grandmother. But the jewelry didn't matter, she only prayed Dovid was hiding and safe. Until now Chavala considered calling on God's help useless, but in this moment . . . "Please God, don't let Dovid come home now, keep him safe, although I know I am unworthy, I beg you." The rest of her pleas remained silent as she heard the clash of her sewing machine hurled against the wall. The bread they ate came from the toil of that machine. Hearing the screams and wailing beyond the confines of where she stood, she knew the wave of horror that had fallen over her people. They were being tortured and beaten, they were being dragged from their hiding places in cellars and garrets and put to death. Smoke rose up from the burning houses and the winds shifted so that she stuck a rag in her mouth for fear she would be heard choking.

Suddenly her fear left and in its place came an overwhelming hatred. How long would it be before this monster discovered her, not only her, but her precious family imprisoned beneath where she now stood? Mama hadn't given her life so that the lives of her children should end in a massacre. If it meant dying, she would die. But not until she killed this crazy devil. Her eyes fell on the large butcher knife. Reaching for it, she inched her way along the wall until she stood to one side of her sewing room. She listened as her heart beat like a drum. It seemed too quiet. She peered through the crack of the wooden slats. His back was turned away from the entrance, and dear God, he was going through her sewing basket. Now he fondled the gold bracelets and put them in his pocket. Taking off her shoes, she walked softly into the room, and plunged the knife between his shoulder blades. As though in a daze, she picked up the metal leg that had been broken from the machine and with all her strength brought it down over his head. The body fell with such a thud that the flimsy floorboards shook. For a long moment he . . . it . . . quivered as the last breath of life was dissipated. Chavala stood trembling. She thought her legs would give way as she steadied herself against the wall. Looking down at the body, an even greater fear came over her . . . what if the devil should be found at this moment? Oh God, what had her vengeance brought down on the family? Why hadn't she let him kill her? That she should even have committed an act so violent . . . but with all her overlapping fears, she brought herself up short . . . she had to deal with them as she had with this monster . . . Quickly she covered the body with rags and the debris he had created, mopped up the bloody floor and shut the door. She went back to the kitchen and sat at the table, holding her face in her hands. Dovid, where was Dovid? Once again, terror washed over her . . . Dovid was dead, she knew it. Nothing else would have kept him away. Should she go out and try to find her husband? But what about the ones huddled together below? She prayed Moishe would survive. He would be the only one to protect the family if anything happened to Dovid and her. As the confusion in her mind flew back and forth, she suddenly became aware of less and less noise in the village . . . was it possible that the wave of horror had ended? She was afraid to hope, yet it truly seemed to be abating. She listened. There was no more shouting of KILL THE JEWS. She looked at the cupboard, which covered the trapdoor, wondering why God had spared this house. She would never know the answer, but for the first time since her mother's death, a rush of tears came down over Chavala's face.

Unsteadily she got up from the kitchen table and walked past the closed door to her sewing room, past her father's bedroom, in front of which lay the broken front door. She took a deep breath as she stood framed in the doorway, then without hesitation found herself standing against the wall on the front porch. Her shock was total. Most of the village was in flames. All she heard were the agonizing, mournful cries of the living. How had the Angel of Death passed over their house? Why had God singled them out to be saved? Why? And then the thought of Dovid rushed back to her, and she managed the strength to run across the road. All that she had feared was well-founded. Dovid lay on the floor in a pool of blood. His hands and ankles were bound with rope. His face had been battered almost beyond recognition. She knelt at his side. Drawing him to her she heard his shallow breathing. He was alive. Cradling him close to her as a child, she whispered, "My dearest Dovid, don't die. Don't leave me. I love you, dearest . . ."

Somewhere from the valley of his consciousness Dovid's eyes fluttered. Still, he knew he was dead. Chavala was, too. They were together. But if he was dead why was the pain so great? Did one suffer in death as in life? Chavala's sweet voice soothed him . . .

"My darling, I'll be back in a little while and we'll take you home. Do you hear me, dearest?"

His eyes fluttered yes, and she gently put the pillow beneath his head, covered him with a blanket and put a cup of water to his lips. They were too swollen to take it. Kissing him, she left and ran across the road.

When the family came up from out of the darkness and saw Chavala, they clung to her, and as though with wings of an eagle she embraced them all and tried to quiet their fears. She poured mugs of milk when they sat at the table and put out the sponge cake. After they had finished she told Sheine to go across the road to Dovid and watch over him, then motioned to her brother to follow her.

Inside her sewing room she tore away the rags and exposed the . . . creature.

Moishe stood back in horror, looking at the huge butcher knife now dried with blood.

"What *happened?*"

Chavala explained with as little detail as possible. There was so much to be done.

"If he's found here we know what will happen. He must be buried so deep that the dogs will not be able to sniff him out. Start the digging near the cherry tree while I wrap him up in rags. Then I'll help you."

When the digging was finished Chavala poured alcohol over the body and the two of them dragged him to the small orchard and watched as he tumbled down the six feet. After the burial was finished they stood back, breathing hard.

In the darkness Chavala said, "Come, let's wash him from our hands."

With the help of everyone, Dovid was brought home and laid on Avrum's bed. Chavala was grateful that the strong cherry brandy had dulled his senses so that he felt very little of that short journey. She sponged his body and spoon-fed him broth and that night she lay on the floor mat next to his.

What seemed to Chavala a miracle not to be questioned, the next afternoon Dovid awoke to full consciousness. She would not ask what happened, it was unimportant. Leaving him in Sheine's care, she and Moishe went to see what they could do to help the bereaved. Except for a few houses all had been burned to the ground. The Chevra Kadisha, the ritual baths, the yeshiva and the *shul* were all in ashes. The cemetery had been desecrated, with many bodies dug up and scattered. The wounded lay in the roads and alleys. Yankel the milkman and his sons were heaping the dead into his cart to be taken up the hill. It was a devastation beyond all comprehension. Not even the devil could have invented such revenge. Manya's family had all perished. Her eyes had been put out and her two youngest babies thrown from the attic to the ground. Rabbi Gottlieb's beard had been torn from his face. He had been beaten with clubs until he lay beyond redemption. Those few who remained helped to bury the dead, whether theirs or not, as though the deceased belonged to them all, as indeed they did. The land of Canaan, from where they had all come, bound them together, one circle without beginning, without end.

Then those same who had survived rent their clothing, sat on the ground and recited the Kaddish, mourning the dead, yet praising God all the same. . . .

Chapter Two

CHAVALA'S APPREHENSIONS GREW. She expected the locusts to come hunting for the buried, but she had kept her fears from Dovid. Dovid's health was returning, and thanks to his inherent strength he had sustained the beating. Her Dovid was a lion.

This morning she could no longer put off telling him of the great danger that hung over their lives. Sitting on the edge of the bed she took his hand in hers. "Dovid, I must tell you something, something I never thought myself capable of . . . the day of the pogrom . . . I killed a man . . ." And she told him every detail, right up to the point where she and Moishe had buried him. "We can't stay . . . I only hope you're well enough to travel."

He would try to absorb what she'd told him about the killing later. It was no little thing to take in about your wife . . . a woman not like others, no question about *that* . . .

"How could I be otherwise with a wife who coddled me like little Chia?"

"I know we must leave. One day he will be discovered, they'll come back looking for him . . ."

"All right, darling, but to get to Palestine is no easy matter."

Palestine? Chavala hadn't thought of going to Palestine. Why had she thought that what *she* so wanted was all that Dovid wanted too . . . So her dream that had looked to America was quieted. She knew her father's wish had always been to die in Eretz Yisroel, and if for nothing else she would have to set aside her own hopes . . . but after he was gone and she had done her duty, well, *then* she would feel free to speak out. But she knew that talking against going to Palestine while still in Odessa was pointless . . . the devotion to Zionism was complete in Dovid now. She was sure . . . hopeful . . . that once Dovid found out the reality of that land he would want America as much as she. Dovid was, she honestly believed, being seduced by an impossible dream. He would have to see that . . .

"Right now there's no way for us to go—"

"Yes, there is . . . we have the money."

He looked at her. "We have the money? From what?"

"From my mother's diamond earrings."

"*No*, that's the legacy she left you. It's my place to provide. I am your husband . . ."

She didn't want to argue that, but this was playing with their lives. "Listen to me, Dovid. I know that they will be back, and I can't eat or sleep for thinking about it. But even if they don't come back because of him, they will come back. Please, let's not be here when the pogroms start again. You've heard what is happening in Kiev, in the Ukraine and in the settlements, you know the violence and burnings that are going on. No, Dovid, we can't wait. Next time we might not be so lucky. That you're alive is a miracle . . ."

Dovid looked at his wife. Actually he'd wanted this for a long time, and it was Chavala that was making it possible, arguing for it . . . he only hoped he could make it up to her. "Chavala . . . I never knew a man could be so lucky . . . you, my darling, are no ordinary woman . . ."

"HOW much do you want for these?" the jeweler in Odessa asked.

Chavala stood nervously as the jeweler looked through his loupe examining the small diamond earrings, wondering how these tiny gems had come to a peasant. Small they were, but perfect and blue-white. "So how much do you want?"

How much? Quickly Chavala tried to figure what it would take them to get to Palestine. "Tell me what they're worth to you, if the price is right, I'll take it, if not, I'll go elsewhere."

He inspected them once again. "Ten rubles."

"Thank you, that's very kind, but give me back my earrings—"

"Fifteen. I should have offered only twelve, but . . . for a pretty—"

"I shouldn't take less than fifty, but give me forty and they're yours."

He laughed, "You're crazy . . . I can buy them in the marketplace for—"

"Thank you, but these are very valuable. I know what they're worth." She, of course, knew nothing of the kind.

"My final offer is twenty-five."

"Thirty." Fire was in her eyes, terror in her heart.

The man laughed, shook his head. Counting out the money he said, "You should be a diamond merchant. To bargain, you know how very well."

With the rubles securely in her hand, she said, "And you know how to cheat."

Turning on her heels she walked with high dignity out the door, slamming it behind her.

As she hurried along the street the echo of the *gonif*'s words rang in her ears. "You should be a diamond merchant . . ." A possibility? Well, a small pair of diamond earrings was buying their freedom. Diamonds meant money and money meant freedom, the power to be free, at least to challenge the world. The words would live with Chavala . . . "You should be a diamond merchant . . ." If they had lived to escape the tyranny and near-death a few short weeks ago, perhaps anything was possible . . .

When she returned home it was with the steamship tickets they needed for steerage. But her greatest pleasure was handing Dovid one gold napoleon that she was able to convert from the rubles she still had left even after the tickets had been purchased.

Chavala took some heart that at least geographically they were in the right place. Odessa was within walking distance and on the Black Sea. Since Jews had never been able to own property, that was a problem they didn't have—there was nothing to dispose of. As always, Jews left with only what they could carry.

So on the twenty-second of May in the year 1906, the Rabinsky-Landau family closed the door behind them. There was nothing to look back on in fond memory, except, perhaps for that small sanctuary marked by a blanket, Chavala and Dovid's universe.

Moishe wheeled Dovid's handcart filled with their bedding, clothing, cooking utensils and little Chia's crib. Raizel carried one basket of food, and Dvora another. Sheine insisted she would be the custodian of her own belongings, which she had meticulously packed in a paper carton.

Dovid and Chavala walked side-by-side, she with the baby in her arms, Dovid holding the rope for the goat to follow.

Avrum clutched his holy books to his chest.

Soon the small assembly was lost from sight, as Yankel the milkman wiped the tears from his eyes and blew his nose on the rag he had taken from his pocket. He stood in the middle of the road long after they disappeared, wishing their journey could have been his own.

WHEN they reached the port in Odessa they were far from being alone. Theirs was hardly an isolated departure . . . from the small towns and hamlets of the Ukraine and the Russian-controlled parts of Poland hundreds of young men and women were packing their meager belongings, and with tears of good-bye to their parents, leaving for, they hoped, something better. Some merely ran away from home when fathers accused their sons of heresy. Zionism was a forbidden doctrine among many of the rabbis and the most devout. Their departure was met with family denunciation . . . *God will send the Messiah* was the watchword that rang through the religious of the *shtetl*, wait, wait. But the youth of that day was the same as that of any other . . . it could no longer hold to the misguided rabbis and the devotions of their fathers. A new time was at hand, and the young were moving with the times. If the Messiah had not redeemed them in two thousand years, then they would redeem themselves. Through Zionism.

On rusting, battered, listing freighters they left Odessa. Some would embark at Trieste, or Constantinople, or Port Said, where they would change to slow cargo vessels to the promised land. The Rabinsky-Landau clan's ancient freighter was bound for Jaffa.

CHAVALA and the children found space belowdecks, where they prepared their bedding on the floor while Dovid went to make arrangements for the goat. Avrum went up on deck, took out his *tallis* and wrapped himself in it, then swayed back and forth with the ancient rhythm and intoned:

> *Hear me, Jacob.*
> *Israel, whom I have called:*
> *I am the one.*
> *The beginning and the end.*
> *My own hand founded the earth*
> *and spread out the skies.*
> *Thus saith the Eternal One.*
> *Who created the heavens and*
> *stretched them out.*
> *Who made the earth and all*
> *that grows in it, who gives*
> *breath to its people and spirit*
> *to those who walk on it.*

The food supplies were rationed by Chavala. The baby had colic . . . the goat's milk had soured. Dvora had dysentery. Raizel seemed to manage the discomforts without complaint, and Sheine became acquainted with a *chevraman* from Galicia whom Dovid distrusted almost as much as the Russian *moujiks.* So far as he was concerned, the Galicianers were selfish *gonifs.*

Knowing how difficult things were for Chavala, Dovid was reluctant to mention the change in Sheine, so he assumed a fatherly role on his own . . . "Sheine, I want you to stay away from this *chevraman.* I don't like the liberty I saw him take with you on deck last night, putting his arm around you—"

"You're not my father. I don't have to listen to you." There was anger in her eyes, when of course it was love she wanted to show. She had allowed the Galicianer to hold her for Dovid to see, to let him know how desirable she could be to a man. Chavala wasn't the only one. If she'd had the jewels he'd given his wife and the black silk dress with the white lace collar, well, she too could look like a queen—

"Sheine, you've changed so I hardly recognize you," he said, shaking his head.

"Oh? You noticed I changed? Did you, Dovid . . . well, good. I'm a woman, I'm thirteen and—"

"I know you're a woman, Sheine. But at the risk of sounding like a boring pedant, I'd like to point out that being a woman doesn't make a person a lady—"

"You have one lady in the family already. I want to be a woman."

Spoken like a true thirteen-year-old, he thought.

She turned and ran until she reached the place that led her to their dark hold below, where she lay down and cried herself into exhaustion.

When they came into the Mediterranean people ventured on deck. There was music from a concertina, a violin, a tambourine, and the dancing lasted until dawn. Still, this night seemed impossible for Dovid. His worry about the future seemed to eat him up, and the festivities above only grated on his nerves.

As they neared Palestine the sea became calm and the air almost stifling. Although he had never mentioned it, in spite of the tightly bound cloth Chavala had made for him his ribs were far from healed and tonight they ached badly. He watched his wife sitting with the other women as she held little Chia, and wondered why still she hadn't conceived. A dark thought passed through his mind . . . his beloved Rivka seemed to have had the same nature; she had conceived late in life, and when he thought of her and her awful death he almost hoped he and Chavala would be childless. After all, there were the girls to raise, and they were like his own. Little Chia would think of him as a *tateh*, and—his thoughts were interrupted as a young man sat down next to him, took out his handkerchief and mopped his forehead. The shock of dark hair receded, although Dovid would have guessed them to be the same age.

"In a few days we'll be in Eretz Yisroel. What do you think of that?" the stranger asked.

"What do I think? I think it's a miracle—"

"Ah . . . the miracle has just begun. Where are you from?" The stranger was short, stocky.

"Near Odessa. And you?"

"Plonsk. What do you do for a living?"

"Make boots. You?"

The stocky man laughed. "I'm a sort of builder . . . of dreams . . . some people say visions . . ."

Dovid looked carefully at this man. "What's your name?"

"David Gruen."

"Mine is Dovid Landau."

The two men shook hands, and Dovid, taken by the man, asked him about himself.

David Grien's mother had died when he was very young, and his father and he proceeded thereafter to have huge disagreements about their beliefs. In the end David defied his father and announced without preamble his departure to Palestine. That was as far as David wanted to go on about the saga of his life. It was as though the rest of his past were nonexistent, no longer of any consequence. "The past is prologue, as Shakespeare said, I come into this old, new world with very little, yet so much. I bring to Palestine young and healthy arms. The love of work, an eagerness for freedom to live in the land of our forefathers, and a willingness to be frugal. If we are to be redeemed, Palestine must be built with our hands. There we will create a model society, based on economic abundance. But above all, political equality." He went on and on, like a missionary . . . with a passion that seemed to Dovid to be seared into his soul. One day, he said, the Jews of the world would rise up, not with arms, not with violence, but with one universal voice . . . "Let my people go, let them live and multiply in the land of their heritage. The land that was their portion when King David brought the Ark to Jerusalem . . ." No question, the man was a spellbinder, and totally convinced . . . and convincing . . .

Now the two sat silently and looked at the midnight sky, sat with thoughts of the future . . .

"Well," Dovid said to the round-faced young man. "I have to go now and join my wife, but I wish you well. I hope we meet again."

"I hope so too, *chevraman.*"

The two clasped hands. "If you come to Petach Tikvah, ask for David Ben-Gurion, not David Grien. I left that name behind in the ghetto of Plonsk. Now . . . *shalom* . . ."

Palestine
1906

Chapter Three

THE LEAKING VESSEL now stood anchored beyond Jaffa. It was early morning, a white mist obscured the distance beyond, but everyone stood at the rail. They had come home at last. As the mist lifted, the shoreline of Jaffa could be seen.

Beauty, promise lay beyond as the pink-and-blue sky seemed to embrace the green waters of the Mediterranean. Suddenly there was a feeling beyond expression. It was as though all their lives had merged into this moment . . . moment of deliverance. Avrum touched the fringes of his *tallis* with his lips, then swung himself into the prayer shawl. For him it was as though God's arms encompassed him. There was joyful singing. Strangers embraced, *minyans* gathered, people bound one another with leather straps around the right arm. On their forehead they placed the minute black leather box that contained the Law, and they intoned the first day of creation as it was written . . . "Let there be light . . ." And now there was. Chavala held onto Dovid as they looked toward what for him was Eden, a trip for her. She looked beyond the horizon—her Eden was America—she would wait.

Moishe could not speak, but he could see it all in his mind . . . the good rich earth where everything grew—oranges, melons, sweet and delicious to the taste like honey, and almonds and grapes. There would be wheat, barley, corn. They would never go hungry again.

Sheine stood watching Chavala and Dovid, then looked directly at Motel, the boy from Galicia. He returned the look. "Will I see you again?"

Sheine shrugged. She had only used the *chalutz* to make Dovid more aware of her. "Who knows? Perhaps . . ."

Their conversation came abruptly to an end, as the whole assembly called out, "Look, they've come to get us . . ."

In the near distance small boats could be seen. The *chalutzim* were rowing fast with deliberate strokes to try and beat the Arabs, who would steal the Jews' possessions and angrily demand, *"Baksheesh, baksheesh . . ."* They would loot anything they could lay their hands on.

Children were running to the rail as the Turkish officers came aboard and demanded papers. Dovid uneasily offered his and a Turk grabbed them out of his hand. The Russian-speaking Turks demanded to know why they were there, and the reply was that they had come as religious pilgrims to pray at the Wailing Wall.

Since no Jew was permitted by law to immigrate into Palestine, Dovid answered each question with caution as the rest of the family stood there, frightened.

How long would they be staying? "Just three weeks," Dovid said, hoping that within three weeks the Turks would be bribed and his family would disappear into the landscape as hundreds of other refugees had done before them. When the Turks' questions seemed satisfied, the red cards issued to all pilgrims were thrust into Dovid's hands. But his papers were confiscated. Dear God, thought Chavala, what would they do? As the red-sashed official moved on, Chavala asked, "What will happen to us without our papers?" Passengers ran helter-skelter, some diving into the water, some throwing their things overboard and jumping in after them, and Dovid said, "We don't have time to think about that, at least we have the red tags."

Now the rowboat bobbed up and down at the side of the ship, and the big *chalutz* bellowed out, *"Jump."*

Although no one could swim it was either drown or be molested, maybe even killed by the Arabs, who were climbing a rope to the deck.

Dovid told Chavala to tear her petticoat into strips, and without thoughts of modesty she slipped out of it. The whole family, in fact, was now involved. Soon the strips were knotted and attached to Chia's basket, then lowered until the *chalutz* retrieved the basket. When Dovid saw the baby secure he told Chavala to jump.

Her heart in her throat, she plunged down into the sea. When she bobbed up to the surface one of the three *chalutzim* was in the water helping her into the small boats. She shivered, dripping wet, then one after another followed until they were all huddled together in the tiny vessel.

"*Shalom.*" The huge *chalutz* smiled his greetings. "Welcome to Eretz Yisroel."

"*Shalom.* Thank God you came out to more than welcome us," Dovid said.

"What will happen to our things and papers?" asked Chavala.

"Don't worry, with money you'll have your things back."

"But we don't have much—"

"Who has?" the *chalutz* said, "but the Zion Agency will take care of it, don't worry. One thing we can depend on as Jews is charity from our own. How else have we survived all these years?"

When Avrum saw the sands of beach that lay just beyond he climbed over the side of the boat, waded to shore and as he reached the beach, bent down and kissed the ground, his black coat dripping, making rivulets in the sand. "This house," he said, "is but a spark, a remnant saved by a miracle from that great fire. Kept by our fathers always upon their altars. You carried us safely to the shore . . ."

Like a small armada, other boats were tying up at the wharf, and as people were being helped out by the *chalutzim* ashore there was a torrent of weeping and embraces with their own *chaverim,* their fellow Jews.

Chavala's tears flowed too, listening to the delighted voices and seeing the faces. They had come as strangers, they had arrived together, sharing, at least for now, a common destiny. Chavala felt most of all the presence of her own as they clustered together. For this moment, at least, she felt at one with Dovid and all the others about the new Zion. Perhaps it would not last, but in this precious piece of time she had come to terms with her desires . . . America would be there when *that* time came, but this supreme moment belonged to those she loved . . . those she would gladly have died for.

Dovid noted one of the members of the Zionist office talking to a Turkish official, and could well imagine what it was about . . . no Turkish official was above corruption. For a price almost anything could be overlooked, forgotten. Corruption was at the very core of the dying Ottoman Empire.

The Yishuv member was bartering for the possessions of the Jews, to have their papers and belongings returned. The money was extorted, then word spread among the newest arrivals that they were to wait and that their belongings and papers would be returned to them soon.

As they waited, Avrum Rabinsky said angrily, "Even here, in our own Eretz Yisroel, we're subject to blackmail? It's not enough, it seems, that we paid in Russia for the right to come here . . ."

A bearded *landsman* sighed, shook his head. "The point is, we don't have a right to be here. Not according to the Turks, anyway. And according to the world we shouldn't exist at all. It's a miracle when you come to think of it, but take heart, friend, they'll never be able to kill us no matter how hard they try. We're still here on these shores even after all the Crusaders have been ground to dust, and we'll be here when we see the Turks in hell."

Right or wrong, the words seemed to make things a little easier to take as Avrum waited with his family in the broiling noonday sun. After what seemed an age they were, miracle of miracles . . . plus a little crossing of Turkish palms . . . once again in possession of their papers and other belongings, even Chavala's goat. Picking up their bundles they started to make their way through the congested narrow alleys of Jaffa. The filth in the narrow lanes was almost too much. This was not exactly what Avrum had envisioned, he had lived his life with a dream of dignity, thinking one day he would sit under his own fig tree. Jaffa seemed worse than any *shtetl* in Russia, but he told himself that this, after all, was an Arab city and for thousands of years Arabs had lived in a backwash of ignorance. Things would be different when he left here and finally reached his resting place —Jerusalem.

Whatever disappointment Dovid might have held couldn't be read on his face. Still, Chavala knew that this was not the land of freedom, or milk and honey, of beauty and plenty that the *Bilus* with their messages of hope and promise spouted in the basements and attics and back rooms of Kiev, the Ukraine, and Odessa. Dovid must be affected by the contrast, Chavala thought. As for her, she had not come to Eretz Yisroel with any illusion, any desire to reclaim the land. Her dream was America, and so not expecting anything, she could not really complain.

But poor papa, who had lived with a fantasy, the effect on him must be devastating . . . she could, she felt, read his thoughts. They had come unprepared for this. Where were the green hills, the wild flowers . . . where indeed were the roses of Sharon . . . the trees, the pastures where David's sheep had once grazed? Where, in fact was a shade tree where any man could sit in peace? At least she and the rest of her family were young, life could change. Coming to Eretz Yisroel was not like a marriage that bound a man and a woman together forever, it was only a stopping-off place for her, but papa had come to end his days with dreams of inheriting the earth. After all, he was the meek, no question of that. But the land he had hoped for had been desecrated by these heathens. There was no fertile land to walk on, only sand and more sand that went on further than the eye could see. No, this was not the place Dovid had promised and papa had hoped for. It was a network of swarming humanity that existed in the narrow alleys. Garbage had to be stepped over. Dead fish lay heaped against the wall. Naked Arab children stood about with vacant faces, hollow eyes and bulging bellies. Children not as old as Dvora were already professional beggars and thieves. The women were dressed in torn rags, and their children sat in the doorways of their hovels. Eretz Yisroel was a small cluster of houses built of mud and pitted sandstone perched on uneven low mounds of sand. This place where they stood was supposed to be one of the oldest inhabited places on earth. Well . . . nothing had changed in two thousand years.

Chavala looked at her father, his eyes filled with tears. Silently he asked what had they done, what had they done to desecrate God's holy earth? His lips barely moving, he asked if they had done the same to Jerusalem, his beloved city.

Chavala put her arm around him. "It's all right, papa. Remember, this is an Arab city. Jerusalem will be as you hoped."

"Then please, please let's go on to Jerusalem."

"We must let Dovid make the plans. Come now, papa."

It wasn't until the reached the Jewish section of Jaffa that Avrum recovered some of his hope.

The young children had not viewed the scene so unhappily. In fact they were enormously excited. Wide-eyed, they walked along the rows of stalls filled with bolts of vibrant colored Oriental silks and cottons, with beads and bangles—this was the one that Sheine especially loved. She tried on the harem rings, the bracelets, and she fastened in her lobes a pair of earrings that looked like filigreed lace and were the color of gold. The sandal shop, where Sheine was sure that harem girls shopped, intrigued her . . . she would have given her young life for a pair.

Dvora's tastes inclined to the less dramatic. Imagine cooking kasha in the earthen pots!

And Raizel seemed just to enjoy the whole excursion.

The children broke out in laughter when Moishe tried on a tropical helmet brought by Christian pilgrims, then a red fez with a black tassel. He wrapped an Arab scarf around his neck, a colorful sash around his middle and stuck a jeweled dagger inside the sash. Trying not to laugh, he asked, "Could I be taken for a Turk?"

"Not likely," Sheine said, "with your red hair."

Standing outside the stall Avrum said, "That's enough, children . . . I've seen enough. We're leaving this Gomorrah."

Sheine looked at the bracelets, at the sandals she would have loved, but to ask would have been futile. They had so little money. But one day, she promised herself, one day she would be back.

Dovid led them beyond the marketplace, and in spite of Avrum's pleadings to go on to Jerusalem, he said they would stay overnight in Jaffa. The journey was too strenuous to begin this same day.

The hotel of Isaac Hirsch was like a true Jewish home. Odors of fresh baked bread wafted through the air from the kitchen of Frieda Hirsch. Wiping her hands on her white apron, she greeted her guests as though they were long-lost cousins from Minsk. *"Shalom,* you are welcome in my home. We are like one big family. Don't hesitate to ask for anything you need. Now, Isaac will show you where the sleeping quarters are. Go rest before supper," she said as she stroked little Chia under the chin. "Such a little beauty. For her I just may have a hard cookie."

When the family was settled and Avrum finally resigned, Dovid went to the Zionist Settlement Office and waited, as the others did. Suddenly he again saw the short, stocky man with the halo of brown hair—*"Shalom,* Ben-Gurion."

"Shalom, Dovid Landau, how did things go?"

"In the beginning a little hectic when we arrived this morning. As you probably noticed. But after today I think we're ready for anything."

Ben-Gurion laughed, then, "Where are you off to?"

"Jerusalem. I've come to ask if we can get some transportation."

"Transportation? If you can get two donkeys you'll be lucky."

"So I'll settle for that. We have a big family and a long way to go."

"We all have a long way to go, my friend, but we'll make it. I'm going to suggest that from now on you should speak Hebrew. When we become a country we must have a language."

Dovid shook his head. "Maybe *you'll* be able to speak Hebrew, but you don't have a father-in-law like mine. To speak in the tongue of the Torah would be to demean God's word. I'm afraid in my house Yiddish will be spoken."

"Then you will have to assert yourself as the head of the family. Ben-Yehudah almost killed himself inventing modern Hebrew. He wouldn't speak to his wife for three weeks because of her resistance. How long can a woman be ignored? She gave in. I wonder if he's so happy now. I understand women can talk a lot."

The two laughed.

"Where are you staying in Jaffa?" Dovid asked.

"In this hell hole I wouldn't spend the night. Plonsk was beautiful compared to this place. As soon as I can get my papers I'm walking to Petach Tikvah."

"You mean today?"

"Today."

"Well, *mazel tov.* Till we meet again."

THE road to Jerusalem was an obstacle course . . . Arab marauders ambushed travelers on the way to the Holy City, possessions were stolen and lives were at extreme risk. The road was narrow, and large boulders had to be cleared before one could go on. It wasn't until they had gone beyond the gorge at Bab el Wad that they allowed themselves to feel even a little safe.

Three days and nights they had traveled, resting at the settlements. Now, within miles of the Holy City, Sheine dropped to the ground in exhaustion. "I can't go on." She hated this place and even, for the moment at least, Dovid for wanting to come here. He had drawn beautiful word pictures of Eretz Yisroel. Well, what they'd seen so far was dirt, sand and mosquitoes that had bitten her so that painful welts were on her arms and legs. Why hadn't they gone to America, like Chavala wanted, instead of this hell on earth? Sheine had momentarily forgotten the pogrom they'd fled from. She looked at Chavala who had ridden most of the way on the back of a donkey because she was carrying the baby, little Chia. How charitable of her to let them ride from time to time. Papa was an old man, so she didn't begrudge him riding the beast, but Chavala! What made her better than the rest of them? That baby was as much theirs as hers. How dare she act as though she'd given birth to it. Her mean thoughts were interrupted when Dovid said, "Why didn't you tell us before, your feet are bleeding—"

"*Because* you were all so anxious to get to Jerusalem by tonight."

"Yes, and the reason is we have no safe place to stay between here and Jerusalem."

Sheine shot back, "What would have happened if we'd have stayed another day in Jaffa? At least there was a little excitement. If we'd stayed another day do you suppose the heavens would have stood still? I hate this place, I wish I'd never come."

Avrum Rabinsky looked at his daughter for a long painful moment.

"I fear for you, Sheine. I think there's a dybbuk inside you, how could six children have been born of your sainted mother and have one such as you?"

Sheine felt the guilt intended for her. She loved her father and she had offended him . . . but he didn't understand her, didn't know that what haunted and taunted her by day, wouldn't let her sleep at night. Dovid . . . If only she could stamp out her love, her obsession with him. All it caused her was pain. Standing up now, she said, "I'm sorry, papa, I'm very tired, please forgive me . . ."

Dovid picked Sheine up in his arms, "Come, I'll carry you."

"I don't need any favors."

Ignoring her, he lifted her up, and as they once again began the journey toward the Holy City she allowed herself to relax in his arms. He felt so good, so strong. It was hard to remember he was Chavala's husband, especially when she didn't want to . . . clinging to him, she fantasized what it would be like if he were her husband, how it would be to lie next to him in the night, wrapped up in his arms, feel his warmth. Then to possess him the way a woman did a man. She closed her eyes and let the fantasy take over. At least he was hers for this moment.

WHEN they approached the top hills just before going down into the Holy City the family stood in hushed silence. Clustered together, they had their first view of Jerusalem . . . Above the ancient wall could be seen the golden dome of the Moslem shrine, beyond the courtyard into the distance lay the Mount of Olives and high above sat Mount Scopus, where the faithful were being called to worship, the church bells tolling in the hush of twilight.

Chavala looked out to the white limestone of the Judean hills. How many millions of lives had been ground into that dust, she wondered . . .

At last they reached the Damascus gates leading to the Old City and slipped through.

When Avrum Rabinsky saw the Wailing Wall he actually trembled, sure his heart had stopped beating. The dream had been dreamt for so long he couldn't believe that such a miracle could have actually happened. He hurried ahead of the family as he held his hand over his heart, and when he finally stood before it, he fell on bended knees and kissed the earth. It made no difference to him how neglected these holy stones had become . . . he was here. Getting up, he kissed the stone and with shaking fingers let his hands wander over its rough surface, repeating the prayer, "Hear, oh Israel: The Lord is our God, the Lord is one. Praised be His name whose glorious kingdom is forever and ever." And then he intoned, "Cause us, oh Lord our God, to lie down each night in peace, and to awaken each morning to renewed life and strength. Spread over us the tabernacle of Thy peace. Help us to order our lives by Thy counsel, and lead us in the paths of righteousness. Be Thou a shield about us, protecting us from hate and war, from pestilence and sorrow. Curb Thou also within us the inclination to do evil, and shelter us beneath the shadow of Thy wings. Guard our going out and coming in unto life, and peace from this time forth and forevermore." He thanked the One Above for allowing him to come to this dwelling place, for letting him be a part of those who had gone before him, of the two thousand years that had brought him to this moment.

Seeing her father embrace the ancient stones, his fingers exploring the tufts of moss that grew between the cracks, Chavala knew that he at least had come home at last, and she was grateful that her own self-centered desires had not denied him this. Those nights as they lay on deck, her secret thoughts had been full of discontent. She remembered looking up to the midnight-blue sky and berating herself for not insisting they go to America. No one had known the demons she'd fought inside herself. At times her anger was almost impossible to hide . . . her feeling that she should have spoken out in her unhappiness . . . She dared ask, silently, why should she have to sacrifice herself for the sake of an old man; he would have lived out his days in the village of his birth if the Russians hadn't turned them out. She tried to convince herself that in America, if their stomachs were full, their feet shod, a roof over their heads and money in their pockets, then his dream of dying in the homeland would surely fade . . . But standing here now, watching her old father, Chavala knew in her heart such thoughts were a lie, a self-deception so that *she* might have her way. But one owed others, she reminded herself. There were debts to be paid. Nobody was born unto himself. Obligations were the kernel of love, and for the first time Chavala did feel at peace with the acceptance of knowing that this was right. Her father's needs and desires were greater than hers, and she embraced her father as a mother would a child. Whispering, she said, "Come, papa, we must get settled. You have your whole life to come back here."

The housing that had been provided for them was a stone hovel twenty-four steps above the street. It sat nestled in a dark, damp alley surrounded by other hovels that looked a thousand years old.

That night they ate in a dismal kitchen. In the other three rooms there were makeshift beds where the family finally lay down.

The next day Chavala, Dovid and the children went to explore this new world. The poverty seemed even more stark than in the little village south of Odessa. It also seemed no better than the streets of Jaffa, and the noise was deafening as they passed the crowded stalls . . . stop it, Chavala chastised herself. Remember why you are here . . . remember what you buried near that blooming tree in Odessa, and remember the fears that forced you and your family to run away. Be grateful . . . be *humble,* Chavala. Still, in spite of herself, the battle went on in her mind.

The poverty was bad anywhere, but here in the Old City Jews had been reduced to living conditions that were barely human. It was a way of life that was accepted and expected. They lived and died on the bounty sent from the Diaspora.

Neither Chavala nor any of her family had ever seen begging in the streets by *Jews.* It was shameful. Children holding out emaciated dirty hands went unnoticed as pious old men hurried on to worship. There was a sickly pallor about them . . . from one generation to the next they had lived in the hovels and dark alleys huddled together. It seemed nature had accommodated their size so that they could fit into their cramped quarters. The men were small compared to both Dovid and Moishe, who was only fifteen. They were round-shouldered from bending over their books and scrolls. The Rabinskys might have been terribly poor in Russia, but it didn't seem so stark, so depressing. Meager as the living was, the Jews *tried.* Yes, there was charity . . . in every home nailed to the wall was the small blue-and-white tin box where a coin was dropped. Those who couldn't make a living were helped, the poor gave to the poor and the poorer gave to those even less fortunate. In her small village there was a feeling of community . . . in spring they picnicked in the meadow, by the cherry tree. It seemed at times, when they were left alone to live in peace, that life had been quite sweet. Maybe it was the smells of mama's delicious cooking, but for the little they had, it still did not seem like this. She guessed it was that people missed the things they knew as children. Whatever . . . there was a quality in their lives she didn't feel here, here in this most holy and sacred of places.

It especially galled her that the food brought to their table was provided by the alms of charity, and she made a pact with herself that her family would *not* live their lives without dignity, and dignity was earned from the toil of their hands and the brains in their heads. Nothing was too menial if it was an honest day's work. She would give them a sense of purpose. If she had an ounce of strength they would not be put in the ranks of the despised and forgotten . . . her family would *not* live in filth, be clothed in rags. Not *hers* . . .

Chavala counted out a few coins and gave them to Moishe to buy soap, a broom and three scrub brushes. When he returned she recruited the girls. Each was given a lecture on cleanliness. There was a good deal of religion talked about here, but if anything was next to godliness, it was cleanliness. They scrubbed the floors, religiously, and the walls and ceilings until they were spotless. Chavala herself washed everything in sight until her hands were raw.

Dovid stretched a rope on the flat-topped roof, then helped Chavala carry up the load. When she looked at the bedding flapping gently in the breeze she forgot her own fatigue and her aching arms . . . it was a good day's work and next time she would save money by making her own soap.

No such satisfaction for Sheine. Chavala, she thought, had become obsessed with cleaning; now she insisted that the front stoop be scrubbed and the stairs washed down. "There's a limit to how hard a person can work, we're not mules—"

"Maybe not!" Chavala snapped back at her, "but we're not pigs either. This place hasn't been cleaned in a hundred years, and if you think I'm going to allow *my* family to live like the *others* you're mistaken—"

"What makes you think we're any different than the *others,* as you call them, no matter how much you scrub, this place will still be the ghetto—"

"But at least it'll be clean."

"A lot of good that will do us," Sheine said, and ran from the room and down the stone stairs, where she almost collided with Dovid. Breathing quickly, she looked at him, and couldn't help thinking, strange that men didn't have to work, only women. Papa went to the synagogue and the Wailing Wall every day. And Dovid? What did he do with his time? Oh, she knew, she'd asked Moishe and he'd told her that Dovid spent his time in the cafe at the old slave market, debating and arguing about very important matters with the Lovers of Zion, like how best to correct those ignorant Jews back in the old country.

"Where were you going in such a hurry?" Dovid asked.

"Out." She glared at him.

"I know, but where?"

"Where I *please*—"

"But why so angry?"

"Ask your wife. She's a tyrant, she'd like to make slaves of us and

I'm sick of it. That's all she wants us to do, is scrub. For what? Look at my hands."

He sighed as he saw Sheine trying to hold back the angry tears. "Chavala wants to make it a little better—"

"Better than what? There's filth all around us. I hate it here—"

"This won't be forever, Sheine."

"I know, Dovid, as soon as the Messiah comes we won't need the Lovers of Zion."

"Please, Sheine, don't be so bitter, and try not to be angry with Chavala. She's trying to make a home for us. Now come upstairs with me."

Chavala . . . always Chavala. Chavala the queen. Chavala the teacher . . . "No, thank you, I'll be back later."

"But it's almost time for supper and papa will be—"

"What are you afraid of, Dovid? That if I leave this holy place and go beyond the Jaffa gate I might be taken by the Arabs and become a bad woman? Oh, don't worry about me. Go see your immaculate wife."

Dovid waited until she disappeared down the narrow cobblestone alley, then stood there, feeling that the responsibility of Sheine's deep hurt was properly placed on his shoulders. Those evenings they'd sat in the dimly lit kitchen and he'd talked about the glories they'd find in Eretz Yisroel. True, things weren't as he'd hoped, but his own devotion, determination still held. Yes . . . if he'd known the realities he would have prepared them in a different way. If he hadn't been so naive he would have understood . . . made them understand . . . that just coming here was only the beginning, not the fulfillment. He'd been so caught up in the notion of building a new life for all Jews he'd deluded himself. The truth was, he'd been ignorant, and his fears now were as great as Sheine's. For over a week he'd wandered the streets, become convinced he would never find what he was looking for in Jerusalem. Now he knew that Eretz Yisroel meant Jerusalem only for Avrum, and that to wrench Chavala away would be an almost impossible task. But what could he do to make a living here? Slowly he walked up the stairs to where Chavala waited.

AVRUM returned home after his day spent in prayer, washed himself so that he could come to God's table with clean hands. As Chavala brought the food to the table, Avrum looked around and saw that Sheine was not there. He frowned and was about to ask where she was when Sheine came into the room, kissed him on the cheek, then sat down next to Moishe.

There was a long, awkward silence as Avrum looked at his daughter. "Where have you been, Sheine?"

"I sent her to the marketplace to buy—" But before Chavala could finish, Sheine interrupted: "I can speak for myself." How dare Chavala treat her as though she were a stupid child! She didn't need Chavala's protection. "I wanted to see the city outside the walls, is there anything wrong with that, papa?" She spoke with more insolence than she had intended. Well, it was her anger at Chavala that had spoken, not her . . .

Avrum looked at Sheine. No . . . she was not like the others. There was a defiance, an arrogance. A child did not speak to a father that way . . . "Yes, Sheine, there *is* something wrong with that. A girl does not go out alone. I forbid it, do you hear me?"

"I hear you, papa, but why should you object? Jerusalem is also outside the walls—"

"For my daughters Jerusalem does not extend beyond the Damascus gates. From now on you will not go further than the old city."

Sheine sat with her head bowed, biting her lower lip. This humiliation was too much . . . in front of the others . . . Papa had never treated his children with such anger, it was Chavala who was at fault . . . Chavala whom she blamed. She waited to settle herself a little, then excused herself and went to her room. Shutting the door behind her she lay down and cried out bitter tears. No one, she was convinced, really loved her. She was alone, she always would be . . .

When she heard the door open, she wiped her eyes quickly and lay with her face to the wall.

"Sheine," she heard Chavala say, "may I please speak to you?" Sheine didn't move.

"Sheine, please . . . forgive me. I know it was me you wanted to run away from. I was too hard on you."

Slowly Sheine turned toward Chavala, her eyes cold as steel. "How kind of you, but why the sudden concern for me? Are you feeling guilty for what papa said to me? That should have made you very happy—"

"Oh, Sheine, *please,* let's not fight. Our lives are difficult enough. All we have is each other. I love you, Sheine . . . you're my sister . . . I just hope you can love me in return." She reached out, took Sheine by the shoulders and hugged her close.

And somehow in that moment the anger vanished and the two sisters cried in one another's arms . . . Chavala because she hoped so intensely that the two would become closer. Sheine's tears, though, were because she knew that she would always be jealous of Dovid's love for Chavala, and not her. She wished she could feel differently, but she couldn't. Maybe there really *was* a *dybbuk* in her. God help her . . .

Chapter Four

AVRUM HAD BEEN so preoccupied with God that he had failed to notice the great changes in his children.

Moishe and Dovid gradually left the tradition of putting on the phylacteries and were absent from the morning prayers. He would have thought that they would have clung to their faith after getting to this holy place, but he came to the realization that Eretz Yisroel for them was not, as for him, a place to drench their souls. He felt in some way he had failed. His children seemed to grow further apart from the traditions of their faith, and painful as it was to face, in the freedom of their newfound hope he trembled that they were becoming nonbelievers. His heart nearly broke when he admonished Moishe for deceiving him, when he found out he was not attending the yeshiva . . .

"Papa, I beg you to understand," Moishe said. "I love God as much as I ever did, but papa, you must understand that if a man is born free he must pursue his religion according to his times and needs. I will observe, but not in your way. I can't go to the yeshiva, because that means to live on charity, and *that* is something I can't live with. I think, papa, the time has come for me to be a man and contribute a man's share to his family. I've taken a job in Mea Shearim cutting stones—"

Avrum clenched his hand out of fear that he would hit his son. But more than his own anger he actually was afraid that God's wrath would descend on his child. Where, he asked himself, have I failed as a father? And how had he failed by not being able to reach Dovid? Dovid wanting to use the sacred words of the Torah was something that Avrum could not tolerate. Dovid's words rang in his ear: "If we are to be a nation we must speak a common language. Today Eretz Yisroel is like the Tower of Babel, a hundred tongues are spoken here . . ."

"If God had intended for our sacred words to be spoken to one another it would have been written in the holy text. I *forbid* it, do you hear me, Dovid, I forbid it." And saying it, Avrum thought how much he too had changed since coming to Eretz Yisroel . . . he would never have imagined that he could feel such anger against his children, or Dovid . . . he had always been, after all, a rather meek man, but his children were demanding things of him he just could not condone. He hadn't come to Eretz Yisroel to change the word of God . . . he'd come here to do God's will, to live and be buried in the sacred earth.

Chavala knew that nothing Dovid could say could convince her father. True . . . they spoke a bastard language, the outgrowth of living in the ghetto, an extraction of German mingled with Russian, a jargon that made it near-impossible to communicate. But Avrum would not give in.

Dovid tried again. Hebrew, he said, was the language of their forefathers two thousand years ago, and it should have been like honey in his mouth, but Avrum shook his head and turned more than ever to his dedication to God through prayers . . . including more for Dovid's and his children's salvation. Avrum Rabinsky's had become a divided house . . .

Chavala lay alongside Dovid and said, "Don't be angry at papa, Dovid. Remember, he's an old man who has only one reason for living —his faith. Please don't challenge him anymore—"

"I don't challenge him, Chavala, I try to explain. All right, I'll try. Still, *we* have to try to fulfill ourselves too. We're entitled to our dreams—"

"I know, Dovid, dreams are fine, as I said so long ago, but we mustn't have our dreams at the expense of other people." She laughed mildly. "I'll tell you what my grand dream is right now . . . to own a sewing machine."

"Well, that's not such a difficult one. For that we only need money."

Remembering the small amethyst brooch that belonged to Dovid's grandmother, Chavala thought she needed a machine much more. Her sisters should be dressed decently . . . "I have the money, Dovid . . ."

"How do you happen to have the money?"

"From the dowry I held out on you," and not wanting to press the matter she nestled close in Dovid's arms and whispered, "We're always so serious, Dovid, do you realize you haven't made love to me for . . . well, I wonder if you still know how?"

Putting his mouth to hers he kissed her and whispered, "I still know how." And, blessedly, there was no more talk that night.

DOVID bought an old sewing machine from an Arab tailor in Jerusalem, which raised Chavala's spirits considerably. In the marketplace she bought material and set herself to making peasant skirts and blouses like the ones they'd worn at home. She made an especially beautiful one for Sheine. As she admired it a sudden thought grew . . . why shouldn't she find a small stall and become a merchant herself . . . ? The idea alone made her excited, even more so when she imagined Dovid sharing the stall with her. Here they were, both of them strong, each with a good trade, and Dovid seemed to be wandering aimlessly about. Good God, why hadn't she thought of this before? She could hardly wait for Dovid to come home.

When he did, for the first time since their marriage, angry words erupted between them.

"I didn't come to Eretz Yisroel to be a ghetto bootmaker."

Chavala stopped her pedaling and looked across to where Dovid sat on the rickety wooden chair. "You're not going to be a bootmaker? What then, a doctor?"

He ignored the sarcasm. "Chavala, we both know that this is not why we came to Eretz Yisroel."

"I thought we came to escape the pogroms."

"That's true, but there must be a deeper meaning to our lives. Surviving isn't enough . . ."

"Not being killed has plenty of meaning for me. At least the Turks don't massacre us."

"Chavala, let's not play games. We didn't run away to settle behind a ghetto wall. Look how we're living."

Her pulse beat a little faster with hope. Maybe Dovid was disillusioned with Eretz Yisroel, after all . . . "Then this isn't what you expected it to be?"

"You're right, Chavala, I didn't come to pray at the Wall. You know what I want."

Of course . . . for a moment she had allowed herself to think he'd changed his mind, wanted to choose America with her . . . Yes . . . she knew what he wanted . . . to live in the wilderness on some Godforsaken kibbutz, but if she gave in to that she could forget about ever leaving Palestine. When the time came she would fight him. She had something coming to her too, her dream of America . . . "I don't see anything so terribly wrong with the way we're living . . . if you wanted to make a living you could—"

"I know . . . I could be a bootmaker. Well, I won't do it, Chavala, not even for you. I want to help build a land—"

"In America you wouldn't have to build a land. It's already built."

"But America is not *our* country. This is."

"Is it? Forgive me, but this country belongs to the Turks and Bedouins, and the decay and rot and pestilence. Please, Dovid, let the Lovers of Zion have their fantasy, but I'm afraid Jews will never have a country. We will always be the intruders who plead with the world to just let us survive. Only in America, Dovid, can you and I really be free."

"*No.* This land, by *rights,* belongs to us, and one day, Chavala, we'll *have* it."

"You're still back in Reb Kaufman's basement, listening to that great sage, the *Bilu* who came from Palestine to save us. To build a country. But how can you build a country when you can't even buy land?"

"Legally, as individuals, no. But in spite of it all, land is still being bought up, settlements are being established . . ."

Chavala loved Dovid so she found it almost impossible to deny him . . . except, she couldn't help thinking, why was it always she who had to give in? But what she said was, "What about my father? You know he'd never leave Jerusalem."

"I've thought about that. Sheine's old enough to take care of him. It isn't that I don't love him, Chavala, I do. But you and I have a life to make—"

"And what about the rest of the family? Have you thought about them too?"

"Yes . . . whoever wants, can come. It's for them to make the choice. But you, little Chia and I will go."

"I didn't say that I would—"

"I'm begging you, Chavala. If we're to find a life, it can't be here in Jerusalem."

But all she could say was that she would think about it.

That night they slept back to back.

The next morning as she watched Dovid leave in anger, Chavala was reminded of another day, a day that now seemed so far away . . . their wedding night. But at least it served to remind her that Dovid Landau was not a man to be wrapped up like a package. For all his kindness and love, he expected his wife to love him enough to go with him. She *was* his wife, and since the days of Ruth a wife went where her husband went. He didn't say when he would return, and her heart beat too fast as she fought back the tears . . .

DOVID had journeyed far into the hills of Metullah, dodging the marauding Bedouins, spurred on by his hope of finding land to settle on . . . But that hope was soon crushed when he found that at the settlement of the Baron de Rothschild only *Arabs* were employed. Not one Jew worked the land—it was cheaper for the baron to hire *fellaheen.* The only Jews to be seen were administrators and overseers, and they had been imported from France, as had been the agriculturists who taught the Arabs how to farm.

He felt duped, deceived by the Lovers of Zion who had filled his and so many other minds with visions of a Jewish utopia.

Angry, frustrated, he left and went back to Jerusalem . . . .

At Mea Shearim Dovid found a job as a stonecutter, working with his brother-in-law Moishe. As he chipped away through the rough rock, he thought, well, at least better this than a bootmaker. "I'm a builder, a builder of dreams," David Ben-Gurion had said to him that night. Here, cutting the stone, at least in a small way he was helping to rebuild the land. This stone would go into new dwellings to build a country . . .

When he returned home that evening his disappointment over not being able to work in the fields was so great he said nothing about working for the diminutive Yemenite in Mea Shearim.

Chavala, though, could hardly overlook his scratched and calloused hands, but since Dovid would say nothing to her, well, she wouldn't ask why he had stayed away, where he had been . . . She wouldn't even tell him she'd missed him . . . oh God, how she'd missed him . . .

That evening was only a prelude to the week that came. Each morning he left for Mea Shearim only to return silent, withdrawn.

After a week Chavala could no longer stand it. That night she moved closer to her husband, waited for him to turn to her . . . he only lay there, rigid, his back to her.

Getting out of bed, Chavala began to pace the small room. Her anger had gone to hurt, and the hurt eventually became guilt . . . he was her husband, and there came a time when it no longer mattered who was right, who was wrong. "Dovid, how long is this going to go on?"

Silence.

"Dovid, please, speak to me."

He turned to look at her. "I don't know how to solve this, I don't."

Again, silence.

"Dovid, there must be an answer, let's try to find it—"

"Do you think you could stand the truth?"

"What's the truth, Dovid?"

"That you are my wife and your place is with me. You know why I came. My reasons are the same."

"But what about the family? How can I leave them—?"

"Look, damn it, I love them too . . . but don't we have a right to our own lives? Maybe it was foolish, but I honestly believed that once your father was settled we would be free to leave Jerusalem. I was even foolish enough to believe that after all we went through in Russia that you too would see that our only hope for survival was an Eretz Yisroel restored. I was wrong. I'm not blaming you, you just don't feel what I do . . ."

"And I'm sorry for that, Dovid, truly sorry, so what do we do . . . ?"

"Chavala, as much as I love you and the family I can't stay here and rot . . . give up my mission. When two people can't share the same needs and hopes, well, I suppose you must do what you feel best. I *won't* beg anymore. The decision is yours, but I tell you . . . I must leave here or I'll just cease to exist . . ."

The words cut through Chavala like a knife. If she did not go with Dovid she would lose him, and if she went her family might be lost, especially her father . . . she tried separating the pieces. In her heart she knew the answer . . . her place was with her husband . . . "All right, Dovid, have you decided where you want to go?"

"Yes, to the Galilee."

She'd never heard of it. "Is it very far?"

"From Jerusalem, yes."

"Isn't it possible to find a settlement closer to Jerusalem where you could be happy?"

"I wish you could have said *we* instead of . . . never mind . . . most of the settlements are failing, Chavala, but at least there's *hope* in the Galilee."

And he proceeded to explain that a strain of wheat had recently been discovered by a man named Aaron Aaronson, whose fame as an agronomist was worldwide. On his recommendation the purchase of a large parcel of land had been made from an absentee Arab effendi who lived in luxury in Beirut. The discovery held the promise that the Galilee could become the most productive farming area in Eretz Yisroel, and five American Jews of great wealth were contacted. Their allegiance to the rebirth of Palestine was as deep and strong as those who had inhabited the land for centuries. They too had once fled the ghettos of Russia and Poland. It took little persuasion to convince them. The money that was sent to the Zion Settlement Office in Jaffa and five thousand dunams of land now belonged to them.

When the effendi signed over his ownership he looked at the document and considered the Jews to be, as always, stupid fools. They had purchased a parcel of swamp and malaria-ridden earth that could never be redeemed. It was a place, in fact, where even birds of prey never ventured, but Jews were children of death anyway and he had properly disposed of this uninhabitable scourge, this abominable cancer in the earth, by selling it to the lowest of human vermin.

Twenty-five men, one single woman and four married couples with small children accepted the challenge. This settlement would be worked for Jews by Jews and when they reclaimed the land, as they were determined to do, it would be because of the sweat and toil of *their* hands. They would be in debt to no one. No foreign administrator and no baron. It would be a commune based on social equality, democratic justice. They would become a judiciary unto themselves. Marriage and divorce, education and the rearing of children would be implemented by the consent of all. And so this small group of people set out to prove to the world that they were more than idealistic dreamers . . .

It was a moving story, but Chavala was still desperately unhappy with the choice she had to make. How to prepare her father? Still, she decided, finally, that her place was with Dovid. The debate was over . . . "I've decided to go, but dear God, how do we tell papa?"

"He trusts you, Chavala—if only you could convince him to come with us."

"Oh, Dovid, you know he would never do that, for him Eretz Yisroel means Jerusalem."

Dovid knew Chavala was right. "We'll do the best we can . . . Chavala, I *will* try to make you happy, I love you very much . . ."

She put her head on his shoulder. "I love you too, Dovid, much more than you can imagine, especially . . . " she smiled " . . . considering the way I act sometimes."

THE next night after supper, the family around the kitchen table, Chavala's courage almost collapsed as she tried to explain the reasons they had to leave, and Dovid felt at once grateful and guilty.

"Papa, please, I beg you, come with us."

His hands shook slightly as he embraced his holy book. "Never . . ." The old man sat with his head bowed, then looked at Dovid. "And you, who I've considered a son, have forsaken me, listened to false prophets

. . . I know about your Zionists, and to them I can . . . I came to this place because it is written that from the seed of Abraham—"

Dovid did not want to hear the rest of the quotation.

Moishe thought back to those days when he'd first heard about the Lovers of Zion and knew that he felt like Dovid. He must not bend to his father's will either. His father was an old man who was like iron in his determination to live out his days as he felt he must. Well, Moishe would do the same . . . "Papa, please try to remember that I love you, but I must go with Dovid and Chavala."

The old man slowly shook his head, it was a new world where respect and honor were no longer important to show a father. He was losing his children.

As if reading his mind, Moishe said, "Papa, if you love Eretz Yisroel as you say, you must see how very important this is to us. We were once a great nation and we must be that again. It's for us, papa, to make the greatness of our people known to the world."

Now the old man was not listening. His children, it seemed, all of them, had become bewitched by the devil . . . "And you, Dvora, what about you . . .?"

Putting her arms around her father she said, tears in her eyes, "Please forgive me, papa, but I want to go with the rest."

Gently he released her. "Better that you should ask God to forgive you . . . and you, Sheine, you will go too?"

"*No.* I'll never leave you. Let them go, papa, we can get along without them. They don't seem to need us or want us—"

"What a thing to say, Sheine," Chavala told her.

"I think what you're doing is shameful, leaving your father. Families don't separate. But don't worry, Chavala, we won't die just because you and Dovid go off. Maybe life is just too difficult for you here. You know, Chavala, you think the whole world will fall apart if it weren't for you—"

Chavala's anger flared and she actually slapped her sister, and then just as quickly it died as she took her sister in her arms and tried to kiss away the hurt . . . "I'm *sorry* . . . this is a time of great emotion, Sheine—"

Sheine pulled herself away from Chavala and stood up. "Oh, I think you'll recover, after all, Chavala, you should go where your husband wants. Now, I think the others should make a decision: How about you, Raizel?"

For Raizel it was like being cut in two. One part wanted to stay with papa, the other to go with Chavala. She too craved flowers and green grass and sheep. She loved the pictures of shepherds and their flocks, and she hated the crowded, narrow stone alleys here where the children had to play. There was no sun here, she longed just to see a blue sky. They rarely went beyond the confines of where they lived. The only beauty Raizel ever saw was when she stood on a chair and looked out to the Mount of Olives, and now, to be separated from Chavala . . . after all, hadn't Chavala been the one who all but nursed her? . . . Still, she loved papa too. And seeing him in such distress, she put her arms around him and said, "I'll stay."

None of them slept that night. The next morning Dovid went to the donkey cart. The mule that was to take them across the country looked sick and mangy, but Dovid could hardly complain since it had been loaned to him by the Sephardic Jew in Mea Shearim, who was no longer his boss. It was enough that the man had trusted him to return it.

Since there were no possessions to take along, except a small amount of bedding and clothing, the cart was ample for them. Dovid strapped the sewing machine to the side of the cart, then tied the goat to the back of the cart, wondering if perhaps he shouldn't reverse the two animals. The goat seemed the more sturdy of the two.

Chavala, huddled close to Moishe, watched Dovid as he stood holding the reins, his face alive with excited anticipation. And her heart ached as she thought of the tears that ran down papa's cheeks, how old and pathetic he seemed as he stood with Sheine on one side and Raizel on the other, watching them vanish out of the city. And Sheine for all her strength of will had broken down at the end and clung sobbing in Dovid's arms. Poor, dear Sheine, who was always so afraid to show her true feelings, always fought the fears of letting anyone know how much hurt she locked away inside. Of course she had held Dovid . . . he was like her brother, someone she had shared her precious, and too brief, childhood years with, as they all had, but now he was also their protector, he had become their strength and she must have felt terribly abandoned . . .

And what about her? . . . well, she loved Dovid, but she was also upset with him at this moment because he was, she felt, sending them into exile, and hadn't the Jews had enough of *that* . . . ? At least when they had stayed together as a family, life seemed bearable, but now . . .

The next four days were almost beyond even Chavala's stamina. They were put up for the night at the settlements along the way. After a meal of thin barley soup and bread and a cup of wheat tea Chavala was only too happy to go to the tent with little Chia. It seemed the only joy she had was in the baby. She had become so winsome, Chavala would never have believed that that shrunken little doll was going on ten months. Instead of the hardships making her irritable, she seemed to thrive. It was almost as though she understood all the reasons not to be difficult.

Chavala, hugging little Chia to her, would fall asleep with the child. Dovid, on the other hand, sat up until all hours discussing, debating, talking with the *chalutzim*. The stamina of *these* people was unbelievable. They worked in the fields from earliest morning, and when the sun became too much they took shelter in the only building erected on the commune, where they repaired tools, made chairs and tables so that when the time came and they had housing they would be ready. . . .

What time Dovid finally crept into the cot beside her, Chavala never knew. But she did know that at four-thirty in the morning they sat with the *chaverim* and ate the usual breakfast of cucumbers, tomatoes, black bread and tea.

This particular morning the meal was sumptuous. One egg a week was what the *chalutzim* had, and the Landaus happened to be fortunate enough to be present for it. Then, amid a cheerful good-bye, they were once again on the road which would bring them closer to their journey's end. Morning, which had started out with the delights of an egg, gave up its early promise as the mule suddenly halted, lay down on the ground and died. Dovid didn't seem surprised, in fact he was grateful that the beast had lasted as long as it had. Chavala was not only disgruntled by Dovid's stoicism . . . fatalism? . . . but the heat beating down on them so brutally made her especially worried about baby Chia, who had a heat rash from head to toe. In her irritation, and as if to underline it, she asked in *Yiddish*, upsetting, she knew, to her husband, "Tell me, Reb Landau, how do you plan to get us to this golden *medina?*"

He pointedly replied in Hebrew, "Chavala, you shouldn't worry, let me do that. I assure you, we'll get there."

"I have no doubt, but I asked *how.*"

"That, my dear Chavala, is no problem. Moishe, you take one pole and I'll take the other."

"You mean *you're* replacing the donkey? You're walking to—"

"Moishe," Dovid said, "come help me get the reins off the mule and out of the way."

Dear God, Chavala thought, at this rate they would arrive by next Chanukah.

Chavala's timing was somewhat off. After an exhausting day, at dusk, Dovid let go of his pole and lifted Chavala out of the cart. Taking her in his arms he kissed her as the sweat poured from his body. "Look,

Chavala, look down below, our beautiful Sea of Galilee. Have you ever seen anything so beautiful?" and then he called out, "Come here, Dvora, Moishe, I want you to remember this moment all your lives."

The sight was indeed magnificent. The sun reflected golden on the gentle ripples. A mist, like gossamer, hovered above. The water looked so tranquil, so lovely, shimmering there, waiting, inviting.

The descent was so steep and the roads so narrow Dovid was afraid the cart might turn over, so, since goats were mountain climbers, he hitched theirs to the cart. Leaving the sewing machine intact, Moishe led the animal down. Dovid helped Chavala, who carried the baby in her left arm. Dvora followed behind. Breathless, grateful that they'd arrived, they stood for a moment regaining their strength.

But as Chavala looked about, reality replaced illusion. From above, the magnificent haze that hovered over the Galilee was now almost grotesque. What they had seen was a mist that rose above the stagnant swamps. The denuded, eroded hills seemed to be weeping, the fields were of rock for as far as the eye could see, the earth was unfertile, thanks to a thousand years of violation at the hands of invaders who had ravaged it and left it to die.

What Dovid's reactions were, Chavala couldn't tell. If he felt as she did, he hid it very well. Too well . . . Chavala followed him until they finally reached the settlement—one flimsy building erected on the edge of the swamps, the rest tents.

Still, they were welcomed and then were assigned to a tent.

That night Chavala lay awake desperately trying to justify Dovid taking them to this Godforsaken . . . not chosen . . . place. She felt haunted by her father's face, her guilt at leaving him . . . she and Sheine had parted without love, and poor little Raizel was losing her whole childhood. She fell asleep from exhaustion, her face still wet from her tears.

THE next morning Moishe and Dovid set out with the rest of the *chaverim* to work. And in the days that followed they labored from sunup to sundown . . . trying to push back the marshland and swamps. By way of America hundreds of Australian eucalyptus trees arrived to be planted, to soak up the stagnant waters. Drainage ditches were dug, handful by handful, the work almost beyond human endurance. They worked waist-deep in the mud, through the terrible heat of the summer and the abominable cold of winter. The rocks had to be dragged by teams of donkeys and the thick underbrush hacked away and burned. Their food was sparse, all they owned was what they wore on their backs, and the labor force was always short, with so many stricken with malaria . . .

Dovid, among them, lay on his bed convulsing with the disease. His condition was so severe Chavala had to doubt his recovery. Day and night she sat by his bed, feeding him quinine, sponging his body and thanking God that she had Dvora to take care of little Chia, and that Moishe had already recovered from this dreadful disease. Weak as he was, he went back to work, although she pleaded with him to rest for a few more days. He shrugged. "When we have a real kibbutz, I'll remember what it took to build this one."

Chavala looked at him and swallowed hard. Moishe, she realized, was proud that he was a part of the land now, and wore his illness like a campaign ribbon.

Finally Dovid did recover, and his attitude was much like Moishe's . . . he went back to the swamps almost as soon as he could stand.

While the work in the fields was going on, three clapboard sheds were erected—one a communal dining room that doubled as a meeting room, the other a tool shed and barn, the third, a community barracks. Although thin partitions were provided for the five married couples to have a little privacy, they would all sleep under the same roof and share common showers and toilets.

When these were completed a much-needed celebration was held. There was little to feast on but they still rejoiced. In the evening a bonfire was lit and they danced the *hora* until dawn. Indeed, they rejoiced. Chavala's pleasure was, as always, tempered by her longing for her family, but when she risked confiding in the other women they all but laughed at her sentimentality. The problem with Chavala, they said, was that she lived too much in the past. She hadn't really escaped the *shtetl* . . . her problem wasn't her longing and love of the old place but her Jewish guilt . . . "Wake up to today," one said, "we've been so conditioned by family obligations, it's become a kind of Jewish disease. Until you leave the ghetto of your mind, there isn't much hope that you'll make it in Eretz Yisroel."

No, Chavala found no comfort in them. In fact, she felt alienated from these women, who seemed to revel with an almost religious zeal that at last they had attained the same kind of rights as men, working side-by-side in the fields, ploughing the earth, draining the swamps, removing the rocks and refusing to be treated as women. Sonia Chernik lived openly without shame with Yudel Liebowitz, which even Chavala found difficult to accept. Traditions were rejected, pushed aside. . . .

Once they'd rolled up their tents and moved into the barracks, a meeting was called. Leah Abramowitz and her husband marched into the meeting hall and sat next to the four other married women. As the proceedings began, Leah, who had been appointed the women's leader, stood in front of the assembly dressed in a pair of her husband's work-pants. "We, the wives of this community, want to voice our disapproval. Since we do the work of men we expect that you men should share the work that was thrust on us only because we are women."

Yudel Liebowitz, the head of the committee, asked her, "What is it that you won't accept?"

"All responsibility for the cooking, kitchen chores, housekeeping and the rearing of children."

There was more than a murmur of dissent from the single men.

Sonia Chernik, the second in command, brought down the gavel. "This meeting will be conducted with decorum. Anyone who wants to debate will have their chance. But comrade Leah will be heard."

Knowing Sonia would be in sympathy with their petition, Leah nodded and began, "As of today I insist that the work be rotated. The men will assume the same amount of hours in the kitchen, cooking and in the tending of children, since this is the responsiblity of the entire community and not ours alone because we are women and wives."

From the back of the room an angry *chalutz* called out, "You forgot to say one thing, comrade Leah, will you also allow us to give birth?"

Jeers and whistles of approval echoed in the barnlike room.

The gavel came down sharply. Yudel called out, "This is a democratic meeting. You've been told that each of you will have an opportunity for rebuttal. Now I call for silence." He looked over the group and asked that Leah please finish.

"I'd be delighted," she said, "but first, an answer to comrade Shmuel's question. Yes, you will be allowed to give birth when you are equal to women and can stand the pain."

Three of the wives applauded.

Leah nodded her thanks. "Now, I ask that the vote be taken."

The twelve members of the committee reached for the ballots and wrote their answers. Then Sonia read them aloud, "Eight against, four in favor. Now it goes to the assembly, since it wasn't unanimous in the committee. May I have a show of hands?"

Of the fourteen members, Dovid voted along with the nine remaining *chalutzim*.

Leah rose quickly and delivered a swift volley of words. "We do not accept this. We will exercise our rights—"

"And what are they?" asked a stern Sonia.

"Strike! In this commune there are no serfs, damn it."

Silence fell over the room.

Chavala looked at Dovid. Since he was against the proposal, and since the committee had said debate was permissible, she raised her hand.

Yudel acknowledged her. "You have three minutes."

That wasn't quite fair. Leah had been given ten. "I don't want to work in the fields. I will, though, take on the responsibility of the kitchen. With the help of my sister Dvora we'll also take over the care of the children." Chavala didn't quite realize that with such words she'd finished herself with the other women. Sonia was so angry she forgot her impartial position as vice-chairman.

"You, Chavala, have been uncooperative since you arrived. You are nothing but a ghetto Jew . . . with the mentality of a ghetto Jew, and I think that's what you always will be."

Chavala lashed back. "And you are very democratic so long as no one disagrees with you. I have as much right to my feelings as you to yours—"

The gavel came down, Yudel announced, "You may be seated."

"But what about taking the vote on my petition?"

"Be seated."

The single men whistled and applauded for Chavala. A woman was a woman, and a woman belonged in the kitchen, never mind that they worked in the fields. They still could not do a man's job, it was ridiculous to think otherwise. What kind of a man would do housekeeping, much less take care of children?

Dovid spoke up to defend his wife. "I believe tonight's meeting has been biased and one-sided. A member of the committee has committed a personal slander that has nothing to do with the petition. The female members, all of them have the right to petition, but a vote was taken and it was voted down—"

Leah stood immediately, shaking her fist at Dovid. "As of this moment, my fellow comrades and I strike!"

And all four women and Sonia walked out.

Dvora looked at Chavala. Yes, she loved her sister with all her heart, but this was different, it had nothing to do with loyalty and love, it had to do with . . . well . . . what was fair . . . she knew that Chavala was not a ghetto Jew, but she also knew that Chavala had tried to walk in the footsteps of mama. She wanted to be like mama and carry on a traditional home, and here she just wasn't able to. Dvora had to admit to herself that she wasn't entirely like Chavala. Her feelings were much like the other women's. She wanted to work in the fields, not be shackled to a kitchen. She wanted the freedom men were privileged to, that Moishe had. She wanted to walk out with the others, feeling the strike was justified, and she would tell Chavala so. . . .

After a week of cooking for the whole community, even though she had the reluctant help of Dvora, Chavala, not surprisingly, collapsed. As she lay on her cot, with Dovid holding her hand, she looked at him and said, "I'm afraid my spirit was stronger than my body; I thought I could do it, Dovid, I honestly did."

"I know, and I love you because you tried so hard, but how in the world could you do the work of five women? Now rest, I insist on it."

Without Chavala, and the other women on strike, the men realized their cause was lost. If they intended to eat they'd better also learn how to cook.

"So," laughed Leah to the victorious women, "It only proves that men are the weaker sex. We really need them only if we want to have children. Once that's over . . . they can't even scramble an egg. We not only can scramble eggs, we can perpetuate the race, we can clear the fields," and on and on.

The men gave in, they had no alternative if they didn't want to starve. Chavala, though, still resented that their lives all but belonged to the *community* . . . she badly missed a home of her own, remembered all too well that first *seder* she and her sisters prepared after mama had died. Sorry, ladies, but she felt like a *woman,* and to her a woman was a very special thing. Yes, she admitted, she missed that little hovel, and living together in these tight communal quarters was almost strangling her. Everything was brought before the governing body. Even the clothes they wore on their backs belonged to the community. Now, even Dvora had alienated herself from Chavala by working in the fields with the other women. She felt more alone than she had at any time in her life. She had no one to speak to, not even Dovid, because she didn't want to add to the other burdens of his life.

In the fall of that year Sonia announced she was expecting a child, and without fuss her marriage was sanctioned by the common consent of the committee. A petition was presented. Since Sonia's child would be the first born on the commune she decided that there was a more advantageous way to accommodate working parents . . . The plan wasn't intended to ignore the children's needs, she said, rather to give them a greater sense of security because the whole community would take responsibility for their welfare. If they were to grow up secure in a country that lived each day on the edge of danger, it was important for them to be raised independent of their natural parents. If these children were deprived of a family, the loss would be less difficult for them to accept. It was suggested that a children's house be built. A vote was taken, and the majority agreed.

Chavala sat in utter disbelief. She would never have believed that Jewish mothers would reject the raising of their children. She had lost her mother, and the bereavement was great, but still she had survived. Actually Chavala suspected Sonia had proposed this because having a child was a burden to *her*. She didn't know if she much liked this new breed of Jews . . .

Chavala's fears grew as she watched the children's house being built. When the building was finished, little Chia, now a year and a half, was installed with the other children, and Chavala was beside herself. The next morning she went to see Chia but was told that if the child was to adjust to this new environment, visiting privileges would have to be restricted to certain hours during the day. Chavala had had enough. She swooped little Chia up in her arms and left without a word.

Leah and Sonia looked at each other. "You're right, Sonia," Leah said, "she has the mentality of a ghetto Jew, obviously this will be taken before the committee."

Sonia nodded. "From the beginning she's been a problem . . . a misfit. . . ."

Dovid found her waiting in their cubicle, and before he could open his mouth Chavala was half-talking, half-crying, "I've *tried*, Dovid . . . I really have, but I just can't go on living this way. I've no one here, not even you. We barely have a moment together. Our lives belong to the *community.* I'm sorry, but our child will be raised in a home, our home, with a mother and father—"

Our child . . . ? "How long have you known?"

"You haven't been listening, Dovid, I said I refuse to go on like this—"

"I heard. I mean, how long have you known that you're expecting?"

"For a month . . ."

He'd resigned himself from the beginning of their marriage to Chavala's not being able to conceive. Now . . . "There are no words to tell you what I feel," he said as he held her close, stroking her hair. "Oh, Chavala, what can I say?"

She separated herself from him and looked directly at him. *Don't be frightened to speak out,* she told herself. And to him, "You can say that we'll leave."

Dovid knew she was right. He *had* been selfish, thinking only of what he wanted. Like an ostrich he'd buried his head in the sand for a year. But he could no longer do that. She was his life, without her there would be nothing . . . "We'll leave, darling. Do you remember the settlement we stayed in at—?"

"I don't want to live on a settlement, Dovid. I just don't fit into this kind of life. Please sit down, Dovid." She seated herself next to him on the edge of the bed, "You want to be a farmer, all of you want to be farmers, but how can that be when none of you know how to use a plough? Darling, you don't know a hen from a rooster. All I've heard in the last year is when the land is cleared the planting will start. Nothing seems to make any sense. Maybe I should thank the women for ignoring me . . . I've learned a lot from the *chalutzim,* among them that your idol Aaron Aaronson has a training farm at Athlit, and that there's a village called Zichron Yaakov. I remember the day when Aaronson rode into the settlement on that white stallion. He's a great man, Dovid, and a great teacher . . . you'll become more than a farmer. With his help you might become . . . what's it called? . . . an agronomist. Dream big dreams, Dovid . . ."

The next day Dovid went before the committee and told them he and Chavala were leaving.

Sonia grimaced and made a show of laying hands on her bulging stomach. She'd gone on working in the fields alongside her husband, even though she was expecting at any moment. But Chavala, of course, was a peasant with a ghetto mentality. She should have stayed in the *shtetl,* the community would be well rid of her kind. The fact that Dovid, Moishe and Dvora had worked as hard as the others was now irrelevant. This commune only had room for those who were completely dedicated.

Dovid went out and looked at the land he'd helped to clear. He had made his contribution, but he felt a deep regret knowing he would not be there when the first crop was harvested. Quickly he went back, gathered his family together and left.

Chavala's happiness could scarcely be contained as the wagon slowly made its way back toward Jerusalem. There had never been a day in the past year she had not dreamed of this moment.

WHEN they finally arrived she all but ran up the long flight of stone steps and threw open the door. At the sight of her father she could not hold back the tears. Holding his frail body close, she was shocked by the change in him . . . he had aged so. Backing off to look and smile at him, she saw that his face was creased with what seemed a thousand folds. His back was more bent, his hands gnarled with painful arthritis.

"You've come home, Chavala . . . my children have come home, my prayers have been answered . . ."

Chavala swallowed, knowing that they had not just returned for him . . . but for her . . . and that they would soon be leaving again . . .

Sheine looked knowingly at Chavala, and in spite of herself took pleasure in her sister's obviously guilty feelings of pain . . . she knew they were going on to Zichron. Chavala had mentioned it in the letter that had come four days ago. "Yes, papa has indeed prayed, welcome back," she said smiling, "and Dovid, you're black as an Arab. But look at you, Moishe. You left a boy and came back a man . . ."

"You're the only one who hasn't changed, Sheine," Dvora answered with anger close to the surface. *You're as spiteful as ever, you haven't forgiven us for leaving,* she wanted to shout out, but for the sake of her father she held her tongue.

Raizel could have told Dvora that she was wrong, that Sheine had in fact changed more than any of them . . . Quite by accident Raizel had found a diary Sheine kept, and although she knew it was very wrong to invade Sheine's private thoughts, once she'd begun it was impossible to stop. Page after page was filled with her love and longing for Dovid . . . how she dreamed of him making love to her in the night. She alone knew the source of Sheine's bitterness, understood it, and so tried to please, even appease her poor, tormented sister. No question, Sheine suffered, had suffered, in her fashion, more than any of them.

The following week's parting was even more traumatic than the first. Avrum wept, beyond consolation. He took his children to him, hugged them with surprising strength . . . the strength of profound fear . . . Would he live to see his grandchild? Only God knew the answer for sure. At least Avrum, in blessed mortal ignorance, could hope.

Chapter Five

IF IT COULDN'T be America, at least Zichron Yaakov was a village that Chavala could understand. True, these pioneers had come from another part of Europe, but the settlement looked as though it could have been transplanted from the *shtetl* she had left in Odessa. Small stone houses stood clustered together, each with its own small vegetable garden, and palm trees dotted the landscape. There were marketplaces in the square, and benches where the women sat and exchanged bits of gossip. The ritual baths and the *shul* truly made Chavala think she was home. Of course if Chavala had seen it twenty-five years earlier, her disenchantment would have equaled that of earlier arrivals . . .

The original founders of Zichron Yaakov were a handful of humble tradespeople who had come in a group from Roumania in 1882, and among them were the parents of Aaron Aaronson, a man who would play a central role not only in the life of the Jewish nation, but in the lives of Dovid and Chavala. They knew little about Palestine. What they found was a remote, neglected Asiatic province in the vast Ottoman Empire. They knew nothing about agriculture or colonization. They knew not one of the languages spoken in Palestine. But they'd come out of love for the land of Israel, a desire to reclaim its soil to enrich their lives and the lives of their children.

When their ship entered the port of Haifa they were faced with this newly issued edict: "Jewish immigrants are forbidden to land on the coast of Syria and absolutely forbidden to live in Palestine. This prohibition is final, any infraction of this law will result in imprisonment and the intruders will relinquish all monies and personal belongings."

The sultan, suspicious of European "philanthropists"—especially British—trying to buy large tracts of land in Palestine allegedly for Jewish settlements, worried that the European powers were merely using the Jews as a front to get a toehold in Palestine. He was, of course, right about that. But this handful of Jewish pilgrims were hardly aware of such political shenanigans. *They* were sincere, driven, and now the door to Palestine was closed to them. They stood on deck, silent and bewildered. There seemed nothing to do but return to Roumania.

Except Ephraim Aaronson thought otherwise. He was a large man, and with a determination to equal his size, he said, "We have not traveled this far and given up so much to return defeated." The Turkish government never officially lifted its restrictions, but a few, including the Aaron-sons and their friends, made it into Palestine and eventually to Zichron, a place steeped in the disease and neglect of centuries. The only signs of human inhabitants on their hilltop were a dozen or more huts occupied by the Arab *fellaheen*, who, left to their own devices, grew only enough to feed their emaciated bodies.

In the beginning the Jews, like the Arabs, lived in huts made of branches covered with mud and roofed with straw mats. Their first perma-nent stone houses had to be built furtively, with the help of judicious bribes, since it was against Ottoman law for noncitizens to build. But their problems had only begun.

The land bought for them was rocky and arid, impossible to till, and the plain that stretched between Mount Carmel and the coast was noth-ing but swamps, breeding ground for malaria. Funds in Roumania that had been pledged dried up when those who intended to follow became aware of the hostile Turkish government. The pioneers in Zichron were forced to fight against a corrupt, hostile government alone.

In that first year everything went against them. Turkish restrictions demanded bribery and more bribery. The limited possessions they still had were all but exhausted. Gold wedding bands were no longer on the fingers of their owners. Rations of food became more stringent, and the small amount of money that trickled in from Roumania was too little to fend off the gluttonous appetite for *baksheesh* that the Turks demanded.

The meager crops failed, malaria took its toll, and no matter how Ephraim Aaronson debated with himself that this settlement would some-day be self-supporting, he knew that their only survival lay in the hands of the French philanthropist Baron de Rothschild, whose plantations were already established in Palestine. Pride at this moment was a bitter thing to swallow, but it was better than certain death.

Aaron Aaronson was six when his parents first came to Palestine. Zvi, Shmuel, Alex and the two girls, Sarah and Rivka, were all born in Zichron, by that time settled with a hundred families.

The Aaronsons were considered the leading family . . . indeed, there was a strange mystery about them, in spite of their friendliness. The style of their lives was unlike any in Zichron. They lived in a rambling, two-story stone dwelling with a wide portico surrounding it. Huge palm trees sheltered the house from the brutal, burning sun. Lace curtains and wooden shutters hung at the windows.

In Zichron Malka Aaronson created a culture all its own for her large family. In a place of honor stood a grand piano, where her two daughters entertained the family with the duets she had taught them. Bookshelves that lined the walls included volumes of Shakespeare, and Aaron's own special library consisted of the oldest and latest editions of scientific agriculture, geology, Latin and botany.

The Aaronsons grew up on their high hilltop, passionately devoted to each other and to the wild country that had become a part of them. Inspired by the Bible, and their parents' ideals, the Aaronsons created a world removed from the grim realities surrounding them. They did not see themselves as children of struggling farmers living in a decadent Ottoman Empire, rather as heirs to an ancient people and a noble heritage. Their ambitions were not for themselves but for the future of Palestine.

Aaron was the idol of the family, and his genius was recognized early, at the age of ten. His curiosity was insatiable, the whole world had hidden secrets that he felt driven to explore. By the time he was twelve he could identify every plant. His quick ear caught the echo of the ancient Hebrew names which the Arabs used. By the time he was fourteen Aaron was the most extraordinary young man in Zichron. His personality, even at that age, was powerful, and the baron became aware of him. At eighteen, under the auspices of his mentor, the baron, he was sent to agricultural school in France. Grignon was heaven to Aaron, a place to gain the knowledge which would allow him to create new agricultural methods in Palestine. Two years later when he returned to Zichron he came back with a degree in agriculture, botany and geology. Aaron was then sent to become an apprentice instructor at the baron's new settlement in Metullah, up in the wild hills of Galilee. For a young man of twenty, Aaron knew that his was an opportunity few were privileged to. Except he soon found that the agricultural instructors the baron had hired were arrogant types from his French-African colonies, their minds closed to all Aaron's knowledge. Aaron knew this country better than they, as well as most of the people who lived there. He couldn't be quiet in the face of their contempt for the Jewish settlers, their indifference to Palestine and their misunderstanding of its needs. Inevitably he was dismissed, in fact denounced as a thief. Rumors were started that he'd stolen much of the scientific data he claimed was his own. Still, the next few years were the time of his greatest scientific discoveries, and they claimed international attention. He was appointed agriculture inspector by the pasha. Now he was able to devote his time to the new settlers and tried working with them, but there were only a rare few that could appreciate and take advantage of his expertise. Besides, a man of science was an oddity in a movement that featured philosophers, religious scholars and writers. Every leader was at least a journalist, if not a writer, and all were orators with idealistic speeches. Committee meetings and conferences were the daily bread of the movement, and to manage *any* agreement before passing a resolution was a major victory. "The committee sickness," Aaron called it. His approach was different from that of the intellectuals who had come from Russia and Europe. Backward as Palestine was at the beginning of the century, it at least was a land of wide open spaces. Aaron was like the great American pioneers whose vision and ambition had stretched roadways across mountains, and created cities out of desert wasteland. The surveys he had taken of the natural resources of Palestine could be used for plans to develop the country. He spoke out against leaders who could only think in terms of buying small tracts of land and building a few houses on them.

Another immigration . . . Russian intellectuals, young men and women who came to create by their own labor a new society in Palestine. They had grown up in the revolutionary movement in Russia. Many of them had taken part in the first abortive attempt, and they no longer believed, as did many of their comrades who remained in Russia, that the overthrow of the Czarist regime would better the position of the Jews. They now were convinced that the Jewish problem was worldwide and could only be solved when the Jewish people had been rooted in Palestine once again, and as an agricultural people.

There ought to have been a bond between Aaron and these young people, but mostly there was an unbridgeable gap. Although they called themselves "the workers" and were known as the "barefoot ones," they were far from humble. They were steeped in the new socialist ideology, were convinced that they and they alone knew the solutions and should control the means for building the Jewish national homeland. Above all they believed that Jews must not be dependent on native labor, like the French colonists in Algeria, and the British. The whole economic structure had to change, as well as the psychology of the old Yishuv. They had to become workers in every branch of the national economy, dependent on no one's labor but their own. Each settlement would conduct its own destiny. The old settlements, like Zichron, that had grown up on the baron's bounty, epitomized the evils of the old society. Well, they'd no longer allow the settlements to maintain themselves on cheap Arab labor. The most outspoken was Dovid's old casual acquaintance, David Ben-Gurion, who in a few years became the standard-bearer of the workers' movement. His and Aaron Aaronson's goals were the same, but their methods very different. Aaron continued to believe that the only way to organize the country was on a scientific basis, but he also couldn't ignore the growing movement of socialism, and he found himself veering closer to it. The thing he most admired about Ben-Gurion's people was their unity. Well, if a national revival was to be a reality, the two factions would have to work together. With science and Jewish labor they would succeed, and with that connection Aaron turned to America for financial help.

For his station Aaron secured funds from such wealthy Americans as Samuel Fels, Julius Rosenwald, Jacob H. Schiff and Nathan Straus, on the indirect recommendation of President Theodore Roosevelt himself . . . the president had been impressed by the young scientist when he'd come to America at the invitation of the Department of Agriculture. Aaron's station at Athlit was under the protection of the American government and he shared the results of his experiments with the United States Department of Agriculture.

Aaron's success at Athlit was so great that Sultan Abdul Hamid II decided the Ottoman Empire had better take advantage of him, Jew or no Jew, and bestowed a gold medal on him, assuring him that, "You are now an Ottoman, the doors of the empire are open to you."

At age thirty-one Aaron was, in a fashion, a kind of founding Jewish prince. The experimental Jewish agricultural station Aaron developed during the next four years was unique in the Middle East, and for his experimental fields he selected a spot known all over the country for its sterility—Athlit . . . on the coastal plain of Sharon, at the foot of Mount Carmel, its sand dunes alternated with malarial marsh. But all about were signs of past populations, and Aaron knew that they couldn't have existed if the earth hadn't been able to support them. The massive ruin of a medieval castle loomed up from the coastline, the last outpost of the Crusaders in Palestine. On the mainland was a rounded hillock that had been a city when the harbor of Athlit had been a place of commerce and seafaring more than two thousand years earlier. The Roman city of Caesarea spread beneath the sand dunes along the coast to the south of the station, and the Phoenician port of Dor lay in between. Behind on the slopes of Carmel were prehistoric cave dwellings, and later excavations proved their inhabitants to have been the earliest known agriculturists, probably the first to have cultivated the wild wheat of Palestine some eight thousand years before.

Aaron chose this spot because he wanted to prove that there was no such thing as worn-out, sterile soil. His station was like a Garden of Eden . . . there was something in fruit or in blossom the whole year round. In drought or rain, his fields of wheat, oats and barley flourished, yielding many times more than those of his neighbors although he used no fertilizer and the same implements as the Arab farmers. Aaron's secret was nothing more nor less than the rational application of the techniques of dry farming. Aaron drew around him a small group of devoted young disciples to work with him at the station, and one of them, Aaron's favorite, was himself a great mind—Absalom Feinberg. Absalom was larger than life—tall, handsome, ardent, a poet, a lover of music, wise, witty, a crack shot, a dashing horseman, and so fearless that the Arabs had adopted him as their own, giving him the name of Sheikh Salim.

Absalom was born in Palestine, his parents Russian intellectuals who came to the country with the first organized group of pioneers in 1882, the same year as the Zichronites. They settled at Rishon-le-Zion, the first Jewish settlement in the south, between Jerusalem and Jaffa, one of the settlements that Baron de Rothschild had adopted and, as at Zichron, a set of tyrannical officials administered the village's affairs and directed the settlers' lives.

Israel Feinberg, Absalom's father, refused to be dominated, and his intense independence led to such a violent protest against the officials that his family was forced to move on, eventually putting down roots at Hadera. Absalom's education was never interrupted . . . from his grandfather he was taught the Bible, but his father Israel, who realized that the Bible was spiritually rewarding, also knew one day the Jews would inherit their land only if they knew and understood the Arabs. And so he sent Absalom to Jaffa, where he studied Arabic as well as the Koran and by the time his studies were finished he could talk and read Arabic as well as any Arab. By family tradition Absalom was a dedicated Jew, steeped in Russian romanticism and French culture. Israel Feinberg observed the changes in his son carefully. He noticed a sort of melancholy that became almost morbid at times . . . the sorrow of the Jewish people? The injustices against them? Their perpetual homelessness became the outrage and challenge of Absalom's life. And his hatred of the Turks was so strong he formed a secret society called the Zion Flag Bearers. For his own sake his father decided Absalom needed to be sent away. His desire to help his people could end in bringing down the wrath of the Turks. Difficult as it was, Israel sent his only child away to France for nearly four years. It did nothing to blur Absalom's thoughts of getting national rights for Jews. "We are so far from it," he wrote to his family. "Why should everyone have a nation and we who have given so much can't even get a charter from the damned Turks. Palestine means nothing to them, not with their vast empire, but they refuse us *only* because we're Jews."

When he returned home his feelings were even more belligerent than when he'd left. The Turks were barbarians, and he swore when the day of judgment came he would be prepared. Always in his mind was the thought of rebellion. He talked to Aaron about his burning discontent, but Aaron's hope and faith was both greater and less bitter than Absalom's. "With the help of providence and the aid of America we will achieve our goals." Absalom didn't quite believe *that.*

Aaron was so absorbed in his work it never occurred to him to introduce Absalom to his sister Sarah, although he spoke of her often enough. They had to meet by chance at a social gathering, and by the time the festivities were over Sarah and Absalom knew they felt something special for each other. She was everything in a woman that Absalom wanted . . . beautiful, tall and with a strength and goodness that seemed to come through in her extraordinary face enhanced by wide-set blue eyes. They were not only physically attracted to one another, but brought closer through their love of poetry, literature, exploring the world. She'd been to Germany, Switzerland and Italy, and Aaron wanted his sisters to see and know the world. But like Absalom, Palestine was the only place on earth Sarah felt content. At *home* . . .

When Absalom was transferred to take over the new station that Aaron had built in Hadera, Dovid replaced him at Athlit, and as the baron had once done in his recognition of Aaron, Aaron in turn took particular notice of Dovid, of his passion and inquiring mind, his *feel* for the land and growing things . . . Dovid was a born agronomist, and Aaron saw him as an extraordinary future scientist. Shoemaker to agronomist . . . such was the potential for *change* in these wondrous days. Change and *growth* . . .

For the first time since coming to Eretz Yisroel, Chavala, like Dovid, found herself fulfilled. She adjusted to the life of Zichron. The village . . . it seemed transplanted from the one she'd left, except her small stone house was better and more luxurious. The kitchen became the center of the household, and, what joy of joys, there were *three* bedrooms. And when Dovid had the time he would add a sewing room, and once again she would take her place as the head of her small family.

Bleak and remote as the village might have been, it never seemed so to Chavala. The household work was no drudgery for Chavala and Dvora. She washed stone floors and scrubbed the wooden tables and benches with sand and water. She reveled in watching her family eating the meals she cooked on the iron stove that stood in the corner of the kitchen. She accepted with pride the praise when she brought the loaves of bread, cakes and cookies to the table. Their first *seder* was bittersweet, with the absence of her father and sisters, but when she saw Dovid sitting at the head of his table she told herself a time would come when papa and the whole family would be together. The family . . .

With Arabic batiks Chavala made colorful bedspreads and cushions. In Haifa's Arab market she bought wall hangings. Gradually this was a home that in her wildest dreams she never thought could happen to her. Russia seemed very far away now, and the dream of America became less and less urgent. Yes, she'd rejected working in the fields of Galilee, but she found planting her own small backyard wonderfully rewarding. With little Chia at her side she planted the seeds that Dovid had brought home to her. Their growth seemed to match the growth she felt in her womb. When the first sprouts came she laughed with delight, and when her small vegetable garden was ready to be taken from the ground, she felt tears in her eyes. Her cherry tree would have made it perfect, but Dovid planted a palm, three olive trees and a few vines for grapes from which she would make wine. Chavala's life was content.

In the afternoon when the work was finished, Dvora and Chavala got dressed up and took Chia for a walk to the village square. Unlike the other women she'd become friends with, Chavala and Dvora's clothes had a bit of style and color. Sarah and Rivka Aaronson, taking their afternoon walks, stopped one day and admired Chavala's loose-fitting garment, which concealed the tiny bulge beneath it. Sarah had come back from Paris several weeks before with the latest fashion magazines. She would be more than happy, she said, for Chavala to see them. Sarah was rare, as was her sister Rivka. They were accomplished, elegant, and the truth was, Chavala was awed by them. She'd never known Jews like this . . . they'd been to France, Switzerland and Italy. For Chavala life had become sweet.

At four of a morning Dovid found her ready to give breakfast to him and Moishe. Then she followed them out the door, standing on the porch and watching as they climbed aboard with the other men onto the wagon that went to Athlit. When they got back in the evening Dovid's exhaustion was quickly forgotten as he looked at Chavala's contented face and abundant belly. After dinner he read his books on agronomy and farming that he'd gotten from Aaronson's library. At times he might look up and see Chavala, a woman beyond anything he'd thought possible for him, and his gratitude for her wisdom in insisting that they leave the Galilee and come here was something almost beyond words.

Everything seemed so good. Be careful, he told himself. Nothing, as a Jew should know, is forever . . .

Chapter Six

CHAVALA GOT UP from her knees from scrubbing, and, rubbing her back, she felt the beginnings of labor. She went into the kitchen and sat down. As though a dam had burst she held onto the table and watched as water poured from her womb. She was not afraid as she called Dvora. But, coming out of the bedroom, the young girl was petrified as she looked down at the floor now flooded with water. The awful reminder of her mother's death nearly paralyzed her . . . what if Chavala died? God, please God, not Chavala too.

Seeing the girl's fear, Chavala said, "Don't be frightened Dvora, I'm young and strong and we'll soon have the blessing mama must have asked God to give us. Believe that, Dvora. Now, sister, take Chia to Mrs. Bronusky and then tell Mrs. Lieberman to bring the birthing stool. Then go down to Athlit and tell Dovid I want him here." Dvora could not move, she could not function. "There's nothing to be *afraid* of. Now, Dvora, do as I say." Without a word Dvora left the room, picked up Chia and hurried from the house.

As Chavala waited, the thought came back to haunt her . . . the face of her father was as clear as when he stood framed in the doorway on another day such as this. "You should not have sent me away, Chavala, I should have been here to hold her hand as she passed through . . ." Chavala would not allow Dovid to be tortured with such demons if it were God's will for her to have the same end. But within herself she knew nothing like that would happen. Still, her hand reached out to the Almighty. Manya was right, God was not to blame for the injustices of man. He had given man a mind that knew what was right and what was evil. Whichever road he decided to take was his choice. This day Chavala felt the presence of God . . .

CHAVALA clutched her fists and bit on the rag while Mrs. Lieberman wiped the sweat away. No, she wouldn't cry out, she wanted this child brought into the world in joy. There would be no tears. Each time the pain gripped her body she shut her eyes and believed her mother was talking to her . . . "Soon it will be over and you will hold in your arms the child that was conceived in love . . ." And Chavala said back, "Yes, mama, yes, a lovely girl child and once more you'll be with us, you'll be reborn in her and I'll have you, dearest mama, I'll see my little Rivkala. You are helping me, mama. *Help me, mama . . ."*

As Chavala lay back in exhaustion, Mrs. Lieberman watched, thinking that in all her years as a midwife she'd never seen such courage. The pain Chavala was bearing in silence frightened her. Why didn't the girl scream out? Where did her strength come from?

When Chavala gripped the edge of the bed, Mrs. Lieberman looked beneath the cover and saw the beginning of life. Bringing the birthing stool closer she started to help Chavala out of bed but Chavala protested. "No . . . this child will not be born until Dovid comes."

"Chavala, you've gone mad, the child is ready—"

"I will have this child when Dovid arrives."

Lying back, Chavala bit on the rag and clutched the mattress. She no longer thought of anything except that Dovid would see his daughter brought to life. God help me . . . mama, take the pain away . . . fill my mind with thoughts of when you were with us . . . those days were sweet with honey and we were happy and your beauty shone like . . . I love you, mama, Dovid will soon be here . . .

The hours had passed, and finally Dovid was there. He went to Chavala's side and took her sweating hands in his. He kissed the palms, then her lips. Of all days he'd been sent to Jaffa for some equipment, and Dvora had frantically been waiting hours for him. When he returned it had seemed an eternity until they reached the hills of Zichron Yaakov. Mrs. Lieberman brushed him aside and helped Chavala to the birthing stool. Breathing heavily and quickly, Chavala had at last found the blessed release from her agony as the midwife gently pulled the child from her womb. Dovid picked up his wife and put her on their bed. "My Dovid, I waited to share this moment . . ."

"I know, my love." Tears were in his eyes.

"You mustn't cry, Dovid, our people have cried enough tears to fill an ocean. Be happy, darling, we have a daughter—"

"No," called out Mrs. Lieberman, "you have a son."

"A son?"

"Yes, a beautiful son. And just listen to him yell!"

Chavala had so much wanted to call her mother's name again, still . . . "Bring him to me." The infant was placed in his mother's arms. Chavala counted the ten fingers and ten toes, looked at the sweet face. He was Dovid.

"Look at your son, Dovid, and never mind what I've said, it's right that this child was born in Eretz Yisroel."

Chavala knew about love . . . for family, Dovid . . . but love of one's own child was of a whole different order. Manya's words rang in her ears about such blessings. Looking down now at the child in her arms, she thanked God for not punishing her for the thoughts she'd once had . . .

To perpetuate life after death, Chavala remembered, Jews named their children for those who were gone. So Reuven Landau became the living spirit of his grandmother Rivka. Chavala had written to her father and all but pleaded with him and Sheine and Raizel to come to Zichron. She would make the arrangements, but Sheine wrote back to say that papa had not been too well and the trip would be too difficult for him. They'd shared so much sorrow, Chavala was disappointed that they couldn't now share this blessing, but life had to go on, and the tears dried. . . .

In Zichron Yaakov the *bris* of Reuven Landau was celebrated with the excitement and joy that all children born in Eretz Yisroel were celebrated with. To be born in the land of their fathers was a great *mitzvah*. These children would know what freedom was. At last, at long last they would grow up with honor and pride in their heritage. They would become the true builders of Eretz Yisroel. For them the ghetto would be dead.

All day the villagers came to the house of Chavala and Dovid. There was feasting and dancing, and even the Aaronsons paid their respects.

Chavala even found herself thinking less and less about the golden shores of America. What still ate at her was that her father and sisters could not share their lives with them. She envied the closeness of the Aaronsons. Well, next week her family would go to Jerusalem. She took out the letter her father had written her, telling how proud he was and that he lived for the moment he could hold his grandson in front of the great Wall.

WHEN they entered the Old City of Jerusalem, Chavala's heart beat quickly in anticipation. She could hardly wait.

She rushed up the stairs, but when she came in Raizel's embrace was not with joy but tears. She looked at Sheine, whose eyes were red and swollen from crying. Breathing unevenly, Chavala asked uneasily, "Where's papa?"

A long silence, then Sheine answered. "He died . . . the day before yesterday . . ."

It was a bad dream, had to be . . . no mention had been made in the letter that he was ill. "It can't be true—"

"It's true, it's true," Sheine repeated.

"What happened?"

"He went to the *shul* in the morning and when they brought him home he was already gone."

Dearest papa, I wasn't even here at the end . . . "But why didn't you let me know he was sick?"

"He wasn't, just old . . . it was his time."

Chavala looked down at her child of three weeks. God took away and God gave. If only she'd at least been there to see him put in the ground. Her thoughts went to a cemetery in Russia, to mama, who should have been side-by-side with him, reunited in death . . .

"Dovid, I want to go to my father's graveside."

He nodded, and the family filed out and walked toward the Mount of Olives. . . .

During the mourning period little was discussed, but now the time was over. "Tomorrow we'll all go back to Zichron."

Sheine looked first at Dovid, then at Chavala. Instead of her love for Dovid becoming less, it now bordered on unreality. Her fantasies were so heightened that at night she thought only of what it would be like to have Dovid's child. In her worst delirium she saw Chavala dead and Dovid, of course, turning to her for comfort. She would punish herself for such evil thoughts, pray that nothing would happen to her sister, but she was obsessed. Finally she decided that only by cutting herself off from the family would she be able to keep her sanity. "I'm staying here in Jerusalem."

"Since papa's gone there's no need for it any longer, Sheine."

"There's a need for *me*. I'm not going to live in a village. What would I do there? Work in the fields like one of your barefoot *chalutzim?* Become someone's *chavera?*"

"It's not that way in Zichron—"

"Maybe not. But I'm not going to live on charity any longer."

"You wouldn't be living on charity, Sheine, we'd all be sharing. And Zichron isn't like the Old City of Jerusalem. It's lovely. I want you to see it, and our little house, and there's a little garden. Please, Sheine, come with us."

Sheine stared at Chavala, who blathered on as though she hadn't heard a word. "You amaze me, Chavala, what happened to that pioneer spirit? Your determination to go to America? You remember when you told me that when papa died nothing could stop you? Not even Dovid

. . . you said he loved you so much that he'd do anything, even give up—"

"Things change, it doesn't seem so important now—"

"Doesn't it? That's shocking, coming from you. You, who more than any of us despise poverty, but I know what's happened. You've let yourself be Dovid's peasant wife . . . what you really want is a stove and a hut and a little plot to plant your vegetables. Yes, you're a peasant, that's what you'll always be. Well, I've waited a long time to get out of here and be rid of all your beliefs, yours *and* Dovid's. *I don't need you,*" and she ran from the room, hysterical.

As the rest of the family sat in stunned silence, Dovid got up and went to the girl. Sitting on the edge of the bed, he tried to take her hand but she pulled away and turned her face toward the wall. Softly he said, "Sheine, what's happened to you? Please talk to me."

You're right, Sheine thought, *my love for you is so painful, to be this close is agony.*

"Tell me, Sheine, say whatever you feel, I'll understand."

She turned slowly and looked at Dovid, and then finally said it . . . "I love you, Dovid—"

"And I love you too, Sheine, and want to help you. That's why I want you to come to Zichron—"

"You didn't *hear* what I said, Dovid. *I love you.*"

The impact of her true meaning hit him like a thunderbolt. "Sheine, you mustn't say that. It's not true . . . I'm married to your sister—"

"How well I know *that.* But you asked, and now, even if I have no pride, at least now I feel free. Dovid, I'm not shameless . . . I love Chavala too, but I can't help my feelings . . . at least now you know why I can never live with the family."

Dovid held his face in his hands. How could he help Sheine, she would never believe that this was only the infatuation of a young girl and that one day she would look back on this as just a childish phase . . . ? "You can't live alone, Sheine, have you thought of that?"

"Yes, but I don't intend to live alone. I'm going to be a nurse."

At least now that he knew, he could understand her behavior. He would have liked to take her in his arms and hold her and tell her that he understood, but under the circumstances that would only be cruel. After a long silence he said, "Come, Sheine, we're leaving soon. See Chavala. I don't want to leave without the two of you coming together again as sisters."

She got off the bed, looked once more at Dovid, then without a word went to Chavala. They sat awkwardly together, then Sheine said, "Please forgive me, Chavala, if you can."

"There's nothing to forgive, Sheine. I know how hard life has been for you with papa. You've had nothing except the worry and responsibility . . . but won't you please try, at least give it a chance and come home with us?"

She took Chavala's hands in hers. "Thank you for wanting me, but I'm sorry. I've other ideas . . . I'm going to be a nurse—"

"When did you decide that?"

"I've been thinking about it for a long time now."

Chavala looked at her sister's hand in hers. "It's been so *long* since we've been a family. Will you at least come with us for a little while?"

"No, Chavala, I've already been accepted as a student nurse."

Nothing could change Sheine's mind. "You'll write?" Chavala asked with tears in her eyes. "We'll worry about you—"

"Of course I'll write, and please don't worry about me. I know for the first time in my life what I want to do with it. And . . . I love you all." And at this special moment she truly meant it.

Chapter Seven

SHEINE, TO KEEP herself sane, had planned, plotted her life with great care. Whenever she had the chance to escape from the Old City, she would wander up the hills to the German hospital and sit on a bench against the wall. She would watch the nurses dressed in their white crisp uniforms that rustled as they went meticulously about their duties. At the end of the long corridor a small group of handsome young doctors stood like disciples, listening to Herr Professor explain the findings of the cases they had seen that morning. This was a special world, a white, immaculate world she longed to be part of. But how? She became aware of her Jewishness. For the first time her Jewishness became an obstacle, something to wish away. This was her first venture into the world of non-Jews, and the feeling of difference, of being separate, came as a shock. They were fair-skinned, blue-eyed and blond. Names she had not heard before sounded melodically in her ear . . . Christine, Helga, Greta, Gretchen

. . . And the German she listened to was softly spoken, not guttural. And speaking Yiddish, she could understand much of what she heard. Compared to it, Yiddish sounded . . . well, uncouth, smacked of the ghetto. She got up unhappily and left this place she felt she could never enter.

Back at her home, she felt so bleak, defeated, she even thought about ending her life that seemed hopeless. But then she thought of all she'd managed to live through so far and told herself to stop the self-pity and *solve* her life, not destroy it. So what if she'd been born Sheine Rabinsky? That could be changed. But what about her raven hair and deep brown eyes, and the olive tint of her skin? Papa had allowed no graven images or mirrors in his house, but she'd hidden a small, broken piece of mirror under her thin mattress. Looking at herself, she thought there was some beauty in her face . . . from her mother she had inherited the delicate features and unblemished, smooth skin. Why, she could pass for some of those French women she'd seen in Odessa who had married Russian men of nobility. She closed her eyes and tried to imagine herself dressed in finery, and the image became alive. If she changed her name, perhaps . . . she suddenly remembered the large bronze plaque that hung in the entry of the hospital inscribed with those who had founded the institution, and the name "Professor Beck" lingered. Why? Who knew? But in that moment Sheine Rabinsky became "Elsa Beck." But what about her coloring? Her mother was French and her father German. Where was she born, something that could easily be checked up on. She'd figure that out later . . . she'd come a long way in her transformation already. She'd need to absorb it, try to adjust herself to it . . .

She took from the small alms her father had gotten and hid the money away until she had enough to buy a German primer. She slowly accumulated more secondhand books, books on anatomy, Latin and the techniques of nursing.

By the time she applied as a student nurse she not only had become Elsa Beck, born in French Equatorial Africa, but she spoke fluent German and her knowledge of nursing was equal to a graduate's. In two years she had taught herself anatomy and even knew most of the generic names in Latin. She was as obsessed with the task she'd dedicated herself to as she had been with Dovid. Not a moment was wasted. Scrubbing, cooking, her head was filled with the lessons she was mastering. A dialogue went on constantly . . . she asked the questions, and she answered them. Sheine knew that one deception created another, but at least, she felt, Chavala had to be told.

So after one especially grueling day, she wrote to Zichron.

CHAVALA sat for a very long time trying to make some *sense* out of it. There were no answers to why Sheine had done this unbelievable thing. Papa had once said there was a dybbuk in Sheine, but who knew what really had made her go to such extreme lengths? All Chavala was sure of was that she had failed. She looked at the letter again . . . "So I ask you, Chavala, to explain to the others that if and when you write it will be addressed to *Elsa Beck.* Please try, if you can, to understand and not to judge me. We all in our own ways must find our own solutions and salvations . . ."

Chavala could just not accept it, not now. Sheine was lost to them, as lost as if she had died. Which in a way she had.

LIFE for Elsa Beck started at five in the morning. The disciplines were rigid, exacting. If a corner of the bed had one small wrinkle, Head Nurse Holstein ripped it off and the student was chastised without mercy and a privilege was taken away. In Elsa Beck's case, no such penalties were handed out. Elsa was, in fact, the most precise, careful and prompt student Nurse Holstein had ever encountered, and for this she gained the admiration of not only Nurse Holstein but the entire staff. Her discipline and devotion did not, however, exactly endear her to her sister nurses. But that didn't bother Elsa Beck. She had become a nurse for the sake of her own survival. She did not fraternize with anyone, and was, not surprisingly, considered a recluse.

When graduation came she held highest honors, and now was ready to become a full-fledged member of the elite. Indeed, the first time Nurse Beck walked into the operating room dressed in her surgical garb, she knew the title of Head Surgical Nurse would soon be hers.

Long live Elsa Beck.

Get thee behind me, Sheine Rabinsky.

Chapter Eight

I‌T WAS NOW 1908.

"Nothing really changed, Moishe," Dovid said, "it only appeared that way. How well off were the serfs when they were freed, did they achieve freedom and equality? No. When slavery in America was abolished did the Negroes really become free? Where were the opportunities for them? And this new rebellion of the Turks . . . Do you really think they will give *us* liberty and equality? A revolution won't change hatred felt for the Jews. It's persisted for over two thousand years."

"But the Yishuv seems to have great hopes that these young Turks will be more sympathetic to our condition—"

"I hope they're right, but Chaim Weizmann isn't so optimistic."

"That's because he's pro-British—"

"Which he has reason to be. Britain is the only nation that has listened to him."

"What about the Germans? The greatest scientists and doctors in the world are German Jews. When the Kaiser came to Palestine he spoke to Herzl and said he was in favor of a Jewish homeland—"

"I know, but you noticed that we still don't have one, and besides, Germany has a treaty with the Turks. No. I believe the way Jabotinsky does, that this so-called rebellion of young Turks was only a political maneuver to gain power and not to create any great changes in Palestine for the Jews. Aaron thinks like Weizmann, but he's in no position to speak out. For years he has worked so closely with the Turks, hoping that eventually the sultan would give Palestine a charter. He may be a dreamer, but he still hopes."

For Chavala, politics was what men constantly, boringly talked about. If a rebellion had occurred, it hadn't touched her life here in Zichron. For her there was one small sacred place that seemed impenetrable . . . her home, and her family.

Chia had now grown into a chubby three-year-old girl with pink cheeks, blue eyes and fair hair. She was cheerful, precocious, always asking questions. Her devotion to and curiosity about the baby Reuven was apparent as she sat wide-eyed watching Chavala nurse him. In her mind she naturally looked on Reuven as her brother, much more than she did Moishe, and Chavala was the mother she had never known.

Raizel had grown in grace and loveliness. There was nothing too difficult for her to do as she assumed chores beyond a girl of eleven. Dvora, on the other hand, was a girl of great spirit who had never forgotten the Galilee, and deeply felt a yearning to go back to the land. For weeks she debated with herself, then got up the courage to tell Chavala and Dovid that she was leaving to join a youth group that had just formed in the Galilee—a girls' training farm that had recently been launched thanks to the determination of Dr. Ruth Levy, herself a member of the second *Aliva*. She conceived the idea of a farm where girls would be taught, in addition to domestic science, market-gardening, poultry breeding and dairy farming.

With Dvora's announcement Chavala's world did seem threatened. She couldn't share Dvora's enthusiasm and excitement. She knew her reasons were selfish, but she'd already lost Sheine and now clung tenaciously to at least try to keep her family together.

Dvora, knowing Dovid would understand, told him, "Dovid, you must help me make Chavala understand I'm no longer a child. This means a great deal to me . . . everything, really. Zichron is fine for Chavala, but I'm not her."

"Let her go," Dovid told his wife. "It's right. To deprive her would only make her miserable, and eventually you too."

"We're gradually losing them, aren't we, Dovid? First Sheine, now Dvora . . ."

"They've grown up, Chavala. Give her your blessings so that she won't need to feel any guilt."

Chavala did, but the day that Dvora left, Chavala felt as though she had lost a piece of herself.

DVORA fitted immediately into life in the Galilee. In the early mornings she would wake up with a special excitement, dress and leave quietly while the others slept so that she could see the sunrise. She inhaled the perfume of the morning air, watched, felt nature all around her. The earth beneath her feet would soon, she felt, reveal all its secrets. She looked up to see the birds in flight. And with it all . . . there was a dream that lay dormant in her, a dream that would soon be awakened. . . .

Three years before, a group called Haikkar Hatzair, "The Young Farmer," had been formed in the United States by twelve young students from the Jewish agricultural college in Woodbine, New Jersey, who were preparing to live on the land in Palestine. After leaving college each member of the group acquired practical experience in a specific branch of farming, anticipating the system that was later adopted by the *chalut-zim*. With $5,000 they appealed to the Palestine Land Development Company to take over the farm, complete with livestock and equipment, for one year. The two youth settlements were within a short walking distance, and when one or the other was in need of a piece of equipment they readily shared . . .

Dvora had just come out of the milking shed when she saw off in the distance a young man carrying a small incubator. Looking in her direction he called out, *"Shalom."*

"Shalom."

As the two came closer Dvora felt a sensation new to her but ancient to females her age and older . . . Now face to face with the young *chalutz*, the feeling was both frightening and exhilarating at the same time. Feeling peculiar, she averted her eyes when he said "I'm from Haikkar Hatzair and I've come to deliver this. Incidentally, my name is Ari Ben-Levi."

"And mine is Dvora Rabinsky," she said so quietly he barely caught it.

As the two proceeded on to the main building Ari said, "How long have you been here?"

"For a month now. And you?"

"I arrived three days ago from America."

"From *America?*"

"It's not the moon."

"I didn't mean it that way . . . you won't laugh if I tell you something?"

"I promise."

"I was just thinking of my sister, who's always wanted to go to America and here you've come to Eretz Yisroel . . . I don't think this is making any sense." She laughed nervously.

"Makes a lot of sense. My family escaped the ghettos of Poland and couldn't understand my giving up the good life to come here and work. It just shows how the pendulum swings."

"Your Hebrew is so perfect, I thought you were born here. I'm afraid mine still has a Yiddish accent. Is your name really Ari Ben-Levi?"

"I was born Richard Levi. Not bad, one generation removed from the ghetto. But it isn't Richard Levi any longer, it's Richard Lee. That's what you call becoming Americanized . . . Well," he said as they got to the poultry station, "it's been very nice meeting you, Dvora . . ."

For the rest of that day she thought of Ari Ben-Levi and absolutely nothing else. Except that she might die if he didn't come back soon. *Very* soon.

On Sunday he did. Looking up from her milking stool, she saw him framed in the doorway. She could *hear* her heart beat, her palms were wet. He was more handsome than she'd even remembered. *"Shalom,"* he said smiling and spreading his hands, "I guess I'm what you call an aggressive American. I'd like to see you today . . ."

Swallowing, she said, "I'll be through in about an hour."

"No hurry . . . I'll wait." He waited, this aggressive American, a week before getting up the courage to come back, a week when his thoughts had been of Dvora and little else. She was absolutely the loveliest thing he'd ever seen . . . her hair was the color of rich brown molasses and her eyes a sort of amber. Her waist was slim, and her bosom just round enough to excite him. If there was such a thing, Ari felt this was love at first sight. And what a sight . . .

WHEN her chores were done Dvora slipped into a pair of fresh white shorts and pulled the blue cotton knit top over her head, buckled her sandals and glanced at herself in the mirror. Her face was flushed in spite of the tan. She ran a comb through her hair and was out the door of the small bungalow she shared with three other *chaveroth*.

At first they just stood awkwardly, then Ari managed, "Since you know your way around better than I, what do you suggest?"

"Let's hike to the top of the hill, the view from there is great."

When they got to the top and looked about, there was a stillness that seemed to make them feel closer . . . as though they were the only two people left in the world. They looked out on the snow-topped peak of Mount Hermon. Pink and white clouds floated languidly in the blue sky, and below could be seen the Sea of Galilee. It looked even lovelier today, standing here with Ari, than the first time she'd seen it, when Dovid had said, "Come, Dvora, I want you to see this and remember it all your life." She would remember it, and she would remember more this moment. Neither spoke. There was no need for words.

They sat down under carob trees, and Dvora unpacked the small lunch she'd brought with her. After they'd eaten they lay back and looked up at the sky visible in patches through the branches.

Slowly Ari's hand found hers, and in the silence of that lazy afternoon he said, "I love you, Dvora. It happened the moment I saw you. I mean it, I don't care how sudden it seems . . ."

"I believe you, Ari. Especially since it's the same for me . . ."

There was nothing awkward, not even hesitant, as he turned to embrace her and their lips met. For them it was more than a kiss, it was a lifetime pledge. As enduring for them as this land they'd both dedicated their lives to . . .

Chapter Nine

By 1914 IT WAS a far different Palestine than the one Chavala and Dovid had first come to. The Jews now numbered some eighty-five thousand. The old Yishuv who had been in the country before the Zionist immigration was still concentrated in the four holy cities and still lived largely on contributions from abroad. They were alien to the new life that was evolving in Palestine and looked on it with a combination of apathy and even hostility.

Their opposition was partly based on religious grounds, but even more on the fear that the funds from abroad would be increasingly for building up modern settlements, thus causing their own sources of income to dry up. The influence of the new worker settlements hardly touched Jerusalem and Hebron. The workers mostly found employment in the villages of lower Galilee. Tiberius was growing into an economic center, and the Jewish population of Haifa and Jaffa owed its development to economic forces rather than to historical or religious associations. The opening up of new shipping, the laying of railroad lines between Jaffa and Jerusalem and Haifa quickened the economic pulse. Jaffa was the principal port of Palestine as well as the center of Judean settlements. Jaffa also became the cultural center of the Yishuv. The first Hebrew schools were opened in Jaffa, the Zionist institutions and workers' federations had their offices there, topped off by the building of the first Jewish city—Tel Aviv. The former settlements were now replaced with kibbutzim that were gradually becoming the backbone of the Yishuv.

At the outbreak of the First World War the Yishuv was numerically stronger and better organized than at the beginning of the Zionist settlements. It had advanced enormously since the unity of the working-class parties. Federations of agricultural workers were formed in Judea and Galilee, and were administered by an elected body, the Merkaz Chaklai. But for all that had been accomplished, much still depended on the Jews in the Diaspora.

Turkey didn't enter the war immediately, but her pro-German leanings were all too apparent. It was to be only a matter of time . . . A state of emergency was proclaimed throughout the Ottoman Empire and general mobilization began to protect Turkish "neutrality." Turkish shipping in the Black Sea and the Aegean was stopped. The Bosphorus and Dardanelles were closed to foreign vessels. Egypt declared war against Germany and went under British protection, whose ships no longer could use Palestinian ports.

In September foreigners came under the jurisdiction of the Turkish courts. They also lost postal facilities, so their correspondence was likely to be tampered with. And so the immigrant Jews in Palestine were cut off from their countries they'd emigrated from.

While the old Yishuv, divided as it had been before into factions and communities, stood by helplessly the new Yishuv was aroused. Its center was in Tel Aviv. Only a few days after the war began an emergency committee was set up.

In spite of all the efforts made in Palestine to cope with hardship, the Jews would have gone under if it hadn't been for help from America. The American warship *North Carolina* put into Jaffa with $50,000. Later on, other American ships entered Palestinian waters. This evidence of America's interest in the fate of the Yishuv not only showed the Jews that they had a friend, it also raised their standing in the eyes of the non-Jewish population and the local Turkish authorities. People with rich friends in America were people who might be worth a little extortion.

On orders of the American donors a central committee was set up to supervise the distribution of the relief funds. Palestine was divided into regions—Jerusalem, Haifa, Galilee, Samaria and Judea. The American Zionist Organization decided what the funds were to be used for. All this American aid was especially timely when on October 31, 1914, Turkey entered the war and the call went out to the Islamic world to join in a holy war against the Allies. Unprecedented hardships now began for the Yishuv. Its very existence was now at stake. Turkey at first ordered all enemy nationals transferred from Palestine to the interior of the Ottoman Empire. Thanks to the American and German ambassadors, though, Jews were at least allowed to opt for Turkish nationality and stay in Palestine. Those who didn't had to leave the country. The Jews weren't happy with the alternatives, but the salvation of the Yishuv depended on it. As for military service, Christians could buy exemption, but the Jews had to serve, and many of them were drafted into labor battalions, where they died of disease or starvation.

Jamal Pasha, commander of the Fourth Army Corps, was appointed supreme governor of Syria and Arabia, and he had a fitting lieutenant in the person of the Baha al-Din, who had gained practical experience in the art of destroying whole groups of minorities in Armenia. The Zionists and Jewish national institutions were considered by Jamal Pasha and his minions as Turkey's real enemy. The first steps taken against them in October

1914 were such things as prohibiting the use of Hebrew in Tel Aviv; all inscriptions had to be in Turkish and Arabic, beneath which Hebrew might appear only in small lettering. Tel Aviv was surrounded by troops. Searches were conducted in the homes of the leading Zionists, many of their papers were confiscated, presumably to expose the separatist aims of Zionism. A number of Zionists were arrested and sentenced to deportation, the use and possession of JNF stamps were punishable by death. Jews were not allowed to protect Jewish suburbs and the Judean settlements. The Hebrew language and the Hebrew script in correspondence were prohibited. The Zionist flag and Jewish administrative institutions were declared illegal. Transfers of land to Jews were forbidden, and the authorities tried to gain possession of the title deeds to land already in Jewish hands.

At noon on December 17, 1914, Baha al-Din issued an order that all foreign nationals had to leave, that a ship was due to lay anchor at Jaffa at four o'clock the same afternoon. Soldiers and police seized Jews—men and women, old people and children—in the streets and locked them up. In the evening they were hustled to the quayside and put into boats, which were to take them out to the ship. Husbands were separated from wives, parents from children. Trials began, indicting prominent Zionists, among them Yitzchak Ben-Zvi and David Ben-Gurion, both by now high in the labor movement. Ben-Zvi's punishment was hard labor for an article describing the brutality used during the deportations. Ben-Gurion was accused of being subversive . . . "It is your aim to establish a Jewish state in Palestine. I decree that you will leave the country . . . meanwhile you will be imprisoned."

At first Galilee suffered less than Judea; but not for long. Requisitioning was intensified. Draft animals, farm implements and stores of grain were seized for the army. The settlements were forced to supply men, horses and carts for work on military installations at Beersheba, and many died from diseases contracted as a result of back-breaking work under miserable conditions. . . .

Dovid's situation was somewhat special. Working at Athlit had its advantages. In the years that he'd worked with Aaronson their relationship grew very strong, Dovid had shown great promise and his efforts had not gone unrewarded. Since Aaron had worked closely with the Turkish government on farm problems and had become a scientist of such renown, the pasha almost forgot—never forgave—that he was a Jew. He was able to intercede with the pasha on Dovid's behalf, reminding the pasha that the men at Athlit were more valuable to the government with their knowledge of farming than in clearing the roads. The pasha went along, not out of charity but because Turkey badly needed food to feed an army.

Moishe's position was more complicated. In spite of his hatred for the Turkish government he had no choice but to join up or be deported, and so he kissed his sister Chavala good-bye and said he would go back to Jaffa to wait for his orders. When he arrived in Jaffa, Moishe suddenly found himself caught up in the storm of arrests. Jews were being pushed and hurried along the streets, and he followed the flood of terrified and bewildered Jews, none of whom was more bewildered than he.

Moishe was on the road between Haifa and Jaffa as Baha al-Din was issuing his expulsion orders. He found old men, gray-bearded, with long coats and broad-brimmed hats, carrying all they possessed in their arms. The crowd was growing in size, as well as the outcries . . . "What have we done?" . . . "Why are you doing this to us?" . . . "Where are they sending us, we'll die in the desert" . . . When the group of displaced Jews was thrown into the detention hall, the rooms were already bulging with people. Families were being separated . . . "Where are you, Isaac?" . . . "My baby, God, where is my baby?" . . .

Moishe could no longer hold in his rage. "I demand to see your commander."

The answer was the butt of a rifle at his head.

Moishe staggered, his hand to his head, feeling the blood. Trying to shake his head clear, he called out again, "I came to join the army—"

The soldier laughed. "In Russia, you join."

People were thrown into a room and demands were made that they turn over their money. After all their possessions were stripped from them, they were herded to the docks and amidst all the madness, walked up a gangplank onto an unfit ship that was set adrift to find its way back to Russia.

As he lay on deck, Moishe made up his mind that he would not go back, he'd rather die . . . Now he became aware of the *chalutz* next to him. They looked at each other, and in that moment with no need to speak, each seemed to read the thought of the other.

"Can you swim?" whispered the stranger.

"No. But if you have a plan, I'll learn quick."

"I have a compass, I know where we might be able to jump ship, with a lot of luck we might make it to Cairo . . . I understand Trumpeldor is trying to convince the British that Jews can fight."

"I don't give a damn about the British, they're no better than the Turks, but back to Russia I'm not going."

"Good. At midnight we jump . . . incidentally, my name is Nathan Zalman."

The two shook hands. "If we don't make it, our names won't matter, but just in case, I'm Moishe Rabinsky."

Moishe, who had never swum, jumped and was surprised to find that he'd somehow come up to the surface of the water. For a while he paddled. His pace was slower than Nathan's, but his determination urged him on until he was almost side-by-side with his new found comrade . . .

When at last they hit the beach, the two lay back in complete exhaustion and disbelief. If they could accomplish this, they'd live to see the Messiah.

CHAVALA was frantic when Moishe did not come back that night. Dovid's attempts to quiet her fears did no good. She sat up until dawn, convinced something dreadful had happened.

When Dovid awoke in the morning he found Chavala standing at the window. He put his arms around her and said, "We have to assume the best, not the worst, darling. Moishe is strong, he's—"

"I'm not a child, Dovid. You know as well as I that something must have happened. He hasn't taken his things, he was coming back after he joined up. What are we going to *do?*"

"Aaronson has connections. If anyone can find out he can. . . . "

Chavala waited, her anxiety growing. Finally on the third day, when Dovid came home, she was sure the worst had been confirmed. She saw it in the look on Dovid's face. Moishe was dead.

Taking her into his arms, Dovid said, "Moishe's in Alexandria with Trumpeldor. Aaronson received this message . . . here, see for yourself, he's in Alexandria . . ."

Tears streaming down her cheeks, she looked at Dovid. "He's safe . . . thank God, he's safe."

Yes, Dovid thought, *but for how long?*

CHAVALA'S world, that only a short time before had seemed so safe and serene, now was unraveling. Sheine had been called up to work at the front near the Syrian border in a hospital unit. Moishe was alive, but for how long . . . ? Maybe he wasn't considered a soldier, but the mule corps faced death as much as any combat unit. And now Dvora had come back to Zichron to announce she was going to marry Ari.

Thinking back on that all too short respite she'd known living in Zichron, she now saw how presumptuous it was to think one was in control of her life, let alone the lives of loved ones. So Dvora was getting married . . . looking at her sister, Chavala remembered how she'd planned that when the day came for her sisters to marry, *she* would sew their wedding gowns and she and Dovid would walk each in their turn to the *chuppah* . . . now that dream was shattered, no amount of argument could convince Dvora. "Wait until the war is over, please, Dvora. I pray Ari will come back . . . but darling, if the worst should happen . . ."

"Then I'll have his child."

Of course . . . Dvora was a woman, and Chavala hadn't even noticed. "Are you carrying his child . . . ?"

"Yes, and I'm proud of it. I love him, Chavala, just as you do Dovid . . . and whatever happens, I'll have to accept it."

Chavala nodded. "When will you be married?"

"Immediately."

After Dvora left, Chavala sat in the lengthening shadows and began to come out of herself, to see in fact that she suffered from a very serious disease—self-pity. Enough. Other people had their troubles too, many of them far worse than hers, and she thought of Sarah Aaronson . . .

Only God knew how Sarah must have suffered when she gave up the man she so deeply loved to her sister Rivka. (The connection with herself and Dovid and Sheine did not . . . not surprisingly . . . occur to her.) Sarah was a woman of great beauty and strength of character, filled with the joy of living and had always been ready for adventure. But Rivka was different, perhaps the opposite . . . she was always the adored little sister, sweet, piquant and vulnerable. Living as she did on the periphery of such forceful people as Sarah, Alex and Aaron, she developed a sense of inferiority, which Sarah not only understood but blamed herself for . . . Rivka seemed to have been all but overlooked. She may have been much adored, but still she could not compete with them. Although she had received numerous proposals, she had rejected them out of her mistaken sense of unworthiness. Sarah decided that once again she was the one standing in Rivka's way. Her sister's love for Absalom was so intense, so complete that there was no question that she would ever marry anybody else. Sarah had seen them together, seen the way Rivka not only looked *at* Absalom, but how she looked *up* at him. And she wasn't wrong. The man was unique, marvelous. After all, she had fallen in love with him, hadn't she? Well, no more thinking about that . . . what she had to decide was whether she was strong enough to give up this man for her sister's happiness, her life, really . . . a life that had been too often limited and frustrated, Sarah felt, because of her own actions, as well as those of others in her family. She thought, and shook her head at the irony of the coincidence, about Aaron and how he was now alone because of a woman he couldn't have, a woman married to one of his closest friends. Aaron had managed to deny himself for somebody else . . . could she do as much for her own sister? Somehow she had to, but how could she stand it? For a while she considered going off someplace so that Rivka would be free to enjoy her love for Absalom, a love she'd been hiding too long. But that would be too cowardly, and Sarah was no coward. What then?

The best she could come up with was a campaign . . . she shuddered when she considered it . . . to make Absalom grow tired of her. She began when he asked her to marry him, with a rather languid, "Let's not be impetuous." Absalom wasn't a man easily put off, not by Turks or short-sighted Jews who couldn't see their future was to have their own land . . . or by the woman that he had made up his mind to spend his life with. What the hell did she mean? Why the sudden change? Being less than self-assured when it came to his attraction to women, he began to think she'd found or preferred someone else. He asked her.

Sarah took the opening to concoct a story that she hoped was more convincing than, God knew, she felt . . . "Absalom, please try and forgive me. I did love you, but more and more lately I've come to see that we are just too much alike, that marriage would only intensify that, and eventually we'd both be miserable—"

He was stunned, even though she seemed to be saying what he was most afraid of. "So you've found someone else?"

"Yes, but please, try to remember the good things we've shared. I know I always will."

Wonderful, he thought. *Live on memories. To hell with that.* Hurt, angry, he left, and his visits to the Aaronson home ended.

Naturally, Sarah's family was bewildered. Sarah tried to explain it to her father by saying love wasn't enough, that she wanted a home and children and not a poet, that Absalom would never settle down, he was a free spirit, a fine man but eventually his way of life would make life impossible between them, and so forth. She was almost getting to believe it herself, as she became increasingly practiced in her lie.

Ephraim was miserable. Aaron had been forced into a life of loneliness, and now Sarah . . .

"You're sure, Sarah, that you won't regret this?"

She could only shake her head, not trusting herself to speak any-more.

Well, there could be no average man for Sarah, and where would Ephraim find another such man? One to take Absalom's place?

He didn't really find another Absalom, but he did find a man, a young man of great wealth, a merchant from Constantinople. Sarah amazed him by agreeing to marriage even though she hadn't even seen the man.

Sarah was quickly married and left immediately after for her new home in Constantinople. That summer, of course, was like an unending nightmare. What Sarah had said to Absalom about being strong and independent was irrelevant only with Absalom. For this man it was like a sentence . . . she'd grown up an independent-minded woman in the free atmosphere of Zichron. Here she was subjected to the world of an Orien-tal-style ménage, where a husband's regard for his wife was at his conve-nience and according to his needs.

Actually he was very fond of Sarah, but he was raised in the conven-tional, rigid, old-fashioned German attitudes his family had brought with them from Berlin. Sarah was never allowed, as his wife, to leave their home alone. She was sheltered, sequestered. Well, it was a kind of atone-ment, she told herself, for all that she'd denied Rivka in the past. At least the ledger was in balance. She hoped Rivka and Absalom—oh, stop it, she told herself. She wasn't *that* noble. She'd done what she thought she had to do. But she was no saint. She was a woman, and she felt like any other woman who had lost her man . . .

IT was the perfect time for Rivka to come to him, to help get him through his bad times. She provided a sweetness, a serenity that he seemed to need so much after the tempestuous courtship and breakup with Sarah. Rivka was like a healing balm.

To no one's surprise, they were soon married.

Like Sarah, Absalom tried hard to make his marriage work, but he still loved Sarah. Rivka knew when she married him that he didn't love her but like a few million women before her, she let herself hope that with time he might.

It didn't happen. It was obvious to everyone that there was no longer enough even to make a show, and Ephraim now understood that Sarah had sacrificed herself, a sacrifice that defeated itself. He felt only pity for the suffering of the people involved, and blamed no one. But as he watched Rivka, now so pitifully silent, he knew he had to take immediate and drastic action. Rivka was sent off to America, where hopefully she would forget Absalom and find something new and better with relatives in San Francisco.

SARAH'S letters went straight to Absalom's heart . . .

> Beloved Absalom, not a day goes by that I don't think about my arrogant selflessness. Not only did I destroy what we had, I made things even worse for Rivka. Let's hope that America can make some of it up to her . . .

And Absalom wrote . . .

> Your goodness, dear Sarah, is as great as your courage. You must not go on berating yourself. It's true, a part of me went with you when you went away. I was hurt, angry. But we two are together even if we're apart. The love between us isn't bounded by geography or time. I admit I'm tempted to come to you, but that would never work. You're married, and I have things to do that might keep us more apart than we are now. Please try to think about me sometimes. I think of you from morning until the day's end, and that is how it will be all the rest of my life.

Chapter Ten

MOISHE AND NATHAN Zalman were picked up on the beach by a British patrol and thrown into a truck. Where they were going, they could only guess, but it wouldn't surprise them if they were hanged as spies. Without papers, how could they plead their case?

Passing the harbor at Alexandria, Moishe was overwhelmed by a sight that momentarily pushed aside his fears. Anchored in the harbor was a part of the giant British armada, the dreadnaught *Queen Elizabeth*, looking as regal as its namesake. The Russian cruiser *Askold* was on hand with its five slim funnels silhouetted against the blue Egyptian skyline. There were French battleships, cruisers, destroyers, transports and smaller craft. Too bad they hadn't come to deliver his people out of bondage, take up the challenge to free Palestine. The reality was that they were in the company of the majority of the world powers—no one cared. Only Jews could save themselves. Including these two particular Jews.

When they were finally delivered to the refugee compound of Mafruza, Moishe was shocked to see the compound overflowing with young Jews, who were undoubtedly contemplating their fate as he was. And like Moishe, they were unaware that their fate lay in the hands of men whose names they had never heard of, although they soon would . . .

VLADIMIR Jabotinsky was considered a genius at seventeen. His prose and philosophies were being read in a land that had created Tolstoy, Gorky and Dostoevsky. He was a born linguist who had translated Shakespeare into Russian, and *War and Peace* into English. By the time he was thirty his name was in the Russian encyclopedia. If he'd been a Russian his life would have been far different, but he was a Jew, and so it was his lot to be hated and discriminated against. His intellect and talents might be rare, but the misery of his people was felt deeply and shared with the lowest of them. He found himself caught up in a struggle that forced him to reexamine his own position . . . did he live as a Russian, isolated from his people, or as a Jew? There was only one answer after he'd witnessed the Kishinev pogroms of 1903.

Jabotinsky rejected the doctrinaire, revolutionary approach of the Russian-Jewish intelligentsia. Instead he went into the ghetto to explore its heart, to understand its hurts, to learn its language. He became an outspoken Zionist, a convert to Herzl and his dream of a Jewish state. He visited the headquarters of the World Zionist Organization scattered throughout Europe, then left for France in the summer of 1914.

One evening as he walked the streets of Paris, he paused at the square where Dreyfus had been accused of treason, and Theodore Herzl had stood that same day in the drenching rain and heard the terrible cry, "Kill the Jews."

Jabotinsky was aware of the echoes of that cry, an echo that gave him his strongest sense yet of linkage with his people.

The next morning France was at war. And after Brussels fell to the German army and the Ottoman Empire declared war on the Allies,

Jabotinsky felt that after four hundred long years of tyranny, the Turks had taken the final step toward their own demise. That would only be good for the Jews.

Now he saw his way clearly. Herzl had tried diplomacy, and for all his valor, had failed. Rothschild's philanthropy had fallen short, and the Jewish revolutionaries of Russia had failed. Now with the Ottoman Empire about to collapse, Jabotinsky knew Jews had to take a direct and active part in the fight for their liberation and destiny. The days of counting on foreign friends and doctrines were over. An all-Jewish military unit was at hand. The Jews would fight on the side of the Allies. And that road would lead to Palestine.

That very night he packed and left for Egypt.

In Alexandria, in the refugee camp, Mafruza, Jabotinsky found the great Russian-Jewish officer, Joseph Trumpeldor. When Jabotinsky saw the one-armed Trumpeldor seated at a crude wooden table, he could barely restrain his anger at the British for showing the man so little respect. Britain and Russia were, after all, allies, and this extraordinary officer had risen to heights in the Russian army that no other Jew had ever managed.

Jabotinsky thought back to Joseph Trumpeldor's beginnings . . . Unlike Jabotinsky, whose family was affluent, Trumpeldor had come from humble beginnings. His father had served in the army for twenty-five years as a conscript under Czar Nicholas I. As a Jew Trumpeldor wasn't able to attend a university. He apprenticed himself to a dentist. When the war between Russia and Japan broke out he was drafted into the army and sent to Port Arthur, Manchuria. For his sacrifice and bravery during the year-long siege he was decorated with the Order of St. George, the highest honor bestowed on any officer. After the war he had a reserve officer's rank, which finally entitled him to attend the university and finish his earlier studies in the law. Still, in spite of the honors, Trumpeldor was a *Jew* in Russia, with no future. He left and went to Palestine, where he worked tilling the soil. And with the deportation of the Jews, he went into action. He knew what would happen to these Jews if they were sent back to Russia. And if they got to Egypt alive, Consul Petrov there would demand the deportation of all Palestinian males. Trumpeldor decided to try his persuasive powers on Petrov. He would go to Alexandria as one of the first expatriates.

By the time his ship landed in Alexandria Trumpeldor had gathered around him a group of young Jewish disciples who would follow him to the ends of the earth. . . .

Now Trumpeldor sat at the makeshift table writing out the plans for his Jewish army that he intended to present to the British. They would have to recognize the huge stake that Jews had in this war. A Jewish legion would be the most dedicated, loyal and effective unit the Allies could possibly have. Men fired by a dream long denied them would fight to the death . . .

Pausing for a moment to collect his thoughts, he looked up and saw Jabotinsky framed in the doorway. No introduction was needed, Trumpeldor recognized the famous journalist and author from pictures he'd seen. Extending his hand, he said, "I'm not surprised you've come. If you were ever needed, it's here. They say the word is mightier than the sword—"

"Only in certain cases. Maybe Zola's, where Dreyfus was concerned," Jabotinsky said, "but for our cause only an army will do."

From that moment on these two were locked together by a common bond; their goals were identical. After dinner they went to Jabotinsky's hotel and Jabotinsky read the memorandum Trumpeldor had prepared to present to the British high command. "None of this, I take it, has been discussed with the British?"

"No. But before anything can be presented, obviously it must be translated into English, and that, my friend, is where you come in."

"I'm more concerned," Jabotinsky said, "about numbers. If we could present the British with a regiment of volunteers, then we might stand a real chance of the proposal's success. How many men do you think could be raised?"

At the moment, Trumpeldor told him, there were two hundred able-bodied men, and each day new refugees were swelling the ranks. They had fled Palestine on anything that would move on water, and one thing they could depend on was that the Turks would expel more. If the Egyptian Jews could be brought out of their lethargy there would be a possibility of at least a few thousand. A regiment would be guaranteed.

Jabotinsky nodded. "You're right, but we still have to convince these Egyptian Jews that Palestine is more important than Cairo. These Jews, who were once slaves for the pharaoh, now employ Egyptian servants. The pendulum has swung. I don't mean to suggest that Egyptian Jews aren't with us, but they haven't lived under the Turks, and the British are here to protect them."

"They're only a small part of the Jews in Egypt. The rank and file are starving and would jump at the chance to earn their bed and board and have daily rations. I've seen them hungry, roaming the streets of Alexandria."

"I know, but the power of the Jewish community here are the rich, influential Sephardim. Whatever action we take must include them. We'll have to cultivate their friendship."

The name Vladimir Jabotinsky opened the right doors, and he brought Trumpeldor. The ladies were fascinated by the one-armed hero. They would certainly use *their* influence in the right places to help him recruit the young Egyptian Jews. The Sephardic leaders were convinced by Jabotinsky's passionate oratory that Britain must accept the demands for a Jewish fighting legion on the Palestinian front for the liberation of Eretz Yisroel, and pledged their support.

Now Trumpeldor was ready to confront the British officials. When he appeared—tall, broad-shouldered, lean, with the breeding of an officer and the dignity of a gentleman (even a British one) he didn't fail to impress Ronald Graham, Minister of the Interior for Egypt. He promised to do all he could. While waiting for a reply Trumpeldor opened a recruiting office. Names were written in Hebrew, Yiddish and Russian.

In London, General Sir John Maxwell paced the floor of his stately office with a petition rattling in his hands. They were daft, those bloody Jews, thinking they could choose the war that they wanted. How dare they even propose such an outlandish thing. There had been nothing about an offensive against Palestine. The British weren't in this thing to gain a piece of real estate for the Jews. What ineffable cheek even to suggest that they could become full partners in the British army. He poured himself a brandy, sat down, sipped it. Still . . . there might be a use for these Jews, even if they were such a bothersome lot. Not as soldiers of the realm, of course, but as, say, *attendant gillies*. It was, after all, a British tradition. In India, in the Sudan, natives were used and had been bloody helpful. He recalled nostalgically how in the Boer War his own personal valet had accompanied him, bringing along his tailored uniforms and sterling silver brushes. That had been a gentlemen's war. Of course all wars were different. There was a need for transport men. The terrain might be . . . well, it might be rugged. getting up the hills at Gallipoli.

So the general's secretary got off a reply . . . the volunteers would be welcomed into His Majesty's Army in the capacity of a transport mule corps. This special unit would even bear arms.

When Trumpeldor read the reply he tried and failed to swallow back the bile. They weren't going to allow a Jew the honor of fighting like a man. The young men around him had lived on this single hope, and in one month of training they had already proved themselves damned good soldiers. Now how the hell was he going to tell them?

Jabotinsky, when told, erupted. "Leave it to the British. They've insulted us, slapped us in the face. Good God, Joseph, you're not really going to accept this, are you?"

Trumpeldor shot back angrily. "What choice do we have? Mules, transport troops, what does it matter? The important thing is that Britain win, and when the Turks are driven out the men will forget that they were porters to haul water and ammunition. In battle all are the same. At least it will give the world a chance to see what Jews are made of."

When the men were told, their faces froze, the British were only using them, they'd refuse to be treated like the animals they were supposed to lead into battle. Trumpeldor waited, then: "A soldier is a soldier, whether he carries a gun or leads a mule. In the army, all are the same. The *important* thing to remember is that this will be a *Jewish* unit with its own insignia, the Star of David. *The first fighting unit in eighteen hundred years.*" He paused a moment. "Be proud, you are soldiers. Company dismissed."

Among those listening to Jabotinsky, and at first with skepticism, was Moishe, who had escaped the hangman's noose only because of the progress Jabotinsky and especially Trumpeldor had made in getting some sort of status for the Jews in the military, even if it was only as a mule corps. Jews were, it was decided, at least a step up now from object lessons with the hangman's hemp around their throats. The days waiting for this day had been ugly ones . . . the British were hardly more civilized than the Russians or Turks, though they spoke at times with impeccable accents as they carried out their abuses. A British-run prison in Alexandria, land of the pharaohs, was a place of swill, despotic discipline and filth. All was scrubbed and shining, including the guards' polished boots—you could see an emaciated Jew's face in the toes clear as a mirror's reflection —but behind the polish was the spit. The sun, they said, never set on the British Empire. It also never rose for those within the gray walls of its prisons. The day they came to let out Moishe . . . he never did find his friend again . . . he thought surely it was his last. The gallows chitchat of the guards who prodded him with rifles hardly was calculated to disabuse him of such expectations. Driven in a truck like cattle, Moishe and others were taken to a primitive barracks, allowed their first bath in weeks, and then led out to hear this great leader. Imagine their surprise when instead of having a British accent he spoke as, and indeed was, a *Jew,* and an officer at that. Incredible. All right, so they'd haul mules, but at least they'd be Jewish mules . . . since when had progress for Jews been in a hurry . . . ?

When Trumpeldor returned to his barracks Jabotinsky was waiting for him. "Well, how did they take it?"

"The same as you, but they'll do their job."

"In that case I'm leaving for London. You were right, sometimes the word can be mightier than the sword. I'll use words to fight for an all-Jewish military unit with the same status that belongs to any British soldier. . . ."

The next morning as Trumpeldor drilled nearly a thousand men of the Zion Mule Corps, a British officer watched them closely. This was a sight to see. Proud Jewish warriors, as proud to be Jews as he was to be Irish.

Trumpeldor brought the men to a halt and attention, and with the aid of a regular army officer, who was to become interpreter, Lieutenant Colonel John Henry Patterson heard himself being introduced in Hebrew, Yiddish and Ladino.

"I wish you men to know," he said, "that I consider it an honor to have been assigned to your ranks. As I look among you I see the spirit that inspired your great general Bar-Kochba. That spirit has risen once again within your ranks. I will be your commanding officer, but only with the collaboration of Captain Trumpeldor. I am proud to be a part of you."

Patterson had led troops in Africa and India, and if a real soldier like him was honored to command a troop of muleteers, there was nothing to be ashamed of, they decided. . . .

Looking at these young men with the Star of David on their caps brought great pride to Trumpeldor and Patterson as they ordered the men out of the compound. It was time to prove themselves.

In full uniform, packs on their backs, Moishe and his fellow corpsmen marched through the streets of Alexandria. What a sight to see. The Star of David on their caps, they proudly held their ancient rifles against their shoulders. Small boys, both Jew and Egyptian, ran alongside and cheered. Jews cheered, young and old—and Moishe noticed more than one wiping a tear from his, or her, eye. Women and young girls threw flowers in their path. They stopped at the great synagogue and were blessed by the chief rabbi in Sephardic Hebrew.

The men had seven hundred and fifty mules. There were twenty horses for the officers. In addition to Trumpeldor, five British and eight Jewish officers had been appointed, the Jews with forty percent less pay, but at least the commands were given equally—in Hebrew as well as English.

The mules, sorted according to size, were now being brought onto the transport vessels, kicking savagely and braying—a strange contrast to the shrill Scottish bagpipes heard from another troopship. Then, accompanied by steamship whistles and commands from bleating horns, the men were brought aboard. Mules before men . . .

Moishe had elbowed his way to stand at the railing and watch. As far as his eye could see, there were vessels. Clearly he was part of a huge operation, dwarfing the awesome vista he'd observed in Alexandria Harbor that first day when he'd arrived. Now he realized he'd seen only a small part of the enormous armada that spanned the narrow sea between Europe and Asia.

On that Saturday afternoon, April 17, 1915, the Zion Mule Corps sailed from Alexandria for Gallipoli under the escort of British warships. A distance away in the harbor, the band of the U.S.S. *Tennessee,* which happened to be in port, played a farewell march. And suddenly a song echoed over the sunlit Egyptian harbor, over the masts of fishing boats, over the stacks of ocean liners, over the towers and superstructures of the British men-of-war. It was a song of sorrow, dignity and surpassing hope too, destined to become the anthem of a nation to be reborn some thirty years later—the "Hatikvah."

The voyage to the Greek island Lemnos in the Aegean Sea, which was a springboard for the invasion of Gallipoli, took two days. The time was uneventful, but as soon as they entered the mouth of the Dardanelles the British let go with a massive burst of cannon fire. Moishe shuddered at the sound, put his hands over his ears, and thought about death. He was . . . face it . . . afraid, and began to wonder just what sort of Jewish warrior he was. Maybe if he'd been fighting for Palestine . . . but here he was on a ship that belonged to strangers, commanded by foreigners, headed for places where he would plod his mules in alien trenches. And even if the British won, there was no guarantee he would get back to his historic homeland . . . Moishe at that moment badly needed some convincing link between his and Dovid's dream of a homeland and the reality of his immediate situation. Well, Trumpeldor had said "Every road leads to Zion." He held tight to that thought . . . Zion was more than a word . . . it was a purpose. He looked up and saw the streaks of red fire across the sky, and felt less afraid. It no longer mattered so much that the huge mountain which lay before him was not Mount Carmel. He understood better what Trumpeldor had meant about fighting for a country that annihilated his own people and for a czar who condoned it. The cause he and the others fought for was greater—and he fought not as a Russian, not for its cause, but fought for his own sake as a Jew, for all Jews

. . . Trumpeldor had been right back in Alexandria when he told them to be proud, that they had to prove themselves, even as mule drivers. It was a major first step . . .

After numerous foul-ups, there was a frenzy to reach Gallipoli on April 25, the date set for the invasion. When they got close to the land, they found the enemy ready and waiting for them directly above the great fortification of Achi Baba. The British armada was choked. The strip was too narrow for all the transport vessels to approach and dig in. Still, the command was given and the men leapt into the water, and suddenly coming up to surface were hundreds of Senegalese, Australians, New Zealanders, Irish and Welsh and English clutching their rifles and struggling to wade to shore. Carnage lay all around them. Those that had reached the beach crawled up out of the water like sea urchins. Bodies floated face down, many with their guns still clutched in their hands, never having had a chance to fire a shot.

An order was given to reverse positions and at last a part of the beach had been secured. The men of Zion could have disembarked then, except there were no barges. From the rail, Patterson shouted down as the vessels passed, "You've got to get me ashore, you bloody fools, I've got your water. If you don't help me get ashore you'll not be dying from bullets but from thirst . . ." Not a craft slowed. Patterson took action . . . he simply requisitioned barges returning from the battle with the maimed and the wounded the moment they were emptied of the casualties. The dead and wounded no longer needed these barges, his muleteers did.

Finally the men of Zion and their mules were able to disembark. The barges were tied together like a pontoon bridge that extended to the beachhead. Trumpeldor and Patterson formed the men into a straight line across the planks and hurried them on.

When the mules were led off, under constant bombardment, the mooring between the barges broke loose and the animals plunged into the water, taking their handlers with them. Moishe jumped back, grabbed a rope and held onto a frightened animal. Most of them ran helter-skelter, biting, kicking.

The Turks were more predictable than the weather. A sudden storm with the ferocity of a typhoon came from out of nowhere. Crates, tins, ammunition boxes were flying like kites in the air, then came crashing down onto the beach. It persisted for two nights and days. The men huddled under any shelter they could find. When the storm broke, the mule corps was ordered by Trumpeldor to salvage whatever it could. Moishe wondered what he had in mind . . . how did you make any kind

of sense out of this chaos, tents blown away, the beach in total disarray.
. . . The work went on until dawn. When some bit of order had been
restored the men slumped on the muddy earth and fell off into exhausted
sleep. . . .

Moishe woke up dazed and disoriented. The pounding headache he
had was ignored as he heard the urgent command that rations and ammu-
nitions were needed on V Beach. In the craziness he'd all but forgotten
that the mules had been led into a safe cove by Trumpeldor, between the
rising and falling terrain under a cross fire that made him wonder how any
of them were missed. Actually the casualties had been surprisingly few.
In the days to come they were not so lucky. With the increasing action
many of the men in Moishe's squad were wounded. The bright sunlight
helped make them targets. A shell would strike and the mules would
scatter, dragging their handlers with them over rocks and falling debris.

As the Irishman Lieutenant Colonel Patterson had privately anticipated, due to their pitiful lack of training, which was hardly their fault,
and lack of communication, the Jewish muleteers and their British officers, full of old and well-tended prejudices, came more and more into
conflict. Finally the third and fourth troops of the mule corps were
actually sent back to Alexandria, which was of course a disgrace for them.
Patterson's Irish dander was not only up, it was over the top. During a
confrontation in his tent with the commanding British officer he listened
to the charge that the Jews had become insubordinate, refused to take
orders, and so there was nothing for it but to return some of them to
Alexandria and arrest and demobilize some others. Their mules were
turned over to the Australians, "who were admittedly bloody barbarians
but at least they spoke the language." Patterson informed the officer that
he was a damned fool, that one month's training hardly added to seasoned
troops. And, true, they didn't speak the king's English, but they didn't
unload ammunition boxes or control a bunch of crazy, frightened mules
with their tongues. Even the mother tongue might have a bit of trouble
with a goddamn mule under fire . . .

When Patterson and Trumpeldor returned to Alexandria to try to
get new volunteers, they got the full story of the British mistreatment of
the mule corps. The men were never allowed to do anything but tote
ammunition and supplies and live with mules, whether on a boat or on
land. Clearly someone didn't approve of the Zion Mule Corps. When
they got back to Alexandria they weren't even allowed to go ashore to see
their families and relatives. Yes, some of them did rebel then, and were
promptly arrested. Their wives had never received support, their widows

denied pensions. The men were demanding they be soldiers, not just laborers, and be treated as soldiers. Patterson tried to get their status upgraded and was turned down by British headquarters. A group then went on a hunger strike. British soldiers proceeded to whip those considered the troublemakers, men accused of inciting the others to refuse to go back to Gallipoli. After their whipping they were tied to a wagon wheel for five hours and put on bread-and-water rations for three days.

Trumpeldor could become angry over such treatment but could do little about it. He also was a soldier, and wasn't entirely in sympathy with defying orders, knowing that any army had to have discipline. But these men weren't criminals. Things had gone too far. He tried to communicate his feelings to Patterson, and in the translation his words were so garbled as to provoke Patterson . . . "Damn it, Trumpeldor," he said when they finally met, "I'm no monster. I have as much feeling for those men as you do. But this is an army and we're in a war. If anybody gets away with refusing to go back to Gallipoli it undermines the morale and discipline of the whole unit . . ." Again the translation was the worst enemy between the two. As he got it, Trumpeldor thought Patterson was holding him personally responsible for being soft on the men and encouraging them to be undisciplined. In the exchange that followed, Trumpeldor, through the interpreter, told Patterson he wasn't going to be intimidated by threats, that if Patterson wanted him out of the unit, then discharge him. And Patterson did just that.

In the end Patterson sent for Trumpeldor, apologized and said he'd had the same kind of trouble as an Irishman with the British. He still thought that sometimes Trumpeldor was a little too soft on his men, but he understood the reasons and respected his work. "I'm asking you to stay and forget what's happened . . ."

Trumpeldor had been waiting for these words and quickly agreed to come back. And when his troops heard he'd been apologized to, they went back with him to Gallipoli. By now the fighting was even fiercer. The casualties increased among the mule corps. The Turks were surprisingly stubborn. Moishe, who had stuck it out this whole time, was a battle-hardened veteran compared to the returnees and new recruits from Alexandria. But this did him little good when, as he was unloading supplies, a shell exploded a few yards from him and he was promptly knocked unconscious in the mud.

When he woke up, his head felt as though it had been put in a vise, and he could not move his left leg, which had taken a chunk of shrapnel.

Well, at least he was alive, and his wound earned him a trip back to Alexandria with the other wounded.

Meanwhile there were few rewards for the Jewish blood that had been and was being shed. The mismanaged Gallipoli campaign was coming to a close. In November Colonel Patterson became very ill, turned over his command to Trumpeldor and went back to Alexandria and then England. At the end of the month the blizzard came with blinding snow and bitter cold. The Jews carried on, delivered their loads and returned to base with their animals, often without coats or boots. As a reward, a month later an order came down to disband the corps. The peninsula was being evacuated. Before they embarked, as many as could went to say farewell to their brothers that they would leave behind on this foreign soil, their graves marked by wooden Stars of David. They chanted the Kaddish, the memorial prayer for their dead, then, like good soldiers, marched to the boat that would take them back to Alexandria just after the beginning of the new year of 1916.

It had been a military defeat, but still a victory of sorts for the Jews. They were, after all, accustomed to not *winning*. But at least they had made a major contribution to a fight that for them was only beginning . . . the revival of a homeland. Yes, all roads still led to Zion, including the road of temporary defeat. . . .

CHAVALA'S hand trembled as she held the envelope in her hand, then looked at the stamp. It had arrived by way of Switzerland. She hesitated before opening it, terrified about what the contents might be, then quickly tore it open. This was the first time she had heard directly from Moishe and now as she read, her tears were out of gratitude that he was at least alive.

> My dearest family:
>
> As you know, there was no way until now that I could have gotten a letter to you, and that was a matter of great concern to me. In fact, I pray that you will receive this. I want you to know that not a day has passed when you have not been in my thoughts. Even in battle it was your presence that kept me going.
>
> Please don't laugh, dear Chavala, but it was not my determination to try to defeat the Turks but the wonderful smells of cooking that come from your kitchen that I fought for. I can scarcely wait to taste

your cakes and cookies. Even now your strudel and *mandelbrot* make my tastebuds water, and the carrot *tzimmes* draws me closer to home.

As you know, the battle of Gallipoli is over. The British could have won there, but they really are such pompous fools. If we had had fifteen thousand men we could have conquered it. The trouble is, they don't know about mountains as well as we do. Well, at least that's over with.

There is so much I want to say, but letters are not like sitting together and talking, the way we used to do, but that time will come soon. I must believe that. I only pray everything is all right with you, and that all of you are safe.

Trumpeldor advised us all to stay together, even though the muleteers have been disbanded. He is on his way to England because it seems that Jabotinsky is making headway with the British. Chaim Weizmann is helping, because now he too believes that we should have an all-Jewish military force. The bravery of the mule corps was evidently more impressive than we thought. The rumors are that any day we will be sent to London. If that happens I will have to forego your baked brisket and those crispy potato *latkes* that could melt in my mouth.

By the way, I was slightly wounded in my left leg. Now please don't start worrying, Chavala, it was just a little shrapnel so they sent me back to Alexandria. It was very minor and in fact I've had a good rest. The nurses have made this more than a vacation. They're not only sweet but very pretty. There's nothing like a pretty woman to help what ails you, especially one that seems to like me. But don't *worry*, Chavala, I won't come home with a *shiksa* bride.

Again, please take care of yourselves, and know how much I love you. Kiss little Reuven for me, and hold him so close that I will be able to feel his warmth.

I love you all more than my words can say,

Your brother, Moishe

It was good for Chavala that she would never know how Moishe felt as he sealed the letter she'd just read, then moving clumsily off the bed, maneuvered himself into his wheelchair and rolled himself down the hall.

Chapter Eleven

Spring, 1916. A plague of locusts. An opportunity for the Yishuv, but especially for the scientist—and secret Zionist—Aaron Aaronson. He traveled to the south to teach the Arab farm-owners and peasants how to combat the plague. And he appointed one of his top associates, Dovid Landau, as supervisor of the Galilee.

The plague under control, Jamal Pasha, in his style, decided that the time was right to execute the elimination of the Yishuv. All nonresident Ottoman subjects, all Jews, were to depart Jaffa and settlements in its vicinity. The order to evacuate Jaffa and Tel Aviv remained in force even though the considerations of strategy that had prompted it had lapsed with the defeat of the British near Gaza.

The evacuation of the Jews of Jaffa was merely the prelude to a new wave of persecution.

Each day was beset with a new crisis. A blockade now surrounded the Mediterranean, stopping the Atlantic crossing of relief funds, gold and foodstuffs. Now they had to be sent by the American Zionist organization, JNF and other Zionist bodies in the form of bank drafts by way of Switzerland.

But the Turkish authorities confiscated all the gold they could lay their hands on. In the absence of gold the market was flooded with Turkish paper money, which was circulated in such quantities that its worth became only a fifth of its normal value. The financial situation grew so threatening that the Yishuv was on the edge of ruin.

The activists took over. Not enough to protect their settlements from Arab marauders and Bedouin murderers. Now they formed a political action committee. Buy arms and train young boys too young for army duty. The "Jaffa Group" began storing weapons in secret places and the training of youths was done out of sight of the Turkish eye on the kibbutzim.

The Turks sensed the climate of insurrection. Yishuv members were taken into custody and viciously interrogated. Among those arrested were Dovid and Absalom. Absalom, still in a kind of mourning for the failure of his marriage with Rivka, but also, to be frank, relieved that she'd gone off to America, took the challenge as a welcome focus for his energies and passions. Dovid, though also a man of scientific talent, as he'd proved in his association with Aaron Aaronson in his work reviving the land and helping keep it free of the terrible locusts whose wake was famine and disease, had never given up or backed off from his determination that the Jews should have their homeland, that danger . . . and even death were concomitants of his dream—and that a dream was measurable after a while by how close it came to reality. He had personally smuggled weapons and kept them on the kibbutz. He had even been shot once and had to be secretly cared for and at the same time tried to calm Chavala and her fears at his actions and what they would mean to her and the family, to their little son Reuven and to Chia . . . "My God, Dovid, our family has already drifted away. One is no longer a Jew. Moishe has been wounded and we pray will fully recover from *his* service as a soldier. I know how much you have worked and risked for what you believe in. I respect it, even though I have other dreams, as you know. But, Dovid, you owe us, yourself, me, something too. Please . . ."

Dovid had understood Chavala's fears, but he was also driven by needs that went beyond them. When he and Absalom were arrested, driven like criminals by the gun muzzles of the pasha's soldiers, they had no idea whether they would survive for a minute or an hour. If they would soon be hanging from the end of a rope. Their worries weren't empty or melodramatic ones. It was Aaron's intercession with the pasha that kept them from the end of the rope, if not from the ugly indignities his soldiers in their sniggering fashion visited on them. At one point Dovid had ignored the threat of gun and rope, and swung around and smashed the face of the guard who had been obscenely taunting him. He was hardly surprised to receive the butt of a gun in his stomach, knocking him to the floor, followed by a knee to the groin—the guards were long experienced in the methods of inflicting punishment which didn't show on the outside, could kill a man on the inside. Absalom, in an adjoining cell, was about to call out, but realized that could only make it worse for Dovid and himself, and accomplish nothing.

When Aaron went to Beirut to see the governor of the territory he was reasonably confident that bribery would at least insure that his friends would be decently fed and not abused. But as he handed over the gold coins to the governor he realized by the smug look on his face that this was only the beginning of the extortion. There was nothing for it but to go directly to Jamal Pasha.

In the pasha's office Aaron came quickly to the issue. "You know that my men at Athlit have proved their loyalty to this government. I want this harassment to stop. Their contribution is too valuable to the war to have them spending their lives in jail."

"Not all of your people, Aaronson, but I grant you that you and others have proved of value. I had no idea, I assure you, that your people were being jailed"—which wasn't entirely the case—"and I give you my word the matter will be taken care of. . . ."

It was at about this time that Dovid was waking up with a terrible knot in his stomach from the blow he'd taken. His surprise, and Absalom's, at the sudden appearance of the guards not to string them up but actually, amidst muttered curses and threats, to escort them out of the prison and to a hotel in Jaffa was beyond belief. At first they wondered if they were being taunted into believing that somehow they were saved and then the string would be pulled and the rope would replace it. The sadism of the Turks was not beyond such behavior. Only when food was *served* them did they decide even the Turks would not go to such lengths for abusive sport, and that their rescue, this time at least, was real.

"You know," Absalom said as he lay back on his bed, which was next to Dovid's, "Aaron either is a man of great importance to the pasha or has gone over to the enemy, and I guess I better quickly say that I believe it's the former that has gotten us out of this."

"Yes," Dovid said, "and we need to take advantage of it, not just be grateful we're not dead. Believe me, only because he thinks he needs us does the pasha hold off from having us hanged. We can't go on forever trusting to that, even with Aaron's influence. What if the locusts don't come? It seems we need a disaster to make us worth keeping alive . . ."

"I agree, let's destroy them once and for all—"

"What's your plan?"

"*Open rebellion.* No more using the cover of the British army—"

"No . . . that would be suicide, and we Jews have done enough of that. That just about got you and me hanged. And for what . . . ? A few boxes of ammunition . . . I'm tired of lost causes . . . let's win for a change . . ."

"Fine, what do you suggest?" Absalom said, lowering his voice.

"Espionage," and now Dovid's voice dropped to a near-whisper.

"Espionage? And you say open revolt would be suicide . . ."

"Absalom . . . we can supply vital information to the British, information they don't have and could never get. They'd listen—"

"I don't agree. The only thing they'd listen to is a Jewish fighting force inside Palestine."

"Maybe, but I still say that would be suicide for us. I want to see the Turks with *their* throats cut, not *ours*. We both want the same thing, Absalom, it's just a question of how best to get it."

The tensions were broken between the two men when Aaron walked into the hotel room. Their greetings were brief, and it wasn't until they'd arrived back at Aaron's house in Zichron that they spoke to him.

Both men smoldered with their own ideas that had taken form in the hotel room back in Jaffa.

Without preamble, Absalom said, "The only way that we can speed up the liberation of Palestine is through rebellion . . ."

Aaron was shocked at the suggestion. He hardly had any love for the Turks, but the notion of insurrection seemed empty and wrong to him . . . "No, Absalom, the British have the arms to liberate Palestine—"

"It's our national *duty* to organize on our own behalf."

"I supose I'm more a scientist than a political activist. But you know my sympathies, and my usefulness. Open rebellion didn't get you and Dovid out of the hangman's noose."

Absalom's eyes flamed with anger. "You're a scientist, Dovid is a believer in helping the British, who treated us like mules. I say to hell with both of you. Let me know when you think we've had enough punishment," and without further word he went out of the room and slammed the door behind him.

Aaron and Dovid sat in awkward silence, both knowing that Absalom's anger, while sincere, was also usually short-lived.

Aaron said, "You must have had something to say to one another in that hotel room. I have a feeling, Dovid, that you'd like to tell me what's on your mind."

"You're right, and I'm not going to be diplomatic. Now, you may be a scientist who doesn't want to get involved . . . and you've said I've some ability in that direction too . . . but whether you like it or not, you're involved in this as much as Absalom or myself. Because of the position you hold within the Turkish government, you're the key that's going to open up doors for us, Aaron. Now, Absalom's angry for good reason, and so am I. We differ only on means. We don't want to wait for the British, on their own, to liberate us. What Absalom wants is revolt and I disagree with that. What I think would be the best way for us would be to use our advantage *and* the British . . . gather information to speed up the British effort against our enemies. I don't for a minute think the British are our friends . . . they use us and we tell ourselves our purposes are served. Well, if that's so, let's help them to use us even more—to get what *we* want. Let *us* control our destiny, by some manipulating of the British, for a change . . ."

Aaron shook his head. "Both of you seem to have got our salvation pretty well worked out for us. Well, I still refuse to become involved in either one of your plans. Now, if you don't mind me saying so, I think it's time for you to go back home to Chavala."

WHEN Chavala saw Dovid come through the front door, the profound anxiety she'd felt in the last days was hardly lessened by what she saw in his face. Her heart went out to him. Quietly she went to him and put her arms around him, "My darling Dovid, it must have been terrible . . . thank God you're home."

"Yes, thank God, and Aaron."

There was something in the tone of Dovid's voice that contradicted his words. He didn't sound grateful. What she caught in his voice was anger at both God and Aaron . . . well, tonight she would not question him. Quietly she said, "Dovid, come, let me get you something to eat." The second greatest offering a woman could make, she thought wryly.

At this moment it wasn't food he needed to offset his frustration. "No, Chavala, I'm really not hungry . . ."

"Then let me fix you a hot tub."

"That sounds very good. Thank you."

After the bath Dovid lay down, Chavala alongside him. But as she clung to him she still felt the tensions hadn't subsided. "Dovid, I know the strain you've been under, the things you went through in jail, but I also know there's something more . . . what is it . . . ?"

"It's nothing . . . or maybe it's everything. I don't know, Chavala, I guess what I'm trying to say is, maybe I would have felt better if I'd joined the British in the fighting. Like Moishe did—"

"Oh, Dovid, darling, everyone fights in his own way. You were wounded, for God's sake . . . and look what Aaron has been able to accomplish . . ."

The muscles in Dovid's jaw tightened. "He has pointed that out. But the fact is, while the Turks are destroying the whole Yishuv, we're safe here at Zichron."

"Dovid, you're all doing the best you can. The problems are huge . . . you can't expect Aaron to be the Messiah. I'm sure he's doing what he feels is right—"

"I'm sure."

Chavala clung close to her husband and knew that this was no time to argue with her husband.

Well, she was still a woman. She knew how to make *that* contribution. And she did . . .

THE next week Dovid made the rounds of the settlements. The complaints were no different than the ones he'd heard ever since the war began. The Turks were requisitioning their wheat and animals, and what the Turks didn't take the Arabs stole.

He journeyed north. The Jewish soldiers in the labor battalion were clearing the roads in the unrelenting heat of the noonday sun. Their lips were parched white from too little water. Because the work was going slowly, many wore cruel lash marks on their backs. Their faces bore the scars of brutality too. Those who dropped from exhaustion were chained to a tree and beaten.

Dovid had seen these atrocities before and hated himself for not being able to stop them. This day, though, his anger was greater than ever before . . . In Tiberius the city was teeming with Turkish soldiers who were abusing old men on their way to prayer. They taunted them by pulling at their earlocks and the fringes on their *tallisim,* which they wore under their black long coats. One old man who protested was thrown to the ground, kicked and left in the dust, hurt and bleeding.

Dovid had to fight himself not to get both of them killed by going after the Turkish soldier. He literally willed himself to leave the scene, and rushed back to Zichron, where he went straightaway to see Aaron.

Still full of anger, he repeated the atrocities he'd seen. He told Aaron that if nothing was done the dissident groups would take it on themselves to take direct action, and that would put the whole Yishuv in more danger than it already was.

Aaron knew the logic of that. He hated that Jews should become involved in espionage but at least it was better than Absalom's suicidal notions of open revolt . . . "All right, call your meeting." He paused and took a deep breath. "But you, Dovid, are going to have to assume the key position."

"I don't mind, I welcome it. Besides, with your contacts with the Turks, it's better you not risk yourself."

THE word went out, and the next evening, in great secrecy, the key men from Hashomer, the Jaffa Group, the Gideonites and Athlit were contacted to meet in Aaron's laboratory.

Dovid stood looking over the group. "Thank you all for coming. In the past we've had our disagreements, but now we must bury them for the survival of our people. You know that what we are about to do is dangerous. To underestimate it would be foolhardy and dishonest. You must consider that you will be an enemy of the country, and if caught, you will be hanged. Those of you who have families should consider what that would mean to their safety. If any of you are undecided about this, the time to back out is now." He paused, allowing the men a brief time to think. But all were in agreement . . . their lives were in jeopardy in any event. Whatever the cost, drastic measures had to be taken.

Dovid looked at Aaron who nodded in agreement, then Dovid went on. "It's my belief that the kibbutzim as well as the Yishuv must know *nothing* about our activities, for their own good and ours. However, it's a little different here in Zichron. The village obviously will be unaware of the activities that will take place, but key men working at Athlit should very gradually move their wives and children to a safer place. Any quick, mass relocation would cause suspicion . . . I now turn the meeting over to the assembly."

Each man began with his own plan.

Yitzchak Lavinsky spoke for the Jaffa Group. "We could raise an army of three hundred men. Already trained and equipped with arms. Their mission would be to blow up Turkish installations—"

"And that," Herman Belkind boomed out, "would bring Turkish reprisals down on the whole Yishuv. As a Shomer my job is supposed to be to protect the Yishuv."

"So what do you want us to do, hire an army and fight the Turks in hand-to-hand combat?" Asher Meged of the Gideonites answered back quickly.

Absalom stood. "As a matter of fact, that's more along the lines that I was thinking. However, mine isn't quite hand-to-hand combat. I suggest a joint operation with the British. Eventually they'll have to move across the Sinai to take Palestine and Syria. If we Jews here help them, it could be done sooner. It would involve the Gideonites, the Jaffa Group and Hashomer. All would be mobilized at a strategic point and the coast would be seized and held. Our flag with the Star of David would be raised and war declared against the Ottoman Empire in the name of the Jewish State. Obviously this action would be coordinated with the arrival of the British fleet and the landing of their army. Backed with their power I feel this plan couldn't fail . . . the enemy would be driven out as they were when they attacked the Suez. And the British would welcome this strategy since it would save them from coming north across the desert."

"And where on the coast could they possibly land, with the coast being patrolled as it is?" said Moses Bartov, the Shomer from Galilee.

"That's just the point," Absalom said. "Palestine will never be in a better position. Jamal Pasha sent the main army to Gallipoli, left only a token force here. A limited British unit could cut the Turkish army in half. While we hold the shore the British could land. Athlit covers the coast behind the ruins of Caesarea. A few hundred of your men could secure our position against an army of the size now in Palestine—"

"It's not that simple," Aaron said, "If you'll forgive a military opinion from a scientist. The shoals at Athlit and Caesarea would rule out landings, even the size you suggest. The area between the shore and the landing area could never be taken. I just don't think military action at this time would be advisable—"

"So," Moses Bartov said, "we sit back and let the Turks do to us what they did to the Armenians? The pogroms we lived through were nothing compared to that. We lost a few hundred villages. But we survived. Compared to these barbarians the Russians were civilized. They rounded up every Armenian. They took people, town by town, hamlet by hamlet, house by house. Just to kill a few, you think? No . . . to wipe out an entire people. Not a man, not a child was to be left. They took them into the forest, the women and children, and left them to die of starvation. They told the men they were going into the army"—Moses spat—"they took them to the army . . . to the army of death. They killed every one of them. The worst massacre in the history of the world, and *nothing* was done to stop it. If nations can stand by and permit a whole people be slaughtered like sheep, then take my word, *we are next.* Jamal Pasha has made no secret that he wants only Turks wherever they rule, only their religion, only their language . . . Well, everyone has to die, but I'll die like a man, not like an animal led to slaughter. I'll die with a gun in my hand . . . I'm for Absalom's plan."

Moses sat down and knew he had moved the group. Aaron was affected too, but he had to remind them that brave words wouldn't solve the problem of rocks and shoals that prevented any large-scale landing.

Aaron had put a damper on the men's spirits . . . and then Dovid stood. "I'd like to ask you a question, Aaron, since you're the one who moves the most freely among the offices of the Turkish government."

"Go ahead, Dovid."

"Well . . . after the Turkish counterattack on the Suez collapsed, the

Turks were beaten and they retreated into Palestine. I waited for the British to take advantage, to make a forward thrust. They didn't. Why do you suppose that was?"

Aaron knew very well the answer, and left it to Dovid to give it . . . "I'll tell you, Aaron . . . the British lacked an intelligence network in Palestine and Syria to tell them the situation in the enemy camp. I believe they know now that they lost the advantage when they were on the offensive in the Suez because of lack of intelligence inside Palestine and Syria. They'd jump at the chance to work with us now. We know this country. They'll accept our plan, Aaron. How can they afford not to? We can offer the British a network of surveillance—"

Nachman Shamir broke in. "You mean spying . . . why don't you call it by its right name, Dovid? And what are we supposed to do in the meantime? It could take months to gather the kind of information you're talking about."

"You're wrong. Every one of us has more information than the British have. The real problem is to keep things quiet enough so that we don't put the Yishuv in danger. So, I'm not asking you to twiddle your thumbs. We can do two things at one time . . . while we're gathering information, you can acquire all the arms that you can and train as many men as possible. Take my word, those of you who want to take up arms so badly will have your opportunity. When the time is right. The Turks will lose, and if the British accept this proposal it will be sooner than you think."

In spite of his former reluctance to become involved, Aaron agreed. "Now, it's very late and tomorrow night we meet again."

IT was four in the morning when Dovid returned home. Quietly he let himself in, hoping not to awake Chavala, but she was waiting. She lit the kerosene lamp and looked closely at him. "What was so important? . . . Something is going on, I know it, I feel it. You don't usually discuss wheat and oats till four in the morning."

How was he going to tell her? Not only that he was now a spy, but that he was also sending her away.

"Dovid?"

He paused for a moment, then, "It's late, it's a long story, I don't know where to begin—"

"With the truth."

He told her as little as possible, but how could he not tell her of his own involvement? He owed that to her. Telling her that she and the families of the other leaders would have to move out of Zichron was the most difficult job. Quietly, he tried to explain . . . there'd be no departure en masse, they'd leave on the pretext of visiting families, sickness—

"*Dovid* . . . what you're saying . . . You are going to be a spy for the British? My God . . . what happens if you are caught?"

"You wouldn't be involved, that's why the less you and the others know, the better."

"*Involved?*" She laughed miserably. "I'm your *wife* . . . I *am* involved. Dovid, you must get out of this before it's too late—"

"I can't do that, Chavala . . . You remember the night I came back from prison? You know how I acted when you questioned me . . . well, I couldn't really tell you what I thought because I had no one to support it. Now I do . . . you said that night that we all fought in our own ways. Well, this is my way, the only way. I devised this plan. I ask you to try to understand how important—"

"I don't give a damn. I suppose I'm a selfish woman who can see no further than that her husband was spared . . . I've no big visions, Dovid. I just want you to live. I want you . . . I want to be with you . . . I won't be sent away—"

"Please, Chavala, don't make this more difficult than it already is—"

"Sheine was right . . . I should have stood up to you, Dovid, insisted we go to America . . . God, it's the only sane nation on earth, that's why they aren't in this war . . ."

Dovid knew that for all her show of spirit Chavala was weeping inside. But he couldn't back down . . . "But we are *here,* and nothing can change that except to try to end this horror as quickly as possible—"

"And sending me away will bring peace faster?"

"No, but it will be safer—"

"Dovid, *please* . . . I beg you once again, tell Aaron and the rest of them that you—"

"*No,* Chavala. I'm doing this for myself, I admit it, as much as for Zion. If I don't, I'll never be able to face my son, or live with myself. Or be worthy of you."

Dovid sat down on the edge of the bed, exhausted.

Dawn had just broken, and Chavala looked out to the small backyard and saw the palm trees silhouetted against the Palestinian sky. Strange, she thought, the things people think of at moments like this. Dovid had planted those trees just before their son Reuven was born . . . that was nine years ago. They had borne the fruits of their labor . . . would Dovid live to see his seed grown to manhood?

Quietly now she asked, "Where will you take us?"

"To Jerusalem, into the Old City. No place is safe, but at least the Turks have left the shrines alone."

Chavala knelt in front of her husband, then put her head in his lap. "What will I do without you?"

"And I without you? In war families are apart . . ."

Chavala tried to remember the years they'd lived here in Zichron . . . such happy days, dancing and singing at the village threshing-floor on hot clear nights after the harvests . . . picnicking and swimming in the ancient harbors of Caesarea. She'd watched Raizel going off with other young people to parties in other settlements. And Dvora racing ahead, laughing as her long hair billowed out against the mild wind . . . Now . . . they were gone . . . nothing was left . . . nothing more to say, except . . . "When will I go?"

"Later today." He was grateful to her for making it easier than he'd have thought possible. Easier for him, but he knew what was going on inside her, beyond the words . . . "Come, lie down next to me, I need to hold you . . ."

They fell asleep close in each other's arms, as though trying to deny the separation that was coming.

WHEN Chavala and Dovid walked up the stone stairs to the old apartment in Jerusalem, they stood in the center of the room, neither quite knowing what to say.

Dovid picked up his son and held him, looked at the soft brown eyes of the little boy and tried to remember all the good things . . . How happy the child was when he would take him to Athlit. He loved the laboratory best. Dovid would adjust the lens of the microscope and Reuven would smile at the wonders of the world he discovered through it. "I'm going to be a scientist like you, *abba.* When I grow up . . ." When he grew up? What kind of a world would it be? Dovid only hoped that what he was now doing would make it a safer, better place for his son to grow up in. And his son's son . . .

He turned to Raizel. He hadn't realized how lovely she'd become. It wasn't possible that all the years had gone by so fast. He could remember seeing her minutes after her birth, and now she was a young woman of almost twenty. Raizel was like her mother. Wise, yet shy. So giving of

herself, she hadn't gone to the Galilee when she'd so badly wanted to
. . . papa came first, and three times she'd refused marriage because she
felt in her heart that Chavala needed her more . . . it was as though she
would make up for the pain of Sheine and the abruptness of Dvora's
marriage and going off . . . and ease the awful fear caused by Moishe's
absence at war, his being wounded . . . And little Chia, for whom he'd
built a shed for her goat, now she was already eleven. So much had
happened to them in that short span of time. They'd known death and
hunger, love and joyous times, and now this war . . . Chia clung tight to
him, calling him *abba,* as she always had. "I'll miss you, *abba.*"

Taking her to him, he forced a smile. "I'll be here so often you won't
have time."

Chavala listened to the sweet deception, wishing it were true . . .

Their parting was so painful no words could say what either one of
them felt. Except deep down in Chavala was a fear she could not force
out . . .

They were at the crossroad of their lives.

Chapter Twelve

THANKS TO HIS great success in destroying the locusts, Aaron Aaronson
had authority from Jamal Pasha to go anywhere he thought there was a
need for his services. He and his designated associates from Athlit were
allowed to go into even most restricted military areas. Aaron, as agreed,
stayed as inconspicuous as possible. His prominence gave him access, but
was also a more visible target. Further, if it became necessary to leave the
country for any reason, it was important for Dovid and Absalom to be
well-connected with Jamal Pasha to carry on in his confidence.

Dovid and Absalom had been with Aaron several times to see Jamal
Pasha and the Turk seemed to relate better to Dovid's low-keyed manner
than to Absalom's extroverted tone. Not that the pasha disliked Absalom,
but Aaron sensed that on those visits when the two had gone to Damascus, the pasha's Oriental mind somehow resisted, even resented,
Absalom's sureness and jocular behavior. Since the pasha's mood
was more than receptive these days, due to the wheat production, Aaron

felt it was best for Dovid to go on this mission. And Dovid agreed.

On the road to Damascus, Dovid closely observed the fortifications, the amounts of food supply for the soldiers and civilians, the size of the army and its disposition. Through contacts in the cities he was given the amount of war matériel coming into the country, how many army units were being deployed and the contact at Gilboa. He found out the approximate number of pilots as well as when they would make their flights.

When he arrived in Damascus he went to the hotel and bathed and shaved away two days' weariness. After he had changed into the fresh aba and adjusted the white kaffiyeh on his head he looked at himself in the mirror and had to laugh. His thoughts went back to a little *shtetl*, to a young man sitting at a cobbler's bench . . . now, dressed like Lawrence of Arabia, going to see one of the most influential officials in the Ottoman Empire. A long way since that morning they'd walked from the little village to the port of Odessa, leading a goat and *shlepping* all kinds of bundles. . . .

As Dovid sat in Jamal Pasha's office waiting for him, his eyes wandered to some papers on the desk. The temptation was near-overwhelming. He realized the consequences of what would happen should Jamal Pasha walk in . . . but did he dare risk it? He'd never have a moment like this . . . did he dare *not* risk it? He got up and bent over the desk. God, this looked like a battle plan . . . amounts of food, sizes of army units, numbers of German fliers, plans for a second attack on Suez . . . too much to commit to memory. His heart pounded as he took out the black notebook he used to make his progress reports that he presented to Jamal Pasha. He wrote as fast as he could. He had finished, just put the notebook back into his pocket when the door opened and Pasha entered. His head pounded like it would split into pieces. Pasha was no fool, to underestimate him would be a great mistake. He may have even left the plans as a test . . . nothing for it but to act innocent . . .

Pasha looked at Dovid, then casually to the plans on his desk. It was too ridiculous . . . he'd had this terrible need to relieve himself ever since that idiot wife had demanded he show her attention right there on his chaise in the office . . . that call of nature was responsible for his lack of prudence in leaving Landau alone with the plans . . . How loyal was Landau? Until now he had had no reason not to trust the man. He had had access to many things and so far there had been no known leaks to the British . . . Still, Landau *was* a Jew . . . He searched Dovid's face carefully for any sign of guilt, even unease. The face revealed nothing, but perhaps his voice would betray him . . . "Well, Landau"—he smiled—

"what do you think of the plan?" A frontal move would, he decided, be most likely to unnerve a guilty mind.

"I'm an agronomist, not a military strategist, I really can't give an opinion," Dovid said with—he hoped—disarming conviction.

"You underestimate yourself."

Dovid smiled. "Thank you, but I do not underestimate *our* government. Look at the British fiasco in Gallipoli. They boasted that a few days and the whole battle would be over. The British lion left with his tail between his legs. And he's not doing so well in Europe. The Germans have him on the run. We will win, I've no doubt no doubt of it."

Jamal Pasha was pleased. "Well, for a scientist, you're an astute military analyst, Landau."

"Not so astute, I just have great confidence in our strength."

"That's reassuring, especially since so many of your people have made the bad mistake of going over to the Allies. I didn't approve, of course, but I understand the mule corps was of help to the British . . . pity for them that they were so wasted."

The bastard was playing with him. *He* was the one who had deported them. His shrapnel had penetrated Moishe's leg . . . "You're right, I'm sorry to say not all of us have the same loyalties."

The pasha twirled the pencil in his hand and looked again at Dovid. If the Jew were lying he was damned convincing. Jamal Pasha almost believed him. If he were to continue using his valuable services, did he have an alternative? It seemed a good, calculated risk . . . "Well, now, how is production from the kibbutzim?"

Dovid took out the black book and read off the amounts of wheat, barley, and fodder as well as all the other essentials. When he'd finished his mouth was very dry. Lying, even to this creature, was not the easiest thing in the world. "We've had to push very hard to deliver this amount of production. I hope and believe that we can even increase it."

"Very commendable," Jamal Pasha said, lighting a Turkish cigarette and handing one to Dovid. "Knowing how the Jews steal and hide what they grow from the government, I must compliment you that they apparently withhold so little from you." Dovid would have gladly slit his throat . . . the Jews were starving, the little they kept was scarcely enough to keep body and soul together. But he acknowledged the compliment with a smile. . . .

Jamal Pasha watched through the window as David went off. You could tell a great deal from the stride of a man, the tone of his voice, the look in his eyes, and he again reassured himself that there was nothing in Landau's demeanor that indicated the plans on his desk were even a curiosity . . . Still, never mind the excuse, he had been foolhardy to leave them out in the open, except how did he know Landau would come in while he was emptying his bladder? Well, he would be sure that he was not again caught with his pants down. He almost smiled when he thought it.

Jamal Pasha's misgivings were more than matched by Dovid's. When he felt safe, he stopped near a clump of eucalyptus trees and wiped the perspiration from his forehead. Fool, he'd been a fool. He could have destroyed the whole operation, and been hanged for much less . . .

Chapter Thirteen

In the laboratory at Athlit, a special tension was in the air as the men sat around the table in the dimly lit room.

Dovid's eyes, and thoughts, lingered on Absalom, whose good and generous words now came back to him . . . "I don't give a damn whose plans we take, nobody needs a medal to destroy the Turks. Dovid and I are brothers. We have faced death together. If the majority rules that Dovid's plan is better than mine, so be it. All I ask is that when the time comes I have the pleasure of pulling the rope that hangs Jamal Pasha . . ."

Aaron's words broke into Dovid's thoughts. "As you all know, in the beginning I was opposed to this idea. However, now I am involved and wish to give credit where it is due. The plan we accepted was Dovid's, he has already begun to carry it out, at great personal risk . . . I think this meeting should be turned over to him."

Dovid was surprised, tried to collect his thoughts. "I would only like to remind you that under certain circumstances the most courageous men have been broken. No man can be sure of his abilities to resist until he has undergone the brutal interrogation that the Turks are capable of. Their barbarism is not understood until experienced. In the event any of you are caught, you will be alone. Expect no help. As I call your names, you will take the oath that your lips will be sealed and no man will inform on another in order to save himself. Is that agreed?"

"It is," the men responded in unison.

Dovid looked around the table at the faces of these brave men, knowing that what he asked of them was too much, but it had to be asked. They were only human, and no man knew what his strengths were until that moment when the pain became impossible to bear. Life was a precious gift, which every normal man clung to. Still . . . the oath might be remembered if the time came . . .

With the Bible in his hand he called out, "Chaim Lazarus . . . with one hand on your heart and the other on the Bible, do you take the oath of silence?"

"I do."

"Lieb Schacham, do you take the oath?"

"I do."

Samuel Guri, Zalman Kishon, Nachman Shamir, Eliave Yitzchak, Alex Aaronson, Absalom Feinberg and Aaron Aaronson took the oath as well. From the finger of each a drop of blood was drawn. "Now we are brothers . . . From the Bible I will read these words. *'Netzah Yisrael Lo Ieshaker* . . . Israel's eternity shall not lie.' We are now members of the NILI."

A small glass of wine was handed to each man. "We drink to the salvation of our people, and their peaceful survival. Let us hope that when future generations hear the word NILI they will know that the cause we fought was theirs."

"Shalom," they said, saluting Dovid.

With his glass held high, Dovid saluted back, *"Shalom."*

The men were given their instructions. Their mission would begin in the morning.

WHILE secretly passing the Samech station, properly disguised, and thoroughly terrified, Chaim Lazarus took note of the war matériel arriving. . . .

At Fuleh station, Lieb Schacham calculated the army units, and the number of officers being dispatched. . . .

In Gilboa, Samuel Guri, outfitted in a uniform stolen by a Teutonic warrior more interested in gold than the Fatherland, drank with the German fliers. Once the wine and beer loosened their tongues, the information on planned air strikes began to flow. . . .

Aaron, the distinguished scientist, went north to gather information on the Turkish army. Everything was written in code and cipher in a small black notebook. No language was discernible, only numbers in groups of five. The Turks would break their brains trying to break the code, even if they should capture the notebook.

Absalom journeyed through Tyre and Acre. In Rosh-pina he discovered a military center and a local school that now served as a supply depot for ammunition. The Turks had apparently, by the equipment on hand, decided to build a new road as a military highway. He would suggest that the British dispatch planes with bombs to the site during the inauguration of the road. . . .

After seeing Jamal Pasha, Dovid went to Haifa, then proceeded to Tiberius and Beirut. He found that the Turks were planning to attack the Suez Canal again. In fact, the German commander, Kers Von Kerstein, had left the Suez Canal in mid-April. It seemed this second attack on the Suez was so close at hand that squadrons of German fliers were stationed in Dagania. Gaza had been reinforced with heavy artillery. . . .

With their staggering amount of information, the men met once again at Athlit. "To quote Herzl," Dovid said, " 'If you will it, it need not remain but a dream.' Now we have something to go to the British with."

"All right, but how do we create a link between ourselves and British headquarters in Egypt?" Aaron's question was in everyone's mind.

"You have to make contact, Aaron. With your credibility they would listen to you," Dovid said.

"I told you earlier, if I leave here it would arouse suspicion. No, the most likely one for this mission, I suggest, is Absalom."

"Why me? As has been pointed out, I'm not exactly a diplomat."

"True . . . but you will make *special* efforts . . . Besides, and more important, when you feel like it, you can affect the manners of a gentleman and that will impress the British. Also, your English is impeccable. *That* is why."

"And what about the *how?* Do I swim or take a rowboat?"

"Neither . . . you will be smuggled aboard an American warship whose mission of mercy is to evacuate all neutral citizens . . . Details later . . ." which meant keep them as secret as possible, even among this handpicked group. . . .

On the way back to Zichron, Aaron suggested to Dovid that he take advantage of the hiatus in his activities to spend some time with Chavala.

"I will, Aaron . . . I miss her very much."

"I can imagine. She is a very unique woman, Dovid. Somehow she reminds me of Sarah, the same combination of beauty and strength. She's been receiving the food?"

"Yes, thank God."

"Thank God, indeed. Who knows when the Arabs will begin their plunder . . . by the way, I have a bag of almonds and a box of dried fruits I'd like you to give to my little Reuven. You wait, Dovid, he's a born agronomist."

"I know, and he thinks I'm a scientist."

"Who says he's wrong?"

"The diplomas I don't have."

"Diplomas don't always make a man a scientist. Some men are born with an original mind, and are committed to what they believe in, no matter what. You, my friend, are one of them . . ."

WHEN Dovid came home to the Jerusalem apartment, Chavala couldn't believe it. For a moment she couldn't even catch her breath to welcome him. Then she ran to his outstretched arms, and they held each other as though they would never let go.

"Oh God, Dovid . . . it's you, thank you for coming . . ." She backed off, patted her hair and smoothed her dress. "I'm embarrassed, the way I look. This is no way to greet my husband . . . the front of my dress is wet from washing . . . oh *God,* I'm so excited to see you I forgot to ask if you've eaten . . . come, sit down . . . no, go in and see Reuven while I change." Then taking Dovid's face in her hands she said, "I'm acting like a moonstruck girl . . . oh, darling, how can I tell you what I feel? Words only get in the way . . ."

That night, after the first burst of urgent passion, they lay quietly, feeling the closeness of one another. Then Dovid took his wife again, this time unhurriedly. In that sweetness no war existed, no hate, nothing at all outside nurturing walls, only love. The world ceased. . . .

In their short time together not a word was said about how Chavala had survived, the fear and anxiety she felt every moment for Dovid's safety. Nor the clawing loneliness. Nor did she ask about Zichron. She did not want to know, in fact.

The night before he left she cooked a very special dinner and refused to think about tomorrow. Life was made up not of days, months or years, it was the moments that counted . . . only the moments.

When he prepared to leave in the morning she smiled as though he would return that evening.

She sent him away with a box of homemade bread, cakes and cookies. "And give this box to Aaron. Thank him for the gift he sent." The parting was swift . . . with no tears. In their precious few moments together there was no time for tears.

IN July, Absalom managed to leave Beirut on an American warship. Equipped with a Spanish passport—the Sephardim were useful even if they were snobbish—he made it past the ports and border checks without serious incident, although he nearly forgot at one point not to speak English but words of Spanish he'd been carefully drilled in. Finally he arrived in Alexandria, but he was prevented from disembarking by the British authorities, who questioned his passport.

Absalom decided the best approach was a direct one. He requested to be brought to British Intelligence headquarters immediately so that he could identify himself. The port officials were unimpressed. The man's English was good but his story farfetched. He decided then to return to Greece and try again. As he miserably walked the deck he met a Jewish student and told him his real name. "They're going to let you go ashore?" Absalom asked him.

"Yes . . . and you?"

"The British refused me entry. I must get into the country. I'd like you to do me a favor."

"If I can . . ."

"You can. I'm going to write out a note for you to take to the manager of the Anglo-Palestine bank in Alexandria. He can identify me."

The deed was done and the note served its purpose. Actually the connection had been set up through a connection in America, a prominent Jewish scientist who had been impressed by Aaron's research and had been contacted by Aaron to help. He in turn called a British colleague who was a brother of the manager of the Anglo-Palestine bank. Shortly thereafter Absalom was permitted to disembark.

He was far less successful in arousing the interest of the British. Once again, their arrogance overwhelmed their self-interest.

That night Absalom returned to the hotel a frustrated and bitter man. After brooding half the night he decided the only possible way to get the attention of the British was to publish an article in *their* newspapers. Maybe they'd believe their own.

He wrote the rest of the night, then hurried to the Egyptian *Gazette* with an article, signed by Anonymous, about the weakness of the Turkish regime and its armed forces. Together with provocative details on the size of their army.

The next afternoon he waited for the newspapers to come out, bought one and hurried to the Pharaoh Cafe, where he ordered coffee and scanned the paper. And there it was:

It seems ludicrous that a people which boasts that the sun never sets on its empire was unaware that the Turkish army was almost nonexistent in Palestine and Syria during the Gallipoli campaign, since most of its units were deployed to defend Achi Baba and Constantinople. Only a small garrison had been left to defend Palestine and Syria. If the British had been less inclined to continue with the tradition of high tea at four, that small piece of real estate could have been taken with little or no effort.

But what should one expect when a nation supposedly as strong as Great Britain did not take the offensive during the attack on the Suez Canal. During that disorderly retreat the Turks almost tripped over one another. The time to have taken the initiative was *then.*

It makes one ponder where British Intelligence was when, right out in front of God and king, the Turks were building the new military highway along the Gaza. How simple it would have been to dispatch a small squadron of planes and bomb the site. Imagine the surprise the Turks would have had if a small sortie flew over during the inauguration.

It now seems a second attack on the Suez is close at hand. Perhaps Providence has given Britain another chance to prove herself. Perhaps it is still not too late if the British will consult with and consider the wisdom of those whose knowledge can, to say the least, supplement theirs.

That was the first in a series of articles he bombarded the British with. To his delight, the articles brought about the desired reaction. At long last, the British were recognizing him . . .

On August 8, almost a month after he had arrived, Absalom finally met with Major Niecomb in the major's office.

"Now, sir, you've been rather bothersome with those articles. I confess they've caused us embarrassment, and quite honestly I don't understand what your reasons are, nor how they can benefit you—"

"The truth is, Major Niecomb, they can benefit both of us."

"How so?"

"You failed in the Suez campaign because you had no intelligence network in either Palestine or Syria. If you had it would have been relatively easy for you to have pushed forward . . ."

Niecomb grimaced, knowing that there was more than a little truth in that statement. "So what are you suggesting?"

"Major, we have formed an espionage network in Palestine, to be put at the disposal of Britain—"

"Of Britain? For no other reason?"

"Of course. The more information you have the faster you can take action in Palestine. And we Jews would naturally benefit from that."

Niecomb lit a cigarette. "And what would we have to pay for this intelligence?"

"Major Niecomb, I haven't come here to sell you secrets. I've come in the name of my people, who believe that by helping Britain we will help ourselves. I'm not a mercenary, nor is this offer made out of altruism. We have something that can be of great help to you—"

"And how large is this network?"

"It's small and secret, but very effective."

Small . . . and secret . . . and no rewards . . . Niecomb was not impressed by Absalom, whom he regarded as a radical Jewish romantic, a dangerous, troublemaking sort looking for some grand adventure. Well, he was not about to be taken in by this Hebrew zealot. Lord, they surely were pushy . . . they really took seriously that nonsense about being the Chosen People.

He ordered Absalom to leave Egypt immediately, and made a call that resulted twenty-four hours later in the dismissal of the manager of the Anglo-Palestine bank.

DOVID and Aaron awaited anxiously for Absalom to return, or for a message from him about the link with British Intelligence headquarters.

Weeks passed without any news.

Dovid became especially impatient. "I'm sure Absalom must be having trouble getting back . . . well, we can't wait any longer. This is too important, I'm going to look for some way to get to Egypt."

"I suppose that's the only answer," Aaron said, shaking his head. "Now, what route are you thinking of? If you go by land that means crossing the Sinai. Aside from the time involved—it's just too dangerous."

"So that leaves the sea . . ." Dovid was not unaware that such passage was also a part of Absalom's plans, but, of course, not having heard from Absalom, he had no way of knowing whether it had succeeded.

IN Haifa a Christian Arab, Tioufit Butaj, who had less love for the Jews than fear of his fellow Arabs, and had decided it wise to support the Jews who might at some point soon be useful to him in saving his own neck, expressed his willingness to take Dovid to Egypt in his small boat—for a fee, of course. Saving one's neck should not obscure commerce. But the British blockade made that transaction quickly obsolete, and so there was nothing left for Dovid except to once again enlist American contacts and procure passage on an American warship dispatched to evacuate people from the war zone. Appropriate papers were prepared and Dovid boarded the ship.

When he arrived in Egypt he went to the president of the Anglo-Palestine bank—the manager (thanks to Absalom) had been compromised, apparently, by collaboration with the Jews, but the president was still above suspicion; actually, he welcomed the opportunity to get back at the British, and the British, in their fashion, never imagined that a Jew who had reached such exalted position as president of a bank in association with the British would ever endanger himself or his position by going against their wishes. After Dovid established his identity with a letter written by Aaron, Joseph Neiman was most receptive. Aaron considered Neiman the one remaining dependable link between Athlit and Cairo.

As the two men sat in Neiman's office, Dovid said, "It is imperative that I meet with the top-echelon British officer in their intelligence establishment."

Born an Egyptian Jew, and occupying the position he did, there were few people in high positions that Joseph Neiman did not know.

"I think that can be arranged. I'll make the contact for you. Where will you be staying?"

"At the Royal Hotel. I'm registered under the name of Dovid Nadar."

The two men shook hands, and Neiman said, "I'll be in touch."

The next day Dovid went to Alexandria, where he tried to find out about Absalom. The most he could ferret out was that Absalom was trying to get back to Palestine, but so far with little success. Hardly encouraging or enlightening news.

Dovid then hurried back to Cairo and waited, not daring to leave his room. Finally the phone rang . . . it was Joseph Neiman.

"I believe I have located your man. Go to British headquarters at ten o'clock tomorrow morning. You might ask for Lieutenant Wooly." He hung up without waiting for Dovid's response.

Dovid was already more fortunate than Absalom . . . though he had no way of knowing it . . . Lieutenant Wooly had replaced Major Niecomb only a week before.

When Dovid was brought in to Lieutenant Wooly, he found him in appearance and manner the epitome of a British officer. He also spoke like one . . . with rather obvious suspicion of Dovid.

"I understand that you have been asking to see me."

"Yes. I'll get to the point, sir. In Palestine we have been gathering a very large amount of information that we believe you can use . . ."

Dovid took out a small black notebook and handed it to Wooly. Wooly could hardly believe what he saw . . . Turkish and German army movements in Syria, evacuation of forces and equipment, an in-depth survey of prices of supplies, sizes of crops, military plans of the Turks, including the one Dovid had seen on Jamal Pasha's desk.

Wooly maintained a British cool he hardly felt. "This is quite remarkable. Tell me, how were you able to gather such information?"

Dovid didn't miss the mixture in his voice of cautious hope and skepticism. He told the whole story, from the inception of NILI, and Aaron Aaronson's involvement, with his reputation, added credibility. Still, only after nearly two hours of close questioning was Wooly able to convince himself of Dovid's legitimacy, and thereby that of his material.

"All I can say, Mr. Landau, is that this is truly remarkable. I will submit it to the high command in London. Thank you for coming to see me, we'll be in touch."

Dovid waited for two agonizing days before he was summoned back to see Wooly. This time he was greeted with open enthusiasm.

"Well, sir," said Lieutenant Wooly, "I believe we can say we have an agreement. Now I think we should discuss how contact can be made."

In a briefing room with four other intelligence officers Dovid said, "The harbor at Athlit will accommodate a small craft. I believe that the information could be handed over to the British by our men at NILI, who would, of course, encode. And I suggest we use light signals. They're simple and fast."

The discussion went on until midnight. Finally, when all was arranged, Dovid was returned to Palestine on a small craft belonging to the British, disguised with Arab insignia.

It was midnight when the boat slowly moved into a cove beyond the huge shoals of Athlit. The lieutenant stood by the rail and shook hands with Dovid. Dovid climbed down into the dinghy. He was rowed as fast as it was thought safe, then stripped off his clothes, tied them into a waterproof sack and jumped into the ice-cold sea. He swam until he came to the familiar rocks. A large wave rolled over his head, the rocks were slippery with slimy green moss, but he somehow managed to hold on, reach the seawall and pull himself up. He was home.

Shivering from the cold that went to the marrow of his bones, he slipped back into his clothes and moved stealthily through the night. He listened to the sounds of soldiers walking along the roads. He heard their laughter, and he held his breath as he lay in the high grass. He darted from place to place . . . until finally he reached the hills of Zichron, and from there to Aaron's door.

Aaron looked at a soaking wet Dovid, a broad grin on his face. "My God . . . Dovid, you *did* it."

"I did it . . . yes, I did it."

Embracing Dovid, Aaron said, "Now go change, put on one of my robes and I'll fix a pot of coffee."

As the men sat at Aaron's kitchen table, eagerly Dovid was pumped to tell everything, from the very beginning.

"Everything would take the two weeks I've been away . . . and before I begin . . . have you heard from Absalom?"

He's *home.* I'll tell you more about that later. Please go on, Dovid . . ."

"I have to give credit where it's due, I was damned fortunate. This Lieutenant Wooly was more eager to work with us, if possible, than we were to make contact. The arrangement is that the contact will be made through a ship. We decided upon light signals. A boat will land near the Crusaders' Castle and from there the matériel will be collected. Now, I think we must decide on dividing our roles. Aaron, you pick the men you feel best suited for gathering information . . . I would like to work with Lieb Schacham, he's a great swimmer, which for a landlubber like me could be a saving grace."

The date of the arrival for the first contact by sea had been set when Dovid was in Alexandria.

On the appointed night Dovid and Absalom waited but the ship did not arrive. "What do you think happened, Dovid?"

"Maybe they were spotted. One thing we know, if they haven't come by now, they won't. It's almost dawn."

Night after night they lay in the bushes, waiting. On the fourth night they heard the low murmur of the ship passing, but it could not come in close enough to anchor because of the foggy weather. And during the next four nights it could not approach because of the storm-driven rains.

Dovid's trip to Egypt had apparently been for nothing—which he couldn't accept. He would go to Egypt once again.

IN the laboratory at Athlit Dovid met with Aaron and Absalom. "How would you like to go on a *hegira* through the Sinai, Absalom?"

"Since I'm practically an Arab, I might as well . . . After all, I'm something of an expert at it by now. It's the way I survived and got back from Egypt after the British turned me down. The British may say they're against the Arabs and the Turks, but the real enemy . . . at least that's the way they made me feel . . . is the Jews." Absalom had regaled Aaron and later Dovid with fairly harrowing accounts of his long journey home, including one encounter with an Arab man and his woman which he refused to talk about, except to say that at the time he wondered if the price of survival was worth it . . . "What is your plan, Dovid?"

"We've got to make contact. Never mind what you and I may think of the British, they are the only hope we have. We must get to them with our information."

"Dovid, how would you get through the border patrol?" Aaron said.

"There's no other way. All the American escorts by now have rescued the neutral citizens. There's no alternative. But with Absalom's knowledge of the desert, and his ability to speak the language, we have a good chance of making it. Do you agree, Absalom?"

"Agreed . . ."

DISGUISED as Bedouins, they left Zichron. As Aaron watched his two best friends go off in the distance he prayed that they would make it safely. A man could stand just so much loss in his life . . .

In Chan-Hunes they were stopped and questioned. Absalom explained that they were representatives from the experimental farms at Hadera and Athlit, and that they were tracing the origins of the locusts.

The local army commander accepted their explanation and, in fact, offered them the use of a telegraph.

Dovid cabled Aaron: "The locusts have not yet been traced." The double meaning was instantly clear to Aaron.

The border was now so close that Dovid and Absalom were sure they'd make it. Their enthusiasm was short-lived.

Near El-Katharan, only a few hours' walk from the front line dividing Turks and British, they were arrested by a border guard. Each man was subjected to a relentless barrage of questions . . . there were no locusts in this area that the interrogators knew of, and if they were the locust officials they claimed to be, then why hadn't they been equipped with a *vasika*, a free access permit?

No story or excuse helped, and they were transferred to Beersheba for further interrogation. When they arrived the German officials were as unconvinced as the border guards had been. They were taken off to jail.

It was clear that the authorities strongly suspected that they were spies, and once again the end of a rope seemed an almost inevitable end.

Within the Yishuv there were eyes and ears everywhere, but to save them immediate action was necessary . . . Max Ben-Eliezer, a Shomer in Ruhama, the most southern village in the country, became the courier between Dovid and Solomon Bartov. At risk to his own life, Bartov went every day to collect the notes and scraps of paper which Dovid dropped from his barred windows. From his hand the notes were then passed on to Nathan Eliav, who rode to Zichron, where Aaron finally learned of the imprisonment.

Separately, the men were interrogated hours on end. When they stood firmly behind their story, the torturing began. Dovid was thrashed on the soles of his feet, then dragged down the stone corridor into a windowless cell, with the door bolted behind him.

Absalom underwent the same horrors, but at least he had not, like Dovid, gotten a violent attack of malaria . . . In the middle of the night he rapped on the stone wall that separated the two cells. No response. He wondered if Dovid were still alive. Sliding down on the cold stone ground he had nothing to do but consider his own dismal future . . . it wasn't so much dying that enraged him, but to die without having seen Sarah . . .

He thought only of her. As long as he could stay alive, she was his bridge to sanity.

Chapter Fourteen

SARAH, SEATED AT the head of the table in the imposing dining room of her husband's house, looked positively regal in her gold brocade, and her emerald and diamond jewels shimmered in the candle glow. Her radiance charmed General Von Himmelstein. This Jewess was enchanting, but how could she be married to such a boor? She made the other women seem pale in every respect by comparison.

"How do you find living in Constantinople?"

"Fascinating, and you?"

"Hardly Berlin . . . but with war, one settles for less."

"I can imagine."

"Then you have been there?"

"Yes, once, with my brother."

"Then you know what I mean."

"Of course." She smiled, but scarcely listened. Here she lived in luxury while her people starved. And for all the indulgences of her husband, he'd not sent a coin to Palestine. He grew richer and richer from the war and was oblivious to the suffering of others. He all but pandered to the Turks.

Her loathing for him had become so great she would no longer even depreciate herself by living with him. Although she had entered into a loveless marriage, in the beginning it seemed unimportant . . . she had sacrificed for what she honestly believed was Rivka's happiness, this man was genuinely fond of her, and that was enough. Children, to whom she could give all her devotion and love, would have compensated for all she'd given up, but she soon learned he was unable to give her the longed-for child. Now she was grateful she had none . . .

She was taken out of her reverie when she saw her husband nod from across the table to her, which was the cue for the ladies to retire to the drawing room so the men could smoke their long black cigars and sip their brandies while talking behind closed doors of how to cheat the government on matériel issued to the army.

Sarah sat on the brocade divan and poured the demitasse for the ladies, who discussed the latest fashions . . . Pity that Paris was a part of France . . . Such a shame the Germans hadn't conquered the French yet . . . Of course these local merchants who called themselves couturiers were too dreadful for words . . . Well, that was war and one had to put up with the inconveniences . . . Sarah thought of the hills of Zichron, about the vague letters she received from Aaron and nothing from Absalom.

After the guests had left, Sarah went uneasily to the bedroom. She undressed, put on her peignoir and sat at the dressing table, brushing her hair. She saw her husband's reflection as he spoke to her while taking off his clothes.

"You were indeed an asset to me this evening, my dear. Von Himmelstein was quite taken with you—"

"And that pleased you?"

"Of course, like the emerald around your neck, a beautiful wife can be invaluable. Your charm hardly hinders my position. In the case of Von Himmelstein, it was indeed important."

"Really? In what way?"

"He happens to admire beautiful women."

"And that doesn't in some way offend you? Most husbands would resent another man expressing his thoughts so openly."

"Not where Von Himmelstein is concerned . . ." She was being weighed by the pound . . . like his gold.

"What makes him the exception?"

"Every government purchase order has to be approved by him."

"I see . . . and the two of you discreetly cheat the government. Instead of an item costing ten dollars, the price the government is charged is twenty and you and the general—"

He laughed. "You're much too bright for a woman. . . ."

After a sleepless night Sarah impatiently waited for her husband to leave. That morning she sat across the table from him as a dutiful wife. Went through all of the usual amenities of pouring his coffee and buttering his toast as he sat like a contented potentate.

As he wiped the crumbs from his moustache and folded his napkin he said, "You will wear the scarlet sari and rubies this evening, my dear. We'll have the pleasure of entertaining a most distinguished Turkish official."

"Will he also be enchanted with me, do you think?"

"Now, Sarah . . . well, I must leave . . . you will remember to be attentive to the governor's wife this afternoon at tea?"

"I'll remember every word you've said."

When he was finally gone, Sarah leaned heavily against the door. Then she went quickly to her boudoir. Her personal maid had already prepared her bath and laid out her frock. She went through the usual routine of the morning except for one variation . . . she wrote a note to her husband.

There was no salutation:

> I will be out of your reach by the time you read this. There are not sufficient jewels in the world to keep me living with a man as despicable as you. If you try to come after me I will expose your illicit dealings. Berlin would take a very dim view of that. For a woman I am indeed very bright, and my brother is not without influence.

She left the note, sealed, on his shaving stand, then opened the safe, took out the contents and laid them on the dresser. With a sense of relief she took off her wedding ring and placed it on top of the jewel case. . . .

When the time came she stepped into a limousine and was driven to the governor's mansion. She was the model of propriety and graciousness that would have made her husband feel his investment in her was worth every one of his jewels.

When it came time to leave, Sarah walked through the huge bronze doors to the street, where her chauffeur waited. "Drive me to Madame Armound's."

When the driver left her off she entered the couturier's shop and waited until the chauffeur parked the car, then slipped out and hurried along the crowded street in the opposite direction. When she reached the marketplace she went into the first shop and purchased a traveling suit, a pair of shoes, some lingerie and a small overnight case. Leaving the shop she got into a cab that took her to the railroad station.

When she had finally been seated and leaned back in the coach, for the first time the tensions eased some.

From Constantinople she traveled to Damascus. The trip was a nightmare . . . trains were being requisitioned for the military, the searches were constant and the malfunctions were endless. For hours at a time she would wait until the parts were repaired. After what seemed like a month she finally got back to Zichron. The tension and weariness still showed in her face, but she would recover . . . she was *home*.

When she stood and looked at her hilltop, the tears came from her eyes. She forgot her fatigue and ran up the incline until, breathlessly, she opened the door to her beloved home. Echoes of her childhood rang in her ears . . . *ema* . . . *abba* . . . sounds of "Clair de Lune" . . . a Chopin waltz . . . Emily Bronte . . . Rivka . . . starched white dresses . . . pink hair ribbons . . . Aaron . . . dear Aaron . . . beloved Absalom . . . And then her mother came into the room. Malka Aaronson stood in hushed silence for a long moment. This was too much to take in. Then they were in each other's arms as their words mixed with tears. "Sarahla, you're *home*" . . . "Oh yes, *ema*," . . . "Dear God, I can't believe it, am I dreaming?" . . . "No, *ema*, it's no dream, I've come home, and you'll never lose me again . . ."

Now Malka held her daughter at arm's length. Suffering was in her daughter's eyes, but there would be time to talk later. "Come, Sarah, you must rest—"

"No, please . . . where is *abba*?"

"In the vineyard. Now go upstairs and refresh yourself. You will see him at dinner, but first you'll want to see Aaron."

Sarah crossed the courtyard to her brother's small house. She hesitated for a moment. What would he say? Would Aaron—or her father —disapprove of her running away from a husband who had given her every luxury? More to the point . . . marriage was a contract, presumably sacred and not to be broken. Would he understand that she *had* to leave to save her sanity? She took a deep breath, opened the door and saw Aaron reading.

When he looked up, his reaction was like his mother's shock. Slowly he got up from the chair, not quite believing she was there, then quickly took her in his arms and held her tight. In that moment Sarah knew she had returned to them. She was home. Without words of explanation, she knew Aaron somehow understood.

"Sarah, darling, you're home . . ." He took her hand and they sat side-by-side on the sofa. Sarah was already feeling a sense of peace she'd not known since her marriage. They sat in silence, looking out at the rolling hills of Carmel, to the vineyard where *abba* was working the soil between the vines. The oleanders were in bloom. God, Sarah thought, this was *home,* and it was as close to paradise as she would ever be. Or want to be.

And then she turned to him, and her story poured out. She talked about her life . . . her husband . . . his insensitivity . . . "I felt as though I was prostituting myself, taking his gifts that had been paid for in blood. In Constantinople we knew what was happening to the Armenians, and life went on. While I sat at my husband's lavish dinners, being the grand hostess, bedecked and bejeweled, an entire Armenian village was being wiped out. As I sipped tea with the governor's wife their villages burned to the ground. A million people murdered. Doesn't that go beyond human understanding? You must have heard about it here in Eretz Yisroel."

Aaron nodded.

"But I'm afraid hearing and seeing are two different things. Some people in Constantinople were even denying it as propaganda against the Turks. They said that the warmongers were deliberately stirring up horror stories to inflame world opinion. But where are the civilized voices? I've heard no outcries. The Turks are so barbaric they left the roadsides stacked with corpses waiting to be buried. And the graves of those who had been were so shallow the human forms could be seen bulging beneath the dirt. Dead children, almost skeletons, were strewn about. Women raped a hundred times, then left to die of starvation. I heard about and I *saw* some of these sights when I traveled, though I wasn't supposed to. The sound of the train wheels reverberated in my ears, and, Aaron, it sang out its warning, 'The Jews are next . . . the Jews are next.' I'd put my hands over my ears to drown out the prophecy . . . Yes, Aaron, we *are* next and the world won't hear our cries, either. We have to save ourselves, Aaron . . . something has to be done before it's too late . . ."

Sarah was trembling so, Aaron brought her a brandy.

When she'd calmed some, Aaron said, "Something *will* be done, Sarah . . ."

"We've said that for so long . . . where does our help come from?"

"Ele'azar asked that on another hilltop. When he stood in Herod's temple at Masada and prayed, he found the answer. We here on our hilltop will find ours. Now, dearest, I think *ema* will be waiting for us to have dinner, and *abba* will be anxious to see you . . ."

Sarah felt a strangeness . . . an evasiveness in Aaron. She had felt something of it in his letters. It was as though he wanted to tell her but couldn't.

"Aaron . . . there's something you're not telling me. What is it?"

"Nothing, Sarah . . . nothing."

"I know you too well, Aaron . . . Whatever it is I want to help."

He looked at her closely. Did he dare put her in the kind of danger knowledge of NILI would bring? Did he have a right not to?

"What *is* it?"

And then slowly he told her about NILI, how it had come about . . . When he had almost finished he said, "The Yishuv knows nothing . . . some of the Shomrim are against us . . . but above all, the village must *not* know. No one except those few who are involved. *Ema* and *abba* do not know and must never find out—"

"What about our brothers? Do Alex, Zvi and Shmuel know?"

"Only Alex is involved. I'm afraid we have a house divided. Zvi is in the Negev, and Shmuel in Galilee. It's best that way, and I respect their feelings."

"And Absalom?"

Aaron tried to turn away.

"What is it, Aaron, please *tell* me . . . I'm a woman, not a child you can protect. I can help."

There was a long pause, "Absalom is in jail."

"Dear God, no! *Where?*"

"At Beersheba."

"Why . . . what is he being held for?"

"I blame myself, I should have insisted it was too great a risk . . ." And he told her the story, from the time Dovid and Absalom had left.

Sarah suspected there was more . . . "Aaron, don't keep anything back from me."

He hesitated then: "I'm doing everything I can to . . . to save them. You must be very strong, Sarah. I'm sure you understand—"

"Are you telling me that they could be . . . hanged?"

Aaron nodded slowly.

For a moment Sarah thought her knees would collapse under her. *"Take* me to him, Aaron."

Aaron looked at his sister's eyes. To deny her was difficult, but for her to see Absalom this way would be more painful. "Sarah, you said you wanted to help."

"I do. This cause is mine too—"

"Sarah . . . somehow I'll bring Absalom back to you. I promise. And you can be of help right now—"

"Anything, Aaron."

"Tomorrow morning I want you to go to Jerusalem and bring Chavala back."

"Yes, of course, Aaron. I'll go. But you do assure me that Absalom and Dovid will return soon?"

He looked at his sister's eyes. "Yes, I promise."

He wished he could be convinced of what he'd said, but if anything happened to Absalom there would be time enough for Sarah to weep.

AARON never took up an issue with Jamal Pasha that could be handled by lesser thieves. But in this case the Germans were involved. Even the bribes that were taken and stashed away did not release the men from prison. When Aaron complained to a Turkish underling, he shrugged and made further promises and more *baksheesh* was extorted. But the sands in Absalom's and Dovid's hourglass were running very low.

This time as a show of strength, he took two of the top agronomists with him, Samuel Guri from Athlit and Zalman Kishon from Hadera. At this moment Aaron had never been more appreciated by Jamal Pasha. His star was high in the royal orbit. The Turkish granary was bulging with an enormous tonnage of grain and fodder, which had been delivered the previous week.

Jamal Pasha greeted Aaron and the two men with Oriental exuberance.

"Ah . . . my dear Aaronson."

Aaron acknowledged the greeting. "You have met my chief agronomists, Mr. Kishon from Hadera and Mr. Guri from Athlit?"

Pasha looked at the two men, then realized he'd never seen them and if he had he surely couldn't remember. "Yes, of course . . . now sit . . . sit." Handing the cigarette box to Aaron first, Jamal said, "These are the finest, they are made personally for me . . . a special blend, so aromatic."

Aaron never smoked, but he took one to oblige, as did Kishon and Guri. To refuse would be a gross breach of etiquette.

"They're marvelous, wouldn't you say?"

"Marvelous," Aaron answered. "Now I believe—"

Jamal interrupted, wanted to savor the moment, knowing the best was yet to come. Aaron was bringing him good news. "You've ridden far . . . let me have some coffee brought."

"That would be fine."

All three despised the dark black bitter brew, but Absalom's and Dovid's lives were surely worth a sour stomach.

After the ritual hospitality was finished, Jamal's eyes glistened as though with lust after a woman. "Now, to the reason you are here. How much wheat, barley and fodder do you have this time—?"

"None," Aaron answered calmly.

"None . . . do I hear you correctly?"

"Yes, and would you like to know why?"

"Would I like to know *why?"* He got up and commenced pacing the room.

Turning abruptly, Jamal shouted, *"Why?"*

"Because you keep putting my men in prison."

"I put your men in prison? Your men have never been molested since that little episode in Jaffa. I gave you my word it would never happen again, and now you sit there with this accusation?"

"The manager at the station in Hadera is now being held in Beersheba as well as my top agronomist from Athlit . . . I can only deliver what you want if I have the men . . . I don't mean the *fellaheen* . . . mere workers . . . to get the yield you want requires the brains of men like Guri here. How much tonnage, Samuel, were *you* personally able to have produced in this last shipment?"

"Five thousand tons of grain this spring, by rotating the crops last fall . . . which, of course, was not my idea but Dovid's."

"And what was your productivity, Zalman?"

"At Hadera we produced three thousand tons of fodder over and above the prior shipment."

"How responsible for that yield were you, personally?"

"Well, I'd say I made my contribution, but without Absalom's scientific expertise it could never have happened."

"And there you have it. Workers to plow, to harvest, to sack, to pick and to deliver, we can get easily. But without men like Landau and Feinberg we have no production."

Jamal frowned. Landau and Feinberg? Those two Jews could grow figs in the Sinai! Never mind if he liked them or not, the important thing was that *they* had been responsible for those yields. Jew or Armenian, made no difference, whoever could produce was vital to winning the war and to his private treasury . . . "Let's begin again. You say your men are being held in Beersheba?"

"That is right."

"Well, you do know, Aaronson, I have a huge country to manage. Every prisoner is not brought to my attention. Why are they there?"

"On a contrived and unsubstantiated charge of *spying*. Could anything be more ridiculous?"

Or true? Jamal thought. He remembered the plans sitting on his desk . . . but absolutely nothing had come of that, and he had carefully watched and waited . . . "Who made the accusation?"

"The Germans . . . in all due respect to their status as our allies, I wouldn't trust them any more than I would the British, French or Russians. I owe *them* no loyalty. My allegiance is to my government, the Ottoman Empire, and to you, who have proven your friendship."

Jamal was pleased. His love for the Germans was almost as great as for the British. "Yes, go on, about the Germans."

"I know they feel a sense of superiority over us Turks. They have the fleet and the air power. Unfortunately, we do not. There is also an arrogance about them, and it is my guess that they would like nothing better than to take a very large slice of the cake when the war is over."

This Jew was very smart indeed. Aaronson was expressing the same thought he had lived with for a long time. "What do you mean by a large slice, Aaronson?"

Aaron knew that he was beginning to gain his advantage by playing on Jamal Pasha's antagonism toward the Germans. He felt it, he sensed it. He hurried on. "By *large* . . . I mean Palestine and Syria."

Aaron was right in his evaluation, he understood the Oriental mind and knew nothing was more seductive than greed. Jamal Pasha sat and stared as his anger visibly grew. He could see himself being thrown out of his office and replaced by some arrogant German . . . *Jawohl, mein Herr* . . . Jamal Pasha would see them in hell first.

". . . To hang them . . ."

"What, Aaronson? My mind wandered for a moment . . . you were saying?"

"An army, they say, fights on its stomach. That's why I sent Landau and Feinberg, our chief agronomists, to do a study on wheat growing in the Negev. But they were arrested by your, if you will excuse me, stupid German patrols. They have a German mentality, and because my men couldn't produce some ridiculous card, they were arrested as spies. Now, I ask you, how intelligent can they be when they can make a big show of arresting scientists in the desert who should be able to go wherever grain can be found to feed the army? In order to make it appear that they perform a useful job here, they are about to hang them to impress the kaiser."

The blood had rushed to Jamal Pasha's face. Stupid, stupid Germans. With their goose-stepping and their blond close-cropped hair, those watery blue insipid eyes and ridiculous Viking faces. The Ottoman army could die of starvation and the kaiser, with his crippled army, wouldn't send a krone. If the empire collapsed he would do a Strauss waltz in Damascus. He was on to them, so was Aaronson. Smart Jew . . .

Jamal called for his secretary to come in immediately.

"Send a telegram . . . Beersheba. Absalom Feinberg and Dovid Landau are to be freed without delay."

FROM Damascus Aaron and the two men went to Beersheba, where they were led down the dark, cold stone corridor to Absalom's cell.

Even the dim shaft of light almost blinded Absalom when the cell door was opened. It seemed he had been in the dark for a very long time, and now he was sure that the end had come. And then . . . was he imagining? . . . no, it *was* Aaron's voice . . . incredible . . . *"Shalom,* I'm glad you dropped by," he said with an ironic bravado he hardly felt.

Aaron raged inwardly at the condition Absalom was in. His normally well-groomed beard was matted with saliva, his lips were cracked from lack of water. His entire ordeal was written in the dark circles under his eyes . . . What barbarians. He would have given his life to choke Jamal Pasha as he watched Absalom trying to get up. "Thank God you're alive . . . we're taking you home. Samuel, get him out to the wagon and I'll see about Dovid. Then come back."

"I can do it, Aaron, on my own—"

"You've done enough. Now, take him out." . . .

Aaron and Zalman found Dovid on a cold stone floor, shaking, convulsed with malaria. He had been given no quinine since his attack. He was beyond recognizing anyone. As they picked him up he could only mumble incoherently.

"Inhuman . . ." Aaron said. "I brought quinine when I was here, they didn't give him any . . . thank God we brought some . . ."

When Dovid lay alongside Absalom in the wagon, Aaron took the reins and whipped the horse into a fast gait. Zalman sat next to Dovid and wiped away the sweat pouring from him. He tried to pour water from a jug, which almost fell out of his hand as they hit a deep rut in the road. Finally he replenished the cup, opened Dovid's mouth and put the quinine on his tongue, forcing him to drink. Dovid's teeth chattered so badly he couldn't swallow. Zalman tried again until he managed, then covered him with more blankets. "Thank God, the quinine seems to be working," Zalman said as he watched Dovid fall into the blessed release of sleep.

"What's been going on at home?" Absalom asked quietly.

"You have a big surprise," Samuel told him.

"The only surprise I know is that they didn't hang us. What else?"

"You have someone waiting for you at Zichron."

Absalom hardly dared hope, but he got out the name . . . "Sarah . . . ?"

"*Mazel tov.* If you can still think of her, I think you'll be all right," Samuel said. . . .

It was two o'clock in the morning when they reached Zichron, and then the Aaronson home. Absalom was carried upstairs, where a waiting Sarah nearly fainted when she saw him. *Here,* bring him into Aaron's old room."

When they were alone Sarah allowed the tears to come. "Thank God, you've come home . . ."

Absalom smiled. "My Sarah? I know I'm dreaming . . . let me look at you . . . no, I'm not dreaming." He took her hand. "It was all worth it if it could bring you back." . . .

When Chavala heard the sound of the wagon in the morning's

stillness she quickly got out of bed. Nervously she slipped into her robe, tied the sash around her waist and ran out of the room, down the stairs and across the courtyard to Aaron's house, where Dovid had been put to bed.

Flinging open the door she asked Aaron, *"Where is he?"*

"In my room . . ."

She didn't wait for any reassurance, instead she rushed past Aaron. When she saw Dovid's face it mattered not at all what he looked like. He was *alive,* and she knew God had sent him back to her.

Quickly she filled a basin of water and put it on the table next to the bed. Pulling back the covers, she called for Aaron, who immediately came into the room. "Help me take off his clothes, and get me some quinine . . ."

After giving him the medication she washed his quivering body, replaced the bedding, then sat quietly beside the bed and held his hand. She was sure she felt Dovid's life ebbing away . . . this was the worst attack he'd ever had. And his condition had deteriorated so badly that it seemed impossible he could sustain it.

For three days and nights she scarcely slept or ate, but eventually, involuntarily, her eyes closed and she fell into a light slumber . . . Dovid's voice came to her out of a dream. It seemed to be saying, "Chavala, dearest Chavala, I must have willed myself to live just so I could see your face again . . ."

She opened her eyes. It had not been a dream. The crisis had passed, and now he lay quite still. He held out his weakened hand to her. Kneeling by his side she caressed his face. "We're together, my darling," and she said it over and over, her words watered by tears of gratitude.

FOR the next week Chavala tended to him like a child. She lavished her love on him, and his heart was nourished by it.

Gradually his strength returned.

As they walked in the vineyard, Dovid stopped and looked at his wife. "I've missed you so badly, Chavala. The world, the war . . . they'll have to wait. Tomorrow we go away for a few days."

"Yes, Dovid, but are you well enough to travel?"

"With you . . . you should forgive the flowery language . . . to the ends of the earth. Far enough?"

The next morning Dovid helped Chavala into the black carriage, took up the reins and they rode high up into the hills of Haifa.

The Moorish inn Dovid had chosen had once housed the harem of an Arab prince, but was now owned by a Sephardic Jew. Royalty to royalty, David thought, and smiled to himself.

Chavala had no sooner stepped over the threshold than the place evoked visions of twirling dancing girls. Shutting her eyes, she could almost hear the tinkling sounds of the small gold bells they wore around their ankles as their exotic eyes peered out above the transparent veils.

From the balcony of their rooms they could see the golden dome of the Bahai shrine and the magnificent gardens that surrounded it. Beyond lay the breathtaking view of the city and its harbor, across which was the bay and the old city of Acre and the mountains of Galilee. Mount Hermon rose majestically with its snowcapped crown.

And then they lay down in the canopied bed, and exchanged the joyous release of their love and gratitude. They lay together, as one, in a kind of sweet exaltation . . . Afterward they still clung to one another, each wishing that they could shut out the world forever. That this moment would be the rest of their lives . . .

"Dovid, I wish there were no war, that we could go back to the way it was—but I know, that's foolish . . ."

Of course he longed for the same things that she did, but to dwell on them now would only make things more painful when this idyll had to end. "We must take our pleasure where we can, Chavala . . . one day this will be over . . . and you and I and Reuven . . ."

Hard as she'd tried not to dwell on the day she left little Reuven and Chia with Raizel, it was impossible not to hear her son's voice once again saying . . . "Take me with you to see *abba,* please . . ." but how could she do that? When Sarah had come to Jerusalem to bring her back to Zichron she was all too aware that she might not even see Dovid alive again. She wanted to spare their son that cruel disappointment . . . Once again she could hear Sarah's words . . . "Absalom and Dovid are in prison and might—" Chavala refused to recall the rest. Quickly she turned her body toward her husband and gave herself to him as deeply, as fully as she knew how. . . .

Chavala knew it would be a very long time until they could know such enchantment again. The four fleeting days had spent themselves, and now Dovid was taking Chavala back to Jerusalem.

When they arrived at their home Dovid found Reuven quietly reading. This was *his* child, and while little Chia especially and the others were terribly close to him, Reuven was different. He was of his flesh and Chavala's. In the war-torn world that he moved in, this was a central, unifying fact for his life. Above all else it made his life seem important, justified going through anything to survive.

When the boy saw him, he didn't immediately run to him, arms outstretched. The boy, understandably, was shy, as though uncertain whether this still-gaunt man was really his father. And, Dovid thought, in a way he was quite right . . . he was not the same man who had left Jerusalem. Nobody went through the imminence of death twice, never mind the ravages to the body, and came out the same person. God, was there a scent of death around him now? Did it walk with him? He hoped not, hoped, instead, that it was more an aura of survival, a will to survive and outlast all the death that the Turks and Germans could try to inflict. After all, they were only the latest in a long line that had tried to extinguish the Jews from the earth. Nobody had quite managed yet. Dovid meant to try very hard to keep up their record of flawed success.

He went slowly up to the boy, just stood there a moment, then reached down and tousled his hair. And then, only then, did the boy get up, and slowly, tentatively and then like he was gripping life itself, put his arms around his father's waist and squeezed very hard. "I'm glad to see you, *abba*. I was worried. *Ema* went off so suddenly—"

"I know, I know, Reuven. Well, you see, the worry was for nothing. Here I am and here she is, and now we'll have a wonderful time together and talk and play and pretty soon we'll all be together again and I won't have to go away . . ."

There were tears in the boy's eyes as he tried to act older than he felt, to be manly. He understood well enough that his father might never come back when he left again, understood better than his parents could know, So for the rest of that day and the next they *lived* together as if they had never been apart, as if they would never again need to separate. Each knew the truth, each, including Reuven, played his role. And when Dovid had to leave, to face them both, the tears did not flow. The love they shared was their bond, their very special hold on life, and each would make the most of it not only for himself but for the others . . .

WHEN Dovid returned to Zichron, Aaron's caretaker told him that he was to go to Athlit.

The lights burned dim beyond the windows of Aaron's laboratory. Quickly Dovid mounted the stairs and found Aaron sitting at the long table with Absalom, Sarah, and the rest of the men of NILI.

Aaron's face was drawn, his eyes could not conceal his anxiety. "Dovid . . . I'm glad you're back. Sit down."

Dovid joined the rest.

Aaron began: "The contact has been broken. No signals, nothing. We have no way of knowing why." He pounded the table with his fist. "And here we wait, night after night. With maps and plans and vital information hidden away in a vault beneath the floor. With all we've amassed, the British could have been close to Damascus by now."

"I'll go, Aaron," Absalom said quickly.

"No, we can't risk you being arrested again. I have other plans for you."

"I know that I could make it, Aaron. There is an old Arab who has a fishing boat, I've spoken to him and he's willing. I could swim out beyond the rocks at Caesarea, where he would pick me up—"

"Remember the last time we tried that. Joseph Lieberman was never heard from again. With all respect to Joseph, your work here is too valuable to risk. The tides are unpredictable. No, there is only one option . . . I must get to Alexandria myself."

Dovid said, "Your absence, as you know, would cause suspicion. The whole Yishuv would be in danger, Hashomer would be down on us. Besides, how would *you* get there?"

"There's a scientific meeting in Berlin. With Jamal Pasha's lust for production, I should have little problem convincing him of the importance of my being sent to Berlin."

"Then what? How does that get you to Egypt?" Absalom put in.

"I'm *getting* to that." Absalom was always in such a big hurry. "From Berlin I'll attend a scientific conference in Vienna. Then, somehow, I'll find a way to get to England."

Sarah seemed puzzled. "Why London, Aaron? Wouldn't it be possible, if you do make a connection, to go on directly to Alexandria?"

"It's my feeling that my best chance of getting to Alexandria is with the British . . . on one of their ships. Well, at least it should be safer than a rowboat . . . or trying to disguise myself as an Arab. I've neither the taste nor talent for that . . . While I'm gone you, Sarah, Dovid and Absalom will be in command. And of course all of you will continue on as though I were still here. Nothing will be changed in my absence."

Chapter Fifteen

In BERLIN AARON became reacquainted with an American scientist who had been sent under the auspices of the United States Department of Agriculture.

Since he had worked with Jerome Harris years back on a sponsoring committee, Aaron felt he had an ally. But how to approach Harris and enlist his help was another matter.

That evening Jerome Harris dined as Aaron Aaronson's guest at the finest restaurant in Berlin.

After a bottle of Rhine wine, which Aaron detested, Aaron explained the importance of his getting to London. Harris was not overly inquisitive; he felt the desire to help his fellow scientist. Besides, he liked this *landsman* from another culture.

He slipped Aaron into his own stateroom aboard the ship returning him to America.

Once aboard, it was not difficult to get off a cable, with Harris's help, to London.

With the British now alerted, the American vessel was halted on the pretext of a routine inspection. In the process Aaronson was taken off and delivered to London.

In London he was taken to intelligence headquarters, where he proceeded to offer all the information about the work that had been done behind Turkish lines.

The British, impressed, wasted no time in sending him to Alexandria.

AARON had been gone since July. It was now September. Waiting, worrying was nerve-wracking for those left behind at Athlit. Further, as Aaron had told them, they'd kept up their espionage activities and escalated them, so that the men were exhausted.

Sarah said to Dovid and Absalom, "Do you think perhaps we should give the men a little break?"

"Obviously the coast will still have to be watched for any signals, but I agree," Dovid said. As did Absalom.

Dovid was especially grateful for the lull. It was an opportunity to see Chavala and his son, whom he hadn't seen for so long.

AS Dovid rode up into the hills toward Jerusalem a shocking thought occurred to him. In a sense . . . well, he hadn't missed her . . . There just was so little time to be lonely . . . it had nothing to do with his loving Chavala as always, but the intense preoccupation with his activities was so all-consuming that emergency squeezed out memory. One needed all one's thoughts on the job of the moment . . . or one didn't have an opportunity for *any* further thought—or breath.

Still, he had a vague sense of guilt about it, and could only hope that Chavala understood the long lapses in communication. She had to . . .

But, in spite of trying, Chavala did not really understand. Or at least could not really accept. With all of Dovid's apparent ability to roam about the country, he seemed to avoid coming to Jerusalem. He even seemed to have forgotten those four glorious days they had spent together in the hills of Haifa. Chavala remembered every touch, every kiss, every whispered word. Did Dovid . . . ? The long letters she'd received at the beginning of their separation had, if she received anything, become brief notes . . . "I hope you're no longer so lonely" . . . "It makes my job so much easier knowing you have Raizel with you, and kiss little Chia for me" . . . "I'll bring Reuven some new seeds" . . . "Stay well" . . .

But Chavala's life, unlike Dovid's, was lived in a void. The nights were the worst. Her nightmares had become so frequent that she awoke in the middle of the night drenched in perspiration. In those awful dreams she saw Dovid . . . and sometimes Moishe . . . dead. It took her days to recover and blot out the sight of blood. . . . If it weren't for the children and Raizel she thought she would have gone out of her mind.

And now she could no longer have the comfort of her sister. At least this loss was a bittersweet one. Raizel had met a young Chasid who lived in Mea Shearim. It was not exactly a marriage to make Chavala overjoyed, although she liked the young man. He was kind and gentle, with a sweet shyness. No wonder Raizel had fallen so in love with him. Her objection . . . and she knew it was selfish . . . was that for the rest of Raizel's life she would live in Mea Shearim and in the worst kind of poverty. Still, who was she to try and persuade her sister? Raizel required so little. Their love would sustain them. But when Chavala saw Raizel and Lazarus Ben-Yehudah joined together, even in that solemn moment she vowed that somehow, someway, she would help bring her sister out of this poverty . . .

They had married only three days ago, and already the longing for Raizel was more than painful. In her aloneness Chavala occupied a dim, shadowy world. Her thoughts, turned in on themselves, vacillated between love and hate, anger and guilt. She no longer even knew how she felt about Dovid. If only he would confide in her. At least she wouldn't feel this sense of . . . of abandonment Her resentments, in spite of herself, built to such heights that she wondered if she would even be able to face him. And such feelings made her ashamed at the same time.

WHEN Dovid arrived she did not greet him as before. They had seen each other, briefly, only three times during eight months of their separation.

This time they went through the act of love almost mechanically. She tried, but she simply couldn't respond to him the way she had the last time.

As they lay side-by-side, Chavala could no longer hold back the hurt, especially when Dovid said, "Sarah sends her love . . ."

Chavala got out of bed and looked out the window to the dismal alley beyond. "Why is Sarah still in Zichron? Is she any less in danger than I would have been?"

Dovid winced. How could he tell her that, especially in Aaron's absence, Sarah was a crucially important person at Athlit? . . . "Well, she doesn't have children—"

"That still doesn't answer my question. Why is she in less danger than I would have been?"

"I can't answer that, Chavala. I can't speak for the Aaronsons. It's *my* family that I want to protect."

She looked closely at Dovid, doubts invading her thoughts . . . Terrible, impossible doubts. But were they really? Dovid *was* a handsome man, and Sarah a beautiful woman . . . She knew Absalom was not always there, and without Dovid realizing it, could it be he was more drawn to Sarah than he even realized? And could it be that Sarah in her loneliness was perhaps reaching out to him?

"Dovid . . . please be honest with me. This will sound strange but . . . well, do you still love me?"

Dovid looked at her, dumbfounded. "Do I still love you? Good God, how can you ask that? Chavala, there's a war, and we're not the only ones that are separated—"

"I know that, Dovid, but I wonder . . . I can't help it . . . if there's more to this than you've told me. I mean, Sarah being allowed to stay at Zichron and not me—"

"What are you really asking me, Chavala?"

"Is there something between you and Sarah?"

Silence. He couldn't allow this to happen between them . . . No consideration of security, or anything else, was worth it . . . He took a deep breath. "Sarah is at Zichron because of her involvement with NILI. In fact, her position at Athlit in Aaron's absence is as important, maybe even more so, as mine."

Chavala felt ashamed, but also hugely relieved. "Forgive me, Dovid. I don't know what else to say, except that I love you . . ."

And, without another word, she led him back to their bed and proceeded to show him in the best way she knew how . . .

BUT when Dovid left, once again the loneliness took over. She turned to Sheine.

She sat down and wrote her sister:

> Dear Sheine,
>
> I greatly regret that we have not been in touch with one another for so long. With the world falling apart it seems crazy that you and I should remain strangers.
>
> I know there are many reasons in our lives that have caused our separation, but we *are* sisters, and there's so much I want to share with you. If you can possibly find time, *please* come to see me . . .
>
> This may come as a surprise, but I'm back in Jerusalem, living in the same apartment that we shared when papa was alive.
>
> Please let me hear from you, and believe that I love you . . .
>
> *Chavala*

When she addressed Sheine's letter to "Nurse Elsa Beck," tears came to her eyes. But she wasn't taking Sheine to task. People were different . . . including sisters . . . Sheine needed to escape the ghetto in her life as much as Chavala, in a sense, knew she had never really left it. That part of her lay buried in a cherished piece of earth, just south of Odessa. But it was also with her.

SHEINE had sensed a desparation in Chavala's words. She had also been surprised . . . and pleased . . . that she had grown so that she no longer feared the sight of her sister. The person who in her old fantasies had taken Dovid from her.

As the two sisters sat now in the dark, sparse kitchen, Sheine wondered why Chavala and Dovid had returned to Jerusalem. But since Chavala didn't say anything, she felt she shouldn't ask. Instead she listened as Chavala answered her questions about Moishe . . . "He was wounded in Gallipoli, and then we heard nothing for a long time . . . but somehow he recovered and made his way to England. I think he was smuggled out by one of our people . . . but they don't tell me so much . . . anyway, I can only believe he will one day be home . . . And have you heard from Dvora?"

"Yes, she wrote me once, she said she was going to be married. I assume by now that she is."

"Yes, she has a little boy, just a few months old."

Sheine felt badly that no one had let her know. "What's his name?"

"Zvi . . . and her husband is in Canada with his volunteer unit. The world has surely changed our lives."

"Yes . . . and tell me about Raizel."

"Oh, Sheine . . . we really have been out of touch, haven't we? Raizel was married two weeks ago and is living in Mea Shearim."

Sheine shook her head. "We've all grown up, haven't we, Chavala? And come a long way from that little *shtetl* in Odessa."

"Perhaps you, more than me. I'm not so sure where we're going."

"We . . . ?" Sheine felt a sudden chill. She sensed an overwhelming loneliness in Chavala. "Where is Dovid? I mean, why are you living in Jerusalem?"

Chavala knew she couldn't tell Sheine about Dovid's activities so without thinking she made up a story . . . "Well, Dovid and I have parted . . . oh, it isn't *permanent,* but . . . Sheine, sometimes things do happen in a marriage . . ."

Sheine sat quietly, in disbelief. There was a time when hearing this would have given her total happiness. But in this moment she felt only compassion. "I don't want to pry, but . . . if you want to tell me . . ."

Chavala swallowed hard. The deception was getting out of hand. ". . . I guess I became a little too . . . demanding . . . you know, a man gets tired of listening to his wife's complaints. You know how I've always hated Palestine. And the years spent living in the village at Zichron began to get on my nerves. Maybe I've outgrown villages, maybe I began to find it . . . well, boring—"

"But you seemed so happy, content there. What changed?"

"We all change." The less said the easier, Chavala thought.

"Maybe it's the war. I suppose you're right. People do change. Well . . . I know that *I* have, and thank God for some changes. I've met a man I . . . like, and have much in common with—"

"I'm so *happy* for you, Sheine! Are you serious about him?"

"Yes . . . in fact, we've decided to marry."

Chavala hesitated, then said, "He's a Jew . . . ?"

"No . . . Chavala . . . this may shock you, but I just don't have any special *feeling* for our faith. He comes from a good family. He's a good man. His name is Gunter Hausman . . ."

How, Chavala thought, could she condemn Sheine, when she herself was no longer observant? But still, the deep reservoir of her *Yiddishkeit*, her sense of Jewishness, was a lasting pull. Chavala was still so warmed by the cherished memories of childhood . . . the lullabies her mother sang when she was rocked to sleep in her arms, the *Shabbes* candles glowing in the silver candlesticks . . . the taste of sweet Passover wine . . . Yes, she clung to the essence of deep faith and was able to separate that from the dictates of form. She did not feel less Jewish for it.

As Chavala looked at Sheine, a painful thought came to her . . . she thanked God that her mother and father were not alive to see a child of theirs marry outside the faith. "Sheine, dearest sister, I feel sad . . . but I don't criticize . . . that you've felt you had to let go of our heritage. It's all we really have . . ."

"It's *also* brought us nothing but heartache and disgrace. . . . I know you're disappointed, Chavala, and I'm sorry, but it just doesn't matter to me that Gunter is not a Jew."

Chavala shook her head. "Does he know about you . . . I mean . . . being a Jewess?"

"It wouldn't matter."

There was a silence between them, and then an awkwardness.

How sure, Sheine asked herself, was she that Sheine Rabinsky had been conquered, and that Elsa Beck had come out the victor? Whatever . . . looking at Chavala's wounded expression, Sheine decided she had to get away . . .

She got up. "I'm happy we've had this time together, Chavala, and I hope that you and Dovid will make up your differences . . . Now, I really must go."

Chavala stood up too and looked at her sister, and then the two embraced. Holding Sheine close to her, Chavala said, "I wish you every happiness, dear. You must believe that. Things can't always be our way . . . I only pray that you're never hurt."

Sheine merely nodded, walked out and closed the door behind her. Or so she thought.

GUNTER was waiting outside the cafe. "Lord, how I've missed you."

Sheine laughed. "That's very flattering. Imagine, we work together and you still miss me."

"If you're away from me for a moment, Elsa, I miss you."

Sheine stood awkwardly for a moment, then the two entered the dimly lit cafe. As she looked around, she felt awkward. Somehow Chavala's words nudged her . . . *Does he know about you?* And her saying, *It wouldn't matter.* Wouldn't it? Could she actually enter into a marriage on a deception? Maybe she didn't love Gunter with the same terrible passion, obsession, she'd once felt for Dovid, but she still loved, deeply cared for him . . .

At first it had been a physical attraction, and then as they worked closely together, she found herself more and more drawn to him. And she found herself more and more drawn to him. And she now walked that fine line between affection and love. Who knew where one began and the other ended?

As they sipped the Liebfraumilch, she peered over the glass, first at Gunter, then at the Jewish girls who were sitting not only with German officers but with Turks as well. Theirs, of course, had been born not out of loneliness but from a need to fill their stomachs . . . to bring food to many of their starving families.

Such was not the case with her. What *would* happen if later in their lives, for some reason, he found out about her true identity? What would he do?

"Gunter," she said softly.

"Yes . . . you seem hesitant. Like you want to tell me something and don't know how. Please . . . out with it."

"You're right. Fear is a bad thing."

"I've never known you to be afraid of anything, Elsa. And I've seen you calm under the most difficult conditions—"

"But there are all kinds of fears."

"Then tell me, darling, what disturbs you?"

Abruptly—how else to get it out?—she said, "I've deceived you."

"Deceived me?" He laughed. "Have you fallen in love with one of your patients?"

"This is *serious.*"

"Then tell me. I love you, Elsa—"

"I hope so, Gunter, I hope you love me a great deal . . . I'm a Jew, and I've thought for some time now that I just can't enter into marriage deceiving you . . ."

Gunter sat for a moment without speaking. At first he was annoyed she'd deceived him . . . Still, when he thought about it, he'd never been prejudiced so why would he be now? He'd not only respected his professors, but revered them, and all had been Jews. He had friends and associates who were Jews. Then why did he feel strange, peculiarly . . . unsure of himself at this moment . . . ?

He looked across the table at Elsa, tried to search deep inside himself. The more he thought about it, the more he was convinced it wasn't Elsa's Jewishness that had shaken him but that she hadn't taken him into her confidence at the very beginning of their relationship. The deception. Well, he loved her, didn't he? She hadn't changed from the exquisite woman who'd captured him, had she?

He reached out for her hand across the table. "My dear Elsa, what difference could this make to me? But why was it important for you not to let me know before?"

She tried to tell him about her life, how she was sure she could never enter his world being a Jew.

"Dear Elsa, it hurts me to know how much you've suffered—"

"I'm not alone, Gunter. My people have suffered for five thousand years . . . Well, I've told you everything now, except that my real name is . . . Sheine Rabinsky."

"Sheine means beautiful. Which you are. I want to be married soon. Would tomorrow suit you?"

It was more than she'd dared hope for. "It certainly would. Let's not waste a moment." After all, she added to herself, he might change his mind . . .

Chapter Sixteen

WITH NO NEWS from Aaron, Absalom became impatient. Sarah watched him as he paced back and forth like a caged lion. Abruptly, he stopped and looked at her. "I've decided to go back to Egypt."

"Have you talked to Dovid about this?"

"No. And I don't want him to know until I'm gone."

"Absalom, you *must* discuss this with him!"

"No, if I did he'd be against it, we both know that."

"That's why I'm pleading with you to speak to him, you're not thinking of the consequences—"

"That's an appropriate word. If we don't make contact with Aaron the *consequences* will be that our work will have been for nothing."

Sarah was beside herself. "You failed to get through last time, and Aaron was able to save you, but he's not here now. Can't you be patient and wait? If you get caught this time they'll surely hang you."

"I won't be caught."

"How can you be so sure?"

"Because I have a different plan this time."

Sarah sighed. There was no way to convince Absalom not to go. "Then tell me, what is the plan?"

"I've located a Bedouin as a guide, and I'm taking Nachman Shamir with me. We both speak Arabic—"

"But that's what you did last time, except for the guide and Nachman. You had to go through the desert. Why is this different?"

"Because this time I don't have to travel to the border, the British are already part way down the coast near Raffa. Sarah, *I have the plan for the defense of Gaza.* The Germans have heavy artillery there, and the British must be warned that the attack should be made by way of Beer-sheeba, that the defense there is very light. They must not make the attempt to break through at Gaza. *Now* do you understand why we can't wait for Aaron?"

She understood, but Sarah was also still terrified, "I still want you to talk about this with Dovid—"

"No, Sarah, this time I do it my way." He looked at her. Taking her in his arms, he put her down gently on the bed they shared. This small room at Athlit had become their private world. Lying alongside her, he said, "Sarah, darling, let me hold you . . ."

Sarah did more than that. She gave herself to Absalom as never before. And throughout the night they held each other, wrapped themselves in each other. . . .

In the morning when she awoke, Absalom was already dressed.

As she started to get out of bed to dress Absalom came to her, sat on the edge, held her face in his hands. "Don't come down with me, Sarah. I want the memory of seeing you this way."

There were no good-byes, and the tears did not fall, at least not until Absalom was gone.

DISGUISED as Bedouins, Absalom, the guide and Nachman traveled south by camel.

The first night they found no difficulty as they passed beyond Jaffa. But when they reached the next Turkish outpost they were stopped by a patrol and questioned about their destination.

With Absalom's knowing Bedouin accent, his dark brooding eyes, dressed in the long black aba with the kaffiyeh headdress, he was very convincing, and so they were waved on as ordinary nomads.

Mostly now they traveled by night, not only because of the treacherous scorching sun, but to stretch out the water supply.

On the third day at dusk, as they continued further south, suddenly in no-man's-land between Turkish and British territory, some forty Bedouins came up out of the desert, swooped down over the high mount of sand dunes. They seemed to come from nowhere, just as the locusts had, charging with rifles in hand.

Absalom's Bedouin guide promptly turned his camel north and went off as fast as the beast would take him.

Absalom and Nachman fell to the ground, took up their rifles and tried holding off the attackers, but it was futile.

Absalom was hit and lay still as the blood came from his mouth. Nachman tried crawling to his side, and Absalom tried to motion to him to get away, save himself. And then Absalom's head rolled to one side . . . and he was still. Very still.

Nachman did try to run but a bullet tore through his right shoulder, he fell and lost consciousness. . . .

In the morning when Nachman came around, he found himself in the back of a truck on his way to a British military hospital. He'd been picked up, luckily, by one of the Australian patrols in the area.

When they finally arrived in Alexandria, Nachman prayed that

Aaron had managed to work out the plan he'd had when he left for Berlin, from which he would try to get to Alexandria via London. He could not even allow himself to think of failure . . . especially not after what had happened to Absalom. Nachman asked the Australians to please make inquiries, try to locate Aaron. He could only hope Aaron's news would be better than his. . . .

Aaron did make it to Alexandria from London, but Lieutenant Wooly, who had been so receptive to Dovid, had been captured by the Turks, and now a Captain Lawrence was his replacement.

Lawrence treated Aaron with a remote indifference. In fact, he refused to see him for several weeks. When Aaron was finally summoned . . . yes, that was the word for it . . . he was left to sit for hours before being ushered into Lawrence's office.

Lawrence, tall, ascetic, didn't greet Aaron, rather he barely tolerated his *foreign* presence. Aaron, of course, already despised him, beyond which he viewed him with considerable suspicion, since it was well known that Captain Lawrence was distinctly pro-Arab. In fact, he had endeared himself so to the Arabs that he became known as Lawrence of Arabia. Aaron was not foolish enough to disregard the fact that Lawrence was also an anti-Semite. He got from Lawrence just what he expected—nothing. . . .

But at least if Lawrence had not kept him waiting when he had first arrived Absalom wouldn't now be dead. That awful intelligence had come to him in his hotel room only hours after Lawrence had dismissed him. He had immediately come to this Australian hospital, at least grateful to find Nachman alive.

For seven days he sat *Shiva* and said the Kaddish.

After the mourning period was over he demanded and got an audience with the highest authorities of British military intelligence.

He stood before them now, barely able to control his rage. "I have been through many things in my life, encountered many people, but I have never been treated as I have in the months that I've been here. Your Captain Lawrence has put one obstacle after another in my way while I have sat here with vital information. Instead of showing interest in this information, let alone trying to understand it, he saw fit to question me about my geographic knowledge of the Sinai. Good God! Instead of all this insane waste of time, if he at least had allowed me to send a signal, Absalom Feinberg would still be alive. Yes . . . I stand here accusing you of the most unforgivable negligence. When Absalom Feinberg came to you, did you listen to him? No, you discredited him, and now he lies buried in the sands of the Sinai, because he tried to get the word to you how Palestine could be invaded. His death is on your hands. And as for your Captain Lawrence, it isn't important that he has personally tried to humiliate me. What is important is that by refusing to recognize a certain competence and reputation that scientists in this country and others have seen fit to acknowledge, he and you and us have been hurt in our common effort. Now I say that either you take my people and me seriously, or we will refuse to go on with this travesty."

The British were finally impressed. A plan of operation was immediately discussed. The main problem was how to create a real link between the British headquarters in Egypt, and the men at Athlit. A link that would work, be reliable.

"Contact," said Aaron, "will obviously have to be made by ship. To camouflage our activities the ship will use a code name . . . I suggest *Menagem.* On board will be Chaim Barash. He will be the signalman from NILI. The crew should consist of three sailors from Tyre, who, as you know, have worked for British intelligence and are familiar with the coast. I would suggest that your intelligence officer, Ian M. Smith, participate and go over the reports from Athlit as soon as they are received on board. Our NILI people will help in the decoding and translating of messages. Is that *acceptable* to you gentlemen?"

Captain Trevor-Brown, not missing Aaron's bitter undertone, nodded. "It's fine." He shook hands with Aaron, smiled. "Welcome aboard, sir. It's damned good having you on our side."

ON February 19 the *Menagem* left Port Said for Athlit.

Aaron was aboard.

At midnight it lay at anchor and signaled.

Dovid, who had been stretched out on the cold ground amid the tall grass could not believe what he had seen. At first he thought his eyes deceived him, but the ship signaled once again.

My God, Aaron had done it. Half-frozen, bone-tired, he signaled back, according to the agreement made before Aaron had left Athlit.

When Dovid finally saw Aaron standing in front of him, soaking wet, the effect was tremendous . . . unashamed, he put his arms around Aaron. "Thank God you're safe and back—"

"Yes, I'm back, but not, I'm afraid, for long. Come, I must see Sarah . . ."

When he entered the small room where she slept he pulled up a chair and just watched her for a while.

When she woke up she could hardly believe her eyes. And of course her first concern was for news about Absalom. It was this moment he'd tried to steel himself for. And, of course, had not succeeded. No words would comfort her, Aaron knew, but still, that was why he had come back . . . "Sarah . . . this is the moment of your greatest testing. I ask you to try to be strong . . . Absalom is dead."

She made not a sound. What she had heard she had expected. What she felt she could not express. Absalom, buried under the sands of the Sinai. Not even their love could stop him from going. He had, she realized, and even greater love, and he'd died for it. Well, she told herself, at least she would try not to dishonor his sacrifice by an unseemly outburst of self-pity. Her private losses . . . first her sister Rivka, her failed marriage and now the man who truly was the love of her life . . . they would stay private . . .

Aaron helped. Take Absalom's courage as a legacy, he said. Carry on his work, the mission he laid down his life for. Let *your* strength be a monument to his name. Help make sure he did not die in vain . . .

Finally Sarah brought herself to ask, "What happened to his body?"

"No one knows . . . a patrol was sent out, he wasn't found."

She still would not cry. "He's buried somewhere underneath the sands of the Sinai . . . well, the Canaan desert is where our people came from . . . Absalom has returned to our land after all." *Sleep well, my Absalom, sleep well, my beloved. . . .*

Aaron remained only a few days longer. The night before he left he said, "Sarah, I'm sorry, but you must understand that no one is to know about Absalom. This must be a secret as well guarded as NILI itself. If the truth were to come out it would inevitably weaken the will of the rest of NILI's men. Absalom was that important and influential. He was our fire, our spirit. Above all, if the news of his death fell into the hands of the Turks it would compromise our whole mission."

She looked at Aaron. "His disappearance will eventually be questioned."

Dovid, who had been standing by, took over.

"You must say that Absalom left to go to London and train as a pilot. We want no mystery surrounding his absence to be questioned. It could affect the inner relationships of the factions we work with." He didn't add how much he wished that he, not Absalom, had gone on this mission.

Absalom's very assets—his language abilities, knack for impersonation—also tended to make him too brave, to take fewer precautions than someone without his special abilities. His advantages had also been his undoing . . .

Sarah nodded her agreement with Dovid's words.

At midnight, she and Dovid silently watched Aaron depart. Who knew which of them would be in the greater danger? No place, or mission, was safe, or for the weak of heart . . .

THE NILI-British operation continued between Port Said and Athlit in the months of February and March. Specific nights were designated for contact so that the men at Athlit knew beforehand of the ship's arrival. But as the seasons changed the operation could not always be carried out. At times powerful waves prevented the unloading of the boat and its safe way to the shore.

Over half the trips ended in nothing. Each failure depressed NILI's men, waiting as they were obliged to do for so many hours on the beach, hiding from the Turkish guard, freezing in cold during the winter nights or suffering mosquito bites during the summer nights. They could not shut an eye after a day's work, and above all else worried that an accident of some sort had happened to the ship.

Menagem could operate only on moonless nights. Coordination between the ship and the group was made by light signals that were changed from time to time to prevent suspicion. On its arrival from Port Said, *Menagem* would first pass to Zichron Yaakov and Athlit during daytime. From aboard the ship, with the help of binoculars, a certain small house in the vineyard could be clearly seen. If the shutters were open, it meant the way to Athlit was safe, and if a white sheet was hanging from the railing, it meant the NILI people would be waiting and it was safe to come down to the shore. For the encounter on the shore, they decided on a password.

Sarah asked that it be "Absalom."

Chapter Seventeen

IN SPITE OF all the hazards, the difficulties, Aaron and Dovid felt that at long last their work with the British had succeeded. The success, though, was achieved at great cost.

During the second disorderly retreat of the Turkish forces from the Suez Canal zone, thousands of Jews died of starvation and disease. On March 26, 1917, the British offensive on Gaza began. Two days later the elders and notable people, Jews and non-Jews, were summoned to the "Soraya" in Jaffa to hear the Pasha's word: "All Jaffa citizens must vacate the area of Jaffa, leave their homes and move to any other part of the country, except Jerusalem and Haifa." Only the Arab peasants and the Jewish grove-owners were allowed to remain after many appeals, but without their families.

Nine thousand Jews from Jaffa and Tel Aviv had to go into exile. The Yishuv was lost; where would they get carts to wheel the old ones, the women and children? What would happen to property?

Still, the tide continued. The British were working against time to build a railway line up the coast to carry heavy cannon, and from the Nile a pipeline was being laid to supply water to the troops. Hashomer and other groups began storing arms, as more and more men began joining the ranks of NILI. In Tel Aviv they gathered to make further plans, when suddenly a burst of cannon was heard. Bedlam was in the streets as people ran in all directions. But Dovid remained sitting, he'd anticipated what was about to happen. He even smiled when he heard the explosion. The ironworks had been hit. He knew that now what they had all worked so hard for was at last, showing some results.

Not surprisingly such results of NILI resulted in the Turks becoming extremely nervous. Restrictions more brutal than before were imposed, the cities were left near starvation. Especially the Jews in Jerusalem. At the Jaffa gate, every day hundreds of people sat and pleaded for alms. By evening a government cart passed among them to pick up the dead.

CHAVALA waited for the food that Dovid had been sending every week, but now she had received nothing for over two weeks. She did not question this, it was only too apparent that the food had been stolen on the way. Dovid would never leave his family in want. She contracted

Samuel Guri, a Shomer who she knew worked with Dovid even before the war, to get a note to Dovid at Athlit.

She waited for two days. When Samuel Guri came back with the news that Dovid was not at Athlit she became frantic. But fear quickly turned into an iron determination. Once before she'd summoned up the courage to kill a man to survive . . . well, she'd heard that a shipment had been sent by the Jews from America, and one way or another she would come back to her family with a sack of wheat . . .

Taking Chia and Reuven by the hand she hurried to Mea Shearim. Quickly she walked up the cracked wooden steps to Raizel's small apartment.

In spite of her pregnancy, Raizel seemed a shadow of herself. Her eyes were hollow, her cheeks sunken.

By God, Chavala thought, she would not stand by and see her family starve.

"Raizel, I want Lazarus to come with me . . . I must go to Jaffa."

"When?"

"Right now . . . today."

"Oh, Chavala . . . today is Saturday."

Chavala was about to ask what that had to do with it when she remembered it was *Shabbes*. What was Raizel's husband praying for today? For God to send manna from heaven? "I'm sorry, with all that's happening I seem to have forgotten the holy Sabbath . . . I'll go alone, then. Chia and Reuven will stay with you."

Raizel's eyes filled with tears. "You *mustn't* go alone, Chavala. It's much too dangerous, especially for a woman."

Starvation can also be dangerous, Chavala thought. "Don't worry, I'll find someone to go with me," she lied.

As she looked up from the bottom of the stairs and saw Raizel with her black *sheitel* on her head, slightly askew, she didn't know whether to laugh or cry. That ridiculous custom of shaving a woman's head before marriage so that she would remain chaste . . . better her husband should have worked harder and prayed less so that his wife would be able to eat. The irreverent thought fled, replaced by her devout hope that she would not arrive too late in Jaffa.

From Raizel's house she went down to the cobblestone alley, where she knew her diminutive Sephardic friend would also be praying to God for the same reasons as her brother-in-law. But since women were not permitted downstairs in the men's section, she waited for God to intervene. Her prayers were answered as a yeshiva *boychik* almost collided with her. He was three minutes late, and God might strike him deaf, dumb and blind. Since it was also forbidden to touch a woman, even by accident, he flushed and mumbled something under his breath. As he was about to enter the *shul* Chavala said, "I would never ask Shimon Halevi to interrupt his *davening* on the Sabbath, but as you know it is permitted in cases of life and death." The boy nodded, remembering what the *Midrash* said. "Well," Chavala said with a faint quiver in her voice, "this is a matter of death. Please tell him I am waiting outside."

Soon the diminutive Halevi was standing in front of her, holding his heart. "Someone died?"

"A great many will . . . if I don't get your horse and wagon."

This was the Sabbath and it would be a sin to be angry before sundown, so he said quietly, "For my horse and wagon you took me from *shul?*"

"Please. While you are talking people are dying."

"Go take the horse, already. I shouldn't even be thinking such things, much less saying them, but you will have to put the saddle on and hitch it to the wagon."

"God will forgive you, and bless you." And if He doesn't, she added to herself, I will.

WHEN she arrived in Jaffa she found bedlam. Crowds were waiting, clamoring, screaming, fighting their way to get to the Jewish Agency.

Chavala's size was her ally. Finding an opening, she wove her way through the throngs. When she found that she needed a ration card she refused to allow that to defeat her. She learned the grain was stored in the adjacent building.

Quickly she got back into the wagon and led it to the side of the entrance. She stood to one side of the door and watched the men heaping the sacks up one on the other. If it were possible to steal she would have no qualms, but the sacks were too heavy. To lie was her only hope, her instincts all she could depend on.

Carefully she scrutinized each man. Who would most likely respond to her? The older ones would probably be less taken in. More likely the young *chalutzim* would be more receptive to a young, vulnerable "widow."

She approached a young, blond *chalutz*. "Please . . . you must help me . . . I *beg* you. I have lost my card and they won't give me another."

The *chalutz* looked at her. Chavala's pleas didn't exactly impress him. If he was to listen to every hysterical woman who begged there would be nothing left in the warehouse. He'd forgotten how many had tried the same tactics this very day. "Go back and wait like the others, you'll get a card."

"*Please* . . . you must believe me . . . I have tried but they said I had already received my allotment, but on my mother's name, I swear it's not so."

He looked at her suspiciously; a woman would do anything to get what she wanted. "I can't help you."

"*Why?* You don't own the flour, it wouldn't cost you anything and I'm a widow with two starving children . . ." Taking the money out of her pocket, she said, "Here, take this. It's yours—"

"Please, don't bother me, I'm busy—"

"If anything happens to my children the curse will be on you. Do you hear? For the rest of your life you'll be cursed."

Before he could answer, Chavala fell to the ground in a heap. It was a convincing act.

He quickly picked her up in his arms and lay her down on a sack, then stood listening to her shallow breathing.

Chavala counted slowly to thirty. Her eyes fluttered, and when she opened them tears started.

The tears helped, as well as the feel of her in his arms when he'd picked her up. She was beautiful . . . a young widow . . . what did he have to lose if he gave her the flour? On the other hand, what did he have to gain?

His thoughts were interrupted as Chavala said, barely above a whisper, "Please . . . help me up. I'm sorry to have bothered you." She stood feebly before him. "Thank you, now I must go to my children."

She started slowly toward the door. He called out, "Wait." She held her breath. Had the pretense worked?

"Yes . . . ?"

"If I give you the flour, can I see you again?"

"Oh, yes . . . yes . . . I will be grateful to you for the rest of my life—"

"Can we meet tonight?"

The world was in a state of chaos, hundreds were starving, and he wanted . . . it was total insanity . . . still, "Yes . . ."

"Where do you live?"

"In Tel Aviv."

"Where?"

"You can't come there . . . I have children, but on my life I promise to meet you in the park at eight o'clock tonight."

He looked at her suspiciously. On the other hand if she wanted more flour she would be a fool not to keep their rendezvous. "All right . . . tonight, and *be* there."

"I will, believe me I will."

After he had loaded the sack into the wagon he held her close. At this moment nothing mattered, except that her family would have something to eat.

As she stepped into the wagon he squeezed her hand firmly, "You won't forget?"

She shook her head.

As she faded into the distance it occurred to him he hadn't even asked her name.

CHAVALA traveled the long, narrow road up to the hills toward Jerusalem, which bordered on the army encampments. It was dusk, and the Turkish soldiers were lying about on the ground. She felt their eyes on her. With her head held high, she whipped the horse to go faster until, thank God, she'd passed the trenches.

She had just passed beyond the gorge at Bab el Wad when she abruptly brought the wagon to a halt.

She waited. Silhouetted against the sky, a black-clad Bedouin blocked the road with his white Arabian stallion.

For a moment Chavala stayed motionless in panic, her mind darted to the body that lay buried under the cherry tree . . . But this time she had no weapon. And how could she overcome this giant of a man?

She watched as he dismounted, slowly came toward her. She grabbed the whip and lashed out as he came to one side.

He only laughed, then grabbed her by the hair and brutally dragged her from the wagon, down the slight incline, and threw her to the ground.

In the nightmare that followed, he lifted her dress and spread his legs over her. She struggled, kicked, scratched his face.

As he undid the sash around his waist, she inched her fingers along the ground until she found a rock.

When he was ready to enter her, she found all the strength left in her and struck him between the eyes.

The blow was sudden, violent. He rolled to one side as the blood rushed from his head.

Fighting for breath, she got to her feet, climbed up the slight incline. How she got back to the wagon she would never know . . . As she was about to climb into the seat she felt something beneath her foot. She looked down, and there in the dirt lay a small red-and-gold tooled Moroccan pouch. Picking it up quickly she got into the wagon, took up the reins and drove the horse with the whip until she reached Jerusalem.

WHEN she arrived in Mea Shearim, she somehow managed to climb the stairs to Raizel's apartment.

"Thank God you're home safe and . . ."

Chavala was too tired and distraught at this moment to tell her anything. "Where is your husband?"

"Resting."

"Get him up, if it won't disturb him too much . . . I have a heavy sack of flour in the wagon. Maybe he can manage to lift it."

While they waited for the man of the house to bestir himself, she hugged Reuven, who, after telling her how glad he was to see her, asked if now they were going home.

"Tomorrow, darling."

The little boy was disappointed, but didn't protest.

When Raizel's pious husband finally appeared to lift off the sack from the wagon, Chavala ripped it open, angrily, and scooped out three ladles for herself and her family.

Raizel said, "But you're leaving us almost the whole—"

"Don't worry, I'll get more . . . just take care of yourself and the children, I'll be back in the morning."

BARELY able to climb the stairs, she could hardly believe she'd reached the door to her apartment.

When she crossed the threshold, Dovid was waiting, and all that had happened to her in that incredible day came crashing down on her. She collapsed in his arms, stayed motionless as he carried her to bed. She hadn't even enough strength to talk. Dovid lay down beside her and held her, gently, lovingly.

Finally she could ask, "How did you happen to be here tonight?"

"When I got back to Athlit from Lebanon I found the note you'd sent by Guri and I came as fast as I could. I've been here most of the day. Now . . . tell me . . . what happened . . . ?"

This time she couldn't control her tears, and as she told him what had happened to her Dovid thought bitterly to himself that he hadn't really protected her at all by sending her away. A woman like Chavala one never protected.

When she'd finished he knew, whether Aaron approved or not, where they belonged. "We'll go back to Zichron. We need each other, and the children need us. Whatever the future, at least we'll face it together."

"Yes, Dovid . . . thank you . . . will you stay the night?"

"*Yes.*"

Chavala got out of bed and went to prepare her bath water. As her garments fell to the floor the small leather pouch lay beside them. Picking it up, she brought it to Dovid. "In all the excitement I forgot about this," she said, handing it to him.

He drew the strings apart and emptied the contents on the bed. Both gasped. Even in the dimly lit room the stones shone. It was unbelievable. A handful of small emeralds, rubies, diamonds, sapphires and opals lay clustered together. Most likely the Bedouin had waylaid a traveler and stolen them.

Chavala said, "You know what this *means,* Dovid . . . after the war we will have more than enough money to go to America . . ."

He said nothing. He would not, *could* not hurt her at this moment by telling her he could never leave. Later he would try to tell her why . . . When he looked at the stones, what he felt most was guilt, thinking about the circumstances under which she'd gotten them . . . "For now, darling, let's only think of being together again . . ."

In the morning they stopped at Mea Shearim to pick up the children and to tell Raizel that they were leaving but that Raizel need not worry, Chavala would make sure that there was sufficient food. The sisters said their good-byes and held one another for a long, lingering moment.

WHEN Chavala stepped over the threshold of her own house, with her family, she wanted to get down on her hands and knees and give thanks that they had, miraculously, all survived . . .

Chapter Eighteen

Robert silverstein's limousine stopped in front of his jewelry establishment on Fifth Avenue. The liveried chauffeur opened the door as Mr. Silverstein stepped out. "Call for me at four. Mrs. Silverstein and I are going to the opera this evening."

In all the years since he had inherited the business from his father this was the first morning he did not pause to look up at the sign, "Silverstein and Sons, Est. 1887." Instead he bought the newspapers from the boy who was shouting, "UNITED STATES DECLARES WAR ON GERMANY!"

In disbelief he read the date, April 6, 1917, in the bold black print. This evening he would not be going to the opera. His only thoughts at the moment were of his three fine sons.

ON the trolley, Mary Kelly was going to work for the Silverstein family, for whom she had worked as a cook for the past seven years. She sat trembling, holding the paper to her chest. Her only thoughts were for her Sean and Patrick, one eighteen, the other twenty. She was very frightened.

IN London at the manor house of Sir Walter Collingsworth, the household staff sat around the table in their quarters downstairs.

"What'll it mean, Mr. Dalton . . . with the Yanks on our side?" the scullery maid asked the butler. "You reckon the war will be over sooner?" Mr. Dalton shrugged, said how the bloody hell would he know.

IN Berlin, Frieda Hockstein said to her husband Fritz, *"Mein Gott,* what will happen now?"

"Calm yourself, Frieda, we will win the war. Remember, *Deutschland uber Alles.* The Americans are run by Jews. Everybody knows that."

IN Damascus, Jamal Pasha paced the floor. "Those *stupid* Germans. As though we weren't having enough trouble with the British . . . they had to get involved with the crazy Americans, with their money, all those men . . ."

IN Alexandria, Aaron read about the event very carefully. The United States' involvement obviously would allow more British troops to be deployed to the Middle East. America would fight on the western front, trying to save the French.

Although Aaron had no political ambitions for himself, he realized this was an opportunity to strengthen NILI's position. He saw this as a catalyst in bringing the problem of Eretz Yisroel to the world's attention.

Since the exile of the Jews from Jaffa and Tel Aviv, the situation in the country had become desperate. The year had been one of hunger and disease. The locusts had destroyed the crops to such an extent that much of the land lay fallow, and those meager crops that were produced the army confiscated. Commerce was paralyzed and the Turks forbade any financial help for the Jews. All of which strengthened NILI's determination to try and save the Yishuv.

Toward the end of April Aaron met with Sir Marc Sykes, who happened to be in Egypt, and through him sent a cable to the World Zionist Organization in London to spread the news around the world of the Jews' deportation. The next day Aaron telegraphed the chief representative of American Jewry, whose support he was trying to gain. Along with such activities, Aaron founded a special committee for collection of funds for Eretz Yisroel. In a few days cables were sent to all the communities of the Diaspora, and Aaron's actions started to get results. In early May, Reuters published his report on the evacuation of Jaffa, and the other press agencies copied the item and spread it around the world. Protest gatherings were held. Jews feared what happened to the Jews under the Ottomans would be the same as what had happened to the Armenians. The American Zionist Organization appealed to Holland, Spain and Switzerland to intervene at Constantinople in favor of the Jews in Eretz Yisroel. Even in Germany, Turkey's ally, protest gatherings were held. In the face of all this, Jamal Pasha decided to ease up a little on the Jews in return for denial of the previous articles in the press. The Yishuv's Jews, the conservative ones, were pleased.

Although the Yishuv was still unaware of NILI's military espionage, still its social and national activities brought NILI's whispered name to many other people who were grateful for its daring. Gradually NILI's influence upon the Yishuv and its institutions spread, including a new wave of enthusiasm among the activists in the Yishuv. The number of NILI members grew. The Hashomer, who knew about NILI's espionage activities, were still divided. Half still saw themselves primarily as protectors of the Yishuv and refused to be involved otherwise. The other half was determined to fight with NILI to the end. . . .

AARON slipped back into Zichron as he had in the past few years. His known absence from the country would have attracted attention and compromised the cause. In fact, he never failed to go to Damascus to see Jamal Pasha.

As he now sat across the desk from Jamal Pasha he noticed the special, almost wild look in his eye. It was now 1918, and the war had escalated. The loss of his men was staggering. Arms being confiscated by the British or retrieved by the Jews was a crushing blow. More and more Turks were being taken prisoners of war by the advancing British, or defecting from the army. And there was the lack of food production.

"*Well,*" he said as he paced the floor, "what is your excuse *this* time, Aaronson? This time you can't say it's because I have jailed your men . . . *why has the production slowed down?*"

Aaron answered without hesitation, "Because you can't squeeze blood from a turnip . . . we're still affected by the locust invasion. It will be at least another year before the crop that has been planted will be ready for harvest. The strain in the country has been devastating, and it shows at the experimental stations too—"

"*Excuses* . . . I'm sick of them. Now you're such a damned smart Jew . . . forgive me, I mean scientist . . . I want some answers. For example, *how do we feed the army?*"

"There is only one way. By buying from the neutral countries."

"Then what are you waiting for?"

"Your permission to travel abroad."

"And with you gone, who is to take over at Athlit for us? That traitor, Absalom Feinberg, went over to the British . . . that's why we're not getting the yield from Hadera . . . I should have hanged him."

Aaron would have liked to have ended Jamal Pasha's ugly life with his bare hands. Very unscientific. He fought not to change his expression, to stay in control. . . . "Nobody is indispensable. I have a very capable man who replaced him. This situation is a little different than before when I said it took brains to provide yields. . . . That still holds true, but you can't fight nature."

Jamal sank down in his chair, "So we have to buy from foreign markets . . ." He sighed deeply. "All right, you have my permission, but do it fast."

Aaron would never tell Jamal Pasha that a shipment was already on its way from Switzerland, that the contacts had been made weeks ago, and that there were men in Greece, Spain and Italy with instructions about at what intervals to deliver the goods.

AT Zichron Aaron found that Sarah had cooked the best Roumanian dinner he had eaten since his mother had died. God rest her soul, he could scarcely believe a year had passed since then. But tonight Aaron was at peace for the first time in so long he wanted to remember the joys she had brought to their lives and not to mourn her loss.

As he sat around the table looking at his brothers, Zvi and Shmuel, who had come back into the fold, then at Alex and his father, his heart was filled. And how thoughtful of Sarah to have included Chavala, Dovid and the children. For the moment, his eyes were on Reuven. Where had the years gone? He remembered the day he witnessed the child's *bris,* and now he was ten . . . it seemed impossible. "Well, Reuven, you're almost ready to become a scientist like your father."

"I just hope I'll be as good," Reuven said, looking at his father.

"I've no doubt . . . and you, Chia? What would you like to be?" She was almost thirteen.

"A teacher, I think."

"Good, that's what we need . . . teachers and scientists. Well, now that we've taken care of the future, I think we should all go into the living room and listen to a little Chopin. Would you do us the honor, Sarah?"

"If I can still remember how to play."

"You'll still remember. And that's also what we need, the sound of Chopin . . ."

After the recital Chavala and Sarah walked the children home. It was long past their bedtime. Sarah listened to Chavala say, "Sleep well, my Reuven . . ." Somehow in Hebrew it sounded so different than in Yiddish. Her mother had always put them to bed with the words, *"Schlaf mit gesund'heit, mein tayere kind."*

Chia kissed Sarah on the cheek and thanked her for the lovely evening. "I had such a wonderful time . . . would you teach me to play the piano?"

Such poignant innocence in the little girl's face. Sarah had to hold back the tears. When would there be time? she wondered . . . "I would love to, Chia."

"When can we start?"

"Soon, dear . . . soon."

Sitting in the front room, Sarah looked about. "It's such a lovely little house, what you've done with it . . . But the children . . . Chavala, you're so blessed . . . if only I had a child," she said, more to herself than Chavala. At least she could speak as a woman to another woman . . . "I still mourn for Absalom. I think about him constantly . . . if only I had his son, the pain would not be so great . . ." Once she'd started she couldn't stop. This was the first time she had spoken openly about him. "But I have my memories. Lord, the things we did. We would ride like the wind, up into the hills of Zichron, and the love between us . . . I still hear the sound of his voice when he read his own poetry to me . . . He was a fine poet, you know. A wonderful man . . ."

Chavala could scarcely answer. "Yes, I know . . ."

Sarah sat there, not speaking, her thoughts on some unknown shallow grave in the Sinai. Getting up slowly, she said, "I am so happy you've come back to Zichron, Chavala."

And Chavala thought to herself, I never wanted to leave, but she answered, "So am I Sarah, so am I . . ."

BACK home, Sarah looked into the living room, saw the men gathered and said a quick goodnight. She wanted to be alone with only one man this night . . .

"*Abba,*" Aaron continued after Sarah had gone off to bed, "I felt the time had come for you to know about NILI. I only hope you understand why I did not tell you more earlier."

The old man still sat in disbelief. "During all the years of this war I ignored the existence of espionage, and the suspicions of the Germans that there were spies among the Jews. I thought it was a despicable, anti-Semitic accusation, but how could I not have known when I worked in the fields of Athlit that my own sons were involved?"

"Because none of them know . . . only the key men."

"I still find it incredible that such a secret should have been so closely kept."

"It was for the good of the Yishuv."

"But if, God forbid, any of you are caught the Yishuv will suffer—"

"No, *abba,* we members of NILI took it on ourselves to do this and we alone will assume the blame, should the time ever come for it."

Ephraim Aaronson was almost mumbling. "I still can't believe that I lived here in Zichron and knew nothing. Why *did* you wait until now to tell me?"

"Because when I leave this time I won't come back until the war is over. You must know . . . you may be questioned . . ."

Ephraim nodded. "How could I have been so stupid, or am I merely growing senile . . . Absalom would never have left Sarah to become a pilot—"

"Yes, *abba,* but that is something only we know. There have been suspicions, though the letters we've arranged for Sarah to receive help make the story plausible."

"I see . . . well, how can I help?"

"Your help is in working with the special committee in allocating money. We have our problems there too. Some of the Zionist organizations aren't too enthusiastic about funds being transferred to the Yishuv by NILI. They want the transfer of funds to go through a special committee of their own in Cairo."

"You mean you're taking the risks, doing the work and they're fighting you? Why?"

"Because, *abba,*" Alex told him, "some of them are afraid Aaron will become too powerful—"

Ephraim was furious. "This isn't politics. Its only purpose is to get information to the British. How dare they accuse Aaron or any of you of such ambitions? Well, enough for tonight. Go to bed, Aaron, I think you need your rest . . . You have a long journey ahead of you. I suppose we all do . . ."

Chapter Nineteen

As the war escalated, it was important that information be gotten at a more rapid pace to British Intelligence in Alexandria.

Although only some three hundred and twenty-five nautical miles separated Port Said from Athlit, they presented the same problems NILI had had since the beginning of the espionage work . . . Only on moonless nights could the ship operate. Good weather and a quiet sea were still necessary. So some other means of communication now had to be found.

A radio link was suggested by Zalman Kishon, but that was considered too risky since the Germans were so sophisticated in breaking codes. Dovid argued that the maritime link be replaced by an air link. But that too was ruled out since the only possible landing site was closely patrolled by the Turks. Sarah, half-seriously, suggested the link between Alexandria and Athlit be not by airplane but homing pigeons.

Aaron consulted a Major Malcolb, an expert on homing pigeons, who said the birds could fly at about one hundred miles an hour, which meant that the distance between Athlit and Port Said could be covered in a little under four hours. Malcolb took over the training of the pigeons. Slowly they were acquainted with their duty, at the same time increasing the distance they could stay away from their dovecote and return to it.

In mid-June the pigeons were put in dovecotes in Athlit and Zichron Yaakov. Three weeks later six pigeons were sent for the first time from Athlit, only one of which reached its destination, this time without any message. Then, two months later, Sarah sent five with a coded message in which she requested the dispatch of the ship *Menagem* on September 10. The next day she sent another five carrying the same message. Four reached their destination, but one was caught on September 3 in the backyard of Ahmad Bey, the governor of Caesarea.

As he was feeding his own pigeons he noticed one didn't belong. He also noticed a feather tied to its foot. He released the feather, and found a message in it. Even though he did not know the message was coded, he was excited by the discovery. He assumed it was the act of spies and immediately contacted the governor of Haifa. The news soon spread to Athlit and the pigeons were quickly killed.

The next day Turkish officials brought the discovered pigeon to Zichron Yaakov and displayed her in a cage in the Graf Hotel. Their hope was that seeing it might encourage some villager to open his mouth. None did.

NILI now had even a graver problem than the damning pigeon. Lieb Schacham was arrested. He had been scouting Turkish military installations, and also had learned that a new Turkish counterattack on Gaza was going to take place between the tenth and fifteenth of the month. He'd tried to hurry back to Athlit, this time traveling southward from Petach Tikvah in order to avoid crossing military guards. So he hadn't followed the seashore but had gone through desert land. Thirst had gotten the better of him, forced him to the ground, where he had promptly been attacked by Arabs, beaten up, his clothes taken away and robbed of all his possessions—including the vital papers and coded messages.

When he was later found by a Turkish soldier he was jailed in Beersheba.

At the first inquiry Lieb denied all connection with any espionage.

General Kers Von Kerstein, hearing that a Jewish spy had been caught, ordered him to be hanged immediately. The Turks, however, wanted to investigate him further and hoped that through torture he would reveal the names of his accomplices. When he still refused to speak the Turks sentenced him to death by hanging.

On September 16 the Turkish authorities announced that on the following morning a Jewish spy would be hanged in the city square and that the public was cordially invited to witness the execution. The hanging did not take place . . . the threat was made in hopes that Lieb would finally give up his secrets—which he *still* refused to do. Once again he was tortured and thrown into the dungeon at Beersheba.

That night Zichron swarmed with a battalion of soldiers. Guards watched every exit of the village. The governor of Haifa, Hamed Bey, gathered together the elders and told them that a network of spies had been found in Zichron, and unless the names of the ringleaders were promptly revealed the Turks would execute one hundred people. A twenty-four-hour ultimatum was given. If they persisted in their stubbornness, not a house or a Jew would be left standing in Zichron.

Terrified by the order, the elders of Zichron debated what to do. The truth, of course, was that until the discovery of the pigeons they knew of no such network of spies.

The spokesman swore on his mother's grave that he had no such knowledge. Governor Hamed Bey called him "a liar, a deceitful scum Jew. . . . You will tell me the truth when we are through with you." The guard was called. "Take him and beat him until he begs us to listen to him condemn his people to death."

His son, who had recently joined NILI, knew that this was only the beginning of his father's torture. All he could think of at this moment was not his safety but his father's life. He went to the authorities and turned himself in. After a punishment that took him beyond the silence he'd pledged himself to, he told the names he knew. His reward was a bullet through the head.

Now, with the information in hand, a systematic roundup began. The prisoners were taken to Nazareth. Fifteen elders were forced to accompany the prisoners of NILI as hostages unless the whereabouts of Aaron Aaronson and Dovid Landau were revealed.

So far, the prisoners taken had either not confessed in spite of the tortures or their innocence had to be assumed, even by the Turks . . . no human being could keep silent under the terrible punishment they'd undergone.

Now Dovid Landau had become the most wanted leader of NILI, both because of who he was and because it was assumed he would know the whereabouts of Aaron Aaronson.

The village was searched. Dovid was nowhere to be found . . . he was hiding in the subterranean vaults at Athlit, almost under the noses of the Turks, listening to soldiers breaking down doors, smashing cabinets, demolishing furniture, and then the crash of glass.

When the experimental station was thoroughly demolished it was suspected that he'd run off to the hills with many other men from NILI. He was not found.

As a last resort Jamal Pasha dispatched soldiers to Chavala and Dovid's house, this time with instructions to intimidate but not molest her. Eventually, he was sure, her husband would try to reach her. After hours of intense, exhausting interrogation she stuck to her denials . . . "I've told you over and over again, I don't know where my husband is, *but* if I did, I wouldn't tell you. You can torture me, kill me, but I will tell you nothing."

They would wait, as instructed. They still needed her alive as a lure to draw her husband . . .

CERTAIN that it was only a matter of time before he was caught, Dovid prayed to be free long enough to accomplish this one last mission . . . At midnight he worked feverishly in the underground vaults with Nachman Shamir and Moses Bartov, taking sacks of gold through the tunnel that connected Athlit to the Crusaders' Castle. When they were finished, Dovid wiped the sweat from his forehead with the back of his hand, then looked at the two men dressed in stolen Turkish uniforms.

"Well," he said, "it seems a long time since we first met at Athlit. You, Nachman, wanted to know that night if you were supposed to twiddle your thumbs."

Nachman managed a smile. "I remember, Dovid. You said we wouldn't have time for that, and you were right."

Dovid nodded. "And you, Moses Bartov, the Shomer from Galilee

. . . you have been a real friend. Now, get the gold loaded into the wagon, you have your instructions which kibbutzim they're to be hidden in. *Shalom.*"

After the men had gone Dovid thought back to that first meeting, marveling that any of them had survived. Well, that was what Jews did best . . .

He crawled back through the tunnel, waited in the vault and listened for any sounds above. He had no way of knowing how much time had passed, but when he felt, hoped it was safe, he cautiously slid back the trapdoor and peered out. Even through that tiny slit he could tell the Turks had been here, could see their ugly trail of devastation. Quickly he lifted himself up and secured the trapdoor.

There was no time for fear. Tonight he had to rendezvous with the *Menagem.* He crawled through the high grass, then along the seawall until he reached the appointed place. He took the small flashlight from his back pocket, lay down on his stomach and signaled the code . . . S-A-L-A-N-E-H I-S A S-I-L-L-Y W-O-M-A-N S-H-E L-A-U-G-H-S. Then he lay very still, waiting for the message to be decoded.

Chaim, his face collapsed in grief, handed Lieutenant Ian Smith the translation. *Salaneh* was NILI . . . *Silly* meant exposed . . . *Woman* was captured . . . *She Laughs* was gold is safe. There was a hush aboard, but this was not the time for mourning.

Quickly the motor started and the *Menagem* made a run for it . . .

Dovid took a deep breath when he heard the sound of the ship going off in the distance, then he waited and listened for still another sound. He'd been through this act so many times he could almost predict when the Turkish patrol would come and go. He heard them pass. He got up and ran from rock to rock until he was almost within arm's reach of the Crusaders' Castle, where, as expected, he was captured by four Turkish soldiers . . .

First he was beaten with the butt of a gun, then kicked when he fell to the ground. To hell with the pain, he willed himself to stand up. His right eye was swollen shut, he felt the blood running down the side of his face. But at least he walked as he was taken off to prison.

THE two-by-four cell was barely large enough to accommodate his body. He sat against the wall, not even able to stretch his legs. Each time he shifted, the pain in his head became excruciating and his bruised body ached almost beyond endurance. As he sat in the dark, there was little else to do except contemplate what would happen to him. Finally, the heavy metal door swung open.

"Stand up."

He did, with great effort, and was led by a guard down the narrow passages, past the death row cells, until they reached an iron gate. Another guard unlocked it. The clang of the ancient metal bolt sounded to Dovid like giant cymbals being clashed together. He wanted to put his hands over his ears, but he was prodded by the butt of a gun down another corridor, to be shoved into an interrogation room.

Hamed Bey motioned to the guard, and Dovid was pushed into a chair.

"What were you doing at the Crusaders' Castle early this morning?"

"I was out for a stroll—"

"Don't try your stupid heroics on me . . . I know you're terrified . . . what were you doing? . . . I will give you one minute to answer."

"I'm a Jew, why would you believe me?"

"Jews are cowards. Little as it's worth, *you* value your life, and I understand you have a wife and child . . . *now,* your minute's running out."

"The truth is, I was a little restless tonight. I enjoy watching the water, it calms me down—"

"Enough nonsense. I know you're the head of NILI. Guard, take him out."

Dovid was beaten and thrown back into the windowless cell. Again he sat in the dark. He remembered the day he dedicated himself to the survival of his people. He heard the echoes of his own voice come back to him, from that night in Aaron's laboratory when he'd said, "Every man has his breaking point . . ." So far, thank God, he hadn't come to his, nor had, so far as he knew, the other seven who had sworn on the Bible that night. He was proud to have been a part of that group, proud of the recruits who were no less dedicated, just less prepared. He did not blame the young man, recently sworn into NILI, who had gone back on his oath to save his father. How could he?

Once again the heavy iron door opened, and once again he was all but dragged down the stone passageway, but this time to a waiting room. Pushed into a chair, he looked at the man behind the desk. Jamal Pasha, no less.

Pasha ignored Dovid for what seemed like an eternity.

"Well, we meet again, Landau, and under unfortunate circumstances. For you. The last time you were in my office I was most hospitable. You smoked my cigarettes and drank my coffee. You also were given an opportunity to look at some very important plans. Now, after all that, I think it only fair that you oblige me with Aaronson's whereabouts."

"I've no more idea than you do."

Jamal Pasha recalled too well the way he'd been tricked into letting this Jew go, how he'd underestimated him. "That's strange, Landau, since I know you're always in contact with him. Well, as you know, I'm a patient man, but there is a limit. Now, once again, I ask you, where is Aaronson?"

"I repeat, I do not know."

Jamal Pasha poured a large glass of water from a pitcher, took a sip, then let it stand on the desk.

Dovid had had nothing to drink or to eat for two days. He said nothing.

"Where is Aaronson?"

Dovid only shrugged.

Jamal Pasha got up from his desk and slapped Dovid across the face so hard that the chair in which he sat almost toppled over. Then: "Guards, take him out of my sight. I assure you, Landau, that when we are through, you'll beg us to kill you."

He was almost right . . .

BY now all of Zichron was put in a quarantine, and every man, woman and child received punishment. Rations were a cup of water per person a day. No one was to leave his house under penalty of death . . .

Chavala was singled out, taken off to jail and tortured when she refused to tell about Dovid's involvement in NILI. When she sufficiently recovered she was asked again and again, "What was your husband's position? What did he do? What were his plans . . . ?"

There were times she almost faltered, but somehow her mind ruled her body as she kept repeating to herself, *They can only kill me once . . . only once . . . only once . . .*

Abruptly she s sent home. Jamal Pasha had decided she was still too valuable as a tool to break down her husband's resistance. He would not kill her. Not yet.

LIEB Schacham was finally to be executed. He had still not talked. When he stood on the scaffold with the rope around his neck, he called out

"NILI! *Netzah Yisroel Lo Ishkahem!* Israel's perpetuity shall never forget thee!"

NACHMAN Shamir and Eliave Yitzchak were escorted to the main square in Damascus, where the gallows had been set up. Nachman told the crowd, "You are near your end, we will liberate our country. We will not betray our true homeland. We are liberating Palestine. Very soon the Turks will be driven out of our land. We, NILI's men, have dug a grave for you. While you are busy hanging our people, the British have entered our Holy City of Jerusalem, your army is running without a battle. On the day of my death, I send you a curse from the bottom of my heart. Be damned forever . . ."

WHEN the Turkish guards came to take Sarah's father and brothers, she received them calmly.

They forced her to watch as old Ephraim and her brothers were beaten on the bare soles of their feet. When she could stand it no longer she told them, "It was *me*, I started NILI . . . I am its real head . . . I started it and I will end it. Please . . . if you have any decency, in the name of your Allah, let my father go . . ."

The old man was "released" from the room, to be taken off to his death when he was out of Sarah's sight.

Sarah had sealed her death warrant. First she was beaten, her fingernails were pulled out, hot rocks were put under her armpits. For three days and nights she screamed out her pain in the black, windowless cell.

When the cell door was finally opened she was ready. At her sentencing she said, "It's customary in civilized countries that the prisoner be granted a last wish. You are civilized people."

"What is your request?"

"To be allowed to go home for a change of clothes. I do not wish to meet my God as I look now."

The inquisitor grimaced. Only a stupid Jewess would think of such a thing, but, as she said, they *were* a civilized people. "Granted."

Sarah was taken in chains through the streets of Zichron. When they arrived she was, after pleading, permitted to go to her room alone.

She locked herself in her bedroom, opened the dresser drawer and took out the small pearl-handled revolver she had carried with her when she left Constantinople.

Strange she thought, I took this for protection . . . Well, that's what it will be used for. Without hesitation, Sarah put it into her mouth and pulled the trigger.

A soldier rushed up the stairs and broke down the door, where he found Sarah unconscious. Beside her lay the small pistol. Her pulse still beat weakly when the soldier felt it. He looked at the blood oozing from her mouth. Knowing how angry Jamal Pasha would be at being derpvied of her hanging, the soldier immediately sent for a doctor.

After an injection she regained consciousness. "For God's sake, kill me, I can't stand any more . . ." She continued to beg for a lethal potion, cursed the Turkish commander, the governor, and especially the police officer, Osman Bey, who had tortured her. For two days she lay paralyzed but semiconscious.

Finally, blessed death came to release her.

Chapter Twenty

Dovid lay on the stone floor. Chavala had been brought to see him, in the hope that her pleading would break his spirit. When they were left briefly alone she had said, "Dovid, please, what will you accomplish now by not revealing where Aaron is? He's beyond reach in Alexandria, so how can you hurt him? *Please*, Dovid. Save yourself . . ."

"Chavala, don't be taken in by the Turks. Even if Aaron were to come back they would still hang me. At least I can die knowing I've betrayed no one. I want our son to know and never forget that I had something to do with the miracle that has happened to our people here. Just know that I love you, dearest Chavala. I have since the day I first knew you . . ."

How long ago, he now wondered, had it been since he'd seen Chavala and said those words? He had no idea. He had no idea what day or what date it was. The beatings had stopped, and now they were using starvation as their last resort. Well, it would soon be over, he almost looked forward to the day of his execution. He only hoped he would have the strength to go to the gallows saying the words, *Netzah Yisroel Lo Yshaker,* Israel's eternity shall not die. And then call out, "Long live NILI!"

DOVID could not know that the British—thanks in part to the information he had furnished—had broken through the Turkish lines, demolishing them, and had dug in. The decisive offensive of the Allies began, and within two weeks the whole of northern Palestine was taken from the Turks.

The prisons were emptied . . .

When the iron door of Dovid's cell was opened by a soldier in khaki shorts, he thought his mind was playing games with him. He was sure he was hallucinating as he lay in the corner of his cell . . . staring, afraid to move.

But the soldier, fantasy or not, came to his side and helped him up. Dovid braced himself unsteadily against the wall.

"It's all over, mate, you walk out any time you like. Good luck, I'd say we got here just in time."

Still unable to take it in, Dovid managed to get out, "What happened?"

"It's all over, chum, we beat them proper."

Dovid slid down the cold stone wall. He finally knew that he was alive . . . and would be going home to Chavala . . .

The litterbearers came for him.

"All right, old chap, we're going to have you attended to right away. From the looks of it, you haven't had a decent meal in a century or so."

Dovid could still not believe it, he'd lived in darkness and fear for so long he was suspicious even now . . . "Where are you taking me?"

"Just lay back, we'll have you good as new in no time. You'll like the hospital we're taking you to—"

"How long do you think I'll have to be there?"

"Oh, maybe three to four weeks."

"What day is this?"

"It's *Armistice Day,* November 11, and in case you're confused about the year, it's 1918."

CHAVALA was holding a basket of wash in her hands when she looked down the road and saw a man approaching.

The change in Dovid would have made him unrecognizable to anyone else, but she *knew* . . . Dropping the basket, she ran to him, and without a word they fell into each other's arms.

That night, as she lay beside her husband, she thought her heart would break when she touched the once strong limbs that were now almost fleshless. She held him to her. She would nurse him back to health. To life.

ALL at once the world had changed. The fighting men of Zion had returned, and a miracle of miracles to Chavala, Moishe, gone so long she had been afraid it would be forever, came home a week later. But in his eyes were the scars of battle, and with them a new bitterness, so foreign to the exuberant Moishe whom she had always known and who had gone off to war with such high spirits and optimism.

When she tried to talk to him about it, he at first only shook his head and said nothing. It was not that he'd found out that Aaron had been in London and not come to see him. He had been upset about that for a while, but later he understood that Aaron had had no opportunity to see him, that he'd had word that he was recovering from his wounds and had the priority of contact with the British for all their sakes. No, it was something more subtle, and more difficult to express or even fully understand. He was a young man grown old too quickly. He had been as dedicated to and sure of their mission as Dovid, but he was too young to sustain that feeling in the face of the violence and death . . . He was a romantic, and like most romantics he was more easily hurt by the ugliness of the way men could treat each other. He wasn't really a hater. He couldn't accept the awfulness of the way the Turks and Germans and Arabs had treated the Jews. And especially the British, he had seen how they had mistreated the Jewish soldiers like himself who were, after all, on *their* side. Who then was left? Where? He remembered his sister Chavala's talk about America. Could it be there . . . ?

Dvora's husband Ari had come back, but Sheine had gone to Berlin.

The war had taken its toll on all of them, Chavala thought, but thank God they were *alive* . . .

Chapter Twenty-one

THE BRITISH WOULD be given the mandate through the League of Nations to protect Palestine, and the Yishuv felt for the first time that they were in the hands of a friend. They had fought with the British, had died for the British, and now would be rewarded by them. The dream was to get on with the building of their lives, in peace.

The grand dream was short-lived. Under the British, the Jews found the restrictions almost as difficult as under the Turks. They were not the cruel overlords that the Turks had been, but the restrictions were nearly as severe. It seemed, in fact, that the British favored the Arabs, and looked the other way at Arab attacks on the Jews. Worse . . . Jews were still not permitted to carry arms, Arabs were.

The Mufti, Haj Amin el Husseini, had been appointed to rule Jerusalem, next only to Mecca and Medina in importance as a holy Moslem city. He had been appointed on the pretext of restraining a religious war as he propagandized that the Jews were going to desecrate the holy shrines in old Jerusalem.

Jewish lives were once again in constant jeopardy.

When Moishe came home one night from being beaten up in an Arab ambush, Chavala made up her mind. This time she would *not* be put off . . .

"Dovid, we've waited a long, long time. The war is over. Remember, we have those jewels. It's time, Dovid . . . we're going to America. This is a country of barbarians, I won't live here any longer. There's no reason for any of us to. You've made your sacrifice . . . we *all* have . . ."

"After all we've been through, Chavala, in your heart, can you really abandon the dream of Eretz Yisroel that, as you say, we *all* sacrificed for?"

"Yes. Dovid, what will we do here? Live on a kibbutz? Zichron Yaakov no longer exists for me. I still hear the wailing, the screaming . . . there's the smell of death here. Where will we go?"

"I can get a job with the Zionist Agency, the need to work for our people is even greater . . ."

"The need . . . it will be here for a thousand years, with us or without us. I can't give my life to a hopeless dream any longer. *No.* And you must not either. Come to America, where we can live like human beings, with our *family.*"

Dovid sat there, his face buried in his hands. The moment had come, there was no putting it or her off any longer . . . But there had to be a reason they had survived, and in his heart he knew . . . as he had always known . . . he could not abandon this land. Yet how could he give up Chavala? She too was his life . . .

Chavala looked at him, knowing the struggle going on inside him.

Finally she said quietly, "Dovid, we've done it your way. At least give mine a chance . . . try, Dovid . . . for all our sakes."

"What would I do in America?"

"I don't know, but let us at least try."

He looked closely at his wife. "Chavala, I said it in jail, I've said it to myself every day I've known you. I love you. You are my wife. I want us to spend the rest of our life together. But I can't live with you if I can't live with myself. I *have* to stay. Tell me, Chavala, what's right?"

"I wish I knew, Dovid. I love you too, you *know* that . . . but I *cannot* stay here. If I did, I would soon be a woman you would not want as your wife. Maybe we are both chasing after dreams that can never come true . . . who knows, maybe the dream I have now will not be what I want. Only time will work that out. But we both must have the chance to find out."

Moishe spoke up. "I feel the way Chavala does, Dovid. We've talked about it, I want to go with her . . . I'm sorry . . ."

Dovid sighed, nodded. For a moment he wondered if he *could* bring himself to leave, but he knew in his heart that in the end the differences between them would tear them apart.

There was nothing left to say.

"When will you leave?"

"As soon as I can, it's the best way . . ." She went to him, held him close. "We've been through hell together, you and I, but this is the worst of all. I love you, Dovid, with all my heart, my soul. I only pray that what we do will somehow justify what we are giving up."

DVORA, Raizel and their husbands had come to wish Chavala, Moishe, Reuven and Chia a safe journey. Each wondered if he or she would see one another again. America and Eretz Yisroel were so far apart. The sisters cried, then walked away, leaving Chavala and Dovid alone.

Chavala clung to Dovid, and he to her. "I'll write," she said, then forced a smile . . . "and please don't be afraid to change your mind." The smile vanished. "And if you need me, Dovid, I'll come back."

If he needed her? *I need you now, Chavala. Now.*

For a moment she wanted to change her mind, to say, *My place is with you Dovid. I'm willing to forget what I want, what I deeply believe is best for our family. You're my husband.*

But then the boarding call came.

They looked at each other and kissed, and then she turned and walked up the gangway to join Moishe, Chia and Reuven. She stood at the rail, watched Dovid below. He looked up at her. They did not take their eyes from each other.

Now the ship was moving out into the harbor, farther and farther . . . until Chavala, his beloved son, Chia and Moishe were finally lost to view. Lost . . . ?

Dovid turned and walked quickly away.

America
1920

Chapter Twenty-two

ON THE DAY Chavala and her family arrived New York had its worst blizzard in ten years.

She was totally unprepared. As they stood freezing in their thin clothes Chavala's mind shifted back. If they'd survived the winters in Russia, survived the pogroms, survived the brutality of the war, then, by God, they would survive this. Unless they froze to death first . . .

Quickly she gathered the children together and they trudged ankle-deep in the snow down Delancey Street until they found a delicatessen. With chattering teeth they seated themselves at a table.

Chia and Reuven could not stop trembling. They had never experienced such penetrating cold.

In Yiddish Mrs. Neusbaum asked, *"Nu,* so what would you like?"

Reuven looked at his mother. He had never heard this strange-sounding tongue. In Hebrew he said, "What did she say?"

Chavala answered back, "The lady would like to know what we want to eat."

This was a frightening and strange world. It was not at all what his mother had told him to expect. He was even more confused and upset than the day he'd left his father standing on the dock in Jaffa. He looked around at the hanging salamis and the glass counters filled with slabs of corned beef, smoked salmon, barrels of herring, dill pickles. Bagels and rye bread and rolls were stacked on the counter. Suddenly he wasn't hungry. "I don't want anything."

Chavala too well understood what was bothering him. This was not, after all, Palestine. It was not *home* . . . everything was so foreign to him.

211

No matter how she had tried to explain the reasons she had left his father, nothing would appease him. But, she told herself, he was still a little boy, one day he would understand that it was only here she would be able to secure their lives. Where they could find their lives . . . What did a child know about building a future free from hunger and poverty, and death . . . ? One day, though, he would understand . . . she devoutly hoped . . .

"*Nu . . . ?*" said the rotund Mrs. Neusbaum.

Chavala said to the family in Hebrew, "I'll order, you'll like it." To Mrs. Neusbaum in Yiddish she then said, "We'll have the dinner."

"Barley soup or noodle?"

Reuven watched the fat lady's lips move.

"The noodle, and the roast chicken."

"For the appetizer, gefilte fish or chopped liver?"

"The chopped liver . . . is that all right with you, Moishe?"

"Only if it's like mama used to make." He smiled.

Reuven was shocked that his uncle Moishe could also speak this strange-sounding language. He sat back awkwardly and observed the small plate of liver with a crater of chicken *shmaltz* in the center of the mound, with the smell of dill pickles and green tomatoes.

He tasted a spoonful of the soup and let it grow cold.

Chavala noticed and did not urge him. He didn't even try the chicken, the *kugel* or the *tzimmes* that lay on the heavy white plate. Well, he would get used to the food, as he would everything else . . . *New* beginnings, always the most difficult . . . But for a moment she recalled her own discontent in Galilee, and then pushed aside the comparisons. The past, it seemed, never let one rest . . .

In Hebrew Moishe said, "I haven't had such a good old-fashioned meal since . . . well, since you and I were children."

"You like it, Chia?"

"It was fine, I just wish we could get *warm.*"

All Reuven heard Chia say was that she liked the food. At this moment he wasn't too fond of her. If she gave their mother the impression she was pleased with everything then he wouldn't have an ally. He knew if Chia and he didn't stand shoulder to shoulder his protests alone would never get *ema* to return to Palestine. Yes . . . he was terribly annoyed with Chia, not to mention his mother and his uncle.

After they had finished eating Chavala told Mrs. Neusbaum, "We just arrived, maybe you could tell us where to stay?"

Reuven felt as though he were on an island listening to his mother and the fat lady speaking.

"Where are you from?" Mrs. Neusbaum asked, wiping her hand on the white apron.

"Palestine."

The woman sighed. "When we left Russia, that's where I wanted to go, to Eretz Yisroel, but my husband thought different, so we're here in the *goldeneh medina. A groisse glick.*"

Life was strange, thought Chavala, just the reverse of Dovid and her, except Mrs. Neusbaum didn't leave her husband . . . enough, already, with the guilt . . .

"You didn't miss so much. It's better here." As though she could tell. But Chavala remembered the echoes of the terrifying sounds that came from Turkish beatings . . . the awful *fear* . . . "Now tell me . . . where is there a place we can stay?"

"Three blocks from here Mrs. Zuckerman has a rooming house. Here, I'll write down the address." Chavala said, "This is very kind of you, Mrs. . . ."

"Neusbaum . . ."

"Nice to meet you, Mrs. Neusbaum, and again, thank you."

"What's to thank? Listen, I was in the same boat once."

Chavala smiled, then said to the family, "You wait here, I'll go take a look."

Although Mrs. Neusbaum could not speak Hebrew, still, she knew enough from the Bible to catch a word. "It's a nice clean place, take my word."

"I'm sure, but you're sure she has a room?"

"She'll *make* a room."

"Come, we'll go then," Chavala said to the family, and to Mrs. Neusbaum, "how much do I owe you?"

Her fingers added up the amount, and then she deducted ten percent. As Chavala took out the money she glanced at Reuven. He still hadn't eaten a thing. "Maybe I should buy a little something to *nosh* on later . . . give me four strudel and a dozen cookies."

With the bag in her hand she said, *"Shalom."*

Lovely sounding word, thought Mrs. Neusbaum. *"Shalom* to you too, and come back." . . .

Mrs. Zuckerman had only one room in the attic. It was cold and the snow came in between the eaves from the shingles that had blown off the roof. But Chavala told herself that for a night they could put up with it. Be grateful for it . . . she told herself, for a night they could put up with it.

Chavala asked Mrs. Zuckerman if maybe she had a little heater? No, Mrs. Zuckerman was sorry but that she didn't have. "That's all right. Maybe you can bring a few extra blankets?"

"That I got."

"Thank you, and if you have some newspapers we can use it to keep out of the snow."

Sure, the Yiddish *Forward,* she had plenty of old copies.

From Mrs. Zuckerman's basement Moishe brought up two extra cots and an orange crate to stand on while plugging up the hole in the ceiling.

Chavala was now ready to assess the day. It had been a *very* big beginning. They all undressed under the covers and slipped into their night clothes.

Moishe was instantly asleep, as was Chia, but Chavala lay in the dark waiting to hear Reuven's even breathing. What she heard was the munching of cookies and strudel. She smiled. He had deliberately not eaten and now, of course, was famished. Moishe as a little boy for some reason had also refused to eat, she remembered . . . what had mama said or done that seemed so important at the time? Chavala couldn't recall, but children, she *knew,* punished their mothers by not eating . . . at least until the stomach took over. She heard the soft crunch again and almost laughed out loud. If Reuven had known she deliberately left the bag at the side of his bed he most certainly would not have touched its contents.

MRS. Zuckerman and Mrs. Neusbaum were Chavala's Baedeker to America.

America the Beautiful was not quite the utopia Chavala had envisioned. What she found was a three-room flat on the fifth floor in an old tenement building on Ludlow Street. The paint was chipped and pitted from twenty years of wear. The plaster that had fallen from the ceiling exploded the lath. The linoleum was patched in a dozen different places and a dozen different colors, not exactly a lovely mosaic. The rooms were dark and looked out to the crumbling building next door. In the alley below she could smell the fermenting garbage coming from the overflowing cans. The porcelain in the sink had worn away and the communal bathroom was down the hall.

Still, they had lived in places as bad as this. It was surely no worse than the hovel in Jerusalem. She was not complaining. It didn't require great insight to know what Moishe, Chia and Reuven were thinking as they looked about. Chavala walked from the dark kitchen to the equally dark bedrooms, inspecting their mansion. With head high and conviction in her voice she said, "When we fix it up, it will be *very* nice."

"Not even God could make it very nice," Moishe said, grimacing.

"God is not a painter. Tomorrow that becomes our profession. You'll see, when I make curtains and . . ." Suddenly she remembered she didn't have a machine. "Don't *worry,* I'll make it look nice." So who was she trying to convince? Herself?

"Why do we have to take this place, *ema?*" Reuven asked almost in tears.

Of course, thought Chavala, he wanted their lovely little house in Zichron, with the colorful batik hangings on the walls. "Because for the moment we can't afford better . . . in time, Reuven." In time . . .

Moishe agreed with Reuven. "Chavala, let's look around, maybe for a few dollars more we can find a better place—"

"I said I couldn't afford it, Moishe." Chavala let some irritation into her voice. He was questioning her, setting a bad example for Reuven, and she didn't like it. It hurt family morale.

"What do you mean, you can't afford it?"

She should never have told Moishe about the little bag of gems. Not that she didn't trust him. He was, after all, her brother, but it was a temptation to spend and had to be resisted.

"I don't ever want you to mention that again. Forget we have them. That's our only security . . . now we'll go eat."

But the next day, behind the closed bedroom door, Chavala took out two small diamonds, put them safely in her purse and left the house.

She found three jewelers on Mott Street. Before selling them she had all three appraise them and found that each had offered a different amount. When she sold them to the one who had offered her the most money she went away with the feeling he had maybe cheated her. But what did she know about diamonds? Well . . . when they got more settled she would make it a point to find out . . .

With the money she bought furniture at Grossman's secondhand store. Paint and brushes, a mop, a pail, and linens and pots and dishes, the essentials to start a home.

But first she outfitted the family with winter clothes and filled the larder. A person needed three things. A roof over one's head, food in one's stomach, and clothes to keep warm with.

After the flat was freshly painted and furnished, she was quite proud of it. Moishe, however, did not share her enthusiasm. "It's so dark, like living in Jerusalem—"

"No, it's not like living in Jerusalem. We don't have a stone wall surrounding us here and we don't have to worry if the Arabs will kill us."

"It's still a ghetto, Chavala, without any fences."

"You want to live in a better place? Go get a fine paying job and you'll live better."

"I got a job."

"Mazel tov . . . doing what?"

"Delivering clothes for a tailor."

"So in no time at all you'll be able to move uptown."

"With the jewelry we could start a little business . . ."

"Ahh . . . I know, that's been burning a hole in your pocket since I told you . . . but Moishe, my dear brother, you have to crawl before you can walk. When the time comes that's what I'll do . . . I'm not married to this flat. I can move anytime I can afford it. Now if you don't mind, I must write a letter to Dovid."

> Dear Dovid,
>
> What can I say to you? That I am happy without you? No. I miss you the way I did when you sent me to Jerusalem. If only you could see how beautiful this country is, and the opportunities are endless. Dovid, my dearest, please just come for a visit. Reuven misses you so. Moishe has gotten a very good job and in the next day or so I will find something to do. I just pray that you will see how much better our life together would be here. Will you at least try to come and see for yourself? I trust you're well and I thank God that some of the family are with you. It would be too much to ask that they come here also. At least you take care of yourself, and know how much I love you.
>
> *Chavala*

DURING the day Dovid found little time to think about his life. It was the nights, the long endless nights that overwhelmed him with loneliness . . . He knew the reasons Chavala had gone to America, knew them by heart, but it still didn't make it any easier for him to live with. Beyond all else he loved her, but in his heart he couldn't quite forgive her. What Chavala hadn't understood was that Dvora and Raizel were happy here. And all he wanted was what he already had. Except for her . . . and to work for a land that Jews could at last call their own. Chavala didn't seem to understand that the quality of life wasn't built on dollars, and what she seemed to understand even less was that no matter what, a wife stayed with her husband. She had married him, knowing what he wanted . . . well, that wasn't quite fair, was it? He had married her knowing that her dreams looked to America. Both had misjudged, or maybe under-estimated, the other . . . She had hoped he would give in to her, and he . . . be honest . . . had hoped and even expected she would give up her idea of America and stay to be part of *his* dream . . . But when he looked back to those tranquil years in Zichron before the war he would have bet his soul that she would never leave. If it hadn't been for the damned war, they would have stayed together . . .

He had gone round and round on this . . . the war *had* come and nothing could change the fact of *that* . . . Holding Chavala's letter in his hand brought tears to his eyes. It was so full of bravado, you didn't need to read between the lines. For her to bend to him would mean unhappi-ness for her . . . she had always disliked Palestine. And if she disliked it before she would feel the same under the British. But one day, he dared to hope, she would come back. This land would be *theirs*. Meanwhile, the waiting . . . could they survive it . . . ?

Dovid sat with the letter in his hand for a very long time. Chavala was not to blame. It was just that he could not stop loving Palestine . . . no matter what . . . Not the past hardships nor the present ones could force him to leave this land. And his life here was changing . . . he'd turned from farming to politics. Officially. He now was involved with the Zionist Agency. His dream was his life. He could only pray that one day it would somehow be Chavala's too . . .

THE weather in New York was as unpredictable as human nature. One day a blizzard, the next lovely as spring. Today was such a day. Unfortu-nately the lovely spring weather did not make Chavala exactly overjoyed. A week ago she had outfitted the family with heavy winter coats and overshoes, and now it was too warm. Again she sold a tiny gem, but this time it was an emerald. Shockingly, she found that the emerald was more valuable than the diamond. Well, she was going to find out once and for all how much the contents in that red Moroccan pouch were worth. But first things first.

After buying suitable clothes for Chia and Reuven, she enrolled them in school.

Now her day began in earnest. With one diamond, a ruby and an emerald secure in her coin purse she pinned the leather pouch to her camisole and walked to the diamond district. And, with each step, she felt an unaccountable quickening in her heart . . . as though she were walking not just for a matter of the moment but smack into the beginning of her future . . .

Chapter Twenty-three

She walked up the Bowery and then to Canal Street. Mostly the district was wholesale. The jewelry sold retail was to the *goyim*.

Not knowing one from the other, Chavala walked into the first store she came to. Carefully she took out the stones and handed them to the jeweler, watched closely as he picked up his loupe, and examined them. After he had given her a price she thanked him very much and left. She wasn't going to take his word, never mind the *yarmulke* on his head. He looked a little like the jeweler in Odessa.

After seeing six rather impatient jewelers, Chavala realized she wasn't as rich as she thought. Nonetheless, when she touched the pouch still pinned to her camisole her spirits lifted. At least they were worth something, they wouldn't starve. Quickly she pushed away any disturbing thoughts and walked up one crowded street and down another.

Breathlessly she looked up at the building she was standing in front of and saw the name of a wholesale jeweler. For no special reason her eyes lingered on "Leibowitz: Wholesale & Manufacturing."

She walked inside and looked at the list of names on the directory. She pressed the button and waited for the ancient elevator to come down. When it came to an unsteady halt she got inside the cagelike contraption and pushed number 4.

As the door of the elevator opened and she ventured out, Chavala hadn't noticed that the floor and the platform didn't meet, and as she stepped over the threshold she twisted her ankle. For a brief moment the pain made her lean against the wall. Was this an omen of things to come? She quickly admonished herself and discarded such superstitious thoughts . . .

Favoring her left foot, she limped down the hall until she stood in front of number 422. A deep breath, open the door, go in. She saw four or five women stringing beads, and beyond a glass enclosure maybe four bearded men in *yarmulkes* examining stones with their loupes. A grinding noise and the sound of water came from the extreme back, but all she could make of the strange object was it apparently had something to do with making jewelry.

Mr. Leibowitz looked beyond his glass-partitioned office and saw Chavala. Getting up from his desk he walked toward her and stood behind a showcase.

"Yes, my dear lady, what can I do for you?"

Chavala smiled . . . winningly, she hoped . . . at the man with the kind eyes and the silver hair, which contrasted with the black *yarmulke*. He was slightly stooped from the years, she imagined, of bending over a workbench.

"My name is Chavala Landau."

"That's nice, and I'm Mr. Leibowitz. Now what can I do for you?"

"I wonder if I might speak to you?"

"About what?"

". . . I want to become a jeweler."

"You know from this business?"

"No."

He shook his head and laughed. "My dear young lady, to become a jeweler you have to learn and it takes a long time and then even after you think you know, you find out you don't know so much."

In spite of his sweetness, Chavala knew she was not going to get a job unless she spoke to him privately and quietly.

"Mr. Leibowitz, if I could just have a little of your time I would appreciate it."

The old man looked at the young woman more closely. The soft but resolute voice, the direct glance . . . she was more than just very attractive . . . there was something that Mr. Leibowitz found beguiling, compelling . . . "Come into my office."

He wiped off the chair with his handkerchief. Chavala sat down across from him.

As she began to speak he suddenly knew why he was so taken with her. He silently wished her a long life, but she reminded him of his daughter who had died of polio five years ago. The thought was still as painful as though it had happened yesterday. He kept silent for a moment as his eyes grew dim, then he swallowed hard.

"Tell me, Chavala Landau, from where do you come?"

"From Palestine."

Palestine . . . What Jew hadn't dreamed of Eretz Yisroel? "You were born there?"

"No . . . Russia . . . in a small village near Odessa."

He shook his head as his thoughts moved back in time. Minsk . . . Poland . . . Odessa, all the same, for a Jew no place was good. But it was easier being a Jew in New York. At least you could walk down a street. No one knocked down your door in the middle of the night and killed you or took you to prison, gouged out your eyes, pulled out your hair. No armband of shame. "How did you happen to settle in Eretz Yisroel?"

"My father, may his soul rest in peace, wanted to live and die there."

"Yes . . . yes . . . How long did you live in Eretz Yisroel?"

Chavala thought of the body buried under the cherry tree. "We left Russia in 1906, I just came here a few weeks ago."

Remembering the money he had sent through his organization, he sighed. "You were there during the war, then . . . it was bad, no?"

Now her thoughts went back, to Jerusalem. She could almost feel the hunger pains . . . see the begging in the streets and the dead bodies in front of the Jaffa gate waiting to be taken away. "War is not so easy, Mr. Leibowitz. It was bad . . ."

No, war was not easy. The irony of it all, he thought . . . he had run away from the old country so he wouldn't have to serve in the army for twenty-five years, which was the penalty for being born a Jew, and his American-born son came back from the war without legs . . . "How were things when you left Eretz Yisroel?"

"Not really better than when the Turks were in control. The British are about as bad, they just seem a little more civilized."

He nodded. "So now that you're here, what does your husband do?"

What did her husband do? *He is very unhappy because he had the misfortune to have married the wrong woman.* A woman who did not stay by his side . . . "My husband still lives in Palestine . . . in Tel Aviv. He works for the Zionist Agency."

The sadness did not escape him. And in his eyes Chavala saw no censure. "You mean you're alone here?"

"No. My brother and one sister came with me, and I have a little boy."

"You'll forgive for asking, it's not really any of my business, and if you don't want, you don't have to tell, but how is it you left your husband?"

A very good question—a question to which Chavala wasn't so sure now, if she ever was, she had all the answers . . . "Mr. Leibowitz, I became responsible for my family when I was sixteen"—and Chavala thought of the night Chia was born—"I knew then that my life did not belong just to me. I have three sisters who need help, and a brother. I will *not* allow them to live out their lives in poverty, and it takes money to make that not happen. And there are nephews and nieces who have to be educated . . . You maybe want to know why I want to get into the jewelry business? Well, Mr. Leibowitz, a small pair of my mother's diamond earrings was able to buy us a little safety. At least away from the pogroms," she said as her hand felt the pouch pinned to her camisole, "and a few little stones bought us passage here to America . . ."

She had almost killed a Bedouin, not for the stones, but maybe it was God's sign . . . his giving her the *chance* for more life . . . Her mind shifted back to Mr. Leibowitz's first question. "I love my husband very much, and he loves me, but we can't melt into each other's mind and body just because we are husband and wife. I want to secure my family and he loves the land. *His* land. Our needs, dreams are so different, somehow we haven't been able to fit them together . . ."

Mr. Leibowitz shook his head, two people with a child couldn't find a way? He heard what she had just told him but still . . . "How long can a man and woman be apart?" He said it kindly.

"As long as it takes."

"That could be years—"

"How many men came from the old country and left their wives and children? I guess you could say this isn't so different, just a little reversed? Because I'm a woman, it seems strange. If I were a widow, God forbid, no one would ask. But in this life, Mr. Leibowitz, we are called on to make a few sacrifices and I don't find mine—or Dovid's—any more tragic than other people's. It's . . . it's the way it is . . ."

Mr. Leibowitz took out his handkerchief, lifted the wire-rimmed glasses, wiped his eyes and blew his nose. For a moment he sat with his thoughts.

And Chavala sat with hers too . . . here she'd been talking about her personal life to a total stranger she'd met only twenty minutes ago. Strange . . . unless there really was a destiny directing poor humans . . . after all, was it *just* chance that she had looked up at *his* window? And that she'd been drawn to his place?

"Well, Chavala, you said you wanted to be a jeweler. You seem a fine young woman, I will be very honest with you. Some people get very rich in this business, but most just make a living. You're not a jeweler and—"

"But a person can learn."

"True. A person can learn to sell shoes, but a jeweler is born. It's handed down from father to son."

"I won't argue with you, Mr. Leibowitz"—destiny seemed to be abandoning her—"but somehow I'll learn."

Chavala's courage, determination impressed Mr. Leibowitz. "I don't know why, but I have a feeling about you." He glanced up at the clock on the wall. It was time for lunch. "The help are eating now, but right after I'll introduce you to Yetta Korn, she's the head lady from the pearl stringing, from there you'll begin."

Chavala couldn't believe it. Destiny—plus old-fashioned Chavala-stubbornness—was back. *"Thank* you, Mr. Leibowitz."

"You're welcome," and taking his lunch from a brown bag he said, "Here, you'll share a corned beef with me and a cream soda."

Chavala was so touched she forgot to ask him how much her salary would be . . .

Later she sat next to Yetta Korn with a tray of cultured pearls, watching as Yetta separated the sizes and colors with a pair of forceps.

After a few days Chavala was knotting the long strands as though she had done it all her life. The years of sewing and intricate embroidery had made her fingers nimble. And her ears and eyes observed everything. She listened to Mr. Leibowitz talk to the jewelers when they came to buy. And she put a million questions to him. She worked while the others took their lunch so she could eat later while the men in the back molded the wax forms.

One day Mr. Leibowitz said, "Chavala, what took me a lifetime you want me to teach you in a week." He said it with a smile.

She smiled back at him. "No . . . sooner. A week, I can't wait."

CHIA and Reuven, Chavala thought, had adjusted to their new surroundings quickly. She was only half-right . . . she was so busy learning and working that she missed the problem with Reuven.

As for Chia, she wanted so badly to become a teacher, as she'd once told Aaron, that she even went to night school. Every spare moment was spent in studying. Not so with Reuven. He hated school, couldn't understand the language and made little or no effort to learn. The only time he felt comfortable was when he went to the yeshiva, and not so much

because he was very religious . . . he just loved the sound of Hebrew
. . . the sound of home . . .

This day had been especially bad for him. On the way home the
other kids had taunted him about his clothes . . . "Ain't he pretty? Look
at them fancy . . ."

Although he could not understand he knew well enough that they
were calling him names.

"Hey, get a load of them shoes!"

"Greenhorn!"

"How do you say screw in Hebrew?"

"That's good, Hymie," a boy named Jake Goldstein said, "you're a
poet and don't know it. Screw and Hebrew, they rhyme!"

The other two boys screamed with laughter as Reuven stood there,
surrounded.

"Let's take his pants down and see if his shmuck's the same as ours."

Suddenly Reuven was on the sidewalk with his pants down. He
struggled and kicked and landed his foot in the face of one of the boys.
His other foot managed to land between another's legs, and the boy
doubled over. But he was outnumbered. He took blow after blow and
would have been knocked unconscious if it hadn't been for Goldfarb the
tailor, rushing out of his shop with a broom in his hand and screaming
in Yiddish, "Get away, you lowlifes . . . you *bonditten!* You'll all be in jail
. . . wait, you'll see . . ."

The boys ran off, less on account of Goldfarb than because Jake was
holding his lower regions in pain and Hymie's nose was bleeding.

Mr. Goldfarb helped Reuven up. "Come, you'll wash up in my
store," he said in Yiddish.

But Reuven stood unsteadily and said in Hebrew, "I don't understand . . . thank you, but . . ."

When Chia came home and didn't find Reuven she went to the roof,
where she knew he would be. Reuven was standing at the parapet looking
out beyond the city.

Chia saw only his legs, the sheets flapping in the breeze obscured the
rest of his body.

"Reuven," she called out.

It took a moment before he answered. "Yes," then viciously tore the
sheets off the line and stood in front of her.

Chia gasped. "What happened to your face?"

"I got into a fight."

"Come here, sit down and tell me."

They sat on two empty crates, Reuven kicking at the pebbles that stuck to the tarpaper. One eye was swollen shut, and there was a long, deep gash on his cheek.

"Reuven, tell me what happened—"

"I *said* I got into a fight."

"I know, but what happened, why?"

"Why?" he said, clenching his fists together as the muscles in his face tightened. "Because *ema* wanted us to live in a *civilized* place . . . I hate it here, Chia, and I've never forgiven her for bringing us here and leaving *abba*—"

"Don't say that about your mother . . . she loves us, don't you understand?"

"No, I don't understand. I think she's selfish, she doesn't care about us, only about what *she* wants—"

"Reuven, you're *wrong*. She gave up her own happiness so we could—"

"Who asked me if this was what I wanted? As soon as I can earn enough money I'm going home—"

"This is your home now."

"No, not ever . . . and it's not my country either."

"You're just upset, come downstairs and I'll fix you something to eat—"

"Thank you, I don't want anything to eat."

"Well then, come down with me while I make supper . . . please?"

Chia hadn't understood a word he'd said. No one was listening. His loneliness . . . he couldn't stand it . . . there was no one to share anything with any more . . . only *abba* . . . a million miles away . . .

But Chia had understood. She was going to spend more time with Reuven, take him to Central Park, where she heard they had ice skating. There was the zoo, and this summer they could go to a beach called Coney Island. She would do things with him and try to get him interested in one of the settlement houes where he could learn to play a game called basketball. And she would talk to her big brother Moishe, convince him to help her . . .

"You won't tell *ema*, will you, Reuven?" Chia said quietly.

That evening Reuven was the center of attraction.

Chavala almost fainted when she saw her son. "How did this happen?" she asked more calmly than she felt.

"Playing ball."

Inspecting the eye, she said, "What kind of ball is this?"

"Something like soccer," he told her, taking her hand away.

"We'll go to the doctor."

"No." What he needed was not a doctor.

"Reuven, darling, please don't be stubborn, we're going to—"

"No." He got up and went to his room.

Chavala shook her head. "I don't know, he seems so angry at me . . ."

"He's at that age, Chavala," Moishe said. He had, of course, noticed it too, the anger at Chavala.

Chavala shrugged. "I know growing up isn't easy, but I don't remember you at that age being so . . . so belligerent."

"It was different with us, we weren't in a strange country . . . we had it easier . . ."

Chavala knew better, but what could she do? Moments like these, she questioned her wonderful reasons for coming here . . .

Moishe got into bed, turned off the light. "Reuven?"

". . . Yes?"

"What really happened?"

"I got beat up, is what *really* happened."

"Did you fight back?"

"I tried, but you can't beat five bullies. *Ema* was afraid of the Arabs. Against them, I had a better chance. I knew what ambushes to stay away from and I always had a chance. At least I spoke their language. I feel like . . . running away—"

"Listen to me, Reuven, no one can run away for long—"

"What did *ema* do?"

"She didn't run away, she came here to build a better life for all of us, *you* included."

"She didn't do such a good job."

"Listen to me . . . she gave up a lot, being with her husband, so we could have it better . . . a few bullies don't count. Arabs or Americans . . . the thing to remember is the Turks. How were we treated? And now the British? We Jews spilled our blood for them, died for them, fought in their war and they loved us like poison. In this country the government's not like that. Here you don't have anyone to really be afraid of . . . except maybe yourself . . . We had to *beg* to fight for them. Remember, Reuven, I was in their army. You should have seen how they treated us, even at Gallipoli in the midst of a war. We couldn't eat at the same table. We were kept in separate barracks in London. And if you have any idea that we'll ever have a country there, you're wrong. There will be a

Palestine, sure, but the *British* will be in it, like the Turks for three hundred years before. They'll rule our people and give the Arabs guns and look the other way. Be grateful, Reuven, that your mother gave you a chance to be free, have something better . . ."

Reuven wasn't listening. He wasn't interested in his uncle's sermon. He would fight the British *and* the Arabs to be able to see Athlit. To walk in the vineyards and swim in the waters at Caesarea . . . he hated the snow and the cold, streets crowded with people babbling in a language he couldn't understand. Life here had no meaning for him. He was an outcast, a stranger. A Jew . . . what else? But in Palestine he could work not to be a stranger . . . like his father was doing . . .

AS Chavala sat at her table stringing pearls she had great difficulty keeping her mind on what she was doing. It was on Reuven . . . he'd become so silent, so distant. She couldn't reach him. Of course he missed Dovid, and so did she. Terribly. But if she allowed herself the luxury of feeling continual guilt about him she wouldn't be able to sustain herself, keep going . . . After all, she was a woman, not a piece of wood. She had her feelings . . . her needs too . . .

Of course she often had huge misgivings about having left Dovid, but she pulled herself up short and tried to reason them away . . . Dovid was a grown man with a strong will of his own, he was trying to fulfill his dream . . . but Reuven . . . Reuven was a little boy. She felt more responsible for him than for Dovid or herself . . . The loneliness, it was hard on adults, but for a little boy missing his father . . . The idea of sending the boy back popped into her mind, and just as quickly she tried to push it out . . . she'd convinced herself that *this* country was where her son would have the best chance not just to survive but to be spared the horrors she and Dovid had grown up with. She had to be strong, not crumble at the sight of her son's unhappiness, remind herself that it would all be worth it to him one day . . . Except the effort was giving her sleepless nights. She was becoming ill. In the last few days she had been unable to keep food down, and this afternoon she felt dizzy and faint. When five o'clock came she was more than relieved the day was over. She had to go home and lie down.

The next morning as she began to dress, nausea overcame her. She sat on the edge of the bed until it passed. Good God, that was all she needed, to get sick. That was *out of the question,* sick she wasn't going to be. . . .

She'd no sooner sat down at her worktable when the nausea started again, but this time she could not will it away. Rushing toward the washroom she held onto the toilet seat and threw up. She was weak and perspiring when she returned.

Mr. Leibowitz looked up from his workbench, saw her, and went over to her. Putting his arm around her shoulders he said, "Chavala, you're not feeling well, I want you to see Dr. Felcher."

"No, I'm fine now—"

"I don't think so. I noticed the last few days you've looked pale and sick."

"I have a few problems . . ." She put her hand to her forehead. And then it started to spill out . . . "Mr. Leibowitz, I honestly don't know what to do . . . about myself I don't care but when you see your children so very—" She caught herself, how thoughtless, she should have bitten her tongue. Yetta Korn had told her about Mr. Leibowitz's children.

"Well, first," he said was saying, "I think you should go to the doctor and see what's wrong. You really don't look well, Chavala."

What a wonderful man. God knew, he had reason to be angry with her, instead he seemed only to be worried about her.

"I don't feel so good, to tell you the truth, but I'm just a bit upset, things are still new—"

"I'm sure, but it wouldn't hurt. Maybe he can give you a tonic for your nerves."

She had lived through more than this without a tonic—Oh, God, the dizziness was back, and she cursed herself for not being able to conquer it. She held onto the table as perspiration broke out on her forehead.

"All right, Chavala, that's enough. You'll go see Dr. Felcher."

Chavala nodded. "Maybe I should . . . how much will he charge me, do you think?"

"It wouldn't be too much. Tell him Leibowitz sent you. Here, I'll write down the address. It's only three blocks away." . . .

THE examination was over and she now sat across from Dr. Felcher. From the look on his face she knew it was nothing. "I feel foolish now for coming, I knew it was my nerves—"

"It's very possible, but the nausea and dizziness is caused by your pregnancy."

Chavala stared at him in disbelief. Finding her voice she finally said,

"That's impossible. I . . . I . . . It's just impossible."

"Why?" asked Dr. Felcher.

"Because I have been seper—" Chavala stopped in midsentence. How could she have suspected this? Her periods had never been regular. Sometimes for two or three months she didn't menstruate.

Maybe the doctor was wrong. No, he was *right.* . . . The night before she left they had made love, so why should this come as such a shock? But it did. Why now, for God's sake? That was all she needed, a baby. "How . . ." She could scarcely get the words out. "How far . . . when is the baby due?"

"You're in your second month."

Chavala sighed. *"Mazel tov* to me. Thank you for the good news, and how much do I owe you?"

It was three dollars because she worked for Leibowitz. Otherwise it would have been five.

She waited until after supper, when Chia and Reuven went to their room to do their homework, to tell Moishe the news.

"Well, Moishe, you're going to be an uncle again."

He looked at her in shock. "How can that be—?"

"Because married women get pregnant."

"But you and Dovid have been . . ." He frowned at his own stupidity. "For how long?"

"About two months."

"Well, *mazel tov.*"

"That's what I said when I found out. You know, Moishe, I think God does have a plan. This child could be just what I need."

Moishe nodded, thought, some good news . . . no husband, no money, they were barely getting by . . . "It's the best news I've heard in a long time."

"Yes it is, Moishe. You see, it takes something like this to make a person come to a decision."

"And?"

"Now I must make a better living."

"And how will you do that?"

"I'm going to open one of those . . . what do they call them? . . . pawnshops. *That's* how."

"Chavala, what in the world do you know about a pawnshop?"

"Nothing. Which was what I knew about most things, it seems. But I also know I can learn . . . I can't go on stringing pearls for the rest of my life. I never really intended to, but the change came sooner than I'd thought . . . You know, Moishe, I truly believe the child is a double blessing."

"I'm very glad you're happy."

"I know . . . now if you'll excuse me, I have to write a letter."

Dear Dovid . . .

Dear Dovid what? Suddenly, and to her surprise, she didn't know quite how to say it.

She started again.

Dearest Dovid,

A wonderful thing has happened. My joy is beyond words. I know you will be as thrilled as I am. We're going to have a baby.

She could well imagine how thrilled Dovid would be. His wife was on another planet and he was going to be the proud father of a child he wouldn't see in God knew how long. What kind of a letter was that?

She pressed on . . .

When I heard the news I could hardly wait to share it with you. Thank God for this blessing. Please be happy, Dovid . . .

She meant that, but also knew it sounded empty, too casual.

Chavala tore up the letter. It was too unfair to use this to try to get him to come to her. Be honest, Chavala . . .

Dearest Dovid,

I know this will come as a surprise to you, as it did to me, but I am two months pregnant. At first I was shocked, but now I feel truly a great sense of joy. This child is very special. For me, it's as though it has bound us closer together. I can't quite explain my feelings, but somehow I know this is a new beginning. In many ways . . . I'm going to open a little store. I feel hopeful about the future for all of us.

I pray that you are happy in what you're doing, and above all I pray you stay well.

Your loving wife,
Chavala

Dovid received the news with mixed feelings. Another child . . . That was wonderful. But it also was a reminder of their situation, which he hated . . . once again he argued with himself for not being able to bend more, and felt resentment at Chavala for the same reason. But he'd gone over and over all this, the reasons, the rationalizations, a million times. And still he couldn't accept it.

He shook his head, and wrote Chavala how happy he was about the child, that things were going fine in Palestine. Everybody sent their love. He missed her with a terrible ache . . . What more could he say? Except what was most in his heart, as it was in hers . . . I want you here, I want us to be together . . . I will do anything . . . Unwritten words of a man to his wife who would have his baby a million miles away.

"WELL, Mr. Leibowitz," Chavala said the next morning, "I didn't need a tonic for my nerves. What I've got is a tonic. I'm going to have a baby."

He frowned, then quickly smiled. Children, after all, were a blessing, weren't they? *"Mazel tov."*

"Thank you, that's what I said to myself when I heard the good news. Now, Mr. Leibowitz, as much as I hate to leave . . . well, this changes things for me. I *must* make a better living."

"Of course, so what will you do?"

"Open a pawnshop."

"A pawnshop? Chavala, what do you know from a pawnshop? That's a very complicated business and a very dangerous one—"

"I'm not unacquainted with danger, Mr. Leibowitz. As for complicated . . . from that I know too."

"But Chavala, you don't understand. What do you think, you put up a sign, open the door and you make money?"

"I think I have to start."

"Chavala, you're a sensible young woman. Listen to me, you don't know a thing about jewelry. How will you know what a thing is worth?"

"I'll learn."

"What will you learn with? It takes money to open a—"

"I have some money."

Mr. Leibowitz stood up. Chavala had money?

Reading his expression she said, "I have some money. Wait, Mr. Leibowitz, I'll be right back."

Going to the washroom, Chavala unpinned the pouch from her camisole and brought it back. "Could we go into your private office?"

He nodded, then his eyes opened wide as Chavala emptied the contents onto a piece of white jeweler's paper.

He looked from the tiny stones to Chavala. Knowing Chavala, even for a short time, he would never question that they were stolen, but how had she come to this? He decided it wasn't his business. "So you want an appraisal?"

"Yes . . . I want to sell them."

Taking up the loupe, he examined each one. When he finished he said, "The lot is worth about twelve hundred dollars."

"I'll take it."

"I didn't say I was buying," he said suddenly.

"Why?"

"Because I don't need any more small stuff."

"Well, if you don't need it, you don't need it."

Chavala carefully put the contents back into the pouch.

"Wait, Chavala, I'll try to sell them for you."

"Mr. Leibowitz, you have been very kind to me, and I'm grateful, but I want to sell them as soon as possible."

"To be in a hurry can cost money."

"And to be lazy, or late, can also cost money. There's a store on Mott Street I saw. An old pawnshop that's empty. I want to buy it."

"So someone else is grabbing it?"

"Who knows? Maybe not, but I'll tell you, Mr. Leibowitz, life has taught me if you don't do something when you feel it's right, sometimes it gets too late, so I don't like to wait."

He truly admired Chavala's spirit, and was so touched by her courage he said, adjusting his *yarmulke*, "How much is the rent?"

"Fifty dollars a month. The fixtures are already there. It even has a safe."

"All right. I'll loan you five hundred dollars to start the business. You leave the stuff with me. I'll get you more than if you sell to the *gonuvim.* "

"I'll never forget your kindness, Mr. Leibowitz." And she leaned over to kiss him on the cheek.

Pleased, he said, "In this world you have to help. It's the real pleasure. Now buy a hundred dollars' worth of musical instruments. I'll tell my friend Goldstein to give you a good buy."

"Why do I need instruments?"

"So you'll have something to sell, and, Chavala, be very careful how much you lend. If you have any doubts, better to do nothing. I'll teach you as much as I can. *Mazel tov.*"

That night she could hardly wait to write to her sisters.

As she wrote, she also thought about Dvora's unhappy situation, but then she consoled herself with the thought that no matter how little she earned, a part of that would be sent to Dvora, who didn't even have a decent pair of shoes.

Putting down the pen, she looked again at the recent pictures she'd received from Palestine. Dvora and her husband, Ari, were standing with their son and daughter in the mud. In the background was the tent they lived in. It looked just like an army barracks. One large tent housed the kitchen and dining room, and she counted, as she had before, ten other tents surrounding it. Still, Dvora and Ari were smiling . . . but Chavala wasn't fooled, she knew what they were going through. She remembered too well the Galilee . . . this was hardly better. In the winter they would live with the wind howling and the rain leaving a river of mud, and in summer they would almost die from the heat. She almost wished that they hadn't sent the picture . . . Dvora had changed from that vibrant young girl who had gone off that summer to the training farm into a woman whose face was etched with the hardships and rigors of their struggles to survive. Her weather-beaten face was wrinkled before its time. Surely Dvora looked too old for her twenty-five years . . . And Ari. When he'd come home from the war he too was greatly changed, not only in his body but in his spirit too. When he'd first come from America, from New Jersey, he was a fired-up pioneer, full of excitement and dedication. His willingness to sacrifice the good life of America was no sacrifice for him. He had the chance to change a world in which all people were distinctly *not* created equal, did not have equal opportunity. He and his fellows . . . and then his wife . . . shared a bold dream of a society where everybody worked for the common good of the community. When he got back from the war they settled in Arazim, a kibbutz in the Jordan Valley, that provided the kind of challenge he'd come all this way in search of. But he soon discovered that there was no such thing as utopia . . . even in Palestine. Here too, in spite of many good things, there was a subtle ruling class, a hierarchy competing for control of the inner workings of the kibbutz. Human nature, it seemed, was human nature. Also, maybe because of the war, he could no longer tolerate the strict discipline, owning nothing for himself and his family. The land still pulled him, but he felt he also had to own a part of himself. He wanted to *see* what he produced with his hands and live in a hut built by his own labor.

The founders of Arazim disapproved.

"Have we done our work here so that now we can sit back like land barons? You talk of private ownership. Being individuals . . . We have invested our lives to claim this land, and here we shall build roots for the future of our children . . ."

Along with twenty others, Ari, Dvora and their five-year-old Zvi moved on. They settled in the Galilee, east of Jordan, a wilderness of marshes, rock-strewn and malaria-ridden swamps, but it fired the imagination and filled them with greater inspiration. The Moshav was divided into equal parcels and cultivated by individual members. They shared marketing and water. A person was recompensed according to his labor. While the land was being cultivated the settlers received a daily wage from the JNF, scarcely enough to live on, but their faith in the future kept them going.

They told Chavala this in letters, but she knew, or felt, much of it was a brave front. Their hardships were so much greater than hers . . . they *must* be suffering . . .

Raizel was expecting her fourth child, and Chavala hated to think of her and her children living out their lives in the desperate poverty of Mea Shearim. It was unthinkable, and it wouldn't be so . . . not if Chavala had to beg, borrow, steal, or all three . . .

Strange, she thought as she began her letter to Sheine, of all the four sisters she was the only one with security. Except, of course, that her husband wasn't of their faith. Well, what was important was that Sheine said she was happy. Chavala didn't hope for Sheine's riches for herself or the rest of the family . . . but she did intend to see them *all* secure, never in need. Never mind the mansion in Berlin, Sheine's husband's ancestral home, where he'd brought her as his bride. What mattered was that Gunter's parents were pleased with her, that his friends had welcomed her. It seemed some *goyim,* even Germans, could be decent. At least for Sheine she had no worries. . . .

Except what Sheine wrote and what was reality were two different things.

Frau Hausman was distinctly *not* pleased with her son's choice of a bride. She was very disappointed that Gunter had married outside his social level. It was young Erica Steinhart that she had always hoped for as a daughter-in-law, but since Gunter hadn't proposed before going off, Erica, a girl of considerable ego, had quickly married so as not to appear jilted.

The war was to blame, Frau Hausman told herself. When men became lonely they lost their sense of things . . . they lived for the moment, grabbing it as though it might be their last. She understood, but she couldn't really accept it. Grudgingly she acknowledged that this Elsa Beck did have signs of decent breeding and some grace. Generally Frau Hausman's opinion of nurses were that they were nothing more than bedpan handlers who wiped people's bottoms and slept with every intern —little more than tramps, really. Well, at least Gunther hadn't disgraced them by bringing one of *that* kind home.

So she was aloof but not hostile to Sheine. Guarded in her manner, she nonetheless welcomed her daughter-in-law. After all, it was that or lose her son. When a man who was so obviously in love as Gunter was, whom would he choose? She would play a waiting game . . .

Sheine, with her long-standing fears and indeed guilts, was grateful for a show of even reserved acceptance. And if at times she wished that Gunter was a little more aware of his mother's lack of warmth, she quickly put it out of her mind. Gretchen Hausman had not been demonstrative to her husband or her son either. Her Germanic reserve was seen by both husband and son as a kind of dignity. They were accustomed to it.

But Sheine knew, *felt* the difference between the coolness she was shown and the long-established manner toward Gunter and his father. The subtleties weren't always so subtle . . . she'd look up and find her mother-in-law scrutinizing her from across the table . . . "You have such lovely *dark* hair Elsa . . . quite lovely. *Nicht wahr*, Frederick?" And then her head would turn to observe Gunther's *blond* handsomeness.

The effect was not lost on Sheine, nor was it meant to be.

In the months that followed, Sheine found herself being taken over by her mother-in-law. (If she couldn't get rid of her, at least she could try to remake her into something more *suitable* . . .) Her clothes were carefully selected. Her hair style prescribed. Nothing was done without consulting *mutter*. If Frau Hausman could have been as adept at controlling Sheine's thoughts, she might even have blessed her seemingly placid daughter-in-law. But Sheine suffered, secretly, and in silence. . . .

Although the *deutschmark* had plunged in value since the war, Dr. Frederick Hausman had no problems. His brother, Otto, was a Swiss banker who lived in Zurich and handled the family's estate. The Swiss *franc* was worth two hundred marks. And Gretchen, thank God, was wonderfully frugal. The best bargains were to be had in the eastern part of Berlin, and repugnant as it might be to Gretchen to buy from these dreadful people, she nonetheless, Sheine in tow, made two trips a week across town to what she and her friends called the Jewish Switzerland.

Inside the crumbling buildings along Dragonerstrasse was an assortment of merchants who had been in the country for twenty-five to fifty years. There was very little that could not be purchased on that long boulevard. There were secondhand dealers, one after another, secondhand furniture stores, markets, restaurants, rooming houses, butcher shops and houses of worship. Among those that mingled with the older Jewish community were the multitudes of newly displaced Jews who had poured in from Poland, Galicia and Russia, holding to their customs and ways of dressing. Young and old women alike wore their wigs of chastity and all in the same color—black. They also brought with them their strict religious codes. Despite that all the butcher shops displayed the Star of David in their windows and that the meat was stamped by the rabbi as kosher, the women would not buy from a butcher who was clean-shaven . . . the rabbi himself was suspect since he too wore no beard. So, poor as they were, they nonetheless chose to pay a little more and walk a little further to buy from Yisroel Schmolivitch in Landsburg *Allee,* who had a long black beard and carved up a side of beef he had just slaughtered. With their purchases packed inside the crocheted shopping bags they wandered back to Dragonerstrasse, where they could find the best bargains in produce. They looked most strange to the blond women dressed in the fashion of the day who hurried into the large mercantile stores.

At Melnetski's mercantile, merchandise—wedding gowns to shrouds —was stacked from floor to ceiling. At the stocking counters, arms reached out feverishly to grab the right size. The place was a bedlam, and the street noises were deafening. At the bakery shop there were queues waiting with bags of near-worthless money to buy bread, onion rolls, poppy-seeded flat rolls with coarse salt and caraway. Hurrying along the streets were eastern Oriental Jews in brocaded caftans, heads covered in the traditional fur-trimmed hats. From the large synagogues, elderly Jews emerged carrying phylactery bags tucked under arm and going into the small *shuls* were long-bearded men wearing wide-brimmed Galician hats, while others wore derbies that sat on the back of their heads; some had short earlocks and untrimmed beards. From the open windows of the yeshiva, chanting was heard.

Outside these holy places the sidewalks teemed with street urchins who begged. Restaurants were jammed with secondhand clothes dealers who had just returned from a morning in the west part of Berlin, where they had waited outside the mansions while the rich matrons bargained for a *pfennig* more. Back at Dragonerstrasse, they lunched with the other dealers and compared the prices they had paid the rich German bitches who tried to cheat them out of a *pfennig* and treated them like *dreck.* At nearby tables pious elderly men said their *broches* before eating. Others sat in the corner playing cards and drinking one glass of tea after another. On the curb outside, vendors hawked their wares, from pots and pans and underwear to secondhand mattresses.

German Jews who had become, they thought, assimilated, tried very hard to ignore these less fortunate refugees. They wanted to run and hide each time the Russian Jews, dressed in their peasant boots and long shabby coats, crossed into their sanctified neighborhoods. They devoutly wished these bearded faces and black caps would somehow just go away . . .

Sheine trembled inside as she realized that she identified more with these people now than she had in her youth. Yes, they reminded her who she was, and Elsa Beck became a shame and burden to her. She wanted to reach out and touch them, *embrace* them.

Sitting in the back of the limousine, Gretchen said, *"Die Juden* are our curse."

Sheine tried to make herself deaf as she droned on and on . . . how the dreadful inflation was caused by this alien scourge in their midst . . . these Russian, Polish, Roumanian Jews who had brought filth and disease to the Fatherland. In *fact,* the terrible influenza was spread by them, and they had desecrated the lovely streets . . . On and on Gretchen ranted.

Sundays were the worst of all. As they walked up the steps of Gedachtnis Kirche, the oldest, most impressive church in Berlin, she faltered slightly, then was led by the arm to sit in the pew with Gunter and his parents. To look up was to see Jesus on the cross, to see the Virgin Mary with her son from the manger to the grave. Sheine wanted to scream out, but fear left her impotent, in silence.

From the pulpit the minister spoke about godless communism assaulting God-fearing, God-loving Germans. The Jews, of course, were responsible. They marched with their banners in the streets, these rabble rousers who were a plague upon the nation. They had spread their poisonous doctrines, even seduced the workers. The government *must* take a strong hand in condemning them, outlaw their Communist party. Only then could the greatness of Germany be free to rise again . . . Greatness exemplified by Goethe, Schopenhauer, Nietzsche, Wagner, Brahms and Beethoven. The Jewish poison of Marx and Engels, *The Communist Manifesto,* needed to be rooted out, banned and burned. Said the minister in solemn tones, had it not been for the international Jewish bankers the Kaiser would still be on the throne and the glory of the Fatherland would still prevail. "Yes," said the minister as he looked into the faces of his parishioners, *"Die Juden bringen nur Ungluck.* They are a blight upon humanity."

Back home for Sunday luncheon after such spiritual lessons, Sheine would sit very quietly, seeing in her mind's eye Jesus on the cross, the Jews of Dragonerstrasse, with the terrifying sound of the minister's words reverberating . . . On Easter Sunday the story of the Resurrection was drowned out by echoes of "Kill the Jews" during the pogroms in Odessa . . . The Jewishness in Elsa Beck Hausman that could not be repressed resulted in blinding migraines, some so violent that she could not get out of bed for days. . . .

This particular evening as the family sat at dinner in the large dining room with the heavily carved furniture, Sheine felt mired in the worst despair she had ever felt.

Frederick Hausman looked at his daughter-in-law, for whom he had great affection, and observed the paleness of her olive skin and the strain in her soft brown eyes. What in the world troubled her so . . . ?

"Elsa, you haven't touched your food. Eat, my dear, or you'll waste away to nothing."

Sheine, her thoughts elsewhere, was startled by her father-in-law's voice. He'd always seemed a man with a sense of humor, and kind. He'd not only welcomed Sheine but admired her achievements as a surgical nurse. Sheine never could comprehend how he'd ever come to marry Gretchen . . .

Gretchen was looking closely at Elsa also, noted the dark hollows under her eyes and was distressed. But, unlike with Frederick, it had nothing to do with concern or affection for Elsa. Gretchen was unhappy because Elsa had given her no grandchildren. Obviously Gunter wasn't to blame, it had to be Elsa. If only the war hadn't ruined everything, Gunter would have a fine German wife and blond handsome German sons, like Erica Steinhart had been able to give *her* husband. But this strange, dark-complexioned woman was tainted with the genes of a French mother . . . Gretchen's dislike for the French almost matched her feeling about the Jews. Because of the French, Germany stood humiliated before the world. Well, Gunter's child . . . *if* one came . . . would be German, and with her influence would be a *Hausman.* She'd see to it . . .

That evening as Sheine, her eyes closed, lay on the bed, trying to cope with the awful pain in her head, Gunter sat alongside her, held her hand.

"Elsa, my dearest, tell me what I can do to help you."

Silence.

"When I sent you to be examined . . . Fritz told me he found nothing physically wrong . . . the headaches, he thinks, are a symptom of something else."

Sheine opened her eyes and looked at him. "He's right. I'm frightened."

"Of what?"

"Don't you really know?"

"No . . ."

"My Jewishness."

"Dear God . . . darling, you've no reason to feel this way—"

"But I *do.*"

"Why?"

"Maybe you can answer that. Gunter, why haven't you ever told your family that I am a Jew?"

Gunter shook his head. "It didn't seem important—"

"Is that the only reason?"

"Yes."

"I don't think so."

Elsa had never spoken to him like that before. "Why shouldn't you believe me?"

"Because you were ashamed to tell them."

"I wouldn't have married you if I'd been ashamed—"

"Then why didn't you tell them?"

"Perhaps because *you* found it so reprehensible to be a Jew you kept it a secret from me." His voice was rising, and then just as quickly was filled with remorse. He took her in his arms. "Elsa, please, let's not do this to each other. The truth is, I didn't think you wanted me to say anything. I'll be very happy to go to my parents, tell them, but I assure you it will make no difference—"

"It will . . . your mother *hates* Jews."

"That's not true," Gunter came to his mother's defense—"you know perfectly well that we have—"

"God . . . please don't say it . . . 'some of our best friends are Jewish' . . . Gunter, don't you understand? . . . They aren't Jewish like I am. They're more German than Jewish, they hope. The Jews from Dragonerstrasse are more a thorn in their sides than your mother's. I can tell you, though, that deep down they're as frightened as I am. They hide behind their German nationalism and pretend they're not Jews. Who knows . . . maybe that works for some of them, but it's destroying me. How do you think I feel, sitting in your church, listening to how the

Jews killed Christ? I tell you, I'm *frightened,* can't you understand that?"

He reached out and drew her close to him. "Darling, I understand . . . I'd actually forgotten you're Jewish. It didn't seem important. It doesn't now. As for my mother, believe me, knowing about you wouldn't matter . . . you're different from people, including Jews, that she may find . . . different—"

"But they're *not* different. *I'm* not different, can't you see that?"

He shook his head. "I don't honestly know what to say, except I can't stand by and see you tormented. Something has to be done. I'll make an appointment for you to see Ludwig Breslauer—"

"I'm living with anti-Semitism, how will that help? No, I won't go to a psychiatrist. I'm not crazy, you know. I'm just Jewish . . . that's my disease, at least to your mother—"

"Elsa, please trust me . . . this is eating you up, and it's coming between us. I can't help except to support you with my love. That doesn't seem enough . . . Will you go, Elsa? Please?"

Gunter was right about that . . . this was destroying them . . . "All right, all right, I'll try . . ."

It took months before Sheine could even talk about being Jewish to Dr. Breslauer. In part, she thought, because Ludwig Breslauer's family had been assimilated Jews for three generations. The doctor said nothing in response to her insight.

Finally, after who knew how many long and analytic sessions, Ludwig Breslauer decided he was getting across to Elsa the phenomenon of Jewish self-hatred, where it had come from and how it could be *dealt* with. The salvation of the Jews, he explained, was to take a lesson from those enlightened Jews in Germany. He was able, he felt, finally to convince this woman that she was far too sensitive on the subject of her mother-in-law's dislike of foreign Jews . . . actually he himself felt that they were too set in their ways, too unwilling or unable to adjust to modern times and to the wonderful country of their choice. He patiently explained that she must now separate herself from the excess baggage of her past. It was debris. She must move forward in her life, not be burdened by her Jewishness . . .

So after a year of intensive psychoanalysis, Elsa Beck found the headaches to diminish and then vanish. She even began to feel a sense of security, as if she belonged. Gunter's mother no longer bothered her. She was one of the family. She belonged, at long last . . .

God help her.

Chapter Twenty-four

CHAVALA AND MOISHE watched as the sign of the Eagle Pawnshop came down and "Landau" went up. She looked at her brother. "This is only the beginning, Moishe."

He nodded. "When you make your first dollar, you'll frame it." He looked up at the sign again. "Well, Chavala, I wish you everything you wish for yourself."

She smiled and held him close. "It's for the whole family, Moishe. It's not just for me. You think I'm going to let you deliver pants for the rest of your life? Chavala's brother is going to be a diamond merchant one day . . . take my word."

From her mouth to God's ears.

The first week in business she sold a saxophone for fifteen dollars.

The next week Mr. Leibowitz came to her with thirteen hundred dollars. "You see, I told you if you gave me a chance I would get top dollar."

His honesty was worth more than the money. "What can I say, Mr. Leibowitz? You're a wonderful person, I owe you so much . . ."

He shrugged in embarrassment, though he was clearly pleased. "Just make a living, Chavala."

"I will, Mr. Leibowitz, with your help I will." . . .

During the next month Chavala began to loan money as well as sell. The first thing she took in was a gold wedding band. What weight it was she had no idea, but she held it in her hand as though she knew. When she examined inside and saw the inscription . . . "With love always," she swallowed hard, and loaned the young woman five dollars. Money was a miserable thing, thought Chavala. She hated herself for the rest of the day, knowing the tears that must have been shed. It could cause a lot of pain . . . but it could also bring happiness . . . Try to remember that, she instructed herself.

Thanks to the hours Mr. Leibowitz had spent with her in the evenings, she knew much more now than when her sign first went up. Looking through the loupe, she could see the flaws. Mr. Leibowitz even taught her how to calibrate the size of a stone. Still, in spite of all she was taught, it was Chavala's own instincts that mostly guided her. It didn't take her too long to realize that understanding human nature was at the root of this business . . . When a customer was both in a hurry and willing to take almost any amount offered, it meant the goods were stolen . . . Merchandise not redeemed by the due date, Chavala put away in the old vault. Sooner than she'd hoped, her goals were beginning to emerge as reality. Her confidence grew, and so did her girth . . .

Reuven looked at his mother's bulging belly. He was going to have his bar mitzvah next month, and he was very unhappy. Both impending events were upsetting reminders that his father would not be with them. The *tallis* and *yarmulke* that his father had sent from Palestine made the sense of loss even greater.

On the day of his bar mitzvah he mumbled through the ceremony. Instead of having his mind on this signal passage into manhood, his mind and heart were in Eretz Yisroel. He couldn't help it, he hated this place. It wasn't his country, it never would be. Who wanted to become a man in a place that didn't want you?

Chavala had different feelings as she listened to her son. Her joy too was limited, but not by the ceremony. Dovid should have come . . . he owed at least that much to his son . . . to her too? She knew he must have wanted to come, that his work must have held him, but still . . . what were the priorities? This was his only son's most important life event . . . Be fair, she reminded herself. If he was the one who had refused to come, she was the one who had insisted on going. Once again she wondered if she'd been right, why was she trying so hard to secure the future if it meant such sacrifices . . . But when she looked up and saw her son standing there at the podium in his *yarmulke, tallis,* and the navy blue suit she'd bought him, her misgivings were quickly set aside. No. Her efforts weren't for nothing. She'd work to provide enough for him to go to college. Chia sitting beside her made her resolve even stronger. Stop this self-doubt, this recrimination . . . gradual as it was, her business had already grown to the point where she was sending money to Raizel and Dvora. Next week Moishe would be able to quit his job in the garment district and become her partner. That was all part of what she was struggling for, wasn't it?

Feeling better, she embraced Reuven. "I was so proud of you standing up there, a man now . . ." And then with an effort . . . "Your father, I know, feels the same way. We're *all* so proud . . ."

Under his breath, without a smile, he managed a "thank you." Anything more would have been too much.

Chia hurriedly moved to save the moment when she hugged Reuven and said, "A rabbi couldn't have done better, you were *wonderful,* Reuven."

He nodded. It was much the same with Uncle Moishe and Mr.

Leibowitz, from whom Reuven with formal politeness accepted a fountain pen.

In spite of herself, and her earlier good thoughts, Chavala wept inside, knowing full well Reuven's feeling of loss.

"NU, Moishe?" Chavala said to her brother on the first day he came to work at the pawnshop. "You see, I told you, before you can walk you have to crawl. And now we're already walking . . . a little bit at first, one step at a time. I told you you wouldn't be delivering pants forever."

He looked at the framed dollar on the wall over the cash register, the first one Chavala had earned. Well, he'd been right about that. He should also have known that when Chavala said she would do something, she would, by God, do it. "So, I'm not as smart as you."

"You're as smart, all right. All you have to do is have patience at the right time, and then run when it's the right time. I may not have the best education in the world, but life has been my training school. I figured out that there's a formula for success, anyone can become rich—"

Moishe smiled. "Anyone?"

"Anyone. You know what the secret formula is? Hard work. Presto. Forget the fine neighborhood, the grand apartment . . . all those things only happen after you've made your mark. So why think about them before . . . ? Come, I'll show you something."

It was quitting time. Chavala pulled down the shade on the door, reversed the small sign to read "Closed," switched off all the lights except the one she left burning all night. Then she walked to the back room, which she used as an office to do the bookkeeping.

Moishe waited, and watched, as Chavala dialed the combination to the safe. When the door opened, Chavala took out four cigar boxes, brought them to the table and sat down.

Moishe's heart thumped as Chavala shoved the boxes in front of him. He looked first from the boxes then to Chavala. "Open them. Nothing will bite you." She laughed.

He opened one, gasped, and then opened the others. Inside were gold signet rings, earrings, stickpins, diamond rings, bracelets and brooches.

He looked from them to Chavala. "These are yours?"

"Ours."

"How . . . I mean, how did you get all this?"

"By doing a service. To be blunt, from someone's *tzuris.* Happy I'm not about it, but I remind myself that I wasn't the one who caused their problems. I gave them money when they needed it, *when nobody else would.*" She stopped herself. So why was she explaining so much . . . ?

"I still don't understand, this is a pawnshop. You have to return the merchandise."

"If they pay. You saw the sign. If not redeemed after thirty days we are entitled to keep it."

"People didn't come back?"

"Some didn't, some of the merchandise I bought."

"I can't get over it."

"I know. I used to go back, take a look and pinch myself."

Moishe still shook his head in wonder, "What do you do now? You sell it?"

"No."

"No? What good is it in a box?"

"Who says I'm going to keep it in a box?"

"Well, then . . . I don't understand. You wouldn't sell it, you wouldn't keep it. So?"

"I've learned a little, Moishe. The stones we take out of the mountings and have the metal melted down. It brings a higher price."

"How did you get to be so smart?"

"From hunger. Pregnancy. Also having a family to be taken care of."

Moishe shook his head. "So you'll sell the things separately?"

"No. Not yet."

"I don't know, maybe I'm dumb . . . but what good is all this if you don't sell?"

"It's good like money in the bank, Moishe. When we have an inventory we'll remount the stones and start a retail jewelry store."

Moishe smiled, still amazed at what she'd done and knew in such a short time. He thought back to his war days. If they'd had more with his sister's guts and spirit the damned Turks would never have had a chance. "When will that be? The store . . . ?"

"When we can take more than one step at a time. There's a time to run and a time to be patient. I told you that. Now I'll teach you the business and we'll start running. Who better could I run with?" she said, as she privately thought of Dovid . . . "Well, we're a family . . . a little spread out at the moment . . . and we have to take care of our own. If not us, who? Dovid is doing it his way in Palestine. I'm just trying to do my part here . . . Now I'll put these back and we'll go home to supper."

When they arrived home, Reuven, for the first time since they'd left

Palestine, was smiling. Excitedly he said, "You have a letter from *abba.*"

Chavala smiled when she saw the letter, addressed to her, had already been read by Reuven. To see the happiness on Reuven's face was worth foregoing the pleasure she always felt when the letters arrived from Dovid. She didn't even have to read it. Reuven almost screamed, *"Abba*'s coming . . . he's *coming . . .*"

He hugged and kissed her. She looked at her son, "You see, Reuven, how things work out?"

He smiled, nodded.

"So take a lesson from this.

THE family was waiting for Dovid. When they saw him begin to walk down the gangplank, Chavala had to restrain Reuven from running up and bumping into people.

He was, though, the first that Dovid embraced. How good the boy felt in his arms. Then he looked at Chavala. Except for the beginnings of a slight silver streak in her otherwise chestnut hair, she actually looked no older than when he had married her. None of the hardships showed. Only the coming child, which swelled her belly.

"Chavala." He said her name like a declaration. Gone were all misgivings, nagging resentments. "It's been so long."

"We're *together,* Dovid. Something I thought would have taken much longer." Dear God, where had she gotten the courage . . . or *chutzpah? . . .* to leave him? And, yes, courage to stay? They embraced for so long Chia finally laughed. "Excuse me, *abba,* we're here too, you know."

He looked at her, took them all in again . . . In nine months? Was that all it took to grow up so? The differences in Chia and Reuven were startling. He had to look twice at his son. Maybe his eyes were playing tricks on him, but he could have sworn he saw a dark, fuzzy down on his upper lip.

Moishe put his arms around Dovid and they embraced as old colleagues, former soldiers and members of the same family. Moishe said quietly, "It means so much to us that you've come."

Dovid thought back to a young boy who worked at a cobbler's bench with him, who sat wide-eyed at the meetings of the Lovers of Zion. He remembered the day of Moishe's *bris,* and now he was twenty-nine. Unbelievable . . . "No more than it means for me to be here with you."

Chavala took Dovid by the arm and the family walked out into the dwindling light of the late autumn day.

Dovid was unprepared for what he saw. The streets of the lower East Side of New York thronged with pushcart vendors hawking their wares, people bargaining. A water hydrant had broken and children slipped and slid under the force of the water, laughing delightedly. This was their park, their playground. Who knew about being deprived? Old, bearded men stood in doorways discussing the *Midrash*, the Talmud. On the roofs the wash flapped drying in the wind. If Chavala had thought Jaffa was confusing the day they arrived from Russia . . .

As they came closer to Chavala's flat Dovid thought Mea Shearim was preferable by far but said nothing. When they climbed the five flights of rickety stairs, Chavala held tight to the unsteady bannister. In the last few days the stairs had seemed nearly to defeat her. Breathing rapidly, she took out the key, unlocked the door and ushered him in.

Dovid, saying little, sat down at the kitchen table and watched as Chavala put the kettle on for tea. Chia put out the sugar cubes and the lemon, then cut the sponge cake. As Dovid picked up his glass he felt the building sway ever so slightly, then heard the sound of the elevated trains roar past. He wondered how they slept, or how the building had remained standing with this constant onslaught.

Chavala kept peering over the rim of her glass at him . . . no doubt about it, he was real. He was also, she decided, more handsome at thirty-seven than when she had married him. But the years were etched in his face too . . . of course the boyishness of youth had gone, his temples were gray, but she couldn't remember seeing the deep lines in his weather-burned face when she'd left. Were they there nine months ago, or did people fail to notice each other as the days merely went on from one to the other? No question . . . Dovid had aged more than he should have. And while she knew she was not the only reason, she was, face it, a part of it. Well, what mattered now was that he had come, and she wouldn't think about the time when he would have to leave . . .

In the double bed Chavala and Chia shared, there was precious little room for Dovid, and even less for lovemaking. Both agreed that to ask Chia to bunk with Reuven would be impossible. Still, for Chavala, just to be held by Dovid, to have him feel the heartbeat of their second child, was almost enough . . .

In the morning Chavala moved awkwardly about the kitchen toasting bagels, scrambling eggs with onions and smoked salmon, putting out cucumbers and scallions in sour cream and cottage cheese.

Reuven, who quickly took up a seat next to his father, announced, "I'm not going to school today."

Chavala looked at him and smiled. "I wouldn't say I'm surprised. And you, Chia?"

"Well, I hope you'll excuse me, Dovid but I have a very important test today and—"

"You go take your test, that's more important. I'll be here when you come home," Dovid told her.

Moishe looked at the clock, saw it was eight o'clock. "I'm going to the store. You'll be by later?"

"Of course," Chavala answered as she started to remove the plates from the table.

WHEN they arrived at the pawnshop, Dovid stopped, looked up at the sign. Somehow seeing the name "Landau" startled him, but seeing the great look of pride in Chavala's face he managed a big smile.

Moishe greeted them from behind the metal-grille partition, and Dovid thought he hadn't seen Moishe this happy-looking since they'd sat in Bernstein's basement listening to the *Bilu* from Palestine, fired up with becoming a member of the Lovers of Zion. Much had happened since then to change Moishe's feelings. For him the old cause had been lost to the treachery of the British. His future was Chavala's . . . this was freedom. With almost nothing Chavala had made a miracle happen, and in so short a time. Dovid understood, but realized he could never agree . . .

Chavala took Dovid into her office, closed the door and took out the cigar boxes. "Well, Dovid, what do you think?"

He listened quietly as she explained the business, how she had come to acquire the inventory she now had. "And you know, Dovid, this is really just the beginning. I have very high hopes . . . it's so important . . ."

To whom, Dovid thought, but said only, "Yes, Chavala, it's remarkable what you've done in so short a time. And it seems Moishe agrees."

"Yes . . . I told you that something like this could only happen in America . . ." She hesitated, took a deep breath . . . "now that you've seen it, Dovid, wouldn't you maybe think about trying it?"

His look said it all. "I'm sorry, darling, I can't, and you know why."

Chavala forced back the tears. In her heart she'd known the answer before she asked it, she was foolish even to think she could change his mind. But to be without him again after even this brief reminder of what it was like together . . . God, why didn't he try to stop her? But she could hear the answer . . . What good would that have done, wouldn't they have ended up resenting, even hating each other? A husband shouldn't have to force his wife to be with him. That wasn't a marriage. If she stayed it had to be because she loved him so much she would do *anything* he asked . . . But was that really love . . . ? In a way it was Dovid's great strength that made it possible for him to let her go. It took a strong man to do that. Chavala only wished she had been woman enough not to leave Dovid . . .

She forced a smile. "Now, Dovid, I want you to meet Mr. Leibowitz."

"Ah . . . Chavala," Mr. Leibowitz called out as he came up to them. He ruffled Reuven's hair. "So how is the bar mitzvah boy?"

"Fine . . . thank you. This is my father," Reuven said with obvious pride.

"Ah ha, so this is Dovid. If I met you on the street I would have known you. Reuven described you very well. Now, come into my office and I'll send out for coffee and cake and we'll talk. I want to hear all about what's going on in Eretz Yisroel."

"Thank you, but we can stay for only a few minutes. I just wanted to show off a little," Chavala said, looking at her husband, "but please come to supper tonight."

He hesitated for a moment, looked at Chavala's stomach and smiled. "I would like that very much, but you're sure it wouldn't be too much for you?"

"I'm only going to have a baby, Mr. Leibowitz, and a family still has to eat."

He nodded, remembering the first time she had walked into his office, a total stranger, and now he felt as though she was a daughter. "I'll be there, and thank you. And you, Dovid, things haven't been the same since the bar mitzvah boy heard you were coming."

Dovid looked at his son. "The feeling was shared. It was a pleasure to meet you, Mr. Leibowitz, we'll see you this evening."

"God willing."

ON the way home Chavala bought a bouquet of flowers and a bottle of seltzer. After she rather laboriously climbed the stairs, she opened the door to the flat to find Chia had already set the table with the new white tablecloth Chavala had purchased for Dovid's arrival.

"Where's *abba* and Reuven?" Chia asked.

"Reuven took Dovid to show him his yeshiva. You notice the change in Reuven, I'm sure."

Chia sighed. "He can't let *abba* alone for a minute."

"I know. I hate to think . . . when Dovid leaves . . ."

"Let's not think about it today, we're together for the first time in a long time. Let's make every moment happy."

It was like old times as Chavala watched the pots. The smells were heaven. The brisket bubbled away in its own natural juices, the kasha simmered slowly, the carrot *tzimmes* needed just a bit more sugar. The one thing Chavala bought were the cakes from Mrs. Neusbaum . . . she was just too tired to make them.

AS Chavala served the food it seemed so *natural* to have Dovid sitting at the head of his table.

Mr. Leibowitz had brought the sweet Passover wine, which he drank all year round. With his glass touching Dovid's he said, "To Jerusalem."

"To the state of Israel," Dovid responded.

"L'chayim," Reuven said.

Chavala hoped with all her heart that Dovid's dreams of a Jewish state would come true. If both of them could realize their dreams then they surely could start together again. It *would* happen, somehow. She willed herself to believe it would . . .

After supper Chavala felt especially tired. She kissed Dovid and said goodnight to Mr. Leibowitz, thanking him for coming.

Reuven was pleased that his mother had gone to bed early and that Chia had gone off to study. He listened attentively as Mr. Leibowitz plied Dovid with one question after another, and to Dovid's answers . . .

"You didn't say so much today . . . but tell me, how are conditions, I mean with the British?"

The lines in Dovid's forehead deepened. "Not good, Mr. Leibowitz. They're trying to make peace with the Arabs, and as usual at our expense."

Mr. Leibowitz shook his head. "They won't let us live, will they? I mean . . . I thought the British would be sympathetic. That's what I read in the Yiddish papers. What about this Balfour Declaration?"

"Not, as they say, worth the paper it's written on. You know . . . for centuries the Arabs lived without lifting a hand to redeem the land and now they've invented something called Arab nationalism. Very convenient. We hoped that the agreement between Chaim Weizmann and Faisal would bring our two people closer together. It was hoped that with the agreement, Jewish immigration into Palestine would flow, but the Arab nationalists were against it. A few weeks ago the settlements in upper Galilee were attacked." He looked at Moishe. "Trumpeldor was murdered at Tel Hai. He fought in Manchuria, in Gallipoli, in Europe, he came home and they murdered him in Eretz Yisroel. Riots broke out in Jerusalem, Jews died. The British authorities gave the Arabs a free hand, the Jewish defenders led by Jabotinsky were wiped out . . ."

Moishe, never surprised by British treachery, was nonetheless in a state of shock. Finally he asked, "What about Jabotinsky?"

"Sentenced with I don't know how many others to a long term, for the crime of defending the Yishuv."

"Are you trying to get them out?"

Dovid laughed bitterly. "The Turks were so corrupt, no one, from the highest to the lowest, turned down a bribe. With gold you could buy yourself out of the grave. The British on the other hand, so civilized and polite, stab you in the back just before taking their tea. They can't be bought off, if the price is a Jew. And it's a Jew, an *English* Jew, Sir Herbert Samuel, who's been appointed Palestine's high commissioner."

"Well, my God, Dovid, why doesn't he help?" Moishe said.

"The British know what they're doing. One mistake and he's labeled pro-Jewish. He can't even be suspected of being lenient. He has to lean over backwards . . ."

"You mean he's done nothing for the Jews?" Mr. Leibowitz said.

"In the beginning he tried to bring in some Jewish immigration, but he had to appease the Arabs. So the Jews that did were put on road projects. He also made Hebrew an official language, side-by-side with Arabic and English as a concession to the Jews, but on the other hand the best government-owned land in the Beth She'an valley was distributed among the Bedouins."

Mr. Leibowitz and Moishe sat in silence. It all seemed so grim. How little, they realized, was written about Palestine's Jews in the American newspapers.

"*Abba,* why can't Aaron Aaronson and you do something like what happened in the war?"

Dovid looked at his son, the boy had been listening so intently he'd all but forgotten he was there. "Because this is a different time, Reuven."

"But you helped the British in the war. Uncle Moishe was wounded—"

"I know, Reuven, but the British aren't exactly grateful to Uncle Moishe or to me or people like us. A few days ago a man named Winston

Churchill who's very important in the British government sat on the terrace of the King David Hotel in Jerusalem and looked out into the distance and there and then apparently decided that the Arabs needed another country, so he created a new place called the Kingdom of Jordan. All that land, Reuven, was once a part of Judea."

"What are we going to *do* about it, *abba?*"

"Fight, Reuven . . . We must be prepared, we can't depend on anyone, especially the British, to even help us get our land. That's why instead of going back and working the land I'm working where I feel I'm most needed, with the Zionist Agency . . . And now, Reuven, I think you should go to bed, it's getting late . . . oh, and don't tell your mother about this, I don't want to worry her . . ."

Mr. Leibowitz couldn't believe it was one o'clock already. He wasn't a bit tired, but he knew he should go home and let these people get some sleep. Getting up he said to Dovid, "If you need me for something, anything, don't hesitate to ask."

Dovid nodded. "I'll remember, Mr. Leibowitz. And thank you for all you've done for Chavala. It makes me feel better knowing she has someone here like you."

"*Shalom* . . . Maybe if you have nothing better to do, stop by and we can lunch in my office?"

But that invitation was not to be taken advantage of . . .

When Dovid started to undress in the dark Chavala said calmly, "Dovid, I think maybe you better go down and get a cab."

He went quickly to her, took her in his arms. "The pains . . . are they very bad?"

"No, they started about an hour ago. Dovid, I love you, thank God you're here . . ."

THE family, as well as Mr. Leibowitz, waited nervously as Chavala was taken to the delivery room at Bellevue Hospital.

Dovid paced in one direction, Moishe the other. Reuven had never seen his father so worried. As for himself, he just felt sort of embarrassed . . . not sure what to do or how to act.

Mr. Leibowitz, sitting next to him, said, "Your *abba* is a wonderful man, Reuven, and your *ema* is a remarkable woman. I know they're both very proud of you."

Reuven barely heard him as he watched his father pacing back and forth.

Chia had her own special, private fears as her thoughts inevitably went back to when Chavala's and her mother had died . . . if anything happened to Chavala, she didn't think she could bear it. Chavala had always been more like a mother to her than a sister . . . The hours seemed endless. She put her arms around Reuven and held him close to her, as much to reassure herself as Reuven. . . .

Nature took over, and on October 23, 1920, after five hours in labor, Chavala gave birth to a son. He weighed nine pounds, three ounces, and from the moment of birth was the living image of his father.

Back in the ward, Chavala asked to see her husband and Dovid was quickly at her side.

Chavala smiled. "Have you seen him, Dovid?"

He shook his head, "No, not yet, but I see you and I love you and—"

"Wait, Dovid, wait until you do. I thought I was seeing a miniature you."

She stroked his head, which lay against her breast, filled with an inexpressibly tender love for this big, strong man who felt no shame in expressing his own love. Trying not to allow the shadow of his leaving her room affect this wonderful moment of closeness, she whispered, "I love you, Dovid. Now go see your new son."

He smiled, kissed her, and walked down the long ward between the rows of beds. He took Reuven with him, and the two walked on to the nursery. The others stayed behind, understanding that this was a special moment between the father and son.

When the infant was handed to Dovid he lowered the child so that Reuven could see his brother for the first time. It was a shared moment they both would never forget . . .

THREE days later Chavala was able to go home, carrying her new son, sharing the joy of him with Dovid, Chia, and Reuven, who almost from the start acted more like a kind of substitute father than a mere brother. He seemed at once fascinated and possessive about the baby.

The day his son was circumcised Dovid proudly held him, surrounded by Moishe, Reuven, and Mr. Leibowitz. After being given a drop of schnapps the infant slept in his father's arms while the men toasted the new father.

Afterward they were joined by others at the apartment for the *simcha.* The pearl-stringer Yetta was there, and so were all the people Chavala had worked with. Mrs. Neusbaum and Mrs. Zuckerman had brought enough food to feed everyone and twenty more, and Mr. Leibo-witz *kvelled* with the pride of a grandfather as he held the child. "Chavala . . . Chavala . . . what a baby, I can't believe it. It was like yesterday that you sat in my office, needing help, and now . . ."

Finally people said their goodnights, and as they did, Chavala thought of a leave-taking to come that would not be so sweet. She'd not let the thought settle in her mind up to now, the joy of little Joshua . . . it had seemed a fitting name when she'd mentioned it to Dovid and he'd immediately agreed . . . had been too important to be sullied with it. But now, there was nothing to do but face it. Dovid had not changed his mind. He had come to America, she now reminded herself, for the birth of their child, in time to be with her when she delivered, even though he hadn't come on the occasion of Reuven's bar mitzvah, which must have seemed almost as important to him. Almost . . . Remember that, Chavala, when you're tempted to feel sorry for yourself, or berate Dovid . . . You, your child, came first. Remember that . . .

They sat quietly in the kitchen on the last night before his departure, and spoke of everything except what would happen the next day.

Suddenly, framed in the doorway, was Reuven. He looked first at his mother, than at his father. Slowly he walked to where they sat. Without hesitation, he spoke the words he had so carefully weighed, and rehearsed.

"*Ema,* I love you, I always will, but I want to go home with *abba.*"

She cleared her throat, swallowed back the tears. What could she say? He had a right to go, and in a way she'd known without admitting it to herself that this was going to happen. It was only a question of when . . . and now it was no question. After all, she had the new child, she had Moishe and Chia. Dovid had nothing of his family. She would not stop Reuven, not even argue. This was not his country, perhaps it never would be. Like his father he belonged in the hills of Zichron . . . the farm at Athlit . . . the coves of Caesarea. Even when the snows of winter melted in America, Reuven would always be cold.

Chavala nodded, even managed a smile. "I'm happy for you, Reuven. I will miss you, my sweet boy, but your father has missed you long enough. And life has a way of taking care of things . . . I think there will come a time when we will all be together again. I believe that . . ." And she did. She had to . . .

CHAVALA stood with Joshua in her arms and watched as Dovid and Reuven walked up the gangplank. She felt a chill all through her, and not only from the sharp winds that blew in from the sea.

The whistle blew, and the ship began to move out. She stood on the dock, flanked by Moishe and Chia, until it was lost from sight. Then they turned and slowly walked back to their life.

Chapter Twenty-five

Dovid and reuven stood at Athlit and looked out to the shoals. They watched the sea roll back and cascade above the high rocks. The spray felt so good on Reuven's face. This might have been the happiest day in his life, except for the look of sadness in his father's eyes. He could guess that it had to do with being apart from his mother, which he realized affected him too. Yes, even though he had not been happy in America and never really understood, or at least accepted, his mother taking him there and staying there, he did miss her. Yes, he *missed* her . . .

And Reuven was right. Dovid did miss Chavala, and thinking about her he also thought of the years they'd lived here. How contented Chavala had been, the pride she'd taken in their small house. But the memories were not all sweet. And filtering through were the sounds of dying, killing. They drowned out the good thoughts . . . Mostly he'd returned here today because Reuven wanted back the memories of his childhood, but for Dovid there was too much to remember . . .

And now there was even more . . . He closed his eyes against the sky. This morning he had heard the news that Aaron had died in an airplane somewhere over the Atlantic. It seemed too much to cope with. Aaron had so much more to give, and he'd somehow always seemed so . . . invulnerable, invincible. He shook his head. Aaron would not have wanted him to be undone by grief. They'd fought too long and hard, too many of them had died to give up now. Their land was still not theirs . . . to withdraw from the struggle would betray the past, and forfeit the future . . .

Reuven stood very close to his father, almost feeling his pain. And determination too. "*Abba,* I know we talked about me living with Aunt Dvora, but I would like to stay in Tel Aviv with you . . . please?"

"I'd like that, Reuven, but my life is too unpredictable. I'm away too often. It's important for a boy, even a big boy like you, to have a settled place to live, and a woman . . . well, a woman like your aunt—"

You're my family, he wanted to say. And *you* need a wife. "Will I see you?"

Dovid knew Reuven's feelings, knew them too well. He'd once been comforted when he needed it most by Chavala's mother, Rivka Rabinsky. His son had been cut adrift too, must be feeling the pain and fear of leaving Chavala and Chia. The next week he'd planned with his son would, he hoped, help ease the change for him.

Dovid put his arm around his son's shoulder. "Will you see me? Of course, as often as possible."

As they walked back to Dovid's car, Reuven looked across the fields and saw the laboratory at Athlit where he remembered his father had brought him as a very small boy. Some of the sounds and sights came back. He had wanted to be a scientist like Dovid, he remembered his father holding him up so he could look into the lens of the microscope. Well, maybe he still would be, but first he would work with his father to create a permanent homeland for the Jews . . .

They drove up into the hills of Carmel, the first time Reuven had seen it, thanks to the war. The view was so breathtaking from the summit he asked his father to stop the car. Together they stood and looked out to the city built on rolling hills. Beyond the sloping landscape lay the harbor and a startlingly blue bay. They looked to the mountains of Galilee . . . Mount Hermon looked regal with its crown of snow . . . the golden dome of the Bahai shrine shimmered in the noonday sun.

Reuven was so taken with this place he felt he never wanted to leave, but Dovid said they had a long ride to Tel Aviv.

They wound their way down the hills, and Dovid became very quiet as they passed the Oriental inn. He slowed the car and looked for a long, lingering moment, recalling those four beautiful days when he and Chavala had stayed here . . . a lifetime, really . . .

When they'd come to the Arab section at the bottom of Carmel, Dovid passed the harbor, turned and continued south. There were few vehicles on the road except for an occasional busload of Arabs and the donkey carts. Further on, they were forced to the side of the road by the sirens of a British convoy as it passed.

Back on the road again, Reuven noticed the contrast between the Jewish and Arab villages. The kibbutzim seemed green, fertile, the earth seemed to come alive as the men plowed the furrows. Passing the Arab villages, he saw the women working in rock-strewn fields (while men sat in the coffeehouses, playing backgammon or sleeping in the sun). Along the roadside women seemed to sway back and forth as they walked along, trying to balance the heavy loads they carried on their heads.

As they passed Zichron Yaakov, Fort Taggert, in the distance, seemed more foreboding, surrounded as it was by barbed wire. Now, abruptly, they saw Hadera in bloom, vast expanse of lush green with counterpoint of orange groves.

It was four o'clock in the afternoon when they arrived at the outskirts of Tel Aviv. Reuven would never forget the sight. A shimmering whiteness, it almost seemed to rise out of the blue Mediterranean. Dovid drove to his apartment on Hayarkon Street. Then he and his son walked down Allenby Road, alive with shops, honking cars and people rushing to catch buses. There was one bookstore after another. The plaza was packed with mothers and children. They strolled up to Rothschild Boulevard to the Old City, which had been a part of Jaffa. The shops in the Arab city appeared neglected, shabby . . . Reuven wanted to go back to Tel Aviv.

They walked through the connecting street of the two cities, through the common marketplace, where both Jews and Arabs traded, then on to the narrow alleys where the multitude of shoppers milled about the stalls.

Finally they returned to Allenby Road, walked passed the Mograbi Plaza, then turned into another wide, tree-lined boulevard—Ben-Yehudah Street was alive, filled with sidewalk cafes, patronized mostly by German Jews, others by sabras, others by bohemians, political engagées . . . all creating a feeling of carnival. A sense of camaraderie seemed in the air. The city pulsed with vitality.

As they sat at an early dinner, Reuven noticed the tensions in his father had relaxed since they'd come to Tel Aviv.

Dovid smiled. "Would you believe, Reuven, that when we came here, right where you're sitting, there was nothing but sand dunes? I don't want to make you feel ancient, but you're a year older than Tel Aviv."

Reuven was pleased to think that he and his age were important enough to be compared to the first Jewish city in two thousand years. "We're both sabras," he said, and laughed.

"I never thought of it that way, but you're right. Tomorrow, though, we'll go to places that are even older than *I* am."

The next morning they journeyed south again. Passing the harbor at Jaffa, Dovid pointed and said, "That's where your mother and I first arrived when we came here . . ." and, encouraged by his son, retold all the events of that special day. As he did, Reuven could visualize his mother tearing her petticoat in strips, then knotting them together so that

Chia's basket could be lowered into the rowboat, he could almost see the *chalutzim* rowing out to the boat ahead of the Arabs as they screamed, "*Baksheesh . . .*"

Eventually they arrived in Jerusalem and wound their way up to Bab el Wad, and as they passed this place Dovid couldn't help but think how different his life, and his family's, might have been if Chavala had not so desperately needed a sack of flour on a certain day . . . Quickly he accelerated the motor and shifted gears as he made the ascent into the Judean hills.

On either side of the road saplings had been planted within the older forests. Somehow their ability to survive in this soil symbolized those Jews who had redeemed the eroded earth.

The ascent made, it was almost impossible not to feel the magical pull of Jerusalem. When they entered the city there was a haunting quality . . . even in this new city of David the stones that went into the buildings were from the same quarries that had built the Temple and Wall that now remained. They drove along King David Street, past the Yemen Moshe, the windmill gently revolving at Mishkenot Shanayim. As they passed the King David Hotel the bells from the YMCA could be heard, and added to the symphony of sounds, the meuzzin called the faithful to prayer in the Old City, and all over Jerusalem on this Friday afternoon the sound of the ancient ram's horn could be heard.

Dovid parked the car outside of Mea Shearim and they walked into the stone courtyard, where, side-by-side, stood old two-story stone dwellings, their balconies outlined with iron grillwork, their shutters opened and laid back against the walls. Bearded men with sidecurls, wide-brimmed hats and long black satin coats walked briskly along with the Yemenites in flowing caftans, Kurds in colorful silks from the ritual bath to the synagogues. The chanting of prayers, the soulful songs rose beyond the synagogue windows. It occurred to Dovid that he hadn't been inside a *shul* since he'd first come to live in the Old City.

The sounds of prayer had faded, replaced by the warm smells of living, as Dovid and Reuven climbed the flight of stairs to Raizel's apartment. Just before knocking, Dovid looked at Reuven and smiled. "You forgot to bring the halvah."

Reuven hit himself on the forehead, "How dumb. Wait, I'll run and get it . . ."

Breathless by the time he got back to the head of the stairs, he said, "I think it's melting."

"It's better when the oil comes to the surface. Besides, it won't be kosher enough for your uncle, but Aunt Raizel will be glad to accept it."

Their knock was soon answered, and when Raizel saw Reuven, she could only say delightedly, "I *knew* you were coming today, your letter . . . but you didn't say what time . . . oh, I'm so happy to see you, Reuven. Come in, come in."

Inside the sparsely furnished living room Reuven said, a bit awkwardly, "Here, I have this for you, Aunt Raizel."

Raizel looked at the wrapping, and knew it was halvah. She also knew Lazarus would never eat it, God only knew if it was kosher . . . "That's very nice of you, Reuven. Thank you. Dovid, how are you? I'm so excited—"

"I'm fine, Raizel."

"We have so much to talk about, but, later, later . . . now I'll just look at the chickens in the oven . . ."

After Raizel left them Reuven asked, "What does Uncle Lazarus do for a living?"

Dovid felt like saying, As little as possible, but he answered, "He has two jobs. He's a *shammas* in his *shul* and he also teaches at a yeshiva."

"Oh, he's sort of a Hebrew professor?"

"I suppose you could say that."

Just then the door opened and Lazarus walked in with two of his four small sons trailing him. They were inches apart in height, diminutive replicas of Lazarus. All that was missing was Lazarus's black moustache and beard.

Lazarus greeted Dovid and welcomed Reuven in Yiddish. Although his Hebrew was impeccable he refused to use it in conversation . . . to do so would be sacrilegious. As he spoke to Dovid, Reuven looked at his father and with his hand over his mouth he asked through clenched teeth, "What did he say?"

Dovid said, also sotto voce, "That you should learn to speak Yiddish."

Fortunately Raizel was now back in the living room, wiping her hands on her white apron. "Good *Shabbes,*" she said to her husband and sons.

"And a good *Shabbes* to you."

She turned to her sons. "This is your cousin, Reuven."

In Yiddish they responded in unison, "Good *Shabbes.*"

Reuven said, *"Shalom."* He was grateful when Aunt Raizel asked them all to be seated. Putting the shawl over her head, she stood in front of her mother's silver candlesticks that Chavala had given her. She lit the candles, placed her hands over her face and made the Sabbath prayer.

Lazarus then said the *motzi,* the blessing over the bread: "Blessed art Thou, O Lord our God, King of the universe, who brings forth bread from the earth." After saying the benediction, he cut the bread and handed a piece to each person at the table.

Soon the plates were being passed back and forth, and no one was more grateful than Reuven. Since he could not talk with his cousins, he felt distinctly uncomfortable sitting across from them, just staring.

They too were staring, all eight eyes, in disbelief. Their mother had said that this was their cousin, so they believed her. But he was very strange, without any earlocks. Uncle Dovid was clean-shaven, but at least he spoke Yiddish.

But Raizel asked her sons to take their cousin into their room and visit. Sighs of dissent in both Yiddish and Hebrew as the five boys walked down the narrow hall to a back bedroom.

When the table was cleared away the three adults sat around the dining room table. Raizel handed her husband his third glass of tea, then sat down. "Well, Dovid, you must be very proud. Chavala writes that the new baby . . . Joshua . . . looks just like you."

These were difficult moments for Dovid. Who wanted to be reminded that he would miss time seeing his son grow up? . . . "Yes, of course, I'm very proud, Raizel."

Raizel quickly changed the subject. "How is Moishe?"

"He's very happy in the *goldeneh medina.*"

"And tell me about Chia."

"Do you remember when I bought a goat so that we could bring her home from Manya's house?" It seems like yesterday . . . and today Chia's growing into a beautiful young woman."

Raizel smiled. "Oh, she should only have a good life. I'm sure she will—"

"I hope so, Raizel . . . well, it's getting late and tomorrow I'm taking Reuven to the Galilee to see Dvora. Thank you for a wonderful evening . . ."

On their way back to Dovid's apartment, little was said between father and son. Little needed to be said. They both sensed each other's thoughts . . . it had been a strained evening, and both would have been happy to see Aunt Raizel alone next time, without the intimidating presence of those holy five . . .

IN the morning Dovid took the road from Jerusalem that led through the Valley of Rephaim, on past Rachel's Tomb near Bethlehem and south through the hills of Judea. Finally they came to Hebron, a city second only to Jerusalem . . . It was here that Abraham's wife, Sarah, died, and it was here that the patriarch bought the field of Ephron for a family burying place. They drove on past the Dead Sea until they came to the fortress of Masada, a place that Dovid wanted his son to see.

Reuven's eyes scanned the red-brown rocks of Masada as his father told him of the courage that had become a symbol of freedom for Jews for two thousand years. It lived in the heart and sustained the spirit when Jews for centuries thought everything was lost, reminded them that no matter what the catastrophe, they were destined to survive. . . .

His arm around his son's shoulder, Dovid said, "I know it has been very hard on your mother, Reuven, but I am glad you asked to come with me. I am glad you feel about this land the way I do . . ."

Reuven felt a bond with his father as strong and powerful as the fortress that lay before them. There was no need for words . . .

Chapter Twenty-six

IN SPITE OF all the struggles, the winter storms, the blistering summer heat, Dvora wouldn't change what she had at Kfar Shalom. She and Ari had been one of twenty-five families housed in black tents bought from British army surplus. Pnina, now two, was born that first winter in the midst of a howling wind. By summer in that first year of her life Pnina was stricken with malaria, and only devoted ministration by Ari and Dvora of quinine and love pulled the child through.

Once the baby recovered Ari told Dvora he wanted her and the children to go to stay at Raizel's for "just a little while." When she protested, as Chavala had once done to Dovid, he told her that the children had already been subjected to typhus and malaria, and that at last night's meeting it was agreed that the wives and children would leave until they had cleared the swamps.

"But we've survived our first winter and summer and we'll go on surviving until we have a house . . ."

The next winter the influenza was at its worst. The storms became so violent that the family tents blew away, and the men were constantly having to secure the communal tent. Still, they survived, and when summer came Dvora saw the first building erected on their own piece of ground—it was the barn, a beautiful sight. A new beginning . . .

Until the terrible day when the shots rang out. Quickly, Ari grabbed up his rifle from its rack and ran to the side of the barn, peered around and saw five Bedouins on horseback. He waited until they rode past, aimed, pulled the trigger and hit one in the shoulder.

The shots had so frightened the baby she began to cry uncontrollably. Ari dove to the ground just before another bullet crashed into the wood siding. From a crouched position he watched as another Arab came closer to the entrance, took aim and managed to wing him in the arm.

Finally they galloped off, but they'd be back. Ari knew it. Now, once and for all, the women and children had to be taken to safety. . . .

Although Nazareth was an Arab city, it could still be a refuge for the women from Kfar Shalom. Arab religious and political nationalism was still in its latent state, and there was some cooperation between the city's Christian Arabs and the Jews of the settlements. Actually, the Arabs of Nazareth and the Bedouins were often at odds . . . in contrast to the Bedouin dislike of the Jews, the villagers of Mahalul accepted the settlers, especially when they realized that the new Jewish settlements would be good for them . . . the Jews bought goods in the Arab shops.

It was hard for Ari to leave his children, harder still to part from Dvora.

Dvora walked out to the truck with her husband.

"How long will we be here, do you think?"

"Until we get the settlement secured."

"That will take months."

"Well . . . if it does, at least in the meantime you're safer here." Jews, as they both knew, were never safe.

Ari took her lovely face between his hands. "I love you and I'll miss you." He kissed her and without another word, walked to the truck, started the motor, and was gone.

AS the truck chugged up the hill to Kfar Shalom, Ari was welcomed by the charred remains of his barn. Quickly he ran across the barren field and saw the men of the moshav still trying to put out a few last dying embers.

Too furious to speak, he could only stand and watch the black smoke rise. When he finally recovered from the initial shock he asked, "What happened?"

Isaac Levy shook his head. "They rode in at five this morning and started shooting and hollering like wild men—"

"Was mine the only building they burned?"

"Only yours."

"Well, the next time I'll be ready for them."

He didn't have long to wait. Like locusts they came riding up into the hills. This time the men were prepared. From behind a large boulder, Solomon's eye followed his rifle and he hit one in the hand. Chaim went for the ankle. The counterattack was so unexpected that the Bedouins turned and started to ride off, but Ari's shot rang out and hit a stallion's right hoof. The beast shook violently, then reared, knocking the rider to the ground.

Fraternity not being a virtue among Bedouins, the other three rode off without looking back.

Ari came from behind the boulder and grabbed the Bedouin around the neck.

The man immediately invoked Allah, divine mercy and love of mankind in his behalf. Also he didn't want to die. "It wasn't me . . . on my father's name I swear. We were forced—"

"Who forced you?"

The fear in the man's eyes was apparent. He would be killed if he told, he would be killed if he didn't.

"You're the one who instigated the raid—"

"*No.*"

"Then who?"

"Sheikh Abdullah Kadar."

Ari stood up and looked at the man cringing in the dirt. "Where's the camp?"

"Near Metullah."

And Ari, mostly because the man sickened him so, let him go. One didn't kill helpless vermin.

"SO what good is it, now you know?" Chaim asked.

"I'm going to use a little diplomacy."

"You're going to make a goodwill call?"

"No, but my brother-in-law Dovid is very good at this. I'm going to see him." . . .

Ari could get to Tel Aviv faster by horse, cutting across fields, galloping over hills past the Arab villages. At midnight he hitched his horse to a lamppost and ran up the stairs to Dovid's apartment.

The men embraced, then Dovid asked, "What brings you to Tel Aviv?"

Ari quickly told him.

"And you'd like me to help?"

"Yes, Dovid. I know where the camp is, I know the leader's name."

"That helps. But what would help more is if you had a harvest. They'd cut your throat for a few sacks of flour."

"So what are the alternatives, Dovid?"

"To bluff . . . but be so believable that you convince yourself. You have to think in terms of your own life. Let me show you what I mean."

Dovid went to his bedroom, came back to the kitchen, and without a word hurled a 1914 German grenade out the open door onto the balcony.

Reflexively Ari dove to the floor, waited with his arms over his head. Then, recovering, rolled over and looked at Dovid. "What did you do *that* for? I could have had a heart attack."

Dovid smiled. "As I told you before . . . if you're going to bluff it has to be *very* convincing."

"You convinced me. Just anticipating the sound of the explosion was too damn much—"

"That's what we have to hope for."

"What about real weapons?"

"We'll hide small ones in our abas, but they won't do us much good if our bluff doesn't work." He went out onto the balcony, brought back the defused grenade and handed it to Ari.

"It looks so damned innocent. I'm not going to say this doesn't seem a little crazy to me . . . but if you think it will work, let's try it . . ."

"I can only tell you I think we have a chance, Ari. I remember during the war, when Yehudah Meir commandeered a ship with a pipe instead of a gun. Fear can be a lethal weapon, Ari. It makes no difference what your color is, or what gods you pray to, a life is a life and no one wants to lose his. *That's* our best weapon."

"When do we leave?"

"Tomorrow morning."

DRESSED as Arabs they rode into the hills of Metullah.

It was dusk when Dovid spotted the encampment. "Look to the left, Ari. Now, let's take a closer look."

From a hillock above they could see twelve black goatskin tents which encircled the camp.

"At this hour they should be eating, Ari, but with that many tents we can expect quite a reception. Are you ready?"

Ari nodded, then shrugged. Which was to say, yes and no.

When they rode in, the women dressed in black robes and coin chains covering their faces ran from the sight of strangers.

Dovid and Ari had just dismounted when twelve men appeared, their rifles aimed directly at Ari and Dovid. Soon after, the flap of a large tent opened and Abdullah walked out, dressed in black robe and headdress. Two jeweled daggers hung below his waist. He stood, hands on his hips, demanding to know what they were doing in his camp.

Dovid had managed something like this once before with Jamal Pasha. He'd survived the torture of the Turks. It would be a waste to die in the hills of Metullah. He didn't intend to. "Much less," he shot back, "than you were doing in our village. How many barns did you burn down today?"

Folding his arms across his chest, his hand inside the aba, he caressed the grenade and waited, but the dialogue ended when Abdullah signaled to have the men brought to his tent. First he would break their spirit, then he would mutilate them, then kill them. A holy trinity all his own . . .

As the men raised their rifles and started to move toward them, Dovid and Ari quickly brought out their grenades, holding them up, poised as if to throw. "There is enough dynamite to blow up Metullah," Dovid said quietly.

The men froze. From the look on Dovid's face, Abdullah quickly concluded he was not bluffing, but in any case he would not risk finding out. "Who are you, what's your name?"

"Dovid Landau." He spoke with more confidence than he felt.

Abdullah decided he'd been right about this one. He'd heard of him . . . he'd been the head of NILI. Abdullah, a sensible man about his own life, cautioned himself to be careful, not even show his hatred. No telling what this Jewish assassin had planned . . .

"What is it you want?"

"For you to stay away from our village."

"It is *not* your village, it is our spring grazing land."

Dovid handed Ari the grenade, then walked closer to Abdullah. "No longer. We paid for it, we *worked* it . . . It belongs to us now. If you or your men come back to Kfar Shalom, we will kill you. I promise you that."

The Arab leader, carefully eyeing the grenades, said nothing.

Dovid turned his back on him, and he and Ari walked slowly to their horses, mounted and rode out of the encampment. . . .

It was eleven o'clock that night when they reached Safad.

"Dovid," Ari said as they sat having coffee and pita, "I don't mind telling you I held my breath."

"As, I assure you, I did."

"Well, I think Abdullah has a healthy respect for you, Dovid—"

"More for those grenades . . . but now I do think you can risk bringing the women back."

"We owe you so much, Dovid. But we still have an enemy. When the marshes have been cleared, then we can bring them home."

Home, Dovid thought. Ari and their home, Chavala's and his son's in New York City. He had news of it in Chavala's letters, but he could not be there. Soon, though . . . soon . . .

THE women and children finally did return to Kfar Shalom. It was spring, the season for life's renewal. The fields were covered with wild flowers. But more beautiful still was what Ari had managed.

Dvora came back to find the beginnings of their farm. Crops were planted in the fields, there was a small vineyard and a vegetable garden. Next to the two-room wooden hut Ari had built a new barn and a stable. Two mules, and a cow whose calf sucked at her swollen udders.

Pnina was especially fascinated by the tiny yellow chicks, which she delightedly chased after, waving her arms. Ari led Dvora into the nursery, and Zvi ran after them, not wanting to miss a thing. Ari had already started the beet root for fodder. Dvora shook her head . . . "Darling, when did you have time to sleep?"

"I didn't . . . without you, who needed to go to bed?"

She smiled. Her hunger had been as great as his.

Such an idyllic new beginning, which did not last long . . . In spite of Ari's efforts, the first wheat crop failed. The vegetables lay rotting in the field; Dvora and Zvi had recurrent attacks of malaria, and Ari had to take care of his wife and children. Worse . . . no sooner had Dvora recovered than Pnina developed an eye infection. Each day the lids became more red and swollen, and the child cried through the night. Ari and Dvora took turns trying to comfort her. When morning came the child's eyes were swollen shut.

"Ari, it's no use. We must take the baby to the hospital in Jerusalem."

He nodded. Each knew the other's fears. Trachoma . . .

When they arrived at the hospital, Pnina was taken down the hall to the children's ward. Dvora, Ari and Zvi were left to sit waiting for the doctor.

It seemed an eternity, but finally he appeared.

"Mr. and Mrs. Ben-Levi, I'm Dr. Haril. I've seen your little girl." Dvora's pulse raced.

"We won't be able to tell about her until the swelling goes down."

"But you must have some idea of what it is, doctor," Ari said.

"We can't be sure, but she's been put on medication to reduce the swelling. She's more comfortable."

As Dr. Haril turned to go, Dvora called out to him, "Doctor . . ."

He turned around. "Yes, Mrs. Ben-Levi?"

"We live in the Galilee. Do you think it's all right for my husband to go home . . . or should he stay?"

"If it's important for him to go home, I don't see any immediate danger."

It was five in the afternoon when they went in to see Pnina. Her eyes were bandaged, a sight that was almost too much for the parents. When Ari held her she said, *"Abba?"*

"Yes, darling . . . it's *abba*. I'm here . . ."

Zvi stood next to the bed and whispered, "When you come home, Pnina, we'll ride on the donkey and we'll pick wildflowers like before—"

"Like before. Promise."

"I promise," and that was all he or anyone else could say.

As they left the ward and walked down the corridor, Dvora put her arm around her son. So young . . . and he'd already seen enough for a lifetime . . . She looked at Ari. "Go home, darling, it's getting late . . . I'll get word to you about how things are going. It will be all right . . . I have faith. You must too. Please . . ."

"I won't let you go through this by yourself—"

She remembered when he wanted their safety and she refused to go. "The doctor said it was all right. You have too many responsibilities at home. Besides, I'm going to Raizel's so I won't be alone."

He knew she was right, but hated to leave her.

They walked down the long corridor and out into the dusk. When they reached the truck she kissed her husband and son, trying to smile. But the moment she saw them disappear in the distance a dreadful loneliness came down on her. She felt shattered, hollow. Slowly she went back and waited in front of the hospital for the bus to arrive.

When it came she paid the driver and sat down, not hearing the conversations around her. As it wound its way down the hills she looked out the window and saw the Mount of Olives, and her father's image now came large into her mind, and with it the thought that if it hadn't been for Chavala, he wouldn't even have had a stone . . .

When the bus stopped at the Jaffa gate Dvora got off and ran to the Wailing Wall. She slipped the lightweight sweater off her shoulders and covered her head with it.

For the first time in a very long time, she truly prayed. Opening her purse she took out a small notebook and wrote a prayer to God. Then she placed it between the moss-covered cracks. She touched the ancient stones, remembering the first day her father had come to this holy place. He'd gotten down on his knees and kissed the ground. Something in the depths of her now compelled her to do the same.

On bended knees she put her body very close to the holy wall and embraced it. Tears that could no longer be held back. And whispering to the ears of God she recited:

O Lord of life, our times are
in Thy hands. One generation
cometh into the world to be
blessed with days.

She lingered a few moments longer, then got up and walked through the streets of Jerusalem until she turned into the cobblestoned alley at Mea Shearim. She passed the ritual baths, and a short distance beyond came to the building Raizel lived in.

After being delighted to see her sister, Raizel had to ask her why she was in Jerusalem . . . alone. Dvora took a deep breath and told her the story. "But, Raizel, I don't want Chavala to know anything about this until later. She has her own problems, I don't want to add to them."

Raizel shook her head. "It's too bad when families are so far apart. Sheine in Germany, Chavala in America . . . well, all we can do is pray that maybe one day . . . Come into the kitchen while I fix supper. Lazarus and the boys will be home any minute."

And when they arrived, the scene was a replica of what Dovid and Reuven would experience when they came.

Dvora did not kiss nor touch her brother-in-law, since that too was against his religious precepts. This man was so very rich. Dvora both envied and loved him for his unending reservoir of spirituality.

"It's so good seeing you, Lazarus . . . you look very well."

"I thank God for giving me my health and the health of my family . . . where are the children and Ari?"

She told Lazarus about Pnina. "Our lives are in God's hands, Dvora. You must believe that."

"I'm sure. But it's not knowing that frightens me."

"You must not be afraid. God is watching over us, as it is written. God will help you, Dvora."

"I hope so, Lazarus . . . and I'm sure your prayers will help." How sure was she . . . ?

That night Dvora slept in Raizel's kitchen on a straw mat. She was grateful for the first light of morning. Quickly she washed and dressed, left a note and closed the door softly behind her.

Although she knew it was much too early to see her child, just sitting outside Pnina's room made her feel a little better. She looked at the clock . . . six-thirty.

The nurses were beginning their morning rounds.

"I'm Mrs. Ben-Levi," Dvora said to the young nurse. "My little girl's name is Pnina. Could you tell me how she is?"

"I'm sorry, but you'll have to wait for the doctor."

Dvora paced back and forth until she saw the nurse come out of the children's ward. She went to her. "Pardon me, but what time do the doctors come?"

"They should be making their rounds in about an hour."

"Do you think I could see my little girl?"

"We are very busy in the morning. A little later."

Bracing herself against the wall, she stared up at the ceiling. Perhaps if she had a strong cup of hot coffee she might feel better. She went to the cafeteria in the basement. Peering over the rim, she kept her eyes on the clock . . . it *never* seemed to move. Oh, God, this waiting was unbearable. After three cups she went back upstairs and sat.

At nine o'clock she saw the doctor go into the ward. She thought she would die until he came out again. Quickly she went to meet him, "Good morning, doctor. You've seen Pnina?"

"Yes."

"How is she?"

"About the same as yesterday. We made a diagnosis. She does have trachoma—"

Dvora steadied herself, then caught her breath. "How serious is it?"

"Fortunately it's in the beginning stages. I think it can be cured in a reasonable length of time—"

"How long . . . I must let my husband know."

"I think she should stay here about a month."

Dvora shook her head. "Thank God." The news was better than she'd feared.

That evening she wrote to Ari:

> Dearest Ari,
>
> Our anxieties over Pnina were exaggerated. I suppose parents always think of the worst things, but you can rest easy now.
> Pnina has a mild case of trachoma. If we'd neglected to take care of it when we did it would have been more serious. I am not going to concern myself with anything other than the fact that we will be home together very soon. Please stay well and give Zvi my love.
>
> Yours forever,
> *Dvora*

After five seemingly endless weeks of anxiety and loneliness, the waiting was over, and Ari was able to come to take Dvora and Pnina home.

When he looked at his family, Ari realized that Dvora had performed miracles with the little girl, but she was working so hard and her hours were so long, he worried about her health. "You can't keep going this way, Dvora." She looked at him and smiled, as though he'd said something too foolish to respond to.

But after the medical bills had been paid and with no crops to sell, their funds were depleted. The work on the new stone house had to be suspended. The children needed shoes, Ari needed seed to plant. Dvora was beside herself. The needs were *so* great she thought of breaking down and asking for Chavala's help. In fact, she'd suggested it to Ari. "No," he said. "We can get a loan from the mutual. I don't want charity from *anybody.*"

"But Chavala's sending us things now and you don't object to it—"

"That's different, they're for the children. But I won't accept from her what I can't pay back."

But Dvora was beyond such worries of pride. A loan would be one final burden too many, she was convinced. In her letter to Raizel it was difficult not to unburden herself.

IT was also too much for Raizel to hold back from Chavala what Dvora was going through:

> Dear Chavala,
>
> I know honor is important and one should never betray a promise . . . But this promise I made to Dvora, I feel I can't honor.
> Two months ago Pnina was stricken with trachoma. Thank God the child has recovered and is doing fine, but because of the illness, they went badly into debt and, as you know, when things begin to go bad it seems that everything happens at once. They've had one failure after another in their crops. They barely have money for seed.
> I know you never would have forgiven me if I had kept silent. I can understand Ari's pride, but when a child's need is so great, one must put their feelings behind them.
> I'm sorry, dearest Chavala, to be the bearer of such bad news, but I had to speak out. I trust that this finds you and Chia and Moishe and, of course, Reuven, in the best of health, and may God bless you for all you have already done.
>
> > With love and devotion,
> > your sister,
> > *Raizel*

When Chavala received Raizel's letter, there was a momentary feeling of anger that Dvora hadn't taken her into her confidence. What did they suppose she was doing here, living without her husband, if it wasn't to help secure the future of the *family?* To help whenever she could? Then quickly the feeling was replaced with worry about Dvora and her family. Obviously Dvora hadn't wanted to burden her with such news. Dvora's courage, her loyalty to Ari so great . . . to go against his wishes and ask for anything would be impossible . . .

Unfortunately, though, at that time the pawnshop was earning just enough to pay for expenses and to send a little something to Palestine. But this was a crisis. Action was required. Chavala went into action.

She went to the back room, took one of the cigar boxes out of the safe, brought it to the table and sat down. Lifting the lid, she took out the largest stones, put the loupe in her eye and examined each of them . . . color was blue-white . . . no carbon . . . carat and a half. They were worth $250 per carat.

She selected five of the best and took them to Mr. Leibowitz.

"My darling Chavala," the old man said when she came into his office. "Business must be too good, I haven't seen you for some time."

"My family complains about the same thing, and they're right, and so are you. But it's not really because business is so good. I must stay in the shop, hoping a customer will come in."

"It's hard for a woman . . . I know, Chavala."

"I don't mind . . . my sister, Dvora, is the one with problems."

She quickly told Mr. Leibowitz about Dvora, then put the stones on his desk. "I must sell these immediately."

He examined them carefully. "These are very nice stones."

"What's the most I can get for them?"

"Well . . . $250 per carat . . ."

"Who shall I take them to?"

"These I could use."

She hugged him. Words were inadequate for what she felt.

She went immediately to the bank and withdrew the thousand dollars she had in her account, which now would show no balance, added it to the amount from the sale of the stones, then made arrangements to have the money sent the fastest way possible.

WHEN Dvora received the $2,500 she was stunned. How Chavala knew, Dvora could only guess. Never mind. It was wonderful to have a family, and she thanked God for both her sisters. And she didn't feel at all diminished by Chavala's help. Instead she felt strangely rich, not because of the money, but because it was a gift of love. From a loved one.

More—and Dvora was enormously excited by this—was the news that Dovid *and* Reuven were coming to see them, that Reuven would be staying with them . . . Looking up from her gardening, she heard the sound of Dovid's car approaching. Quickly she picked Pnina up and went to greet them.

After the introductions between Reuven and little Pnina, Reuven went out in the field to see his uncle and cousin, and Dvora and Dovid could settle down to a chat.

"The house is almost ready?" Dovid asked.

"Yes. We'll be moving in in about a month . . . I hope Reuven will be happy with us, Dovid."

"He will, I'm sure . . ."

"Does he say much about Chavala?" She knew it was a risky subject, but felt it better to bring it up now and in terms of Reuven rather than Dovid.

"Not much . . . not yet . . ."

"You know, Dovid, Chavala never complains. I only hope you know . . . oh, I'm sure you do . . . that this separation isn't easy for her either. You may not agree with her, but what she's doing isn't for herself—"

Dovid was grateful when Ari and the two boys came in and interrupted them.

"Dovid, how good to see you."

Dovid nodded, a bit stiffly. "Everything looks good Ari. It's remarkable what you've accomplished in just this last year."

"Look at the help I've had," Ari said, smiling at Zvi. "And this year should be even better with Reuven here . . . you think you're going to like being a farmer?"

The thought had never been far from Reuven's mind . . . times at Athlit and especially the night at dinner with Aaron . . . the echoes came back . . . "I want to be a scientist like my father . . ." That had been the dream. Well, even at Reuven's age, with what he'd been through, he knew you sometimes settled for a little less than the dream . . . Not grudgingly, in fact happily, except . . . if only he could reshape his world so that his mother and father would be together, be a family, and he and his father would work the land the way Ari and Zvi were doing . . . and his brother Joshua would know the feeling of sacred earth beneath his feet. Could he ever understand his mother? For what she had done? . . . He looked at his father, then at his uncle Ari. "When I was in America that's all I ever thought about . . . yes, Uncle Ari, I'm going to like being a farmer . . ."

Dovid looked at his son, felt a deep bond that went even beyond the two of them. The flame of Zion would *never* be put out. It would be passed from generation to generation. It was eternal. And with the sweet joy of that conviction came a deep sadness about Chavala. If only she could understand that, despite everything else, their lives without one another were incomplete . . . and that all the desperation Raizel and Lazarus endured, the hardships Ari and Dvora shared, were part of the riches of life. But then . . . he was responsible too for them not being together . . . his love of Eretz Yisroel, how did he square that with his love for Chavala? Well, he could only hope. In his head he knew the truest legacy in life was the deep abiding love of a man for a woman. When would he and Chavala know that in their hearts . . . ?

He was so deep in thought he scarcely heard Dvora say, "Reuven, darling, go get your things from the car and, Zvi, you bring uncle Dovid's."

When the boys left, Dvora said to Dovid, "I'm sorry, Dovid, for . . . well . . . for the circumstances that brought Reuven back, but since he is here I can tell you it means so much to Zvi. He's talked about Reuven like a big brother."

Dovid hesitated for a moment. "I'm glad some good comes out of this separation . . ."

Fortunately, the two boys came in then with the suitcases. "Where do you want these, Aunt Dvora?" Reuven asked.

She smiled. "In *your* and Zvi's room. We'll unpack them later, after dinner . . . And welcome to our home, Reuven."

He pushed the thought of his mother aside. "It's good to be home . . . I mean in your home . . ."

Dovid did not miss his son's slip of the tongue. Perhaps it had somehow been planned for his son not to be a stranger living in an alien place. Reuven was part of five thousand years of Jewish history . . . maybe it was no accident he was here at this moment, to help claim the heritage that had been promised so long ago . . .

AT four o'clock in the morning Reuven was initiated into the life of a farmer.

"Time to get up, Reuven," Dvora said, nudging him gently.

Stretching, he shook off sleep. "What time is it?"

"A little after four." She laughed. "Your father has already milked the cows. In fact, he couldn't wait to get started this morning."

Reuven jumped quickly out of bed, shivered slightly as he put on his robe and went to the outhouse. When he returned he dressed hurriedly, walked into the kitchen and joined the others in a breakfast of cucumbers, tomatoes, cheese, homemade bread and tea.

Afterward, Dovid placed the plow in Reuven's hand. "All right, let's see you plow a straight line."

Reuven looked at his father. "What do you think I am, a genius? A straight line . . . I can't even move this thing—"

"You'll learn."

By noon, after hours of sweating, Reuven stood back with Dovid at his side and looked at the furrows, then looked at his father. Both laughed.

"Did you ever grow crooked wheat?" Reuven asked his father.

"Once or twice . . . after lunch it'll be straight."

"I see, you were just testing, is that it?"

"Just testing. You see, I did think you were a genius."

At the end of that day when Reuven gratefully got into bed, he said goodnight to his father and added, "I'll plow a straight line tomorrow if it kills me."

It wasn't precisely "tomorrow" that Reuven managed that wondrous achievement, but after four days he could say to his father as he followed alone, "You're going to have to keep up the seeding a little faster."

EXCEPT for the Shomer guardsmen to defend the settlements, no Jews could carry or own guns, by order of the British. Well, that was a law Dovid would not honor, not when it came to his son. Taking his German carbine out of its case, he handed it to Reuven. "I'm going to teach you how to defend yourself. Now remember this is to be used for that one purpose and *no* other . . ."

Each morning at dawn Dovid took Reuven to the furthermost reaches of the farm. He taught him the safety devices, how to load and unload the gun, how to clean and care for it. At first Reuven missed every empty bottle, every tin used as a target. But then, gradually, under Dovid's patient tutelage, he was able to take aim and split a rock as Dovid threw it up into the air.

Reuven's next lesson was how to defend himself with a bullwhip. The first day Reuven thought his arm was going to fall off, but after a while he began to catch on to the technique until, finally, with a flip of the wrist he could cut a leaf to shreds. It was not a lesson Dovid was happy his son had to learn, but it was, like survival, a fact of life . . .

A week had passed since then, and now, as Dovid looked across the field watching his son plow, the sight brought a special joy to him, tempered by the thought that his son would almost surely have to live all of his life with a plow in one hand and a gun in the other.

And the thought nudged him . . . shouldn't he have considered the dangers when Reuven wanted to return with him? In a way Chavala was not so wrong after all. She wanted peace and safety for her family, her sons especially, and how could he blame her for that? She'd known more than her share of violence and tyranny and bloodshed. This morning

Dovid wasn't so sure of himself. And yet, sitting on the fence watching Reuven parting the soil into deep furrows, with Zvi behind planting the seed, how could he really question that this *was* their heritage, and that it was worth fighting for?

At noon Dvora came into the field with food to feed her men. She put down the basket and stood resting her hands on the fence where Dovid sat, then looked out at the two boys in the distance. Neither spoke for a moment, then she said, "Reuven's so much like you . . . it's amazing how quickly he's learned . . . I only hope what we're doing will make it easier for them—"

"I'm not sure anything will make it easier. But at least they'll grow up never knowing what it feels like to be a ghetto Jew. They'll be free men, and that's really what this is all about . . . they'll be able to live their lives in dignity, with *pride* in their Jewishness. I think that's about the best legacy we could give them."

She nodded, but felt more at ease with less grand notions . . . "Reuven is going to miss you when you leave tomorrow."

"I know . . . if only I didn't have to be away so much. On the way back from America I even considered getting a small farm and working it with Reuven. It's what I've always loved the most, using my hands. But that was foolish, I can't go back, too much has happened, too much to do . . ."

The valley that Dovid for so long looked to made up the southern Galilee. Few knew and understood the land better than he did . . . those years in Athlit had earned him the reputation of a man who knew how to make the desert bloom. He knew that beneath those marshlands lay a floor of fertile, black, yielding soil. What was needed were money and knowledge to teach the new settlers how to farm and not to fail. The dream of that valley had lived with Dovid. He'd gone to work with Myer Benei, a French-Jewish architect who'd designed many of the moshavim and kibbutzim in the Jezreel Valley. With the restrictions lifted by the British, Dovid was free to go to the Zion Settlement Society with a whole plan. "If you will it, then it need not remain a dream," Herzl had said. The Society voted favorably on Dovid's idea, and he was sent to Beirut to make the purchase. The parcel included an area between Haifa and Nazareth. The Jezreel purchase fired Jewish pride and funds poured in from world Jewry. That one step opened the way to the establishment of hundreds of new kibbutzim, and with them the cities grew, houses were built in the hills of Haifa and apartments began to spring up in Tel Aviv. A building boom started in Jerusalem outside the Old City as the need grew for the Jews to expand the restricted old community. It seemed that the Yishuv could begin to believe that after two thousand years of persecution they had found some justice. The Yishuv Central became a kind of government to speak for the Jews and be a link to the Zion Settlement Society and the world's Zionists. Although Dovid had no political ambitions, he became deeply involved and was personally responsible for much of the planning. He was well-known for his Jezreel Valley feat. He'd given his heart and soul to it. So although he hadn't sought it, he was elected to the Yishuv Central. It became his life's work . . .

Well, that work now had a new frontier. "Next week," Dovid was saying to Dvora, "the Agency is sending me to Paris to try and negotiate a tract of land Baron Rothschild owns. He's been adamant about selling, but I'll wait till hell freezes if necessary. We need it for resettlement and we need it *now.*"

"Where is the land?"

"Near Trans-Jordan."

"Why there?"

"When we become a nation—as I know we will—eventually we're going to have to secure our borders, and the more settlements we have in that area the stronger our position will be."

"Dovid, you really think that we have a chance of becoming a *nation?*"

"If I didn't, then I'd go to America and get into the jewelry business with Chavala." He tried to keep the trace of bitterness out of his voice, and didn't entirely succeed.

Dvora shook her head. She remembered well how much Chavala had sacrificed. Without Chavala the farm wouldn't be so green and lush. Without Chavala, Pnina might have gone blind. She only prayed that Dovid could permit himself to remember also, but it would not do to remind him now. "Well, I pray you're right, Dovid . . . I mean about us having our own country . . . And now I had better get on with lunch."

Dovid got down from the fence, picked up the heavy basket of food and walked with Dvora across the field.

REUVEN, not surprisingly, had refused, been unable to face Dovid's leaving. He'd closed his mind to it, but the wonderful days with him had come to an end, and now he stood looking at his father in their parting moments. "When will you be back, *abba?*" he asked, trying to keep his voice even.

"As soon as I return from Paris."

"Well . . . have a good trip." He looked away.

"Better than good, please. Hope I succeed. Wish me luck."

Reuven nodded. "I do . . . you'll write?"

"Every day." They looked at one another, then slowly, Dovid placed his hands on Reuven's shoulders, drew him close. Then he quickly separated himself from his son, "Take care, Reuven . . . and remember what I told you about the gun . . . only in self-defense . . . only when there is no other alternative."

"I will."

"Good . . . I love you, son."

Quickly Dovid got in the car and started the engine. Reuven stood watching as the car disappeared in the distance, then walked slowly to the fields, where he lay down among the clump of eucalyptus trees and cried until he fell asleep.

Chapter Twenty-seven

THIS PARTING HAD been even more difficult than the first for Chavala, but as the days became weeks and the weeks turned to months, she worked harder than ever before. Her goal . . . to make enough money to bring *all* her family together . . . was reinforced by her need to blunt the pain of separation.

On this particular day Chavala sat in the shop going over the books, as she did so often, but today she just could not concentrate.

After closing the store, Chavala pulled down the shades and to Moishe, "I went to see Mr. Leibowitz."

"What about?"

"Well, I told him that I was very grateful for the kind of living we're making, but that it's not really enough for our needs. He sent me to Hammerstein's, and I've been offered a line on commission."

Moishe could hardly speak.

"Why are you so shocked, Moishe?"

Which was the same question she had asked Mr. Leibowitz. He hadn't exactly sent her to Hammerstein's the way she said. She'd asked,

"How can you make money in jewelry *without* owning a retail store?"

"Well, for you it's not, I want to tell you that right away, but a man can take on a line, go on the road and make a good living. They pay five percent on gross sales."

"So, if I sold twenty thousand dollars' worth, I'd get one thousand dollars?"

"Well, not you, Chavala, but a salesman—"

"Why *not* me, Mr. Leibowitz?"

Her even considering it was so out of the question that Mr. Leibowitz could only shrug.

"Why are you so shocked? Just because I'm not a man?"

He nodded, mumbled, "Yes . . . I suppose that's what I mean . . . Chavala, a woman does not go on the road with a line. It's not for a woman, *believe* me."

Chavala smiled. "You know, Mr. Leibowitz, we Jews had a general once, *her* name was Deborah, and I bet she didn't even go to college, let alone on the road."

Mr. Leibowitz had to smile back.

"Listen, I read the newspapers, not just Yiddish, but the *New York Times*. I read about a lady who's helping women plan their families, not get worn out by so many kids they all starve. And also about one woman being responsible for having no more whiskey in this country . . . You know, Prohibition, it's called. Well, if those women could do that, then certainly I can take a line."

The smile froze. "This is a different story, they didn't have to *shlep* a case of merchandise from one city to another—"

"True. One, however, did *shlep* an ax." She laughed. "Besides, I figure there are enough stores right here in New York so I won't have to travel. Now, Mr. Leibowitz, as my dear friend, please tell me who would give me a line."

He shook his head. If Chavala said she wanted a line, nothing would stop her. "All right, already, you'll go see Hammerstein. Maybe . . . maybe he would listen to you." But he devoutly hoped not. For her own good.

"Mr. Leibowitz, how can I thank you? And please come to dinner tonight . . ."

Now it was Moishe saying, "A woman salesman? I don't understand, Chavala—"

"Listen, Moishe, I can sell as good as any man. I know it . . ."

"That's not the point. A woman shouldn't travel alone, and besides, what will you do with the baby?"

"I'll answer the first. I wouldn't travel, only at most to upstate New York, and mostly right around Manhattan here. As for the baby, thank God he's getting along fine, staying the days with Mrs. Zuckerman. I'll still pick him up in the evening, like I do now."

Moishe, who understood what it was to be outgunned, shrugged and said, "I can't stop you. God help you and good luck."

"Thank you, Moishe, you'll see. And soon we'll be able to open a store."

Chavala had her hair bobbed, which had become the style, and she carefully watched how the ladies in Manhattan were dressed when they walked on Fifth Avenue. She shopped for a nice matching skirt and jacket at Gimbels, navy blue, and a white silk blouse. She bought navy shoes and a bag, then went to the cosmetic department and for the first time bought lipstick.

Not only was Moishe shocked by the transformation in Chavala, but Mr. Hammerstein was speechless. She was beautiful. If he had had any misgivings about Chavala as a salesman he surely didn't now. Besides, he'd been won over by her charm, her smarts, her ability to make him feel her confidence that she could sell anything she put her mind to. But *this* he hadn't bargained for.

AND Chavala proved she could do just what she said. She didn't worry about failure. She wouldn't let herself even consider it. And fear . . . ? She'd killed two men so her family could survive. She should worry about being turned down by a buyer, about looks or questions? It made no difference how long she had to wait to see the buyer, she waited. She was never coy, she didn't use womanly devices to sell, except to try to look good. Sure, at first there was some resistance because she was a woman, but it could be handled. She obviously was a curiosity. Well, the little white lies she told didn't damage the quality of her merchandise. How long had she been in the business? . . . All her life. She had been born a jeweler. Came from a long line of European jewelers. Cut her eyeteeth on her mother's diamond bracelet, and so forth.

After the initial resistance was worn down the buyers even began to take *her* to lunch. Lunch? Fine. Dinner was politely declined . . . she was tired, it was a difficult life for a woman but also so rewarding . . . look at the people one met . . . And the commission checks grew and grew.

Until late one afternoon, after having returned to Mr. Hammerstein's with her case, she felt his warm breath on her face and his thick arms around her waist.

Well, well . . . it seemed Mr. Leibowitz wasn't all wrong. Being a woman did have its disadvantages in a man's world. Or maybe to some its advantages . . . she may have come from the *shtetl* but she knew a woman could make more money on her back than she could with commissions. But *not* her.

She disengaged herself from Mr. Hammerstein, looked at his flushed face, turned away from his uneven breathing. Grinding out the words she said, "You're a fool, Mr. Hammerstein. You're low. Don't think I'm flattered, and don't for a minute think I'm afraid. I'm just disgusted and angry. Take a look at the pictures of your grandchildren. I'll wait outside for my check." She walked out, slamming the door behind her.

Yes, she was offended by Mr. Hammerstein, but far more, she was angry that her growing success with his line was so short-lived. Yes . . . she could probably get another line, but then what? There were more Mr. Hammersteins out there . . . she was sure they came in all different sizes and shapes. So Chavala went back to the pawnshop, but said nothing to Moishe about her real reasons . . .

"But you seemed so happy," Moishe said as he watched Chavala look through the loupe at a small ring they had bought this morning.

"I was, but you can't get real money that way . . . and besides, I like being my own boss." And not being Miss Available, she added to herself.

"To tell the truth, I'm happy you're back. I never liked the idea of your *shlepping* around all that jewelry. A woman has to be more careful than a man—"

"You're right, Moishe . . . Listen, it's almost time to close. Pull down the shade and lock the door."

Chavala obviously had something on her mind. She never closed the store on time, often stayed open for an hour or two beyond closing time.

Sitting in the back room Chavala said, "You know, Moishe, I've been thinking . . ."

When she started a sentence with that opening, and the faraway look in her eyes, Moishe knew for sure Chavala had something coming . . . "All right, what have you been thinking?"

"That we now *must* open up a jewelry store."

"That's a very good idea, but it seems to me you once said it took an inventory we still don't have. Besides, we make a living here—"

"I didn't give up my husband to *make a living* . . . I came here to make a great deal of money. I have my reasons . . ."

Moishe laughed. "I wouldn't be unhappy if you made a million dollars, but tell me, what do you plan on using for capital?"

"My brains. Plus take some chances. We both have done that before." Chavala swallowed hard. "I can get stock—"

"Someone will give it to you on consignment?"

"Who? Don't be foolish, and I wouldn't ask Mr. Leibowitz. Besides, the insurance alone would be so high we couldn't afford it."

"Well, then?"

Chavala folded her arms across her chest and took a deep breath, exhaled. "I found a . . . a fence . . . his last name I don't know and I don't care. But I spoke to this . . . *landsman,* that's what he's called, and after a while he agreed to sell to me . . ."

Moishe just sat and stared.

Chavala hurried on. "Would you believe it, Moishe, he looks like a *tzaddik,* although I know better, but still you would be surprised how nice he seems—"

Moishe found his voice and all but yelled, "We could go to jail."

"I know . . . and I'm not proud to have to do this . . . or too proud to do it . . . but it's the only way, Moishe—"

"Why is it the only way? Where are you running, who's chasing you?"

"Time, that's who. I'm over thirty and we have a *family* in Palestine, and they need help. I'm not going to tell you if you don't know what bad times they're having. Listen to me, Moishe, we could be here for twenty years and in twenty years I'll be over fifty and then it will be too late. You think I'm going to stand by and see my family starving? Right now I have two children with no future, and Chia has to go to college, and what about you? If you found a girl and wanted to get married, how would you support her? It's not *kosher,* and I don't want to do this, but honestly believe I *must—"*

"I see, you have it all figured out . . . well, I don't want any part of it."

Chavala sighed. Moishe the firebrand . . . the lover of his people . . . the idealistic warrior . . . That was yesterday . . . She was sorry she had even told him, she should have gone ahead on her own. "That's up to you, Moishe. It's my decision and my risk. I'm going to take it."

He shook his head, got up and paced the floor. "How did you find this . . . this *tzaddik?"*

"You ask enough questions, you find answers. Besides, you don't really want to hear."

Moishe stopped pacing and looked at his sister. "You mean you would actually try to take this on by yourself . . ."

"I didn't have a policeman with me when I *shlepped* the jewelry. I could have been robbed. What's the use of talking, Moishe, I've made up my mind. It's the only way I can see open to me . . . It wouldn't be forever, only to get a new start."

Moishe knew he was out of his mind to say yes, but how could he let Chavala deal with the . . . the underworld by herself? Finally, not finding any alternative, he said, "All right . . . I'm against it, but—"

"I'm *for* it? Of course not, but I've got to do it." She laid out the plan. "You'll take care of the pawnshop and I'll run the new store."

Moishe merely nodded.

That evening when they went to pick up the baby Joshua, Chavala held the child tightly. He was, incredibly, almost a year old, and what a beautiful child. Why not? He still was the image of his father . . . When he held out his arms to her she wondered if she deserved such a blessing. That he even recognized her made her grateful . . . in all the months she'd been able to spend not more than a few hours a day, in the early morning and evening and Saturdays. Maybe love was time . . .

Maybe . . . but she still had feelings of guilt. She thought back to the children's house in the Galilee when she frantically picked Chia up and ran back to her cubbyhole and waited for Dovid to come . . . no child of hers was going to be raised without its parents, she'd told herself. Well, times changed, and sometimes you had to make sacrifices. So what was perfect in this life . . . ?

This morning she was especially happy it was Saturday. All the businesses closed down on the Sabbath. And if they opened it was only after sundown. No one defied tradition on the lower East Side. So today forget the bookkeeping, they were going to have an outing.

"Chia, Moishe, we're going to have a day in the park," she announced as though a great event were going to take place. And for them it was.

Chia was thrilled. She never complained, but she missed the close relationships they'd once had. Since her older sister had become so involved in her affairs there were less and less family meals, fewer and fewer chances to talk over her personal life with Chavala who, after all, was really more a mother than a sister. And she badly missed Reuven, never mind how they'd disagreed when he'd been here.

As for Chavala, she'd almost forgotten how lovely it could be to spend a whole day with the family. Dressing the baby, she talked to herself, but at him . . . "My darling little Joshua, you don't think for a moment that I don't love you. I hope not. God knows . . . not to mention some others . . . I'm not the best mother in the world, but if loving you counts . . . well, you can count on me. Listen, I'm trying to do the best I can. What can I do? I know I'm missing a lot, so are you, but you have a crazy mother. So while you're still this young, maybe it won't matter all that much? What do you think, Joshua?" She smiled at him. He cooed and laughed back. Almost as though he understood.

IT was 1922. Chavala found a store she could barely afford on the fringes of Harlem. A start. She bought the least expensive showcases she could find, which she and Chia painted green. She padded the inside of the cases with green felt. When the store was scrubbed clean and refurbished, she wasn't too unhappy. Park Avenue it wasn't, but better than the pawnshop it certainly was.

Through Mr. Leibowitz, she found an old jeweler who removed diamonds from their mountings, then melted down the metal. One day, Chavala told herself when she went to pick up her merchandise, she would have a place like his. On Fifth or Park Avenue . . . Why not? If one had a dream, at least make it a big one.

But she set aside the dreams for another time. Soon her low prices attracted the people . . . she tried not to look too closely at them . . . who came by their money she didn't want to know how. They paid cash, no receipts and no returns. If some Jim Dandy wanted a five-carat stickpin, Chavala spoke to the *landsman,* and one way or another he made it possible for her to satisfy her customer. The ones she felt the most antagonism toward were the Jewish pimps, prostitutes and gangsters. What the *goyim* did, she didn't care so much, but her own . . . In spite of the money she made from them, Chavala wished they would take their business elsewhere. Their money seemed especially tainted, and she felt it tainted her. At other times she almost welcomed their business as a kind of poetic justice, instructing herself that she was a fine one to put on holier-than-thou airs. Oh yes, she had her good reasons, but maybe they did too . . . Once she woke up in the middle of the night, startled out of a bad dream. A very bad dream. What would happen if she were found out? What kind of mother was she? What kind of a person would do what she was doing?

No, at least Chavala did not excuse herself, but on the other hand her needs, the demands on her, were becoming more urgent. In June Chia was graduating from high school, and they couldn't live where they were any longer . . . what kind of friends would she be able to make? To bring home? Matters in Palestine were more and more pressing . . . she was sending Raizel more money, more clothing. Her contributions were important, weren't they? So she went on . . .

Now Joshua was two. And Chia was about to be a *graduate*.

On graduation day Moishe and Chavala watched with enormous pride as Chia received her diploma. If there was a time when maybe she was entitled to cry a little, it was now. She had kept her promise, part of her plan had come true . . . For now, at least, anything she had done against . . . well, set it aside. For now . . . she was back in the little hovel south of Odessa and she stepped outside herself for a moment, seeing the sixteen-year-old Chavala cutting the cord, then rushing to the kitchen and dunking the newborn first in warm water, then cold, until she shocked the child into life. I kept my promise, mama. Your little Chia had it better than you and I. You're sitting here, mama, alongside me . . .

She was brought out of her reverie when she saw Chia standing in front of her, dressed in the lovely white organdy dress. She had grown into such a fine and beautiful young woman . . . Yes, whatever she had done, whatever she would have to do was worth it when Chia said, "Oh, Chavala, I don't know how to thank you."

"Thank *you*, Chia, for being you. I wonder how many *mothers* can say that? Now, darling, I have a little treat for you, today we're going to celebrate."

Chavala wasn't, for a change, going to worry about the cost. Not today. Chia was going to have a memory she could always look back on with special pleasure.

Then had lunch at the Plaza Hotel. A grand and imposing place none of them had ever been to. How did Chavala even know about such a place? Moishe asked her.

Simple. When she'd sold to the jewelers, many was the time she had walked into the lobby and looked. And looked. It didn't cost to look, and besides, a person should know about things. The world didn't begin and end with Ludlow Street. She even had the *chutzpah* to have a cup of coffee once at the Waldorf-Astoria Hotel. Came in the Park Avenue entrance too, not the Lexington entrance, if you please. Moishe was indeed impressed.

As they sat over their coffee, Chavala looked at her sister and brother. Strange, she thought, Chia had never seemed interested in boys, hadn't even had a date, so far as she knew. Why did that suddenly come to her as such a surprise? The business consumed her so, she hadn't even thought much about anything else. Maybe just as well, with the *bochers* on Delancey Street . . . When Chia went to college she would meet a nice young man . . . She looked at Moishe. By now he should already have found a girl. He was over *thirty.* If not now, when?

"Moishe, you should go to some of the dances at the . . . Jewish Center?"

Moishe looked at her. "Did you ever take a look at the girls who go to them? *Yentas* . . . do me a favor, please don't worry about my love life."

"Well, I'm not worried . . . I just feel that you should think about settling down?"

"I will, when the right time and the right girl come along."

Chavala gave it up for now. When the three of them walked into the June day she said, "Well, I think I have a surprise for you . . . We're moving . . . Moishe, get a cab."

Getting into the cab, Chavala gave the driver the address.

"794 Riverside Drive."

Moishe had to know, "Where are we going?"

"You'll find out. Just enjoy the scenery and be grateful you have a day off. Remember I gave you a vacation. You should thank Chia, she's the only one with an education."

Chia laughed. "With your brains, Chavala, you don't need an education."

Chavala shook her head. "Everyone needs an education. There's a big difference between being a little clever and having knowledge. If I had knowledge I wouldn't need to be so clever."

"You're doing all right without the knowledge," Moishe said, and for a moment Chavala wasn't sure if he was being sarcastic or not . . .

Soon the cab came to the curb, and Chavala forgot all her questions, put aside her uncertainties about herself.

"*This* is where we're moving?" Moishe asked, looking up at the lovely building.

"This is it."

"I can't believe it."

"Believe it. Come," Chavala said, as she led them to the elevator.

On the seventh floor she took out the keys from her purse and unlocked the door to the apartment. Even her heart seemed to miss a beat when she saw it again today.

The foyer separating the dining room from the living room was large and square. Down the hall were three bedrooms and two baths. The kitchen was modern with a new refrigerator and a four-burner gas stove.

The sink was porcelain and the drainboard yellow tile. It was beyond words. The three of them stood in the center of the living room and looked out to the bridge and the spectacular view beyond.

"Who would ever have imagined that New York was so beautiful," Moishe said.

Any city could be beautiful, thought Chavala, if one looked out of the right window. And it took money. Well, Chia was going to Hunter College, and she needed a home where she could bring her friends . . .

"Well, Chia, what do you think?"

"I *love* it! Oh, Chavala, I can't believe we're going to live here—"

"And why not? Nothing is too good for the Rabinskys. Formerly of Odessa and Palestine."

Moishe shook his head. Chavala had indeed performed miracles. At this moment, he even forgot what it had taken to perform such miracles.

To Chavala it was no miracle. It was, though, some satisfaction. She'd set her goals, she'd achieved some of them . . . Dvora had shoes and money for food. Raizel could buy a new *sheitel* and Lazarus could now go to *shul* with no outside pressures to interfere with his devotions. One prayer he no longer had to beg God for was to please help him keep a roof over his head and help to feed his increasing family, which had now grown to five children.

"Well," she said, "let's go see the furniture. I hope you approve."

At Axelrod's on Third Avenue she had carefully selected a peach-colored brocaded chesterfield with two matching armchairs, occasional tables and lamps, a French-type bedroom set. The dining room furniture was the best Grand Rapids could make. If she was going to spend, it was going to be for good things. A few dollars more or less, she'd learned, didn't make a person richer or poorer. From scrimping and saving on the food money a person did not get rich. You made money by hard work, invested it with care. That was how it was done. Cheap people, Chavala didn't like them. To know how and when and for *what* to spend was what counted.

"So, Chia, you pick out the set you want for your room, and you too, Moishe."

A WEEK later they moved into the apartment. Joshua would sleep in one twin bed, Chavala the other. But the first night Joshua slept with her. Not so much for him but for her . . . she needed to hold him. He was two very much going on three, and she was missing precious time with him

He'd become so attached to Mrs. Zuckerman he cried when Chavala hired an Irish girl to take care of him during the day. At Mrs. Zuckerman's it had become like family. . . .

SEPTEMBER was a month of joy, and tears. Chia enrolled in Hunter College, and Chavala received a letter that very Friday that on his way to the Wailing Wall, Lazarus had been killed when a bomb exploded just outside the Jaffa gate.

Chavala immediately closed the store and went to see Moishe at the pawnshop.

The moment she entered, Moishe knew something terrible had happened. Chavala stood there, actually shaking. He came from behind the counter and helped her to the back room.

For a moment she just sat staring at Moishe. Oh God, the nightmare of it. If only her family hadn't stayed . . . for what? This? Were things going too good in America? God didn't like that. . . . ?

"What is it?" Moishe's words finally got through to her.

"Lazarus was killed."

Moishe sat down. A long silence between them, then Chavala said, "I'm going to Palestine."

"We should all go."

"No . . . nothing can help Lazarus now. But I can help Raizel. You stay here, keep things going. The needs are going to be even greater now. I'm going to take Joshua. His father and brother should see him . . ."

"And the store?"

"Close it, what else can we do?"

"We can take the merchandise out and bring it here."

"Yes . . . well, what more is there to say? Raizel left with five children . . . there's no end to it, is there, Moishe?"

"I guess not. I can't get over it . . . When will you leave?"

"As soon as possible."

Dinner that night was a very quiet affair.

"I feel I should go with you," Chia said.

"No. Raizel will understand, you can't leave school."

"Chavala, I'm part of the family too, you've always talked about family. I'm no child, I can help. I can miss school and make it up later or—"

"*No.* It's different. I mean, it's different for me. My sister's husband has been killed. I must go, she has asked for me and I couldn't live with myself if I weren't with her now. But you have your own life, darling. Yes, you're family, of course, it's your sister too. But I think you can see it's different. I thank you for wanting to come, I wish I could accept. Believe me, I'd much rather go with you, have the comfort. But in the end it would hurt you too much, set you back too much and I'd only be indulging myself. I know it sounds trite, but it's true. Life does go on. It has to. And it's never more important to remember that than at a time like this . . .''

Chapter Twenty-eight

THE CLOSER THE ship came to Palestine, the greater Chavala's anxieties. She had the time and atmosphere now for her old guilt about separating from Dovid to surface. And guilt because she lived in comfort and safety now while much of her family not only struggled but lived with danger every day. She had been through this a thousand times in her head, but she still felt it . . .

As she dressed Joshua, her hands were unsteady. This was the first time since Joshua's birth that Dovid would be seeing him. And if it hadn't been for the tragic death of Lazarus, she wouldn't have been coming back now.

When the ship anchored in the harbor at Haifa, Chavala was on deck with Joshua. She scanned the crowd, and when she saw her family . . . Dear God, the loneliness, the feelings of isolation came back with a jolt. All the good reasons for leaving them four years ago didn't seem as convincing or important today. The price she paid for America seemed terribly high as she walked down the gangplank.

DOVID watched as Chavala and Joshua walked down the gangplank, and he scarcely recognized her . . . it wasn't the years that had changed her, it was the look, the air of elegance . . . He thought she was beautiful, but nearly a stranger, surely not the same woman from four years ago. This was not the peasant girl he had loved and married. This was a woman of the world, and he realized . . . feared . . . that they were worlds apart . . .

Face-to-face now. For a moment neither spoke, the awkward silence. Finally: "How wonderful to see you, Dovid." . . . "Yes, Chavala . . . it's been a long time."

Even the embrace seemed stilted.

Everything seemed out of focus to Chavala.

She felt rather than saw Joshua being taken from her, watched as Dovid all but devoured the child before he got to Chavala and held her close.

Ari was speaking . . . "We're so happy you've come . . ."

Chavala nodded, looked at her older son.

At first Reuven seemed reluctant to embrace her. Chavala understood, and fought back the tears. Well, it was up to her to try . . . "Reuven . . . I've missed you so," she said. The words sounded empty even to her.

Dvora saw the difficult byplay and felt for Chavala. In spite of her affection for Reuven, she did feel the boy tended to be a bit rigid . . . she remembered how she'd sat with him and he'd criticized his mother so sharply for not staying in Palestine, for having gone to America, where he was never happy. She'd tried to explain to him that Chavala had made sacrifices and denied herself in ways he perhaps was still too young to understand, and that she had done it not just for herself—not for herself at all—but for all of her family . . . Reuven didn't seem to be listening, or didn't want to listen, was probably more like it. Dvora, realizing that she could only expect so much from the boy, left off with reminding him that whether he understood or not about his mother, whether he approved or not, he ought to remember that Chavala was his mother. She deserved at least his respect . . .

Quickly now she went to Chavala with Pnina. Chavala looked down at the little girl with the incredibly blue eyes and suddenly her life didn't seem so empty. . . . She swooped the girl into her arms, "I read your letters all the time, Pnina. They make me very happy. I want to thank you for them."

"And thank *you*, Aunt Chavala, for the dolls."

Chavala blinked back the tears. "You're very welcome, I'm sure . . . And now, Zvi, my, what a big boy . . ." Looking at the small boy, now eight, the past came back swiftly. How well she remembered the day when Dvora came to tell her she was marrying Ari and she'd said, "There's a war going on, why don't you wait?" . . . She tried to push away the next remembrance, and failed . . . "If he doesn't come back? . . ." "Then I'll have his child . . ." And now the child of that love was in her arms. How good he felt. She thought of all the years that had passed since that day, and felt suddenly old.

Dvora, again sensing the tension, went to Dovid and said, "Let me see my nephew . . . Joshua, I'm your Aunt Dvora."

The little boy looked at her and quickly lowered his eyes. So many things were happening . . . so many strange people were holding him. He reached out to Chavala, but Reuven took him from Dovid. From the moment he had first seen his baby brother, Reuven had felt a special affinity, a special *bond* that seemed a physical thing . . . went beyond the notion of this is my brother—more like a pledge . . . to the child and to himself that they would always be together, that he would protect this infant all through his life. That feeling was reawakened now as he said, "It's too bad we have to be introduced, but I'm your brother Reuven . . ."

A bit cruel, Dovid thought, though he also suspected the feelings that were below the surface of Reuven's words. Still . . . And Dvora shared his thought . . . "I think we had better get started, Raizel is waiting," she said quickly.

DVORA had tried to prepare Chavala, but there were no words to describe Raizel's grief, or her sons'. She sat silently, like a helpless child.

What could Chavala say? Nothing would bring Raizel comfort. "Raizel, please try to remember the good, the happiness you brought Lazarus, and he brought you . . . you have your lovely children to live for, Lazarus would want you to remember that . . ."

"What will I do without him, Chavala? He was my life . . ."

"He lives in your sons, Raizel, and in your memory of him. And . . . well, please don't worry . . . I mean, I can help, *whatever* you need . . ."

Raziel finally allowed the tears to come as she embraced her sister.

When they left, Dvora said, "I'm afraid Raizel's like papa. He never recovered from mama's death. Well . . . we'd better get some rest, it's been a long day."

When they arrived at the small pension where the family had been staying the last few weeks, they walked to the second floor and stood for a moment in front of Dvora's room. Dvora kissed Chavala goodnight, and she and Ari, with Pnina, closed the door behind them.

Reuven and Zvi shared a room, but tonight Reuven asked if Joshua could sleep with them. Chavala said yes, but somehow felt vaguely threat-

ened by the request. It was a fear she could not articulate or justify
. . . she decided she was just overtired, worrying about shadows . . .

But when she found herself alone with Dovid again, the same uneasiness came over her. They said little. When finally she lay by her husband's side she sensed a distance, and was terrified. But what did she expect? Could a man like Dovid live his life as a celibate? In the darkness Chavala said softly, "Do you hate me, Dovid?"

Silence. Then: "No, I love you, although sometimes I've wished I didn't."

"I can understand that . . . I know I'm depriving you of your new son, and myself . . . but I don't know what to do . . ."

"Only you can find the answer, Chavala . . ."

If only I could, she thought . . . find a way to fulfill her need to see her family secure, take care of Raizel and her children, and still be with Dovid. How?

"Do you want to be free?"

The question came shockingly to her. It seemed he was asking for *his* freedom . . . The next thought was too painful to keep to herself . . . "Dovid . . . is there someone else?"

"No, but one can't live alone forever . . . What about you? You're a beautiful woman, and one day—"

"Don't say it, Dovid. Don't even *think* it. There will never be anyone else, you must know that."

"Time and life can change people. No one can be happy alone."

"Then *you* want to be free."

"No, that's *not* what I want. But what I *don't* want is ever to be unfaithful to you—"

"Then you've met someone—?"

"No, but I'm lonely and being lonely makes one reach out. If I met someone I liked, I'm not sure I would not be strong enough to walk away. I'm only human—"

The whole prospect was too much for her. "Dovid, I'm willing to come back, give it all up. I don't want to even think about you and someone else—"

"You say you're willing, and at this moment you mean it, I know . . . but being willing isn't the answer, darling. You'll never be able to come back until you can let go. Raizel's needs, Dvora's farm, Chia's and Moishe's future . . . They're still your overwhelming concern. I can't blame you, I never have. But I won't pretend I've not been bitter at times, driven half out of my mind with wanting you . . ."

Chavala wept quietly. "Love me, Dovid . . . love me, please, in spite of myself . . ."

"I love you for what you are, not in spite of yourself. My God . . . you're a very extraordinary woman, Chavala, but for some reason you don't feel your life belongs to you. You owe too much, *you* think . . . Love you? Yes, God help us both . . . I do love you . . ."

Nothing, of course, was resolved, but then Dovid turned toward her, held her close and proceeded to make love to her, washing away, for the moment, all the uncertainties, resentments, guilts . . . in the moment of union a singleness that shut out the world and all its diversions. . . .

SINCE Lazarus's death the family had been in Jerusalem. Several weeks had passed, and now, with the harvest underway, it was imperative that Dvora's family return to Kfar Shalom. Chavala felt she would stay on at least a little longer with Raizel.

The morning of departure Reuven made it clear by the way he looked at Joshua that he wanted to spend more time with his brother. He said as much, and in a kind of demanding fashion that Chavala could have done without. Still, she gave in, realizing that the atmosphere at Raizel's was hardly ideal for Joshua and that he'd be better off at Dvora's house and with her family. Well, at least Dovid would be staying in Jerusalem . . .

Chavala could barely get through the next week with Raizel and her mourning. When it was simply no longer supportable she told her sister it was time for Dovid to pick her up and take her to Dvora's, after which, unfortunately, she would be leaving for her home in New York. The final morning, as they sat in the kitchen waiting for Dovid, she said to Raizel as she had so many times before, "Come with me to America, you and the boys. In Brooklyn there's a community of Chasidim. You'll feel happy there. Please, Raizel . . ."

Raizel shook her head. "Chavala, I thank you, you know how grateful I am for what you've done for us, but I can never leave Jerusalem . . . never . . . who would be here to watch over papa's and Lazarus's graves? Besides, this is *our* home, we belong here . . ."

"Then come with us to Dvora's for a few days. You're not sitting *shiva* anymore—"

"The boys say Kaddish."

"But can't you get away for a few days? I mean, they're old enough now and—"

"I know . . . but I *belong* here . . . I'm sorry, Chavala . . ."

Chavala nodded, knowing the answers in advance. At least she would take some money to see her through the next few months, and, Chavala swore to herself, beyond that Raizel would *never* be in need . . .

DURING the following week Reuven thought his mother seemed happier at Kfar Shalom than he could ever remember seeing her. Memories of the little house they lived in at Zichron were evoked when he saw her baking bread in Dvora's kitchen, and he dared hope that, maybe, being here would make her want to stay. For his father's sake . . . he'd seen how much he liked having Joshua here . . . And each day Reuven took Joshua to the fields with him, wanting his little brother, even at the age of three, to feel the soil, to plant a seed. Joshua was obviously delighted, and none of this went unnoticed by Chavala.

Including how intimate and closely knit the families of the village of Kfar Shalom were. She was proud that her sixteen-year-old Reuven was not only respected and admired but had in fact become a leader among his peers.

On Saturday the family was up earlier than usual. Today they were going to climb to the summit of Mount Tabor. Chavala and Dvora were busy with the preparation of the food as the men were attending to the farm chores. Then shortly before dawn, with their knapsacks on their backs, the journey began. Dressed in their sandals, white shorts and blue tops, Reuven and Zvi took the lead. Even Pnina came along with Joshua. The air was crisp and invigorating in the early morning.

Mount Tabor rose to more than two thousand feet. From time to time as they stopped for food and drink Pnina romped with Joshua while Zvi and Reuven scouted ahead, not because they were unfamiliar with the sights they were about to see but because it was a never-ending source of wonder and beauty.

Along the hillside there were dozens of goatskin tents and in the distance grazing flocks of small black goats. It was four in the afternoon when they reached the large round plateau of Tabor, to the south the entire Jezreel Valley opening before their eyes. For Chavala the sight was staggering . . . the valley was a symphony of color, in the distance square-cut fields sat like jewels in a setting of green. White clusters of Arab villages dotted the landscape all the way to Mount Carmel, and to the north lay the Sea of Galilee.

Dovid pointed to the place where Gideon was buried and where Saul and Jonathan had fallen in battle to the Philistines. Reuven, obviously deeply affected, broke out into: "Ye mountains of Gilboa, let there be no dew, neither let there be rain upon you nor fields of offerings. For there the shield of the mighty is vilely cast away, the shield of Saul . . ."

Chavala was understandably impressed, and Dovid proud. "That was beautiful, Reuven," Chavala said. "You certainly know your Bible—"

"All sabras do. That's our history book, the Bible." Then he picked Joshua up so that his brother could see and, he hoped, never forget.

Chavala didn't miss the message for her. She could be proud of Reuven, but she could also wish he were just a little less *righteous* . . .

Now they moved beyond the forest until they reached the pinnacle. The remains of ruined Crusader forts stood there, along with a Saracen castle. Finally they reached the campsite. Chavala walked to the eastern rampart and looked out to the valley and the Sea of Galilee. A chill went through her as the mild wind blew through her hair. She stood at the wall and remembered the first time, so many years ago, that Dovid had taken her to what she then considered a place of wilderness and self-imposed exile. But the earth had yielded to Dovid's dreams, and somehow she stood unfulfilled for her . . . lack of faith?

Dovid, standing now behind her, brought her back to the moment. "Dovid, what can I say when I look out there and see this land and what you've accomplished?"

"It wasn't what *I* accomplished. I had only a small part—"

"But it was you who saw what this valley could become when you said over and over that it belonged to our people, and managed to acquire so much of it by your own efforts. I've hardly been a devout Jew, but I must say, when I stand here and look out to the land there I really feel a sense of God . . . of what you have felt for so long. I envy you, Dovid . . ."

Joshua broke into the mood of communion with, "Let's play ball, *abba.*"

Dovid looked down at the little boy and picked him up and held him close. "Right, big fellow. Let's go."

By dusk the boys and girls of Kfar Shalom reached the summit. Immediately a pit was dug, wood was gathered and four lambs were prepared and spitted for roasting. The sun moved down behind the Jezreel Valley and, suddenly, there was a burst of laughter and singing as the fire was lit and the lambs placed over the pit.

After the feast the mountaintop rang with song, and the dancing began. Meir Zeid sat cross-legged, beating the drum made of goatskin.

The rhythm of his beat was accompanied by the playing of an ancient Hebrew melody on a reed flute. Each song gave way to a new dance. Against the starlit sky the young dancers cheered and clapped as they sprang into the air, and then half a dozen jumped into the center and started a *hora*. The ring grew larger and larger and the dancing went on for hours until they collapsed in breathless, delighted exhaustion.

As Chavala watched these strong, free sabras, it occurred to her . . . grandiose though the thought might be . . . that in their fashion they were the young lions of Judea, the ancient Hebrews reborn. Their faces were the faces of twelve tribes . . . they were Reuben, Simeon, Judah, Zebulun, Issachar, Dan, Gad, Asher, Naphtali, Benjamin, Ephraim and Manasseh. The strength of God, and His children, was in their young hearts and souls. The comparisons were perhaps too grandiloquent to express, but she deeply felt them at that moment . . .

TIME once again took over Chavala. Never mind whether she wanted to go back, she simply had to. She had her own obligations that pulled her back to a very new and different place. Moishe was waiting for her. Chia. Was she to allow Raizel and the boys to live on the charity of strangers? If indeed even that were available?

"But what about *your* life?" Dvora insisted. Dvora had, of course, prayed that by some miracle Chavala would feel that Eretz Yisroel was where she belonged. But Chavala could not honestly say that was so. Oh yes, she'd felt something special with Dovid and her children looking out over the land, but there was another need, and the pull . . . Still, one day . . . "Dvora, with all the dislike I came to Eretz Yisroel with, somehow in the last few days I've had the thought that if Dovid and I had a house in the hills of Haifa, and the whole family was free of financial difficulties, well . . . Palestine could look far different to me than it did looking out of the windows of that hovel we lived in when we first arrived. People change, countries change, and I've seen the changes here . . . yes, Dvora, if that day came it could make all the difference."

Dvora could only say, "I can only hope your dream will come to life. You and Dovid deserve it . . . God knows, you do . . ."

On her way back to America, Chavala tried to hold to those last words of Dvora . . . repeated them over and over, as if the repetition itself might make them come true. But as she neared the shores of Manhattan, more pressing reality crowded in . . . Moishe, Chia, the store . . . other lives had their claims on her too . . .

Chapter Twenty-nine

AND OTHER LIVES were being lived, and changing, in America, new challenges for Chavala Rabinsky. . . .

ON this particular crisp Friday evening in October, after closing the store, Moishe conducted a momentous debate with himself about whether to go home and fix dinner for himself or to eat downtown. A grown man's kind of decision? The truth was that this short time away from Chavala made him realize that his life had become wrapped up in a neat, small package of routines . . . days spent behind a cage in the pawnshop, nights roaming about the streets, a movie now and then, an occasional release with a professional woman. The restlessness had been building for some time now. He was thirty-one and suddenly he wanted a home of his own, children. The ex-warrior had damn well better begin now . . . or forget it, he thought grimly.

He called Chia and asked if she wanted to join him for dinner, but she said she had a date with one Lenny Moscowitz. *Mazel tov . . .* He ate alone. As he sat in the restaurant, poking at his food, it occurred to him that everybody's life in America had changed except his. Take Chia, for example . . .

Shortly into her first semester at Hunter she met an outgoing girl named Joannie Joseph, born and raised in Lawrence, Long Island, daughter of a successful attorney who specialized in entertainment law. Joannie Joseph became a signal influence in Chia's life. Knowing something of the "show-biz" realities, so-called, of life, clothes and hair—nice short bob, silk stockings, red lipstick, she also changed Chia's name to Cherie. At first Chia felt uncomfortable with that, but she had from the first been the most susceptible to assimilation, and after repeating it over and over and over to herself she found the name almost familiar. To complete matters, the "sky" was dropped from Rabinsky and "Cherie Rabin" emerged. Like any normal young American woman, she found life had become more than academic, her noble dreams of becoming America's great educator were not unnaturally put aside in favor of weekend parties on Long Island. The condition of grim was an acquired, not an inherited, characteristic. Chia's . . . or Cherie's . . . environment allowed her to shed that burden . . .

At a soiree at the Josephs' Tudor-style home she met, and was almost instantly captivated by Lenny Moscowitz, who, after graduation from Columbia Law School, had become a junior member of the firm of Joseph, Joseph, Abrams & Joseph. A friend of the family—but also a talented and decent young man. And about ten thousand cultural years from the men Chia had known before . . .

Thinking on the events—and the speed of them—that had taken place in Chia-Cherie's life, Moishe decided he was barely alive and living on Riverside Drive. Quickly, he got up, paid the check and left, wondering what in the world he was going to do this night. He ended up at home and alone.

On Saturday he went to Central Park to ice skate—a skill he'd learned about by accident, or rather osmosis, having spent hours watching the skaters before he ever came to try it himself. Strangely, he seemed to have strong ankles—and a weak head, he thought ironically. By the time he'd gone around the rink a few times he found himself bored rather than exhilarated, as he once had. Maybe he should find a girl. It helped the tensions . . . helped him to forget. He left the rink, walked down Fifth Avenue, looked in the store windows, seeing little except for the reflection of his own less than devastating image. He looked again . . . *where* was he going? He turned and continued on, up one street, down another, passing the Stage Delicatessen, reversing himself and going in. Pastrami might not be a woman but it was damn close to God's food. As he sat eating a pastrami sandwich, he noted and then fixed on a young woman sitting at the table next to him. He didn't notice the color of her hair or her eyes. He wanted only to reach out and touch her. But that, of course, was damned foolish. Lately he'd begun to want to do that to every girl he saw. Quickly he got up, paid for his meal and left.

Nine o'clock on a Saturday night. Moishe let himself into the apartment. He looked about and asked himself what his life was . . . he had only a room in his sister's house. He was a *boarder.*

The next morning, as Moishe waited at the elevator, New York City's unique capacity for first isolating and then abruptly, as if with a mind of its own, putting apartment dwellers into unexpected relationships, took over his life, as well as a co-apartment house dweller's named Julie Kahn.

Moishe noted the young woman standing alongside him. Noted . . . my God . . . was smitten by . . . which, of course, in the impersonality —alleged—of New York was supposed to happen only in stories and be relegated to myth. Yes, never mind the implausible, he was indeed smitten by this lovely young woman with her tawny hair and mischievous but warm eyes. Slim, actually trim more than slim, nearly the same height as he, she carried her purse in one hand and a book in the other . . . and wore no wedding ring.

He tried to spot the title of the book. "Are you liking it?" he asked. "I mean the book, of course . . ." Lord, that was clumsy, probably that would be the end of him with her, if indeed there had ever been a beginning.

Julie Kahn scrutinized him frankly. Attractive, a weathered skin, could be any age from thirty to forty. A *man,* which in this city, and in this building and area wasn't all that common. Married? Who knew? . . . but there was an air about him that seemed to promise honesty. Go by her instincts . . . "Yes and no," she said. "It's about how the Jews are fighting for a homeland and having a tough time of it, but at least they're fighting. Sometimes I feel sort of guilty the way I've been brought up . . ." And then she stopped, realizing that she'd already confided too much to a perfect stranger. Except that strangely—the pun in her thought amused her—she didn't feel like he was a stranger . . .

Moishe, of course, couldn't believe his good fortune. My God, this woman and he had more in common than he could have dared hope. Too good to be true. Well, up to now, his romantic life in the land of opportunity had been almost too bad to be believed, or tolerated. Maybe the old balance wheel was coming around.

Small talk quickly established what was self-evident—as small talk usually did—that she lived in the building, that her name was Julie Kahn and his Moishe Rabinsky, and so forth. But no follow-up, no promise about future meetings or even where she was going, or he, when they exited the apartment building and went their separate ways.

Except for Moishe, at any rate, there was no separation. All day as he went about his routine in the pawnshop he thought about nothing and nobody but Julie Kahn. That night when he came home, he found Chia studying.

"Well," he said, more casually than he felt, "how are things with you and the irresistible Lenny?"

She frowned, then, "I *think* he's going to ask me to marry him—"

"What do you mean, you think? Doesn't he know if he wants to get married to a gorgeous thing like you?"

"Moishe, be serious. He's just starting his law practice and feels maybe we should wait—"

"He's crazy . . . if you love someone you get married." He was surprised by his own certainty, vehemence.

"What about *you?*"

"All I can say, when I find someone I'll ask her. Now, what do you want to do about dinner . . . *Cherie?*"

"Maybe we'll order Chinese, *Maurice.*"

They both laughed. At first Chia's name adjustment had annoyed him, but he'd gotten accustomed to it, realizing that it was more a matter of being Americanized than abandoning her faith. At least that's what he told himself . . . "Well, just be sure it's *Jewish* Chinese. Some things, after all, are still sacred." He felt like hugging her, he felt so good, but held off.

After dinner, when he took the empty cartons to the garbage chute, impossibly but truly, there she was. A coincidence. A fortuitous circumstance. Even if it was at the garbage chute. An omen? Stop worrying about it, he instructed himself, and start reacting . . .

"Well . . . hello." A terrific opening gambit, he thought to himself sarcastically. How about some straightforward talk? "I take it we're neighbors."

"Yes, as a matter of fact, I live just down the hall."

"How is it I haven't seen you before?"

"Just moved in last week . . . well, it's been good seeing you again." And it had been, she thought as she turned and walked down the hall.

Moishe didn't sleep that night. Among other things, it took some *chutzpah* to think this lovely young woman would be interested in him. She no doubt already had someone, but even if she didn't, who was he? A pawnbroker. Hardly a romantic occupation. Face it, he'd be reluctant to tell her. But he was going to see her, whether she knew it or not. Because he *had* to . . .

The next night at seven o'clock he knocked on her door. No answer. He looked her up in the phone book. Not listed. Called information, no such listing. Well, she'd just moved in . . . He continued to try her door during the next few days without any results. And then—the romantic muse of New York at work again?—they met one evening coming home. He'd lived with the fantasy of her for what to him seemed so long that somehow he felt as though she'd been avoiding him. He forced a smile as they got into the elevator. "Hello. Do you know what I've been doing this last week?" For God's sake, can't you be more subtle . . . ?

She smiled back. "That's all I've wondered about . . ." which, in fact, was true ". . . what?"

"Standing at the damned garbage chute, hoping lightning or something would strike twice."

She laughed, an open, warm sound. "Did you ever think of knocking on my door?"

"I tried, no luck."

"Of . . . of course . . . I've been visiting my mother, she hasn't been too well."

"Sorry to hear that."

"She's better . . ."

"Good . . . Julie, are you free Saturday night?"

"Saturday night? I'll have to check." Have to check indeed, she thought as they walked down the hall to her apartment. She unlocked the door, stuck her foot out to hold it open, and said, "I'll let you know . . . about Saturday, I mean."

Moishe had had enough suspense. "Why don't you look now?"

She looked at him. Thank God he persisted. "I'll let you know later, okay?"

"*Okay* . . . I'll be around. Just knock three times." She was driving him crazy.

"I will, I promise . . ."

Which was enough for Moishe to feel happier, more hopeful, than he had since he'd come to America.

"You seem a changed man," Chia said as they sat down to dinner.

"Maybe so."

"I think you've met someone. A girl?"

"It shows, huh?"

"It does . . . who is she?"

"A lady who lives down the hall."

"Down the hall? Really? That's very convenient. How come you haven't said anything about her?"

"There was nothing to say . . . until tonight."

"Have you been out with her?"

"Not yet. But I plan to Saturday night."

"That's great . . . what's her name?"

"Julie Kahn . . . and I think I'm in love with her."

"How long did you say you knew her?"

"About a week. That is, I met her once before . . . at the garbage chute . . . that's where you really get to find out about people."

"You're crazy. What did you find out about her at the garbage chute?"

"That she likes Chinese food, she was throwing out her cartons too."

Chia laughed. "I'm glad, Moishe, I'm really glad you've met some-one."

"Me too, I assure you. And we've more in common than Chinese food. She cares about what's happening to the Jews in Palestine. She's no"—and he broke it off, not wanting to offend Chia—but he was about to say that she was no *goyishe* Jew. Finally he recovered with an assurance that she was no superficial, spoiled American girl . . .

After dinner Moishe walked down the hall and stood in front of Julie's door, then rapped firmly. It seemed a few years before the door opened. She had a towel around her head and wore a bathrobe. She seemed surprised. "Well, you are insistent." And to herself, Thank God. "As you can guess, I just washed my hair."

"Yes . . . about Saturday night? And while you're thinking it over, do you suppose I could wait inside? I'm getting sort of tired of this hall."

She opened the door wide, motioned him to a chair as she disappeared into the bathroom.

Yes, she *liked* this man. He was direct, he flattered her by his persistence and her early good instincts about him had deepened. A man . . .

When she came back, dressed in a housecoat and with her hair framing her lovely face, Moishe had trouble restraining himself from just going to her and kissing her. Besides, he'd done it a few hundred times in his daydreams.

She sat across from him, and she marveled how *natural* she felt with this man who was still a stranger. No need to play the boring dating game, no need to pretend, which she was thoroughly sick of. He had that effect on her.

"Would you like a cup of coffee, tea?"

"Coffee."

She went into the kitchenette, measured out the coffee, then the water. When she brought the coffee she said she was sorry she didn't have anything to go with it. "Truth is, I still haven't gotten settled in."

"The coffee's just fine . . . now, tell me about yourself."

He'd just stolen her line. All right, she'd go first, and hope he wouldn't be bored . . . "Grew up in Philadelphia. The place they have the joke about . . . I went to Philadelphia and it was closed . . . well, never mind . . . anyway, I came to Manhattan. Graduated from N.Y.U. Art history, what else? I manage a small dress shop now on Madison Avenue.

Also, what else? When my father died two years ago my mother moved here too. That's it, dull, duller, dullest."

"I don't quite accept *that*. What about . . . friends?"

"You mean men?"

"I guess that's what I mean."

"Well, I practically grew up with a guy *everyone* thought I . . . should marry . . . my parents, of course, included. I was in the minority. Result: at twenty-three I'm a premature old maid . . . I've lost track of how many well-intentioned people lift their eyebrows and declare, 'You're not *married?*' As though that was the only thing in a woman's life."

"But it could be rewarding to share your life—"

"With the right person, I suppose. I just haven't met—"

"I have, and it's great."

Very American, Julie suddenly took leave of her sense of humor . . . here he was asking her out when he had a special girl . . . "Well, how is it you're not taking her out on Saturday night?" She sounded more irritated than she intended.

"I am. Julie Kahn, the first time I met you I knew I liked you very much, to put it mildly. That's not so strange, is it? A man you'd known all your life didn't attract you. I'm thirty-one and you're the first girl . . . it's true . . . I have ever felt this way about. I think I love you."

Julie sat there, mouth literally open. Finally, all she could say was, "As they say in bad novels, Sir, this is so sudden."

"They also say that truth is stranger than fiction." With that he got up and stopped resisting himself. He took her in his arms. "Yes, Julie Kahn, as I said, I think I love you."

When he kissed her, she wasn't at all sure she didn't feel precisely the same. He was right . . . a lifetime of familiarity could breed nothing, even contempt. She ought to know. An instant could make a lifetime . . . take advantage of it, Julie. Let it *happen* . . .

That night Moishe got back to his apartment very late. Both he and Julie were astonished by the quickness, and the *naturalness,* of the intimacy that had happened between them. It was as though, he thought later, they had somehow telescoped time . . . minutes, hours had literally developed the force of months and years. Their lovemaking had had the excitement of newness, of course, but also the most mystical depth of familiarity. Both knew, without a lecture, that this was indeed something special. And both were determined to take hold of it, nurture it and be grateful for it.

They saw each other every night after that first, except when Julie had to visit her mother, who lived on East End Avenue, across town. A few times Moishe went to dinner at her mother's, and Julie cooked, which was not her greatest talent—she still majored in Chinese, ordered in—but, as she said and Moishe more than agreed, nobody was perfect. He'd take her and be damned glad for what she was. And she felt precisely the same about him. Moishe was a new phenomenon to her—not only as a man, and she'd been so right about that early feeling about him, but in terms of his remarkable background. Here was a man who had fought for the Jews, fought and been wounded and almost killed to help make a homeland. They didn't grow them like Moishe Rabinsky in Philadelphia, or at N.Y.U. either, for that matter. And God knew, the men who occasionally accompanied the ladies who came into her shop were on another planet from the likes of Moishe. She loved this man, face it, she told herself. And what was miraculous, he felt the same about her. Chemistry was working overtime in their case, and they were both deeply grateful for it. . . .

WHEN Chavala arrived back from Palestine and found Moishe in his new and welcome condition, her happiness for him was almost . . . even for her . . . beyond expression. And here she'd been so worried about the absence of romance and marriage in not only Moishe's life but in Chia's. Well . . . the Rabinsky family could use a new infusion of love, she thought wryly.

Julie was everything that Chavala had ever hoped Moishe would have the good fortune to find and marry, although their coming together had altered the plan she'd devised all during her journey back to America. Well, she would think about that later, but there was no doubt in her mind now that Moishe could not, would not, continue to spend his life in a pawnshop. Not after Julie . . .

She was sitting in the darkened living room, thinking about the alternatives, when she heard the door open and Moishe walk in.

She called out to him. "I'm in here."

He turned on the lamp. "What are you doing sitting here in the dark?"

"Thinking."

He sat down. "When Chavala thinks, it's usually serious business. What's it this time?"

"It's you, and one or two other things. How does Julie feel about the shop?"

"She hasn't said anything. I doubt she would."

"Well, I wouldn't blame her if she did. A pause. "Moishe, are you getting married?"

"Yes, I think I told you that. And soon. Julie knows a good thing when she sees one—"

"Stop the jokes, please . . . Moishe, I was thinking that maybe I would have to take a little trip. Not for long. Now with your getting married, well, I'm not thinking, I'm knowing—"

"What do you mean, a trip? You just came back a few months ago."

"Moishe, we have to expand our business. And upgrade it. This family is growing, obligations, needs . . ."

"So how do you plan to expand, upgrade?"

"I plan to open a very fine jewelry store—"

"And what are you going to use for money to buy stock?"

"Well, that brings us to the little trip . . . While I was crossing that big Atlantic Ocean a lot of thoughts occurred to me, and one of them was that the best buys in stones are in Europe. I've always heard that . . ."

"Europe? This is a little complicated, Chavala, and maybe I've missed something, but since you haven't the money to buy from the wholesalers here, and we've been getting the goods from your friend the *landsman,* I ask you, what are you going to use for money to bring merchandise in from Europe?"

"I'll find a way . . . please trust me, Moishe. Now, the only detail left for you is to get somebody to fill in at the Harlem store while I'm gone. It will only be for a short time. I'm sure you can handle that."

He shrugged. "I suppose, but I don't think you're telling me everything. I also can see you don't intend to, so I'll let it go. But please, Chavala, whatever it is, don't get in over your head."

Chavala forced a smile, thinking, what have I been over all my life . . . so what's new?

CHAVALA walked into the dismal alley, scarcely aware of the debris around her, and knocked on the *landsman*'s door.

He looked through the peephole, then the door leading to the basement was opened. He was delighted to see her. In fact, of all the people he did business with, Chavala was his favorite. "*Nu*, Chavala, what can I do for you?"

As she sat across from him she prayed that God . . . her family . . . would forgive her for what she was about to ask. "I want to make a good deal of money . . . and quickly. I want you to tell me how to do that."

He laughed. "That's all you want? Better you should ask for the moon."

"That *is* what I'm asking for," she answered, thinking of Dovid, Reuven, Raizel and the rest.

"You could open up another operation . . . like the one you've got. I know just the location—"

"Another one like the one I have I don't want . . ."

"So?"

"What do you mean, 'so?' That's what I'm asking you. You're the expert. Who knows more about what I'm looking for than you do?"

He hesitated, then: "All right, so I'll tell you. It's called smuggling."

Chavala thought her heart would jump out of her throat. "Please go on."

The *landsman* shook his head knowingly. "I could sit here for hours and tell you how, but diamonds, gems are just about the easiest things in the world to hide." He went on to regale her with a dozen different ways that, for example, a small diamond could be secreted. A fortune could be concealed in the knot of a tie. A ten carat diamond could be put inside a false molar. The naked body could conceal enough diamonds to live in a mansion in Miami for the rest of one's life . . . How? "I don't want to be vulgar, dear lady, but . . . the mouth, the navel, the rectum, an ear, an armpit, between the toes. And, if necessary, they *could* be swallowed. Toothpaste tubes were common carriers. A box of face powder, packets of tea, cans of coffee, the false bottom of a suitcase. One of the best was the hollowed-out heel of a shoe." He sighed, gesturing with his hands. "Listen, I even knew someone who used the socket behind a false eye . . . What can I tell you? There's no end to it."

"Well," she said, "I certainly came to the right party. But it sounds almost too easy—"

"It *is*. Take it from me . . . The *kosher* merchants puff out their chests and deny that the traffic goes on, and they keep their mouths shut about what they know, even though they hate the way what they call submarine goods cuts into their business. The diamond syndicate, people like the De Beers, would like the diamond world to feel that goods can only be bought from them."

Chavala tried not to think about what she was asking. "So tell me, where do people get the stones from?"

"Different places. Amsterdam is one."

"And where does Amsterdam get them from?"

"Russia."

"*Russia?* A communist country deals in diamonds?"

"Of course. They pretend they're only selling their revolution, but they're competing in the world market in other commodities, believe me . . ." he laughed. "Like a regular democracy, they happen to like the decadence of money too. What do you think, the Kremlin doesn't like money? Think again."

"How do people get the stones out of Russia?"

"That's not too hard. They have a license to sell, courtesy of the government—"

"From there, though, what countries do they do business with?"

"South America, Marseilles in France, but one of the biggest markets is Amsterdam."

Chavala sat silent, almost afraid to ask the next question. "How do you get back into this country?"

"Well, sometimes that's the tough part. Although diamonds are the easiest thing in the world to conceal, still the customs are smart and they eventually get to know the operators."

"So, if I understand right, unknowns would be the answer?"

"Obviously, and without records."

Chavala sat thinking it over. If she were going to be a smuggler, thief, what would she do? "What thief do you know that can be trusted?"

"Oh, Chavala," he laughed out loud, "that's what I like about you. No matter how serious, you have a sense of humor."

"All right, so start laughing a whole lot. Who do you know?"

"I know plenty, as you might imagine, but I wouldn't recommend them. They cheat you blind."

"What about your Benny?" she said quickly.

"Benny? He was a sad kid I picked up off the streets, an orphan, penniless. And, God help him, a clubfoot. You'd have to be a stoneheart not to care about that kid. I'm still trying to find a doctor to fix his foot . . . He's become like my son, you know that . . . A thief he's not. Sure, he delivers goods . . . but that's not being a thief—"

"So what am I? A hardened criminal?" What she didn't say, though she was sure the *landsman* was aware of it, was that, sad as it was, Benny's special shoe with its five-inch platform would be a likely place to hide diamonds . . . "But just suppose I took him to Amsterdam and he helped me bring in the stones, that wouldn't be stealing. That would make him more like a helper."

The *landsman* laughed again. "Benny? He'd be scared to death."

"To tell the truth, so am I. We'd give each other support."

"Suppose I let Benny go, how would you get through customs?"

"As Chasidim."

Chavala's imagination was working overtime, he thought. "Chasidim? How did you come up with *that* idea?"

"Because, what Chasid would smuggle? They still live with the teachings of Baal-Shem-Tov like two hundred years ago. They still live with the code of honor . . . God should only forgive me for even thinking about them like this. But what customs officer would have the *chutzpah* to search prayer books and *tallisim* going to Brooklyn? To say nothing of a woman who wore a *sheitel* . . . especially a pregnant woman with a *sheitel.*"

The *landsman* shook his head. "You know, Chavala, you have the mind of a thief, and by me that's no criticism. And you've got more guts than anybody."

She grimaced. "Thank you for the great compliment. But do you think it would work?"

He took a little time to think about it. He nodded. This woman was one of a kind, no question.

"So you think it will work?"

"It's possible. Maybe sixty-forty. Not bad odds."

She hoped he was right. "Now I have something that I find very difficult to ask you."

"Ask."

"All right . . . I need your help like I've never needed it before. Will you loan me the money?" she asked quickly, then hurried on to add, "I swear I'll pay you back with whatever interest you want."

That he had to think about for a long time, not because he didn't trust Chavala, but if it didn't work Chavala could even end up in jail and he'd be out the money. Happy about that prospect he wasn't, not only because of the loss, but for Chavala's sake. On the other hand, the whole thing was just crazy enough to work, and, above all, he knew Chavala could talk her way in and out of anything she set her mind to. More than that, he truly liked this incredibly spunky woman. Admired her too. He knew, without all the details, what drove her on to take such crazy risks. Chavala Rabinsky, by God, believed in *family.* He liked that. He had no children, only a lot of money to leave to the State of New York and lawyers in the event of his demise, which he'd prefer not to think about, thank you. He was remembering now when Chavala had first come to him and pleaded for goods because she had to support her family. He thought about Palestine and the troubles they were having. Even a fence was a human being, never mind he hadn't been exactly the most honorable person in the world. Not that he was taking himself to task . . . who did he hurt? . . . but life hadn't treated him to a bed of roses . . . He'd been born in Siberia, where his mother and father had been exiled. They died when he was nine and he escaped when he was thirteen. During his wanderings he'd been starved and beaten. By the time he was sixteen he'd finally gotten out of Russia—mostly by walking—and managed to get to the Black Sea. He'd wanted to go to Palestine but the only ship he found available was headed for America, so that's where he went, to the land of the free and the home of the brave, and the one place where it was possible even for a man like him to better himself . . . He considered himself one of the fortunate ones . . . So who the hell cared if Yussel Melnetsky lived or died? Sure, he stole . . . well, life had stolen from him and he only started to get even when he became the *landsman.* Then, finally, people respected him. Affection? Who cared about him? Who asked them? But somehow Chavala had touched him in a way nobody else had. In her case he wanted to be a *mensch.* He also wanted to do one thing in his life so that he wouldn't have to stand in front of his Maker and say he hadn't helped a living soul. "All right, Chavala. On you I'll gamble."

She smiled. "I don't know how to thank you. The first day I met you I said to my brother Moishe that you looked like a *tzaddik* . . . I think you are."

Funny, he thought, it felt good to do something nice . . . not for money, just to feel good . . . and this was the first time in his life he'd felt that way.

AND how did Chavala feel? A smuggler, now. Well, let's see. Let's put it up against who she was and where she'd been . . . A Russian dead in Odessa, by her hand. A Bedouin dead in Palestine, so that she and her family could have something to eat . . . and out of that had come the gems that had made it possible to get a start in the new land. They were times of life and death, and that was how, now that she thought about it, she had been living almost since she had memory. Her mother dying, her pledge to protect little Chia, her caring for and saving the life of her family . . . so what was new? She had been doing it a long time, she was still doing it. It was what she *did.* Some people fought for big causes . . . like Dovid, God bless him, and no doubt Reuven was following in his footsteps. And Joshua . . . ? She didn't want to think about that now. Thank God she didn't have to. Not yet. Well, her life was her family, and whatever and wherever she had to pursue its survival, health and, yes, someday prosperity. Did they think she loved this life away from a man like Dovid? Did she enjoy the nights when she woke up in a sweat and wondered about him, if he had maybe—God forbid, but she wouldn't blame him—found another woman to take her place at night, even for one night—she would die if she knew . . . and what she felt in her own body, not willing it, even trying so hard to will it away, the feelings of a woman, which she still was, thank you . . . But that was her choice, don't complain. But don't apologize so much either, Chavala Rabinsky Landau.

Who said it was noble to survive? Who said it was easy or cheap or pretty and clean? Not her. That wasn't the life she'd known. So who was she to get so squeamish about masquerading as a pregnant Chasid, maybe even use the ritual things that may have been sacred to some, but who did they save when blood was being spilled in Palestine, when children were starving, when a little girl was maybe about to lose her eyesight? They were so devout, God bless them, but even as a Jew . . . and she *was* a Jew . . . there was more than one way to serve God. She would do as well as she knew how, and take her judgment later. Meanwhile, she had a little private admission to make to herself . . . Face it, Chavala, you like it too, the danger, the craziness of what she'd done and the outrageousness of what she was about to do. It was, it seemed, in her blood. Who would want it tranquil? She would probably die first . . .

BY the time Moishe and Julie did marry a month later, Chavala's new partner in crime Benny looked very much the proper Chasid. Even being underweight helped. To be pious also meant to go hungry, which, Chavala hoped, added to his credibility. His earlocks were curled as prescribed, and the beard he'd grown was just right. When Chavala put on the black *sheitel,* she looked like any dutiful Chasidic wife. After the purchase of the traditional clothes, as a dress rehearsal she placed the small, round pillow under the petticoat and, lo and behold, she took on the aura of a saintly if pregnant spouse of a holy Chasidic husband.

Yussel felt it his duty to take over the responsibility of all the negotiations as well as the arrangements. Their passports were arranged, funds were deposited in a Swiss bank, and all the contacts in Amsterdam were taken care of.

Their passage was booked, second class, and Benny was equipped with an import license for the purchase of religious items. Well, their trip did take a kind of blind faith . . .

NOW there remained one last cover story to manage. How would she handle it with Moishe? . . .

Sitting in the dining room of Julie and Moishe's new apartment on West End Avenue, she tried desperately to seem at ease, delay the inevitable with small talk . . . "How did you learn to cook so good, Julie?"

Julie laughed. "I manage with the help of the *Good Housekeeping* cookbook and Moishe's uncomplaining temperament, not to mention his non-gourmet palate."

"You manage . . . Moishe, you're getting fat. With all due respect to you, Julie darling, but you're treating him too good. From my cooking he didn't look so good."

"From *your* cooking nobody would look good. Besides, when did you ever cook?"

Julie scowled at her new husband. "Don't be nasty, darling. Your sister's numerous talents don't have to include cooking . . ."

After dinner they retired to the living room, and the moment was at hand. All week long Moishe had put questions to her, and she had replied, "When the time comes you'll be the first to know." Now was the time . . .

"I know you said the place to buy stones was in Europe, but I think it's only fair that you should tell me where you're getting the money, and also, where this big market is," Moishe was saying.

She poured herself a little schnapps, sat up almost primly, looked at Moishe with deep sincerity and began. "The first question I'll answer first. A few dollars I've got, right? So that I'm taking. And the answer to the second question is Mr. Leibowitz, who as you know, Moishe, has always been our good friend, signed a bank note for me."

"That was very nice of Mr. Leibowitz. But then, as you say, he's always been a friend. But what I want to know, where are the bargains?"

"In Germany."

"Why Germany? That's not exactly the jewel center of the world."

Chavala closed her thoughts. At least this was good practice, a sort of dress rehearsal for what she'd soon be going through . . . "It's not the jewel center of the world, you're absolutely right about that . . . but unfortunately, Moishe, after the war all the Jews that came from Eastern Europe and went to Germany came only with what they could carry. And what did they carry? The same thing we carried when we left Russia, a few diamonds—" she took another drink of schnapps "—well, multiplied by what we had, imagine how the pawnshops there must be bulging with jewelry. Don't you realize, Moishe, with American dollars you can buy a fortune? The Germans are carrying their money around in a wheelbarrow to buy a loaf of bread. That's what the mark is worth. There's a lot of money to be made, Moishe, and although life is very sad, one person's misfortune can become another's opportunity . . . Listen, Moishe, to say I'm happy, you know I'm not. But we didn't create it, we didn't make the world what it is, but we do have to make a living. For all of us. And *that's* why I'm going to Europe."

When she'd finished, the story sounded so convincing, she just *might* investigate the German situation . . . yes, she just might . . .

"And what's the *duty* on all this going to cost?" Moishe said.

The magic word "duty" meant going through customs. For the moment, she forgot about the pawnshops in Berlin. With a grand effort to reassume her composure she quickly answered, "First of all, there is no duty on anything over a hundred years old" . . . a good guess . . . "and besides, what I'll be buying it for, it'll be a pittance. I mean, it's to develop a business. America likes that. I'm being like an American . . ."

Moishe decided not to press, in spite of his misgivings. For whatever they were worth, Chavala at least seemed to have all the answers. "When are you leaving?"

"Tomorrow."

"Well, dear sister, I can only say go with *mazel,* and come home safely. What time does your ship sail?"

She really swallowed hard. "At midnight."

"So late? Well, the family will see you off anyway—"

"At twelve o'clock midnight? . . . don't be silly. You think I'm going to wake up Joshua to see me off? Absolutely not! Besides, for this family there've been enough hellos and good-byes from docks. It's very sweet of you, Moishe darling, and I do appreciate it but somehow I don't feel in the mood for more long tearful good-byes . . . When I come home we'll have a reunion." She smiled brightly.

DEPARTURE day she rented a room in a downtown hotel, she didn't even notice the name. Taking shears out of her bag, she cut her hair very short. After she dressed that evening, complete with the *sheitel* and the small round pillow, she examined herself in the mirror. So, Chavala . . . you're a mother and a wife, *and* a smuggler. *Mazel tov.* Somehow, though, she managed a secret smile, then quickly put it away.

"MR. and Mrs. Moses Epstein" (better known as Chavala Landau and Benny Bernstein) shared separate bunks. The pious Mr. Moses Epstein was to stay away from any of the young ladies aboard and *never* to leave the stateroom without his Bible.

He managed to do that, and the entire week's voyage was a smooth one in every way. People tended to leave the Epsteins alone—they were hardly a gay couple—and the ocean cooperated by not getting out of order and upsetting Chavala's stomach.

A more incongruous, a more outlandish-looking pair of smugglers had never, Chavala was sure, arrived in the stately city of Amsterdam. After checking into a *kosher* hotel in the Jewish section, they proceeded to the carefully memorized address they had been given.

All the way across the Atlantic Chavala had been in terror of what was to happen next . . . the actual acquiring of the "goods," as they were referred to. She'd pictured terrible men and floozy women . . . guns, knives, who knew what . . . and then in the middle of the transaction police whistles, handcuffs, jail and the firing squad. It didn't happen. It all went so smoothly that she was a little let down. The men were polite, if close-mouthed. No floozies. The packets were ready, the vouchers and money quickly exchanged. By noon Chavala and Benny behind locked hotel-room doors were carefully arranging the contraband. The narrow bands around the *tallisim* were taken apart, filled, carefully sewn back. Inside of Chavala's *sheitel* some twenty carats were taped. The largest amount was secured in the heel of Benny's five-inch platform shoe. All necessary items were put into the paper valises they'd carried from the shores of Manhattan. They would not risk staying; it was unwise even for the night. As they were about to leave, Chavala could no longer hold back the idea she'd had since they'd left New York . . . "Benny, let's find out how far it is from here to Germany—"

"Germany?" He all but screamed. "I want to get *out* of here and get this whole business *over* with. I don't know whether you know it or not, but I haven't slept a night. And you may notice that my clothes are practically falling off of me—"

"I know, Benny, I know, and what can I say? It's *you* who've been my greatest jewel through this whole nerve-wracking ordeal. But you see, dear Benny, I have a sister living in Germany that I haven't seen in a very long, long time, and to be this close and not see her . . . well, it would be something I'd never forgive myself for . . . Do you think, for my sake, you could eat a little more?"

Happy, he wasn't, but her words did get through to him. A family was a family, which was what he'd never had, except for the *landsman*. "All *right,* all right . . . we'll go find out how far it is . . ."

To their surprise, they didn't need a ship—all those canals, all the water in Amsterdam somehow suggested the sea and ships. Actually, there was a regular train service between Amsterdam and Berlin.

When they arrived in the strange city, they stood for several minutes, clinging to their suitcases, watching the crowd scurrying in all different directions. To keep up their masquerade, their choice of hotels would once again have to be in a Jewish section. But where was that? After searching the platform, asking questions in Yiddish, English and variations thereof, they found a bearded Jewish peddler and Chavala asked him in Yiddish where they might stay. He happily told them how to get to the eastern part of Berlin, where they would find not only Chasidim like themselves but restaurants that prominently displayed Stars of David, signifying that the food was strictly *kosher.* Also, they should have no problem getting a room.. . .

Chavala, of course, felt as though every policeman they passed on the street knew that sewn inside her wig were diamonds, and whenever she looked . . . in spite of herself . . . at Benny's five-inch heel she was sure she lost another pound to the ten pounds she'd already worried off . . . she hadn't been able to eat or sleep properly during the past weeks, she'd had nightmares that the gendarmes would break down the door and find this holy couple's business was illicit gems instead of the word of God. The rest of her life, she'd spend it doing penance in some European jail . . . Each night she'd wake up soaked in perspiration, and in those moments she just knew her soul would burn in hell. Yes, true, Jews didn't believe in purgatory, but she was a Jew that knew it was there, never mind what you called it . . . if this wasn't a living hell, what the hell was it . . . ?

Finally they did manage to find a guesthouse, faded and crumbling, on Dragonerstrasse. When at long last she'd locked the door, she lay down and Benny, feeling none too good himself, went to the adjacent bedroom and decided to do the same.

As she lay there, she decided that for all its interesting challenges, she really didn't have the temperament for this jewel-smuggling business. Added to that rather belated insight was the thought that maybe Sheine hadn't gone to the post office to pick up the message she'd sent.

For three days she lived in her anxiety, never leaving the room, Benny dutifully fetching food she couldn't eat. By now she'd almost given up hope that Sheine had received her message and debated with herself about taking the risk of calling the Hausman residence. Why not? She could merely ask, "May I speak to Mrs. Gunter Hausman?" . . . "Who's calling?" . . . "The milliner, her hat is ready." She'd try it . . . she had to do something or go out of her mind altogether.

Handbag over her arm, she tapped on Benny's door, gently opened it. "Don't leave the room, Benny, I have to try and see if I can get in touch with my sister by phone."

Benny laughed. "You think you can trust me with the merchandise while you're away?"

Chavala smiled weakly. "Any friend of the *landsman*'s is a friend of mine," she said, and shut his door.

When she was about to leave her room there was a knock on the door. Her stomach turned over. Sure, it had all been too easy up to now, the righteous wrath of God had fallen down on her head, right where it belonged. Who could get away with such a thing? . . . It was the police coming to take her away . . . "Who is it?" A little girl's voice she barely recognized as her own.

"Me . . . *Sheine* . . ."

Quickly she opened the door, hugged Sheine to her in happiness and relief. When the pleasurable shock of seeing one another had subsided, the two scrutinized one another. Sheine was chic and blond. Chavala looked like she had just arrived from Pinsk.

Sheine asked, "Why are you dressed like this?"

"Well, darling, it's a long story. The truth is it's so silly I don't know where to begin. You see, there's a lot of jewelry to be bought here in East Berlin . . . because of the refugees . . . it's like when mama had the earrings. You know what I mean? Well, anyway, they like to sell to their own. If I was dressed up they would think—" She couldn't go on with this travesty. "Why should I lie to you . . . you're my sister . . . but no one else knows. No one. The truth is, Sheine, I'm doing something very bad. I came to Europe to buy diamonds on the black market . . ."

Sheine, not surprisingly, took a few moments to absorb *this,* not to mention its consequences . . . "You mean . . . you're *smuggling* jewels into—"

"That's what I'm doing. Aren't I terrible? Don't answer that."

"But why?" Sheine shook her head. "You were making such a good living . . . that's what you wrote in your letter—"

"I am . . . but not enough. Not enough at all. Oh yes, you heard from Dvora, but she didn't tell you how bad things have been for her . . . It took money, a great deal of it, with the baby being sick, and what you don't know is . . . I'm sorry to say to you . . . poor Lazarus was killed and Raizel had nothing. Chia goes to college . . . oh, did I tell you? She's going to get married, you know Moishe already is. What can I say? I could work myself up to poverty in one generation."

"And if you get caught? Have you thought of that?"

"Of course I've thought about it, that's all I've done since I started this whole *meshuggene mishegoss.* Why do you think I look like an old lady of ninety? I'm sure that under the *sheitel* is plenty of white hair."

"I really don't know what to say—"

"Neither do I, except that if I have the *mazel* to get away with this it will be the *last* time, take my word . . . Now enough about me. How are you, Sheine?"

She hesitated for a moment, then: "Pride is a foolish thing, Chavala, and in the beginning of my marriage I didn't want you to know how unhappy I really was, so I made the letters sound like life was all sunshine and roses . . . but since we're sisters and you've been so honest with me . . . Well, in the beginning, when I first arrived in Berlin, I had a very difficult time. Being a secret Jew and living with an anti-Semitic mother-in-law almost gave me a nervous breakdown. Maybe it did. Anyway, with Gunter's support and the help of a psychiatrist, I'm able to live with the deception . . . You see, Chavala, I've learned that life has its price, and we have to pay for our sins. I've paid for mine." She said it simply, directly. No tears or wringing of hands.

"I wish you had told me sooner, how terrible it must have been for you—"

"It *was.* But it's better now. Not perfect. Better. I've learned to put things in their proper place. At least I think I have. Anyway, something wonderful has happened. *I'm expecting a child.*"

"Oh, Sheine, I'm so happy for you."

"And what a joy it is to be sitting here telling the news to you."

"And your husband? How does he feel about it?"

"Gunter is beside himself . . . I suppose my nature is a little bit like mama's when it comes to having children, we'd almost resigned ourselves to being childless at first. But it seems miracles do happen."

Miracles indeed, Chavala thought . . . "When are you expecting?"

"In eight months." She laughed rather bitterly. "At least I seem to have redeemed myself in my mother-in-law's eyes. Maybe she's forgiven Gunter for marrying beneath himself—"

"*Beneath* himself? Some nerve—"

"I was born Sheine Rabinsky, and Sheine Rabinsky didn't exactly fit her Germanic ideal, wasn't one of the fair *frauleins* she'd hoped Gunter would marry and make babies with."

Chavala looked at Sheine more closely now. "Does all that explain your blond hair?"

"Partly. And at least I don't stand out like a sore thumb in the blond world we move in. Besides, what does it matter? I made my choice . . . I'll make the best of it . . . Now, tell me about the new baby, and Reuven . . . and Dovid . . ."

"The new baby's not so little any more. Joshua's four, and Reuven's not too pleased with me for not living in Palestine. I can't say I entirely blame him, and I do miss him terribly . . . As for Dovid, he's very involved with politics, with the creation of a homeland. He's quite a man . . . as you well remember, Sheine."

From the sound of Chavala's voice Sheine knew that much was left unsaid. Just as she had kept to herself for so long her early passion for Dovid. Still, she asked, "How are things between you?"

"I'm not sure. Can we let it go at that for the moment?" She just couldn't bear thinking the unthinkable about Dovid and another woman, let alone talk about it. Not even with Sheine . . . maybe especially not with Sheine . . .

The shadows of dusk shone through the dingy lace curtains. The hours had fled too soon. Today's reunion had been so rich that Sheine almost was able to forget that they weren't back in that little village south of Odessa, sitting around mama's kitchen table drinking tea the way they'd done when they were children . . .

But now the time had come to leave the past. Getting up, she looked closely at Chavala, then said, "Chavala, seeing you is the greatest gift you could have given me, and if ever there were times in our lives when we were not close, well, I regret that. This has for me more than made up for it. I love you, and I pray that everything you want happens. You deserve it. Please tell the others to keep in touch. Now I'll miss you all more than ever . . ."

THE next day Mr. and Mrs. Moses Epstein, their suitcases filled with prayer books and religious objects, took the train to Hamburg, where they immediately boarded a ship bound for New York City. Traveling on U.S. passports, they had no trouble with customs. That prospect was yet to come on the other side of the ocean. Chavala and Benny decided not to think about it. And for once Chavala welcomed rough seas . . . she could focus her attention on her queasy stomach instead of the prospect of being led off to jail . . .

CHAVALA and Benny looked out to the magnificent harbor of Manhattan, and there stood that lady with the torch held aloft. Her welcoming "Give me your poor" did not apply to these two standing on deck. When they finally reached customs the supposedly pregnant Mrs. Epstein trembled inwardly as the officer asked questions, then went through a cursory examination of Mr. and Mrs. Moses Epstein's paper suitcases.

Everything seemed in order. The asthmatic Chasid, Moses Epstein, stood at attention during the procedure. It was that or collapse. His wife merely died a thousand deaths. At last they were dismissed and waved on. As they were about to get into a cab, Benny's shoelace, already loose, became untied, and the shoe with the five-inch hollow heel became detached from his foot. By the time he'd retrieved it and pulled the laces tight, Chavala had nearly fainted into the cab.

CHAVALA sat in the basement of the *landsman,* her recovery nearly complete. After a warm greeting, he proceeded to take inventory, going meticulously through every packet. To Chavala it seemed hours. Finally he smiled. *"Mazel tov.* You have more than enough merchandise here to open two stores. The goods is good. Believe me."

She took a deep breath, let it out. "What can I say, how do I thank you?"

"When I see the store with your name on it, that will be my thanks."

She put her arms around him. He did look like a *tzaddik.* "I'll never forget you for this, and I'll pay you back every dime. *You* believe *me.* "

He shook his head, "I know . . . I know. Worried about you, I'm not."

She kissed him on the cheek. "I love you."

For once in Yussel Melnetsky's life he felt loved. Mumbling under his breath, he said, "That's better than money. *I* owe *you* . . ."

THAT night was a busy, happy one at Moishe and Julie's apartment on West End Avenue. Joshua was so happy and relieved to see his mother again, he scarcely left her side. Although none of them knew it, the presents they received had not been purchased in Berlin but at Macy's department store. Well, Joshua cared nothing about the geography of the train set (made in Germany) that went over trestles and under bridges. But he wouldn't, not even for his mother, wear the Tyrolean suit with the lederhosen and the gray felt hat with a feather, which Chavala bought in a shop on Fifty-seventh Street and Madison Avenue—made in Germany. Maybe he already had more sense than she did, Chavala thought.

From the dining room Julie summoned everyone in to dinner. Julie's mother, an attractive if frail woman, was there, as well as Chia and Lenny Moscowitz and his parents.

"Well," said Moishe, standing with a glass of wine in his hand, "I have an important announcement to make . . . Julie and I are going to have a baby."

Squeals of congratulations.

Then Chia looked at Lenny and said with a straight face, "Well, I hope it won't be in June . . . because Lenny and I are getting married then."

Chavala had to hold back the tears, remembering the night Chia was born. The memories were too many and the past too close tonight. In her mind she was standing with a new child in her arms, back in that kitchen south of Odessa . . . "You are mine . . . you were given unto my keeping . . . little Chia . . . mama's life will be lived through you . . ." *I've kept my promise, mama. For all the bad things I've done, all the mistakes I've made, this makes it worthwhile . . .*

Compared to the great announcement they'd just heard, hers about the new store seemed insignificant. It could keep. Tomorrow was time enough.

Chapter Thirty

IT SEEMED A century since they'd first reached the shores of America. Chavala had never dreamed how she was going to make a living. A day to remember. It was the worst blizzard that New York had had in years, and they'd barely had sufficient clothes to keep them warm. The snow fell between the eaves of Mrs. Zuckerman's attic, and Moishe had complained about the apartment on Delancey Street . . . Well, maybe it was a century ago . . . it was 1920, and in the short period of five years she'd worked herself up a very long way. Only in America . . .

CHAVALA signed the lease on a store at Fifth Avenue and Forty-first Street. It was 1925. America was riding the crest of her prosperity wave. Chavala wanted her store to fit the times. The lighting was soft. Muted pearl-gray silk covered the walls, and in front of the gold French tables Louis XV chairs were positioned so the customers could contemplate the merchandise in comfort.

Chavala, Moishe and Julie stood in front and watched the sign, "Landau's," being hoisted in all its splendor.

The pawnshop was now operated by a close friend of Mr. Leibowitz who was too old to stand on his feet any longer; his honesty, of course, was beyond question.

Since the *landsman* felt it was time for Benny to become a respected merchant, he suggested to Chavala that the one-time "Mr. Epstein" should run the store near Harlem. Chavala agreed quickly; it was the least she could do.

All that was left was to manufacture her own jewelry. It was also a matter of need. So as not to be obliged to show records of wholesale purchases, Chavala and the *landsman* realized that the smuggled loose diamonds would have to be mounted. She found a loft on the Bowery, where the rent was right and where there were men out of the labor market so far as their ages were concerned but not their valuable experience. Some were stooped, most white-haired, their pants bagging on frail limbs and with belts taken in too many notches. They had been skilled and respected craftsmen, first in the old country, then for years in America. But age had overtaken them, or so they were told. Chavala's offer to them was a simple one, and they blessed her for it . . . Do what you do best, gentlemen, and name your price—within reason, of course . . . They smiled and went about their jobs like reborn human beings. Someone had given them a chance to get out of the alleys, the dark corners, literally and spiritually. Her name was Chavala Landau.

Chavala also became a designer, thank you very much. She designed what the old men executed, and maybe she wasn't educated at some fancy school for design, and maybe her sketches were all in her head, and she didn't talk like she had her lips buttoned and didn't know whether she was a boy or a girl, but she managed, along with a little help from those noses-in-the-air Cartier, Van Cleef & Arpels, and, not to be a piker, Mr. Tiffany too. So she used her imagination—under the spur of necessity—to make a few adjustments . . . a diamond instead of an emerald, a blue star sapphire instead of a ruby, but depend on it, the designs, whatever they were, she *sold* like a master craftsman. And who was hurt? Nobody, just like with the smuggling . . . except a few dollars in duty that didn't get collected into somebody's pocket . . . And who could argue that many, many were helped?

Between the three stores and the manufacturing plant, Chavala began truly to acquire a sizable bank account. She provided for her family, now they would never be in want. Every month Raizel received a check. As for Dvora, she was more cautious with her since she knew about Ari's resistance. It was a delicate subject, but she'd found out about an outfit called Harvester that made large farming equipment, and she knew what Ari needed was a mechanized plow. Except she couldn't just send it to him tied in a red ribbon and say Happy Chanukah, so she decided to ask Dovid to help, welcoming at the same time an opportunity to be in touch. That evening she wrote a letter:

My Dearest Dovid,

As always my thoughts are of you and Reuven. I pray that all goes well with you and, especially, that you are happy. Joshua is a lovely little boy and talks about you constantly. In my heart I know that the time will come when we will be together. Permanently.

Now, Dearest Dovid, I need your help. Knowing your ability to handle delicate matters, I would like for Ari to have a mechanized plow. Let me know what you think would be best for his use and suggest the necessity of it. I will arrange to have the money transferred to Jerusalem. Of course he must think the loan is from you or he will not accept it. When he pays you back, the money will be put into an account for the children. What else can I say except thank you, thank you for your help.

Now, about things here. As you know, Chia is getting married in June to a wonderful young man I've written you about before. As you already know, I still cannot get over the fact that the family, and *you*, Dearest Dovid, will be together on that memorable day. Well, Darling Dovid, what can I say, except that I live for that day.

With all my love,
Chavala

As June approached, the excitement over Chia's wedding took precedence over all else. But when Chavala sent the tickets for the family, there was an exception that made her terribly sad . . . how could she call it a reunion of family if Sheine would not share in the important event? And how could she? Her husband, son of an anti-Semitic mother . . . Sheine still having in her heart to live a deception about what was left of her true feelings . . .

For several days she could not even wait on the trade, instead sitting in the office and trying to work on the books.

Moishe went upstairs to Chavala's small office, sat in front of her desk. "You know, you and I have shared a lot of things. Now, tell me what's bothering you."

"Nothing . . . what brought this on?"

"The way you're acting."

"How am I acting?"

"Sad."

"Why should I be sad . . . that's nonsense . . . I have a lot of things on my mind—"

"Such as?"

"Four businesses."

"But that's not new . . . for God's sake, Chavala, don't always be so brave. You have a problem, talk about it."

She looked at him. Maybe it would help to talk about it. "I want Sheine at the wedding . . ."

"So? Why don't you write and ask her?"

"Well, as I told you when I came back from Berlin and I'd seen Sheine, she told me she's expecting a baby and—"

"So . . . pregnant women don't travel? What is she going to take, a horse and wagon? She'll be on a luxury liner."

Chavala said nothing.

"To ask wouldn't hurt."

But Chavala was thinking about her anti-Semitic mother-in-law. Still, she told herself, she wasn't inviting the mother-in-law. "Well, maybe you're right . . ." She was grateful to him for making her face her reluctance, and helping her overcome it. Including the worrisome prospect of meeting a true-blue Aryan like Gunter.

As soon as Moishe left, Chavala took out a piece of stationery headed "Landau's Fine Jewelry," and began:

> My Dearest Sheine,
>
> The memory I have of the last time we saw each other in Berlin becomes more vivid with the passing of each day. Even a brief moment can become a timeless gift, which is the case with you and me. I long to see you.
>
> As you know from my last letter, Chia is getting married and the family are all coming from Palestine. The only sadness will be if you aren't here. If I had one wish it would be to share this joyous time with you. Do you think it might be possible for you and Gunter to come? Please try, my Dearest Sheine.
>
> I pray that you are well and happy. Write soon, as I will count the moments for your reply.
>
> Your loving sister,
> *Chavala*

Sheine opened the small metal box at the post office and found the letter from Chavala. Quickly she sat on a wooden bench and opened it. After she'd finished, there was a long moment when she wondered if it would be possible . . . there was *nothing* in this world she wanted so much as to be reunited, after all these years, with her family.

She thought of little else that day, and in the evening when she and Gunter were alone in their rooms, her pulse raced as she handed him the letter and even more so as she watched him reading it.

When he'd finished, he handed it back to Sheine, then said, "Obviously, dear, you want to go, and that's understandable. But how do you think your family is going to accept me?"

Forgetting the rejections she'd had from his family, she put her arms around him, grateful for his not saying no. "You mean that we can go?"

"I wouldn't want to deny you . . . but the question remains. Will they?"

"They'll love you—"

"That's a bit more than I was asking."

"They're very happy for us, the baby . . . that's all they want . . . my happiness . . ."

He hesitated, remembering the reaction of her family when they'd married. Still, time could change things . . . look how his mother had mellowed about his wife . . . "Well, if it means that much to you, then, yes, we shall go."

Amidst her rush of gratitude was a sobering thought . . . "What will you tell your mother?"

Poor Elsa—he still thought of her by that name—she still lives with ghosts. Of course, it was all unfortunately the residue of her Jewishness, her apprehension about her past. He sighed to himself, determined to put her mind at rest. Taking her in his arms, he smiled down at her. "Darling, my mother is not our keeper. We'll tell her we are taking a holiday. There, do you feel better now?"

She did. How could she not with such a sweet understanding husband . . . so unlike his mother . . .

When Gunter retired that evening, she could scarcely wait to write Chavala.

And when Chavala received the letter, her world was finally complete.

WAITING for the family to arrive strained Chavala's self-discipline to its outer limits. She marked off each day that brought them closer. But it seemed that when one waited, time never passed.

Still, in the next month there were a million things to do, which made the waiting a *little* easier. The ceremony would be held in the large chapel at Temple Rodeph Shalom, accommodating two hundred and fifty people, and the reception at the Plaza Hotel. The bride's dress was purchased at Bergdorf Goodman, and the bridesmaids' dresses at Bonwit Teller. This was going to be the wedding to end all weddings. Chavala worked for hours at a time with the florist on decorations for the *chuppah*. White roses, small orchids, peonies, baby's breath and green maidenhair fern created the dome from which hung satin ribbons entwined with lily of the valley. White streamers and tall standards filled with gladiolus would line the aisle, and on the pulpit would be large roses, gladiolus stocks and lilacs. For the table centerpieces, baskets of pink peonies sitting on pink damask tablecloths.

The next project on Chavala's agenda was more complicated. Going over the menu with the caterer at the Plaza, it was decided that the food would not only be the finest but also strictly *kosher.* Raizel and her sons were especially to be considered in this connection . . . including not having Beef Wellington, out of the question. Chicken, but strictly *kosher,* was the compromise. On the five-tiered wedding cake, there would be no compromise.

The orchestra . . . Chavala had auditioned them personally . . . had been engaged, as well as the photographer, a man whose pants were too tight, but what could you do? . . . he had a very good professional reputation . . . And all none too soon. Tomorrow was *the day.* The family was arriving.

CHAVALA was a nervous wreck as she stood at dockside waiting with Julie, Moishe, Chia and Lenny. Each moment seemed an eternity as the giant steamer was nudged by the tugboats into its pier. When it finally had stopped, Joshua looked up, then screamed out, "There's papa . . . Reuven, look over *here* . . ."

Although the little boy's voice could not be heard from the deck above, Reuven saw his brother being held up on the shoulder of his uncle Moishe. Reuven waved back furiously, laughing with excitement at the sight of Joshua.

And then things began to happen at what seemed a furious pace as the passengers began walking, running down the gangplank. When the family was finally assembled, laughter, tears, excited conversation overlapped . . . "It's unbelievable . . . "Chia! I can't believe it's you" . . . "Oh, Dvora, and Ari" . . . "Aunt Chavala" . . . "Pnina, what a beauty . . ." Reuven kissed and hugged Chavala. "I'm very happy to see you, mother . . ."

In spite of the excitement, Chavala was not only touched by this open display of affection from her previously disapproving son, but surprised that he'd called her mother instead of *ema.* "You've learned English," she said, and laughed a little nervously.

"I had to. Aunt Dvora's a slavedriver. It's all her fault . . . I'm glad you approve . . ."

"Oh, I do, it's wonderful . . ."

And then came the moment when not only Joshua was in Dovid's arms, but so was she, being embraced. The deep thrill that went through her, right to her very soul . . . "Dovid, oh God, seeing you, I don't have the words . . ." And then in a whisper . . . "I love you, Dovid."

"Those are the best words, Chavala. And they are mine to you—"

Suddenly it occurred to Chavala that neither Lenny nor Julie had been introduced. In Hebrew she said to the family, "This is Julie, Moishe's wife, and come meet Lenny, Chia's *chatan.*" Excitedly, the family greeted the new additions. A slight problem, however . . . since the acknowledgment was made in Hebrew, Julie and Lenny couldn't understand one word. Moishe came to the rescue and interpreted.

The preparations had included housing for the family. Raizel and her sons were driven to Mrs. Zuckerman's, where everything would be *kosher.* A suite of rooms was reserved at the Waldorf-Astoria Hotel, since *kosher* was not a problem—nor would the language be a barrier— Ari, after all, having been born and bred in New Jersey, U.S.A.

After the family had been settled, Chavala went back to her apartment to supervise the preparations for dinner that evening. She suggested that, since she would not be available, Dovid and Reuven take over the role of family guide.

After an hour's rest, the family was gathered together, and the sights of Manhattan loomed before them. Each place they stopped at was awesome. New York was a city of towers that seemed to reach up and touch the sky. As they walked the streets, they had to step aside to allow the ongoing flow of this multitude of humanity that passed them. Zvi looked at his father, "I don't like it, *abba.*"

Ari laughed, "To tell you the truth, I'm not crazy about it either, Zvi. I never was, but then, the whole world isn't Palestine."

Overhearing the remark, Reuven said, "It is for me." Reuven was still Reuven.

When they finally stopped at Schrafft's Restaurant to rest their weary feet, the family all agreed Manhattan wasn't Tel Aviv.

Raizel, seated close to her sons around the large round table, felt all but forgotten until the waitress asked for orders. She looked at Ari and in Yiddish asked, "What did the lady say?"

"She wanted to know what you want . . . we're going to have coffee and cake and ice cream sundaes. What would you like?"

What she would like was to be back in Mea Shearim, where she didn't have to contend with this dreadful *trayf.* From these dishes and cups she wouldn't drink. "Thank you very much," she told Ari, "but I'm not hungry."

Her sons followed her example. They sat and observed as the coffee cakes and ice cream sundaes were being served and delightedly consumed. Watching the family, the two oldest sons, sitting there with their black broad-brimmed hats, looked meaningfully at one another . . . it was Sodom, said the first with his eyes, and the other's silent response was, Gomorrah.

AT seven they all arrived to be greeted by an ebullient Chavala. No denying it, Chavala's apartment was magnificent, though Zvi said to his father, "I like our place better."

Reuven agreed.

But Dvora did not share her husband's or Reuven's feelings. She was proud of Chavala, and grateful to her. "This is beautiful, Chavala . . . I'm so proud of you."

Chavala thanked her and told her how proud she was of Dvora . . . of *all* of the family . . . "And to think I have you all together. Would you have believed when we left that little *shetl* that we'd be here in New York City tonight waiting for little Chia to be married?"

"No, I surely didn't, I wouldn't even have been able to imagine it. But thank God it happened."

Thank God, Mr. Leibowitz and the *landsman,* Chavala thought, and kissed Dvora. "Now, then, I think we're all ready to go to dinner."

THE next day the family collected once again for the arrival of Sheine and Gunter. Again the kissing, the hugging, except for Gunter, who stood awkwardly aside until Sheine took his hand in hers and said to the family, "This is Gunter."

Uneasily, formally, he acknowledged the introduction.

Dovid greatly helped by holding out his hand. "It's a pleasure. I'm sorry we took so long, but, welcome. You've made all of us very happy by coming, and helping to make this family gathering complete."

Sheine, deeply grateful for those words, could barely control her emotions as she stood now in front of Dovid . . . She had married Gunter because of Dovid, her frustrated love for him being so great at the time. It was almost a perverse reaction. And, now, as she and Dovid, she too close to the middle of her life, embraced, she knew her love was even greater than before, but so very different . . . love had so many faces, disguises . . . now Dovid was once again the brother she had had as a little girl. Now her love for him had come full circle, back to reality. It was a great relief . . .

THE next day the shopping for Dvora, Pnina and Sheine began. For Raizel, there was no choice . . . she would wear black silk with a white lace collar, as well as a black *sheitel.*

Standing in front of the triple mirror at Bergdorf's, Dvora looked at herself in the pink flowered chiffon and hardly recognized herself. A far cry from overalls. Viewing her reflection in the mirror, Chavala said, "It's perfect, Dvora, that's the one, it's lovely . . ."

Looking at the price tag, Dvora said, "I really don't know what to say."

Chavala understood. "What is there to say? It's gorgeous. Of everything you tried on, that's the one. End of discussion."

Dvora was still reluctant.

Chavala decided she needed an ally. She went to the adjacent fitting room and brought Sheine back with her. The two sisters then surveyed Dvora solemnly and with great care.

"Why in the world are you hesitating?" Sheine finally asked.

"Well," Dvora said, "it's so expensive, and when will I wear it again—?"

"To Zvi's bar mitzvah. You're taking it. Am I right, Sheine?" Chavala said.

"You're absolutely right. Now, what do you think of mine?"

"What could be better with your coloring? You were always at your best in blue."

Sheine laughed. "I wasn't thinking so much of the color. How does it look with my bulging belly?"

"Like tailor-made. With all those flounces, no one will even see. Now, let's see how Julie's getting on with *her* bulging belly."

The three sisters walked into Julie's dressing room, just as she was slipping into a hyacinth silk maternity dress. Julie looked first at herself in the mirror, then at her sisters-in-law. Laughing, she asked, "Do you think anyone would know I was pregnant?"

"Never in a million years," Chavala said. "And now we have the most important dress of all to buy . . . Pnina's."

Dvora asked, "What about you?"

"Mine I already have. I am, after all, big sister of the bride-to-be."

THE day of days for Chia had arrived. Chavala, up early, brought her sister the nuptial breakfast on a bed tray. Placing it before Chia, she said, eyes gleaming, "It's very important for a bride to eat. You'll need your strength this day. Now don't take too long, we have a million things to do . . ."

Chia looked up at Chavala, reached out her arms and hugged her. "Chavala. I don't know what to say. You've made us . . . me in particular . . . so happy. We owe so much to you . . . you're what's held us all together . . ."

Chavala could say nothing, but allowed herself the thought that maybe the decision she made that day so long ago, standing on the dock in Jaffa, had been the right one after all . . .

BY two o'clock the pews at Rodeph Shalom were filled with family and close friends. As the organ played softly, Chavala, Dovid, Chia, and the wedding party waited in the foyer. Chavala looked at Chia, dressed in her white jewel-encrusted satin gown and fifteen-foot train edged with heirloom lace and could not quite believe her eyes. She quickly kissed Chia on the cheek and placed the short veil over her face.

Dovid looked at Chavala . . . at his wife . . . beautiful, a queen . . . the mauve of her tissue taffeta gown, trimmed with Alençon lace, embellished the delicacy of her porcelainlike skin. Her deep blue eyes sparkled and there was an inner peace that seemed to shine in her face. But she was just as beautiful that late Saturday after *Shabbes* when they'd stood shivering in the dirty, cold little *shul*, pledging their troth. He saw her clearly, dressed in a peasant skirt and blouse, a shawl over her head. Yes, indeed, Chavala was beautiful, perhaps even more so then than today . . . the world had been so new, just like their love. What they had done that day had been an act of faith in themselves, in life. He only hoped it would not be lost . . .

His thoughts were interrupted as the sounds of *Lohengrin* filled the sanctuary and spilled out into the foyer. The moment had arrived. As the doors opened, Pnina, dressed in white embroidered organdy with a pink satin sash around her waist, was the first in the procession, scattering rose petals from a basket she carried. Dovid, in a gray cutaway, stood at Chia's right—he would give her away. Chavala was at her left. The three walked slowly into the sanctuary with the bridesmaids, dressed in delicate pink tulle and carrying nosegays of baby roses and orchids, following.

To one side of the altar stood Lenny with Reuven as his best man. Joshua, as ring bearer, held the satin pillow. On the other side stood the four ushers. When they reached the altar, Dovid kissed Chia's cheek, then took his place and stood next to Chia, as Lenny's parents approached the altar, standing for their son.

The ceremony began, the rabbi explaining the responsibilities of marriage and the sanctity of union . . .

Chavala and Dovid listened, each with their private thoughts, each remembering *their* wedding day, feeling a renewal and also a fear over the effect of their separation. Well, each in his fashion was a survivor, Dovid thought. Especially Chavala . . .

For all Chavala's planning, though, Raizel had declined to attend the ceremony; her sons would not worship in a place where women and men were not separated and *yarmulkes* were not worn. Chavala had respected their feelings, but their absence hurt.

Well, the loss was theirs, Chavala thought, as she heard the rabbi say the magical words, "Do you, Leonard, take Chia to be your lawfully wedded wife, to love and to honor, to cherish until death do you part?"

Solemnly he answered, "I do."

"And do you, Chia, take Leonard to be your lawfully wedded husband, to love and obey through sickness and health until death do you part?"

"I do."

The rabbi asked for the ring, which Joshua proudly came forward to offer.

Taking up the ring, Leonard held it as the rabbi said, "Repeat after me . . . With this ring, I thee do wed."

The ring was then placed on Chia's finger as the rabbi said, "I now pronounce you husband and wife, and may you live according to God's laws. You may now kiss the bride."

Picking up Chia's face veil, Lenny looked at her for a moment, then kissed her, deeply and fully. He then proceeded to stomp on the wine glass inside the napkin, and the new Mr. and Mrs. Leonard Moscowitz turned and walked five feet off the ground until they reached the foyer, where once again, Lenny kissed her and said, "And I meant every word of it, Mrs. Moscowitz."

"And me too, Mr. Moscowitz."

Quickly now he took her by the hand and they hurried down the steps to where a hired limousine waited. Shortly after the newlyweds arrived at the side entrance of the Plaza two additional limousines stopped in front of the main entrance and the family was helped out by the doorman.

When Dovid stepped into the lobby and saw Raizel and her sons sitting on the red damask sofa in their long black coats and wide-brimmed hats, he bristled. They had been waiting here during the ceremony. Instead of following the family to the main ballroom he walked over to them and said, "Take off those hats and check them. You are not in Mea Shearim. You will show manners and respect. And as for you, Raizel, God would have forgiven you had you seen your youngest sister married . . . temples are also houses of worship. And as for you," he said to his pious nephews, "when you lay *tefillin* tonight, ask the One Above to forgive you for offending your aunt Chavala." With that, he walked away and joined the others in the reception line.

Finally, after the good wishes and congratulations, the guests moved into the ballroom, where corks began popping.

Champagne glass in hand, Chavala wove through the crowd to where her very dear friends stood back, observing the festivities. Putting her arm around the *landsman,* she said, "You look so handsome dressed in your navy blue suit. I think you're the best-looking man here."

He laughed. "If you think so, I wouldn't contradict you, Chavala," and then, almost shyly, he said, "I can't get over you asking me to your beautiful *simcha.* "

"Would I have anything as important as a wedding and not have you, and Benny?"

All he could say was, "God has blessed me by knowing you."

She looked directly into the eyes of her friend. Without him this *simcha* could never have happened. "And God blessed me with your generosity." She kissed him quickly on the cheek, then went to her friend Mr. Leibowitz, who stood with Yetta Korn. The memories *they* evoked . . . how lucky for her the day she walked into his shop . . . Kissing him too, she said, "You shared so much with me . . . helped me so much. For that there are no thanks. I'm proud to have you share this day with me, and you, too, Yetta. Today would not be so rich for me if you hadn't been here."

"The pleasure is mine," she said laughing. "It's always a pleasure to see a pearl-stringer get up in life . . ."

NOW the guests were seated at round tables, and dinner began.

Chavala looked down the length of the bridal table at her family. Imagine the miracle of it all . . . from the ghettos of Russia they had come, from the pogroms they had fled, and today they sat at the Plaza Hotel in New York City . . . indeed her cup did runneth over, until she noticed Raizel and her sons not eating.

Casually, she hoped, she got up and walked to the end of the table where Raizel and her sons were seated.

"Are you feeling all right, Raizel? The boys?"

"We're fine."

"Then why aren't any of you eating?"

"Because my mother won't eat off the plates, and she wouldn't eat the chicken," Boris, the oldest, answered promptly, ignoring his uncle Dovid's earlier words. Well, neither he nor anyone else would make them go against their convictions.

My God, thought Chavala as she looked down at the chicken sitting untouched on the plate, this was really too much. "I ordered a *kosher* dinner—"

"My mother still won't eat it."

Chavala, fighting her annoyance, called for the maitre d' and asked for *kosher* cottage cheese to be substituted, adding that it should be served on paper plates. She then went back to the long table and sat down once again next to Dovid. Her face, in spite of her efforts to conceal her emotions, was tight. She did not touch her food.

"What's the matter?" Dovid asked her.

She shrugged, "Nothing, dear, nothing. Everything's fine—"

"No it isn't," he said as he saw the food being placed in front of Raizel and her sons. "Raizel's become a *meshuggeneh,* a fanatic. And as for her sons, I'd like to wring their necks. How do you put up with this nonsense? If the food's not *kosher* enough for them, then let them starve."

"Don't be upset, Dovid . . . please . . . the day is far too important for that." She took up her champagne glass. "Here's to you, Dovid . . . to the best man a woman was ever lucky enough to have as a husband. I mean that, darling, even if sometimes what I do doesn't seem to live up to my words—"

Before he could answer, the photographer began to gather the family together for picture-taking. First the bride alone . . . then the bride and groom . . . the flashbulbs went off as the five sisters, Chia in the center, stood beaming . . . the in-laws together . . . Sheine and Gunter with

Chavala and Dovid . . . Ari, Dvora and their children . . . Julie and Moishe . . . then all the children, Joshua stage-center. The last photograph was of the whole family.

The music began, the bride and groom danced alone to "Oh, how we danced on the night we were wed." Then Dovid and Chavala, Ari and Dvora, Moishe and Julie, Sheine and Gunter joined them on the dance floor.

When Joannie Joseph, Chia's mentor at Hunter, danced with Reuven, she almost forgot he was a mere eighteen. Feeling herself in Reuven's strong, muscled arms, she thought it would take very little to convert her into a dedicated Zionist . . . Damn, if only he were a little older . . .

Dovid and Chavala laughed as they watched five-year-old Joshua dancing with seven-year-old Pnina . . .

Dvora and Ari watched their ten-year-old Zvi dance with one of the bridesmaids, who barely came up to his shoulder. "You know, Ari," said Dvora, "I think we've produced a generation of giants . . . Zvi's taller than the girl."

"It's the wide open spaces of Palestine . . . gives them plenty of room to grow in." . . .

And now Chia was in Dovid's arms. "This is the happiest day of my life, Dovid, and not only because of Lenny. You were here to give me away in marriage . . . I've always thought of you as my father . . . thank you, *abba.*"

"Well, Chia, you were always my little girl . . ." In fact, my baby, he thought, remembering the night she was born . . . "I only hope for you to be half this happy the rest of the days of your life," and then he relinquished her into the arms of her husband.

The band struck up "Hava Nagilah" and the circle formed. An ancient tradition was perpetuated. The bride and groom were hoisted on chairs held aloft on the shoulders of her cousins, who circled the room with the newlyweds. The rest of the guests joined in the procession.

As the *landsman* sat watching, he said to Benny, "You see, that's what you call *tradition.* At another wedding in this fancy Plaza Hotel, this you wouldn't see. I guarantee you."

And Mr. Leibowitz remembered that at his wedding in Minsk more than fifty years ago he too had been held aloft, high above the crowd with his wife . . . like a king and queen . . .

And Lenny's mother and father, third-generation Americans, well, they thought the scene a little strange.

Gunter didn't quite know what to make of it, the Jewish weddings he had attended in Berlin were little different than the non-Jewish . . .

And Sheine thought that Chavala had managed to combine the unorthodox with the orthodox, the beauty of the old that did not seem out of place with the new . . .

Introduced by a drum roll, the orchestra leader asked that everyone be seated for the cake-cutting. Chia, her hand in Lenny's, made the first cut as the camera recorded the moment.

And now, all the months of planning and preparations came to an end as the bride, dressed in her tea-rose yellow silk suit, and the bridegroom in his gray flannel, rushed down the steps of the Plaza Hotel to the Buick convertible that Chavala had given them as a wedding gift.

THE guests dispersed. The family went back to Chavala's apartment to spend a quiet evening together.

A light supper of cold cuts was laid out, along with a sterling-silver coffee service. Everyone helped himself, then took coffee into the living room, where the men talked about politics and the sisters about the past . . .

As usual with such reminiscences, the good was remembered, and what at the time had seemed sad, tragic, now became almost humorous, its sting drowned by the palliative of time . . . Nobody made strudel like mama . . . once again they heard the sounds of Yankel's rickety milk cart making its morning rounds . . . Itzik, the butter-and-egg vendor, falling in the mud, all his eggs broken. Looking back now as they sat in Chavala's well-appointed living room, the hut in Odessa seemed a place where they'd spent their most treasured years . . . Passover was remembered with mama and papa, Rosh Hashanah, Yom Kippur and the simple joys at Chanukah . . . Chavala laughed as she told about the time she'd almost become intoxicated stealing and sampling the cherries from mama's jug of brandy . . . the winter nights huddled around the warm tile oven. In their poverty it seemed there was a feeling of togetherness greater than any of them had ever known since . . . Or so it now seemed . . .

The moment lightened as Chavala said, "And the thing I'll never forget is when we were on our way to the Galilee. The donkey lay down and died. Dovid wasn't a bit upset, he just picked up one pole, told Moishe to take the other, and lo and behold, we finally somehow made it . . ."

Sheine remembered the day "we walked through the bazaars at Jaffa. I never said anything, but I wanted those harem bracelets and gold jeweled sandals so badly I thought my heart would break. I dreamed about them for weeks . . ."

Julie, listening, tried to build images for herself. "What was Moishe like as a little boy?"

The sisters looked at each other, and Dvora finally answered. "You know, I don't remember him ever *being* a little boy . . . but I do remember the way he looked in the red Turkish fez . . . and the gold dagger in the sash around his waist. He asked if he could be taken for a Turk and Sheine told him no, not with his red hair—"

"His hair was that red then?" Julie said, surprised.

"Like fire . . . I'm glad it calmed down some, and with the streaks of silver I have to admit he's almost handsome . . . even if he is my brother."

"And I'd have to agree, even if he is my husband . . . Well, since we're on that subject, I think I'll have Mr. Handsome take his future son's mother home. It's been a long and wonderful day," she said, getting up and taking Chavala's hand. "The wedding was perfect . . . I'll never forget it, Chavala."

As they all followed suit, Chavala suddenly had a sinking feeling . . . when would they do this again, be together like this?

The sisters looked at each other, all sharing Chavala's thought. It was Sheine who said, "Julie's right, none of us will ever forget it. But the very best of all was the family being together."

AFTER the door had closed on the last of them, Chavala returned to Dovid in the living room. "Well, Dovid, we've seen them all grown and married. Let's pray that God lets us be present at our grandchildren's weddings."

He took her in his arms. "From your lips to God's ears."

Before going to Chavala's bedroom, they stopped at Reuven's door, looked in on their sleeping sons.

The night now belonged only to them.

Chapter Thirty-one

CHIA SAT AT the dressing table in their suite at the St. Regis Hotel, only a few blocks from the Plaza, the scene of her wedding reception, and studied her reflection. Was that the face of the girl of yesterday? Hardly. A woman had happened last night. She'd heard stories about what a letdown the wedding night could be. Well, not in her case. Not by a long shot. Lenny had been tender, and then fierce, she had been able to respond, the new feeling in her body as much a surprise as it was a profound pleasure and relief. She was brought out of her delicious reverie by Lenny kissing the back of her neck. Draped in a towel around his middle he said, "The bathroom, madam, is yours."

She turned and kissed him. "I thought it was ours."

"You should have thought about that while I was taking a shower. Don't forget it next time."

"How about aboard ship? A date?"

"A date . . . now, darling, you'd better get it moving. We've got exactly one hour before sailing."

They arrived at dockside just in time to say good-bye to the family, who'd been nervously waiting for them. Then, amidst serpentine streamers, confetti and boat whistles they waved good-bye to the family below as the ship made its way out of New York harbor on its way to Bermuda.

IT seemed to Chavala she was spending her days in good-byes.

Two days later Sheine and Gunter were bound for Berlin, and in the next forty-eight hours the others would be going back to Palestine.

The morning of their departure, as Chavala, Dovid, Reuven and Joshua sat having breakfast, she tried very hard not to think about the moments ticking away. For the moment she was tempted, very tempted, to give it all up in America, to go back with her family to Palestine, especially in the glow of having been with Dovid, having her body renewed by the nights together with him. But it wasn't so easy, even though the rationalizations were powerful . . . she had come a long way, built her business. But the need of her family once they returned to Palestine would not have disappeared. And could she leave the whole burden on Moishe, newly married, or Chia? Of course not . . .

And then the temptation turned almost to a demand, a challenge, when Reuven, all unexpectedly—except, if she thought about it, it really shouldn't have been so unexpected—looked across the table at her, hesitated, and then blurted out what he'd been thinking about almost since the first minute he'd come to New York . . . Could Joshua come back with them to Palestine? At least for a visit?

Seeing the expression of dismay on his mother's face, Reuven realized he hadn't exactly said it right. "What I meant, mother, it's only June and Joshua won't be starting kindergarten until September and . . . well, it would be great to have him for even a little while . . ."

Dovid, as surprised as Chavala, held his breath, waiting for her answer. Of course her first impulse was to say no, it was out of the question, but that impulse gave way to what she knew was only fair . . . after all, Dovid, and Reuven, had been deprived by her of Joshua all these years. How could she begrudge them a few months . . . even if she did have a chill at the prospect, reinforced by the fear that somehow a vacation, a visit, might turn into something more permanent? Well, get it over with, she told herself, and smiling a smile she didn't feel, said, "All right, Reuven, I think that would be all right." She couldn't bear to look at them when she said it.

Reuven immediately got up and kissed his mother. "Thank you, thank you, mother, and I only wish that you could spend the summer with us too."

"That would be nice . . . maybe next year."

Dovid well understood what this would cost her, and his heart went out to her, knowing all too well the loneliness she would feel not only in his absence but now Joshua's too. If ever he'd resented her denial of his younger son, it surely was *not* at this moment. "Thank you, darling . . . I always said you were a remarkable woman. You just keep on proving how right I am." Getting up from his chair and going over to her, he took her in his arms, held her tight and kissed her.

Joshua happily missed the whole drama of the moment. All he knew was that he was going to spend the next few months with his father and his brother Reuven, whom he adored. . . .

AFTER all the good-byes, Julie and Moishe sat in the cab, feeling Chavala's melancholy. The last months had been filled with such excitement, and the last weeks spent in the wonderful coming-together of the family, that there was a distinct letdown for them too.

Julie, feeling it keenly, said, "Chavala, why don't you come and spend a few days with us?"

Tonelessly Chavala said, "Thank you, but I guess not."

"I think it might be nice. For all of us."

Chavala shrugged. "It's always nice, being together. No, darling, thank you, but I want to go home, be by myself a little while."

She wanted no such thing, Julie suspected, but also was sensitive enough not to press.

WHEN Chavala was finally alone in her living room, she looked about at all the *things.* They meant nothing. Self-pity rushed in to fight loneliness . . . What was *she* left with? Nothing. Dvora was much richer than she, and even Raizel, who at least had the comfort of her sons. All of them now had made lives of their own, all except her. Her father had warned her about false prophets and he'd been right . . . She went to her bedroom, undressed and looked at her body in the mirror. All those lost years away from Dovid, soon she'd be middle-aged—oh, shut up, for God's sake . . . you made your bed, now lie in it. Which, she discovered, was easier said than done . . .

JULIE couldn't bear to see what amounted to Chavala's bereavement, trying to camouflage it as she might as she attended to business every day, smiling too brightly as she waited on the trade.

It was noon of the fifth day when Julie went upstairs to Chavala's office, and found her staring out of the window. Chavala was so deep in her own thoughts she didn't hear Julie come in, and so was startled by the sound of her voice when she said, "Chavala, I think you need a vacation."

"What . . . oh, Julie, I didn't hear you come in . . . I'm sorry. What did you say?"

"I said I thought you could use a vacation."

"A vacation? Why, you think I'm overtaxing myself going to the bank?"

Julie ignored her try at humor. "I just happen to think a change would be good for you. Moishe and I have talked it over, and for once, Chavala, you're going to do something for yourself—"

"So, how good should I be to myself?"

"By taking a trip."

"What would you suggest? The Bronx? Or, better still, Albany? That's the capital of our beautiful state . . . maybe I could even have lunch with the governor."

"Joke all you want, you're outnumbered. Moishe and I already have the tickets. You're going to Florida. And don't tell me Florida is only for winter. This is an emergency."

Chavala shrugged. Maybe they were right. Not maybe, they *were* . . . "So, when did you both agree that I should go?"

"As soon as you can pack a bag."

"Fine. I'll travel light, without my mind, which I think I lost a long time ago."

That night she packed, and the next morning Julie and Moishe saw her off to Miami.

THE first night she arrived at her suite of rooms in the Fountainbleu she thought the hotel was big as Manhattan, and the dining room a runner-up to Grand Central Station. A few hours later, asking the maitre d' for a table for one, she looked about the room at the elaborately gowned women, with varying shades of blond hair, bedecked with jewels, seated at tables with husbands and friends, and decided this definitely was *not* for her. She did an about-face, red-faced, escaped to her suite and dined in on room service. As she forced herself to eat, she decided one was, indeed, a very lonely number. At four o'clock in the morning, with the *New York Times*, *Harper's Bazaar* and *Vogue* strewn about on her bed, she turned off the light and fell into a troubled, restless sleep.

The next morning, after breakfast served in her room, she decided it was enough already. *This* kind of loneliness she certainly didn't need. She got into her bathing suit, went downstairs and out to the pool. It was no better. Glamorous widows, happy married couples, seductive singles. Still . . . to go home without giving it a chance . . . no, she'd stick it out to the bitter end.

But at the end of one week, Miami had defeated her. She surrendered and caught the first train to New York.

WHEN she arrived home, she wasn't happy, but at least her misery wasn't costing her anything, and there wasn't the *obligation* to have a good time . . . What there was, though, was a letter from Joshua. He was having such a good time he only wished he could stay there all the time. Wonderful news, exactly what she'd worried about in the first place when she'd agreed to his going.

The next letter was from Sheine, and suddenly she was smiling. Sheine had given birth to a nine-and-one-half-pound baby boy.

Chapter Thirty-two

SHEINE'S JOY AT giving birth to Erich Dieter Hausman was less than complete when, shortly after his birth, Frau Hausman showed her disappointment that the little boy looked so much like his mother, "With that dark hair and those brown eyes . . ." For nine months she had seen herself cradling a blue-eyed, blond-haired cherub. Privately she bitterly resented the fate that had tainted the pure Hausman bloodline. By the time of the christening, Gretchen Hausman, at long last a grandmother, had almost managed to forget the infant's alien genes. As they stood in the church, her thoughts were determinedly on the future, he would be a German to the very marrow of his bones, and *she* would direct his upbringing.

Sheine, watching her son being baptized, felt like shouting out, He's my son too, he's a Jew and should be circumcised, in our faith a child of a Jewish mother is a Jew . . . If only she had the courage, but did she really have the right . . . hadn't she forfeited that the day she became Elsa Beck Hausman . . . ?

Chapter Thirty-three

IN SEPTEMBER, A agreed, Reuven brought Joshua home.

As pleased as Chavala was to see them, she was especially gratified that—whether it be because of Dvora's giving him a greater sense of reality, or an unbending from maturity—Reuven seemed to have overcome his belligerence, even to have come to terms with her.

He had forgiven her, true, but what he still resented, could not reconcile himself to, was being separated from his brother Joshua.

But when Reuven left to return to Palestine, Joshua seemed morose. He stayed in his room as much as possible, he spoke to his mother with underlying tones of irritation bordering on impudence. Chavala felt at a loss to reach him, and so turned to Julie and Moishe for help.

They reminded her that he was still a little boy, that at his age he was very impressionable. And Palestine, after all, could be seductive, and of course Reuven had become his idol. She shouldn't, though, worry about it. When he went to school and made friends he'd forget about it.

Chavala was not convinced. Joshua had become so remote, sitting like he did for hours, gazing out the window. At what . . . ?

At Palestine, that was what. America was a place he no longer felt was home. At night in his darkened room he would lay in bed staring up at the ceiling, reliving the events of the past summer. It was as though he were there now, remembering how uncle Ari had loaded the wheat into the wagon for Reuven, Zvi and himself to take to the mill to be ground into flour. Reuven, strong and tall, carried a bullwhip. "You always need to be prepared for an Arab ambush," he said, and explained how from behind boulders along the road Arabs had a tendency to attack and steal the wheat. Joshua almost anticipated the ambush, it sounded like cowboys and Indians. When they traveled home his eyes would shift from place to place, and he would imagine piercing black eyes watching them . . . He remembered the time Reuven had held his hand when they climbed the mountain at Masada, and how at the top of it he told about the few zealots holding out against the powerful Roman legions for over three years. It was a story to fire his imagination. And then they'd tramped over the route through the desert where Moses had led the twelve tribes . . . What stories!

Autumn had been beautiful, a time between summer harvest and winter planting, and it was a favorite time for hikes and outings. Reuven, in his zeal to imbue Joshua with a sense of their homeland, suggested to his aunt Dvora that she allow Joshua to spend a week with Zvi and himself exploring the countryside. Knowing the dangers, Dvora said no, that Joshua was only a little boy. Ari, on the other hand, felt that Reuven was more than equipped to handle the situation. For all her reluctance, Dvora finally gave in. The expedition was carefully planned. They were equipped with two canteens each. Ari briefed Reuven the night before, reminding him not to roam too far, that if they did, their canteens could be taken away by the Bedouins, and what would they do without water?

Reuven laughed. "I've done this a dozen times, Uncle Ari. I know how to handle it."

"*Mazel tov.* But you better be very sure this time, or your mother will have your scalp if anything happens to Joshua, to say nothing of you or Zvi."

From the money Chavala had sent him, Reuven took twenty-five Palestinian pounds, as well as the camera, and off they went. . . .

As they entered the Arab city, the first stop on their adventure, Reuven's heart skipped a few beats, though he tried not to show it. He was doing exactly what he'd been told not to do. Kabayah was a small Arab town known for its hostility toward Jews. As the boys passed the coffeehouses and bazaars the looks they received were hardly friendly. Still, they'd come this far, so shoulders back, chin out and head high, Reuven all but held his breath until they left the city behind them, without incident.

Now they went on the road down to the Jordan. It was noon when they arrived and collapsed in a clump of eucalyptus. Joshua was exhausted, even though Reuven had carried him on his back a good part of the way. The little boy immediately fell asleep on the spread blanket, and Reuven watched protectively. It made him feel especially good to be his brother's protector.

When Joshua woke up, out came the hard-boiled eggs and tins of sardines from their knapsacks, all consumed with gusto. After they'd finished they changed into the extra clothing they'd brought along, Reuven took out the map and scanned it carefully.

The middle of August was a month known for its hot, dry eastern winds, so to insure a supply of water the boys were obliged to walk close to the riverbed. But this in turn meant that Reuven and Zvi had to hack away with their bare hands at the dense vegetation, not to mention the difficulty of crossing the deep ravines.

Toward evening as they neared the Damiya Bridge, they caught sight of a large Bedouin encampment pitched on the riverbank. To avoid it they circled west until they reached the main road through the Jordan Valley. By now it was dark. With very little water left in the canteens, Reuven decided that to conserve both their strength and water they should sleep where they were, alongside the road, rather than look for a place that might be free of thorns, snakes and scorpions. A vote was taken, the other two agreed.

At dawn they began their trek back to the riverbed, avoiding the Bedouin camp, and continued on their way south. The day was a long tiring one, and by the time it was over and they'd gone to sleep the last of their water was gone. Several hours later they woke up with parched tongues. Reuven looked at his watch, it was midnight. The dry, utterly still air was beginning to choke them. He worried about Joshua, thought back to what Ari had said and now realized he shouldn't have subjected Joshua to all this. He'd been so cocky . . . well, they were here now and he had to deal with the moment.

Nothing for it, in spite of the danger involved in passing the Bedouin camp, but to go back to the river. Reuven warned Joshua to keep as quiet as he could, try not to be afraid. Actually, Joshua was not afraid . . . not with Reuven along . . . Slowly, with Joshua on his back, Reuven led them toward the riverbed—

Suddenly the night's silence was shattered by the barking of dogs. In the darkness they had stumbled into the middle of the Arab encampment. Reuven's first impulse was to run, but then, with more bravado than he felt, and telling himself that to run would only invite capture, he suggested they walk right in and face the Arabs.

Zvi said, "No. Remember what my father said. I think we should run for it—"

"*My* father told me never to be afraid, that if you don't show any fear things have a way of working out."

Zvi yielded to Reuven, always the stronger, but was hardly convinced.

As the three now stood in the circle of darkness Reuven called out, "*Ya zalame, ya zalam, ya nass* . . . O men, O man, O people." And then: "We've come to pay our respect to your noble tribe."

Within moments the Bedouins appeared from their tents with lit torches, saw the three boys trying to look self-confident. Silence.

In the dim light the boys caught sight of the Bedouin chieftain, who seemed surprised and perhaps a bit impressed by such courage. Maybe Dovid had been right. "It's kind that you should honor us with your presence. Now, what can I do for you?"

"We would be grateful, son of Mecca, to share your water," Reuven got out.

The old chief actually laughed. "As a reward for your bravery, you shall have it."

Zvi trembled inside as he watched the water streaming into their canteens. Reuven said, "For your kindness, I would like to present you with this gift."

The old sheikh looked questioningly at the camera. Reuven explained the mechanics, then took out the film, inserted it. The boys were asked to spend the night. They slept on goatskin rugs, and in the morning they were given breakfast and left not only with canteens full of water but with camel-milk cakes. Reuven decided he'd been vindicated, Joshua was proud of him, and Zvi was just happy to be alive. Not to mention surprised.

They traveled on a crowded bus to Gaza, then went directly to visit the old fort. But before they could explore, an Arab policeman arrested them and brought them to the local police station. They were suspected of being illegal immigrants. The police were, in spite of themselves, impressed by Reuven as he refused to be interrogated in Arabic, refused to be intimidated, and kept insisting that he was born a Palestinian. By the time he finished, Reuven was quite impressed with himself, sure that he had been believed. The Arab policeman, though, was not nearly as benign as the Bedouin chieftain. Until he could definitely establish that the three boys were not aliens, they were put into a cell, despite Reuven telling him in a rising voice that "My father's name is Dovid Landau, he's with the Yishuv Central. If you don't believe me, get in touch with them. Besides, you have no right to keep us here. This isn't a Turkish courtroom . . ."

The policeman walked away, leaving his protest hanging in midair.

Dovid was contacted, and several hours later appeared, not at all pleased with Reuven. "How could you have done such a stupid thing? Endangering not only yourself but Joshua and Zvi. You mean to tell me you went into Arab territory?"

"I know, *abba,* but you told me never to be afraid—"

"I *also* know that I told you never to be a fool."

Dovid finally managed to free them, but not without embarrassment to himself as well. . . .

When they arrived back home their exploits quickly became known to Reuven's peers at Kfar Shalom and in spite of what Dovid, Ari and Dvora thought, Reuven emerged a young hero . . .

THINKING about those wonderfully exciting months, Joshua felt intensely his love and admiration for Reuven. He badly wanted to be a part of the youth group that Reuven was the head of. He longed to walk the length and breadth of Palestine to the sites of ancient battles and visit the tombs and the cities. He admired the traditional blue shirts and shorts the young people wore, and their songs about the homeland:

Who will build
Galilee?
We! We!

And the melodies of "Elijah the Prophet," who called out:

Come unto us,
Come in our time.
Bring Messiah
Of David's line.

The echo of that ancient chant reverberated in Joshua's mind. He would, he determined, keep his promise to Reuven to come back, to dedicate himself to Eretz Yisroel too. . . .

JULIE and Moishe had now become proud parents of a lovely daughter named Laura. Chia and Lenny made up for lost time . . . they had the blessing of *twins*, a boy named Gideon, a girl named Aviva—since they had been born in April, Aviva, meaning spring, seemed especially fitting. . . .

In Palestine Zvi had become, Reuven wrote, not only proficient in Hebrew, but devoted most of his time to the Zionist youth movement. . . .

For Chavala, life had not stood still either. The year was now 1928. The country seemed to be flourishing. The stock market was climbing to untold heights, and so was Chavala's business. Still, the demands on her had escalated too. Not just because the family had expanded. Palestine was in terrible need financially. Family . . . Palestine . . . they became one for her. She expanded her operation. The pawnshop on Mott Street was doing so well she spoke to the *landsman* and it was decided that five more shops in different areas should be established. By now the operation of Landau's on Fifth Avenue had become *totally* respectable. Chavala bought wholesale from Mr. Leibowitz, and so was able to produce statements. She added to Landau's on Fifth Avenue by opening a fine jewelry shop in Miami, and another in Los Angeles. Chavala Landau was a national enterprise.

Chavala was also on a treadmill, or so she felt. Time nudged her. She knew that Joshua had grown away from her. His needs had grown as consistently as Chavala's business. And, unknown to Chavala, his determination to rejoin Reuven also grew. . . .

IN September of 1929, the world stopped spinning, fell apart. But not for Chavala. By the time the crash came, Chavala had amassed sufficient liquid assets to buy up properties at unheard-of bargain prices. She bought a six-story apartment house on Sixty-eighth Street between Fifth Avenue and Madison Avenue, two office buildings on Lexington Avenue, and a sizeable parcel of land in Jamaica, New York, just outside of Manhattan. She set up trust funds for all the children, including Sheine's little Erich.

The needs of Raizel and her sons were especially great. Since their capacity to earn was so limited, Chavala supported them. Raizel, frugal as she was, never, Chavala was convinced, used any of the money for anything as frivolous as, for example, a new dress. Chavala knew where it went . . . beyond the basic necessities of life her sister gave to charity and the *shul.* Well, if that was what her sister felt was most important, it was fine with Chavala . . . except she did wish just *once* Raizel would be a little selfish, do a little something for herself . . .

What especially pleased Chavala was that Ari no longer seemed to resent her contributions, she didn't have to use subterfuges as in the past, thank God. He seemed to realize that without her help Dvora's life would have been drudgery. He also felt no need to apologize to the rest of the *chevra.* The *important* thing was Dvora's life, and to the extent Chavala could help lighten the load, he not only accepted it but was able to be grateful. Dvora had her new stone house with four bedrooms. Even more exciting was, when electricity came to Kfar Shalom, Dvora could have a new refrigerator and stove, and miracle of miracles, a washing machine.

Chavala was also grateful to Julie and Moishe, and to Chia and Lenny, for allowing her to make available for them apartments in her new apartment house on Sixty-eighth Street. Without apology she lived in the penthouse. It was, she thought thankfully, a good deal of family under one roof. Family . . .

BUT if Chavala's life seemed to be fulfilling itself, one of the main sources of her inspiration, indeed, her calling, was coming onto harder and harder times.

The year 1929 was not only the year of the crash of the world's economy, it was a time when Palestine was beseiged with turmoil, betrayal and revolt. The emergence of the dynamic kibbutzim had sparked a cultural revival of Jews . . . School systems emerged, political affairs were managed through the Jewish Agency, of which Dovid was a prominent official, and independently of the Arabs—and increasingly of the British. The Arabs, made nervous by the higher living standards of the Jewish community in Palestine, as well as its tendency to act like a separate nation, felt the Jewish institutions were somehow alien intrusions. Not surprisingly they worried that the Jewish example might spark unrest and rebellion among the *fellaheen* masses—whose standard of living hadn't changed materially in a thousand years. The Yishuv's progress was seen with bitterness and suspicion.

As for the British, they were caught between conflicting promises made to Jews and Arabs. But it was the Arabs that they saw as their allies, the Jews as their threat. The Arab world was increasingly discontented, and so it had to be appeased. The British proceeded to make it illegal for the Yishuv to own weapons—despite that the Jews had always supported the British. The British, experts at rationalization, reminded them that they had, after all, allowed Jewish settlements . . . Besides, Jews owned land, but the Arabs owned oil.

The British would welcome an Arab leader, one to emerge from the inner squabbles of the Arabs. The most powerful effendi family was the El Husseinis, who had inherited Trans-Jordan, a state invented by the peacemakers after the First World War. The most feared of them was Haj Amim el Husseini, a former supporter of the Turks, who saw a power vacuum and proceeded to fill it. The Ottoman Empire was kaput. The British were nervous about the Jews, who had taken the Balfour Declaration seriously and proceeded to try to secure a homeland—even, it seemed, create a Jewish state. The British embraced the doctrine of divide and rule. And into the breach came Haj Amim, backed by over a dozen Arab leaders, to grab off what he could of Palestine and proclaim himself mufti of Jerusalem. If there was violence between the Arabs and the Jews, the British could protest they were doing their best to put it down, at the same time looking the other direction when Haj Amim seized power, and proceeded to stir up the *fellaheen.*

On the birth date of Moses, when the Moslem holy day was also celebrated, he inflamed the *fellaheen* against the Jews, ranting that the Jews were stealing their land, desecrating their holy places . . . Not surprisingly, blood flowed. Kibbutzim able to defend themselves were avoided. But in the holy cities of Safed, Tiberias, Hebron and Jerusalem pious old defenseless Jews were murdered.

The British, seeing too much of a good thing, needing to swing the pendulum, for show at least, a bit in the other direction, brought Haj Amim el Husseini before a British commission of inquiry, where he was chastised. And then pardoned. And once the pardon had been granted the British Colonial Office restricted Jewish immigration. Arab goodwill at all costs . . . it was mandatory for the British in retaining their control of this hugely oil-rich area.

SOMETHING had to be done for the Yishuv, or it would perish.

The Zionist Settlement Society called a secret meeting. From London to Palestine flew Chaim Weizmann. Dovid Landau was there, as was Yitzchak Ben-Zvi, David Ben-Gurion, and Binya Yariv. Many felt that Yariv, a large, impressive man of the Third Aliyah who had come to Palestine with an impressive war record from the Russian army, was a most likely candidate to lead the Jewish defense.

Arguments went far into the night . . . the British were too important to be sidestepped . . . the British were devils, replacing the Ottomans only in uniform and diplomacy since both were exploiters. Many favored retaliating against the British now, while Ben-Gurion, Dovid Landau and Binya Yariv, with others, counseled a more middle-of-the-road strategy. They agreed the need for arms was pressing, but to ensure a positive world opinion legal means were preferable. But one thing was agreed on—the Yishuv could not be left defenseless. Arms would be obtained. A militia would be formed, in secret. The militia would be used for defense only. Yariv was voted to head the new, secret organization, and so with this army of self-defense, the Haganah was born.

DOVID was best-known for his success in developing the settlements, but now there was an even greater challenge for him. His experience with NILI well qualified him—to find where arms could be purchased. A supply of arms was literally a life-and-death matter for the Haganah.

Given the Yishuv's shortage of funds, Dovid quickly proceeded to the benefactor he was closest to. That night he took the late flight out of Lydda Airport. Destination, New York City.

CHAVALA never thought the day would come when he would ever ask for her help. At long last, she could perhaps believe her reasons for having

left him. For all these years she had often been at war with herself
. . . well, but now there was an even greater war to be fought. A war for
not only her family but the whole Jewish family . . .

When Dovid, sitting in her living room in Manhattan, finished
telling her what was happening, she simply asked. "How much money will
help, Dovid?"

He wouldn't even mention the enormous sums it would take to
protect the Yishuv. "At this time, as much as we can get our hands on.
Put it that way."

Without another word she got up and used the telephone. Nervously
she waited for the ringing to stop. When she finally heard, "Hello," her
heart jumped. Thank God her friend the *landsman* was there on the other
end. "This is Chavala."

"*Chavala.*" He was delighted to hear the sound of her voice. "You
want more goods, this time of the night?"

In spite of the tense situation she laughed. "This time it's not goods
that I need. Just money . . . only this time I mean a *lot* of money."

"So by you, what would be considered a lot of money?"

"Two million dollars, maybe. Give or take."

The *landsman* stared into the phone. When he recovered his voice
he asked, "What do you want it in, nickles and dimes? . . . Chavala, where
would I get two million dollars?"

"Tomorrow morning I'll come to see you, and then I'll tell you how."

Dovid was in shock. "Chavala, that's insane. Not that we couldn't
use it, but two million dollars?"

"Have a little patience. If things work out my way, it won't seem so
much." She went to her desk drawer, took out her checkbook and handed
Dovid her own personal check for $200,000. He sat there, staring down
at the six figures. And this was the little girl from Odessa who'd never
given up a dream. She was the giver, and he, in fact, was somehow the
taker. Her love of Eretz Yisroel was just as great as his. It had only taken
a different direction. Come from a different direction, source . . . love of
her family . . .

NEXT morning, as the two sat in the *landsman*'s basement, he adjusted
his *yarmulke* on his sparse head of hair, adjusted the wire-rimmed glasses
and said, "I'm afraid to ask, Chavala, because I know you. I know your
plans and your schemes and your determination . . . but still I'll ask. Now,
where will I get two million dollars?"

After explaining Dovid's mission, Chavala said, "Obviously, knowing you, you'll make a good-sized donation. But two million dollars I don't expect. But from your association, with your friends . . . it should be no problem . . ."

"Listen, Chavala, *kosher* I haven't been, but then on the other hand, I never got mixed up with gangsters in New Jersey. Not even Jewish gangsters."

"But you're intimate with—"

"Intimate?" He shrugged. "I knew them when they were little kids, just starting out. So what do you want me to do?"

"Call a meeting tonight."

He sighed, "What, you think it's so easy to pick up the phone and call Bugsy Siegel, or Harry Teitelbaum and say, 'Come over tonight and we'll break a few matzohs together.' . . . Chavala, you don't understand, they're not ordinary people, face it, they're gangsters—"

"Yes, but they're Jewish gangsters . . . who would you expect me to go to, the Italians?"

The *landsman* shook his head, shrugged and gave up. When Chavala had a plan, nothing would stop her. "All right, already, let me see what I can do. *Oy vay,* Chavala, the things I do for you."

She laughed. *"That's* what friends are for, and tomorrow night you'll come to dinner with Dovid and me . . . Now, darling, get on the phone."

It was no easy task to convince the boys he'd known in their youth to meet at Chavala's apartment, but he talked and he talked and he talked and explained and explained and explained that for old times' sake they should do him this favor.

WHEN he'd hung up, Bugsy Siegel said to Waxey Gordon, "You think it's a setup?"

"With the *landsman* I doubt it . . . in fact I'm sure it's not. But where the hell is Palestine?"

CHAVALA knew that God was on her side, and even if the world was against them, and they never had a friend, God was also on the side of Eretz Yisroel. She knew it the moment she opened the door and in walked the *landsman* and his boys, formerly of the Bowery.

Chavala didn't know whether Jewish gangsters were the same as just ordinary Jews, but she'd bet they could be reached, that a Jew was a Jew, whatever his profession. Or so she hoped. She put in a supply of whiskey she'd got from the *landsman,* which he'd gotten from his bootlegger. The table bore an assortment of bagels and lox, cream cheese, kosher dills, chopped liver (formed, God forgive her, in the shape of a Jewish star), as well as platters of corned beef and pastrami.

In the beginning, there was a distinct reserve on the part of her guests. But soon Chavala put them at ease with her mimicry and jokes. Even Jewish gangsters laughed . . . Well, she thought, if she could get them to laugh, maybe she could get them to give. The source wasn't important. Now when the British had turned their back. As they always had, the Jews would survive, by whatever means left to them.

When the table was cleared, silence prevailed. Chavala looked from left to right: Doc Stacher, Bugsy Siegel, Harry the Lip Teitelbaum, Lepke Buchalter, Big Greenie Greenberg, Shadows Kravits, Dopey Shapiro, Little Farfel Kavolick, Little Hymie Holtz and Waxey Gordon. Next she looked at Dovid for moral support, and also to God that he should put the words in her mouth. To mention the money would be the kiss of death, she knew. No, the approach was to the Jewish heart that beat beneath their bulletproof vests. Standing to her fullest stature, she said, "You cannot believe the honor I feel this evening, that you gentlemen have agreed to come here."

They looked at one another, wondering just exactly what it was that made the *landsman* persuade them.

Chavala continued, "All of your parents escaped the pogroms of Russia and Poland and other places. We have all been cut from the same piece of cloth, and because your dear parents had the wisdom to come to this great country, you have been given the opportunity to become prosperous men. I'm sure that all of you are aware that only in this country could such a miracle occur, that you men who came off the streets of the East Side were able to avail yourself of the great freedoms and gifts that this country offered us. But Jews all over the world are being killed, annihilated, thrown out of one country to another. For *them* there is no hope. And those Jews that live in the land of our ancestors have been deprived of the right to defend themselves. Deprived of weapons, *guns*" —she emphasized the word, knowing it was one they'd understand. "The British are the worst *mamzerim* in the world. To the Arabs they give guns, yes. But to our people, they give *drek.* If we don't help them, our very own, who can they depend on, Lucky Luciano? Capone?"

Mention of the Italian competition was a masterstroke. Quickly she forged ahead to take advantage of it. "We must help our own, and the only way we can do that is to supply our Jews with the ammunition to fight all our enemies. You are as much involved as myself . . . and my husband. (Forgive me, Dovid.) Jews fight for Jews, and we will win the battle with the help of God, and your money."

Little Farfel Kavolick's parents had barely escaped the pogroms. "How much guns do you need?"

Chavala thought she would faint. "That, my husband will answer in just a few moments, but at this moment I'm giving three hundred thousand dollars, because it's more than guns we need, we need big equipment . . . tanks, an airplane or two . . ."

Bugsy Siegel looked closely at this wisp of a woman. It had almost become a game, and Bugsy loved gambling. "I'll double your ante," he said.

She didn't know whether to laugh or cry. She'd stretched the truth a little, but it was working.

"Thank you very much, Mr. Siegel."

"Call me Bugsy. Now, what are the rest of you guys gonna come up with?" He had now taken up the lance. This was for his people.

Nobody outdid Big Greenie Greenberg. What would it mean? A few more boats of illicit booze coming in from Canada. "I'll match you."

Dovid was speechless. By the end of the evening, they had raised their two million dollars. When Chavala shut the door after her guests had left with the promise that the money, in cash, would be at the *landsman*'s in the morning, she allowed herself a yelp of joy. Running to Dovid's arms she said, "Oh, Dovid, we did it."

"No, Chavala. You did it, as you've done everything else you ever set your mind to." He held her closer. "I love you, my darling. My God, how I love you."

"And I you, Dovid. Hard as it may have been for you to believe it."

And they went to her bedroom, to reaffirm what they both felt so overwhelmingly.

IN the morning Chavala was singing as she fixed breakfast for Dovid and Joshua. A woman well-loved, she thought, was a happy woman. How could she ever have forgotten, or lost sight of that . . . ?

At the breakfast table Joshua looked intently at his father, scarcely listening to the conversation that went on between his parents. Did he have the courage to discuss what had been eating at him? When he'd come home from his summer in Palestine his mother had said that from now on his vacation would be spent at camp, at Lake Minnetonka. Who cared bout that? He wanted to see Lake Kinneret. Finally he blurted out his long hidden thoughts: "I want to spend this summer in Eretz Yisroel too . . . is it all right with you, *abba?*"

Dovid looked at Chavala. She'd already given up one son, and now Joshua? It wasn't merely the suggestion of another summer spent in Eretz Yisroel. Both knew that this was only a prelude to his ultimate goal of living there. Joshua, smart as he was, didn't give his parents credit for being perceptive enough to read his deeper feelings.

He waited for what seemed a very, very long time, watching the exchange of looks between his parents.

At long last, Chavala nodded slightly to Dovid . . . It was he who had been asked the question by Joshua. He should be the one to answer.

Knowing too well how painful that apparently simple nod was for Chavala, Dovid also knew it meant she understood and respected her son's need to be where his heart was.

Still, for a moment Dovid was tempted to say, some other summer, but seeing the look in Joshua's eyes, and not wanting to demean Chavala's sacrifice, he said, "I think you should ask your mother."

Joshua was afraid. Wasn't it a certainty that mother would say no? If only his father had just said yes, not placed him in this position. But his father had always said to Reuven, and to him too, "Never be afraid." All right . . . "Could I . . . mama?"

Without hesitation she answered, "Of course. I'm surprised you didn't ask sooner . . . In fact, I want you to go." She would kill herself if she allowed a tear to come.

For a moment he sat there in disbelief. Then slowly he got up from his chair, put his arms around his mother and kissed her. "Thank you, mama . . . I love you very much."

She smiled. "Well now, that's the best gift I ever received. We'll call it your vacation going-away present."

WHEN Dovid returned to Palestine, it was at least with a feeling of hope that the Yishuv would be protected and that the Haganah could have its beginnings. No sooner had he gone to his apartment in Tel Aviv than he sat down and wrote a letter to Chavala. He told her of all that had been accomplished, the careful smuggling of weapons, the building of an arsenal, and ended by saying . . .

And one day, my dearest Chavala, when we are a free and independent state, I can proudly tell the world that my Chavala contributed to its birth.

With my deepest love,
Dovid

He also wondered if he should tell the world about the gentlemen from New Jersey. Would it ever be ready for that? He had to smile . . .

AFTER the bloodshed and riots of 1929, Kfar Shalom joined the Haganah organization and began receiving arms and military instructions. The whole community of men, women and children was, of course, sworn to secrecy. Sentries were posted and warned that adults should police all approaches to the entrances of the moshav. Lessons in judo and pistol shooting were given, but handling weapons seemed less important than belonging to the Haganah, especially for the boys. As for Reuven, firing a carbine was not new. His father had taught him when he was only thirteen. . . .

On a December night in 1932, the settlement of Kfar Shalom was jolted by a loud explosion. Rushing out into the rainy night it was discovered that Eliezer Har-Zion and his eight-year-old son, Dov, had been killed. There had been recent attacks on Jewish settlements in the Jezreel Valley during the year, but still, this assault on Kfar Shalom was a terrible surprise. Since its establishment, the settlement had experienced nothing more serious than an occasional quarrel with Bedouins over property rights.

After months of intensive investigative work by the Haganah, and with the help of the police, Ahmed el Gala'eini and Mustapha el Ali were arrested. After their arrest three other suspects were rounded up. All five had one thing in common—wildly unkempt beards—and thereby was uncovered a terrorist group that had become known as the Bearded Sheikhs, also as Kassamai'in, named after their leader . . . Syrian-born el Kassam preached insurrection from a mosque in Haifa; his recruits were the disenchanted quarry workers, mechanics, and blacksmiths—in fact, anyone who had access to explosives or knew metalcraft. He and his small band specialized in making homemade bombs, which he used to kill the Jews. A religious fanatic, he customarily read passages from the Koran before sending his men out to kill. . . .

By dawn the farmers of Kfar Shalom were in the fields.

Ari, Zvi and Reuven were plowing the west section when a tire blew and Reuven went back to the barn to bring back another while Ari and Zvi took off the old one.

Dvora was fertilizing her newly planted crops of vegetables in the far east field.

Pnina was in the barn, milking her cow, Shoshanna.

Just before Reuven reached the slight incline into the courtyard, hell erupted . . . guns firing, curses of "Kill in the name of Allah," "Destroy the Jews . . ."

Chaim Zadok's farm was ablaze in the distance, billows of smoke rising from the northern sector of the moshav.

And now the terrible sounds of vengeance for the Bearded Sheikhs were coming closer.

Reuven dropped the tire, ran to the house. When he came out with the carbine his father had given him, he heard Pnina screaming from the barn, then saw her being dragged out. The whole world spun. The terrorists had infiltrated the moshav. Without hesitation he positioned his rifle, aimed, shot the Arab through the heart. He ran to Pnina, picked her up in strong arms. He stroked her hair, holding her closer. "Shh, Pnina, it's all right . . . it's all right, I won't let anyone hurt you."

And feeling his strength, she did feel safe. She lay still in his arms, head cradled against his shoulder. "I love you, Reuven . . . I do and I can tell you now. Is it all right . . . ?"

"All right? God, I feel the same way, darling Pnina. I love you." A simple declaration.

Except Reuven didn't quite accept that she loved him like a woman, that her love had grown from childhood to this . . .

He carried her into the house, put her down on the bed and hovered over her for a moment. Finally he said, "I think they're leaving . . . Now, you stay here, I have to go . . . join the others. You'll be safe, please trust me . . ."

She reached up and kissed him. "I love you, Reuven, my dearest . . . just believe that . . ."

In the fields Reuven saw his family standing with the rest of the moshavim, and thanked God that, in all this destruction, at least Ari, Zvi and aunt Dvora were alive. Ten others were not so fortunate . . . They had given their lives to protect their sacred piece of earth.

When they reached their farm and Ari saw the dead body in the courtyard, he sent Dvora into the house, then looked at the face of the dead man. It was the face of the same man who had massacred hundreds in the name of Allah . . . it was the face of Az-el Din el Kassam. Ari felt no sorrow or compassion. The body was removed and placed along the roadside, where it was taken to Jenin. A fitting place, since it was there that they had decimated the bodies of twenty-three Jews in prayer.

This day irrevocably set the course of Reuven's life. His first dream had been to become a scientist, an agronomist like his father had been. But, like his father, other pressures intervened. Both had wanted to be farmers, to live in peace, work their land, but from this moment on, Reuven knew his mission was to be a defender of his people. From this moment on, he dedicated himself to the Haganah.

Chapter Thirty-four

IT WAS 1933. Hitler had come to power. But the consequences of that awful fact were hardly on Joshua's mind. The only one he felt able to turn to, as he had through the years of his young life, was Reuven. Sitting down at his desk, he wrote in Hebrew . . . Reuven, of course, was fluent in English, but it made Joshua feel closer to Eretz Yisroel to write in Hebrew.

Dear Reuven:

As you know, even though I was only five when I came back after that first summer in Palestine, I felt America was no longer really my country. I live here, but my heart isn't here. I'm too far from the land I love. From you.

I've friends here, but I feel like a foreigner because I belong to a different world than they do. I want to be with you and *abba*. That's not to say that I don't love *ema*. We both do, you and I, but we're different from her. Even the Americans in the Zionist youth groups I work with don't seem to be the same as Zvi and Pnina. I am one of them. Of you—

I hope you'll forgive me for bothering you with my small problems when I know that yours are so big, being an officer in the Haganah. But still, Reuven, I feel that only you really understand. This letter isn't only to tell you once again, as I always do, how much I want to live in Eretz Yisroel. As you know, my birthday will be this October, and *ema* is planning a bar mitzvah as elaborate as the wedding she gave to Chia. Of course she plans that the whole family will come to America. She never asked *me* what I want. What I want is to be bar mitzvah standing at the Great Wall in Jerusalem.

I wish I were like you, but I think I'm sort of a coward. Over and over again Uncle Moishe, aunt Julie and Chia tell me that her sacrifices have been so great, how much she has done for all of us, and how hard she works. I can't bring myself to hurt her. So I suppose I'll just wait until I'm of age, so maybe then I'll be man enough to tell her that it's time for me to have my own life.

I know this letter sounds as though I'm feeling very damn sorry for myself, and I suppose I am. But at least it makes me feel good inside that I have you to tell about my own secret feelings.

Please stay well and safe, and give *abba* and the family all my love, as I give you mine.

Your brother,
Joshua

P.S. Please write soon. I've saved every one of your letters.

REUVEN was more than touched by Joshua's letter. He was twenty-six now, but it seemed like yesterday that he'd stood in his mother's dirty cold flat and announced he was going back to Palestine to live with his father. Strange, he thought, he'd been thirteen too, like Joshua. He remembered too well his feeling of desolation that his father wasn't present on the day of his bar mitzvah . . . "You belong to one another," he'd been told . . . the echoes of Dovid's words were never stronger than at this moment. Never mind his important work, Reuven turned it over to his lieutenant and left for Jerusalem.

Fortunately for Reuven's purposes, Dovid had just returned from an important Zionist conference in Basel. Dovid said, "They're keeping you pretty busy these days with all the mischief Haj Amim is making . . . he doesn't seem to give up, does he?"

"Not so long as there's a rotten breath left in him. But then you wouldn't have had to go to Basel if it hadn't been for Haj Amim's dear friend, Adolf Hitler. But we have another problem that has to be taken care of," and Reuven handed Joshua's letter to his father.

Dovid read it, looked at Reuven. "Like brother, like brother, or so it seems."

"Yes, I think he should be here, don't you, *abba?*"

"I'm not as positive as you two are . . . For one thing . . . a *very* important thing . . . your mother must be considered. We both know . . . and so does she . . . that once Joshua has his bar mitzvah here in Eretz Yisroel, nothing will pry him loose. Your mother will be heartbroken. To be deprived of two sons, Reuven? That's a lot to ask, wouldn't you say . . . ?"

"But what about Joshua? Maybe if we give him the bar mitzvah it will satisfy him . . . well, for a while, anyway . . ."

"You don't believe that, Reuven, any more than I do."

"Whether I do or not, for God's sake, *he* deserves it . . ."

Dovid nodded slowly . . . in a way he had no choice, no more than did Chavala . . . "Your mother has to be eased into this . . ."

"Write her a letter. You can convince her."

"Stop buttering me up. You're not as brave as I thought you were. You're pretty good in the word department yourself."

"So, I'm a coward . . . but the truth is, only you can help make her understand."

Or accept, Dovid thought, what she had understood . . . and dreaded . . . for a very long time . . .

IN spite of Dovid's sensitive and careful letter, Chavala's heart sank. It was as though she had been in the room and heard the conversation between Reuven and Dovid . . . Once Joshua went to Palestine for his bar mitzvah, she would have lost him and that she knew as well as she knew that her name was Chavala Landau. But she also knew she could not deprive Joshua of this, even if it meant . . .

When she announced to Joshua that she had decided it was only fitting and proper that his bar mitzvah should take place in Jerusalem, he could only say, "I'll never forget that you're doing this, mama . . . I love you. Don't you please ever forget that . . ."

ON the twenty-third of October the entire family—all but Sheine—stood near the wall and saw Joshua taken into the covenant of his faith. It was a simple, brief ceremony. It needed no trimmings. A boy had entered the state of manhood at the most enduring place in the history of his faith.

AFTER visiting in Jerusalem for a few more days, Chavala, Julie, Moishe, Laura, Chia, Lenny and the twins said their good-byes and were airborne. Joshua stayed. As Chavala sat on that flight, Joshua's words came back, the ones he'd spoken to her as a man . . . "Mama, I love you more than words can say. But the greatest gift you can give me is to let me go, let me live where I feel I belong, here in Palestine . . . I'll go back if you insist, but the day will come when this will be my home. I ask you, let it be now."

From the night Chia had been born, Chavala had had precious little time for tears. Now, it seemed, there would be the rest of her life to shed them.

Chapter Thirty-five

IF JOSHUA'S WORLD now took on a new meaning, for many others in this year of 1933 life became a hellish terror.

Few knew what Hitler's new order would bring to Germany, and at first the Jews of Berlin actually waited with high hopes that Hitler would not harm those Jews who had given their devotion to the Fatherland for three hundred years. Hopes quickly faded, though, as lawless bands of youths roamed the streets, actually looking for Jewish blood. Not only the once-derelict and street brawlers, but university students from "good" German homes swarmed over the city, seeking revenge against "Jewish traitors."

Platoons of men dressed in brown uniforms marched in the streets, raced in cars and motorcycles, carried torches to the accompaniment of martial music blaring from loudspeakers. Worst of all was the terrifying, constant marching, the pounding of knob-heeled boots.

In the beginning of the Third Reich the Jews were urged to leave the country, with the provision that their property be confiscated, their possessions taken from them. All they could leave with was the clothes on their backs. The relatively few who accepted these terms . . . most Jews still lived in the delusion that as Germans first and Jews second they would be spared . . . found that few countries wanted them. To appease the Arabs the British restrictions in Palestine remained in effect. In the

Yishuv's most desperate hour of need for open immigration, the British turned their backs. The Balfour Declaration was not worth the paper it had been written on.

Desperate to help those who wanted to leave Germany, Dovid—by now one of the Yishuv's most important troubleshooters—was sent in search of foreign governments to take in those Jews. He flew from Lydda Airport to London, though with little hope that the British High Command or the foreign office would honor its commitment of 1917. He was right. In France the government agreed to accept a token number, provided that they were self-sustaining. They could not become citizens nor avail themselves of any of the benefits of French citizenship.

With the aid of American dollars, all of five hundred Jews were issued visas to come, without possessions, to Paris.

Aside from France there were few other countries left to appeal to. Italy was fascist . . . Russia communistic . . . One thousand were sent to Sweden, 750 to Denmark and 600 to Norway, with the provision that they would be supported by funds from world Jewry. Holland's doors, however, were open without question.

Still, the country most looked to was America. Dovid flew to Washington, D.C., where Chavala joined him in his crusade. The best America would do was allow a limited amount of immigration provided that affidavits were signed by reliable American Jews that they would take full responsibility for the support and employment of these refugees. They would be entitled to no other benefits. Bonds of good intention were required to be posted.

Chavala herself signed two hundred affidavits.

In New York, for the first time Chavala noticed that the enormous strain of the past few months was written in Dovid's face. The silver streak in his full black hair had widened. There were wrinkles around his eyes, it seemed to her, that had not been there even the day before. Looking at him, she realized that he was giving himself to a dream, a cause, that had become more precious to him than life itself.

She went to the bar and brought back two highballs. Handing one to him, she said, "Here, darling, I think you need this . . . *l'chayim.*"

They touched glasses. *"L 'chayim . . .* to life, and to you Chavala, for all you've done—"

"What have I done? . . . I only wish I could get Sheine out."

"Well that, my dearest Chavala, I'm afraid is something not even you can do . . . Remember, she's married to a German. We have to hope that will protect her." He could hope but he didn't believe, though he wouldn't tell her and add to her anxieties.

"Yes," she said uneasily, "we must hope. At least you've been able to help so many. Without you and others, who could we depend on?"

"Not the British," he said bitterly. "They sacrifice us to appease the Arabs—"

"Drink your drink, Dovid darling, and try to relax for a while."

He settled back and sipped slowly, but his mind did not stop working. "How do you plan to insure jobs for two hundred people?"

"Simple. When I signed those affidavits I had a plan . . . Since I arrived in the *goldeneh medina* things have changed. In those days the diamond district was down on the Bowery, Canal Street and Maiden Lane. It changed. The wholesalers moved uptown and took over Forty-seventh Street between Fifth and Sixth Avenue. Tomorrow I'll show it to you . . . Unfortunately as a people we never had much *mazel*, but brains we had. Maybe we should thank the *goyim* for our knowledge. For hundreds of years the best diamond merchants, artisans and cutters in the world have been Jews. I'm going into wholesale manufacturing. There's a building I want you to see. I have my dreams too, Dovid. By the time my *chevra* arrive, I'll have the operation ready—"

"But Chavala darling, not all Jews have been in the diamond business—"

"True . . . those who don't know will learn. If I could, why not them? Now, don't worry. Trust me and everything will work out. Now, if you'll excuse me, I have a few phone calls to make. I figure I can get a few hundred more affidavits signed."

Dovid shook his head, and even allowed himself a laugh as he thought about the night Chavala had raised two million dollars. "Your Jewish gangsters have been indicted. I read the *New York Times* too, I know about Thomas Dewey, your district attorney."

"I know about that *mamzer* too. Imagine, putting nice Jewish boys in jail. But in this case it so happens I wasn't planning to ask them. I have a few friends in the trade. I can promise that every one of them will sign affidavits."

Dovid put down his drink and reached out for her. "What would I do without you? What would *all* of us do without you . . . ?"

Not wanting at the moment to deal with the full weight of what that really suggested, she only said, "Where is it written you have to do without me?" Smiling what she hoped was a seductive smile, she took him by the hand and led him down the hall to her bedroom. . . .

AFTER breakfast next morning Chavala introduced Dovid to Forty-seventh Street. His first look was from the corner of Fifth Avenue and Forty-seventh Street. It was not the jewels occupying the store windows that dazzled him, it was the street scene . . . For a moment he thought he'd been transplanted back to the ghettos of Russia and Poland. The noisy, crowded streets were lined with energetic bearded Chasidim dressed in black frock coats and wide-brimmed hats under which earlocks fell. They stood in groups of twos, threes and fours, quietly discussing their deals. Within their pockets were small packets which, if combined, would represent millions of dollars' worth of gems. The exchanges seemed better suited to a village marketplace in the squares of Pinsk. The street was alive with people, hurrying, dealing, and talking with their hands. Hands reached upward in exasperation . . . hands clasped over an owner's head in chagrin . . . hands shook one another firmly after a deal had been consummated, followed by a *"mazel und broche."*

When those words were uttered the deal had been made—no contracts, lawyers, not a slip of paper as a receipt. A handshake constituted the basis of trust and faith. It was a commitment which encompassed the ethics of Maimonides, the Talmud and the Torah.

Weaving between the crowds, they made their way to the building Chavala was negotiating on, looked up from the store on the street to the top of the fifth floor. Smiling, Chavala looked at Dovid. "Well, what do you think?"

Smiling back at her, he said, "I think it will do."

"I'm glad . . . Now, my plan is this . . . the street store will be strictly retail . . . with a little wholesale only to the *goyim,* which really means in the trade that *goyim* pay retail, and then some . . . Why not? What, they've been so good to us? Then, for now, the first three floors will be used for manufacturing. After that, as we get more affidavits, we'll take over the rest. You approve, Dovid?"

He merely nodded, still smiling.

"In that case," she said, "you are now looking at The Landau Building on Forty-seventh Street . . . Not so bad for a couple of greenhorns who left Odessa with a little wagon filled with pots, pans and bedding, and you leading a goat. You're a big *macher* in the cause of our people, I'm a little *macher* in the diamond business. Not so bad . . ."

Late afternoon of the next day they arrived at the Airport just in time for Dovid to board. As he kissed her, she said, "We have the best long-distance marriage in the world. For Chanukah I think I'll buy you an airplane."

"Thank you, and I'll call it Chavala, the Angel of Eretz Yisroel."

Just before boarding, her cheerful facade rapidly failing, she managed to say, "Give my love to the children," and then she kissed him, quickly turned and went for the exit.

Dovid stood looking after her, then, shaking his head in admiration, turned and hurried down the ramp for his plane.

Chapter Thirty-six

CHAVALA'S CONCERN FOR Sheine the day she had asked Dovid if it were possible for Sheine to leave Germany was more terribly well-founded than she could imagine.

Stormtroopers, their numbers growing, resounded through the streets of Berlin. *Wenn vom Judenblut das Messer spritzt dann geht's noch mal so gut, so gut,* boomed out so that every word would penetrate deep inside the houses of those they intended to impress. Houses also in the best neighborhoods, houses of rich Jews . . . the house Sheine lived in, lived in growing apprehension for her son Erich . . .

The effort it took to hide her anxieties, to go on as though the events surrounding her had no relationship to her grief, was almost unendurable. She envied those Jews she'd known who had left. She was aware of the plight of the thousands of beleaguered, abused Jews in eastern Berlin, but she was helpless to do anything about it . . . she was married to a German, it was imperative for her own and her son's safety that she maintain the social posture of Mrs. Herr Doktor Gunter Hausman. . . .

As she dressed this evening, her head pounded with the thought that she and Gunter would be the guests of one of Berlin's most extraordinary hostesses, Erica von Furnstein.

Frederick von Furnstein's family controlled some of Germany's most prestigious banking firms. For two hundred years his had been a family of assimilated Jews, turned Christian, and not for one moment when he heard songs about the spilling of Jewish blood did he consider that his own life was in danger. He was not only a convert but married to a Christian wife, and he was an important board member of Gedächtnis Kirche, the oldest church in Berlin. His home was graced with the most important government leaders. Whatever happened to the Jews would certainly not effect him.

Sheine wandered through the rooms, listening to the fragments of conversation . . . "allegiance to Germany above all . . . the Jews must not continue to corrupt and demean us . . ."

By evening's end Sheine went home sick to her stomach. Next morning she felt worse . . . In the papers there was an account that during the night Frederick von Furnstein's house had been broken into by a group of youths, among whom were those that had sung in the streets about spilling Jewish blood. If one had a drop of Jewish blood, it would drip from their daggers. Late that night von Furnstein was dragged from his house and thrown down a narrow stone stairway into a cellar sour from years of neglect. He was stripped naked and beaten until he fell to the ground. *"What have I done?"*

"You were born a Jew."

"But you're wrong, I'm a Christian—"

"A Christian?" The gang leader proceeded to beat him further with chains.

The pain became so terrible he now pleaded, "Kill me, for God's sake, kill me."

"Not quite yet."

He was kicked and battered until, finally, his head rolled to one side. Just before dying he whispered, "Dear God, the God of my people, forgive me for my sins."

After hearing about von Furnstein's brutal murder, Sheine knew even her son was not safe. Lying in bed with a high fever, Gunter sitting at her side, she took hold of his hand . . . "Save me, save my son, our son . . . send me away. *Please* . . . I can't live this lie any longer . . ."

Gunter understood her fears, of course, but honestly believed they were misplaced. Taking her in his arms, he held her tight and stroked her hair . . . "Dearest, you are in *no* danger, you must believe me. You've nothing to fear. You are my wife . . . the mother of my son . . . nothing, no one will hurt you. You are Elsa Beck Hausman . . . Now please, my dearest, remember what I have told you. As soon as you feel better I will take you and Erich on a holiday to Switzerland."

Gunter's holiday plans would be indefinitely postponed.

Chapter Thirty-seven

If HITLER EVER had a natural ally, it was Haj Amim el Husseini. What could be more convenient than having the mufti of Palestine to fuel the propaganda machine?

The scenario could not have been written better by Goebbels himself . . . The Jews were stealing Arab land under the control of British imperialism . . . Hitler would one day rule the world, Haj Amim el Husseini was convinced. Hitler was his answer to how he could seize control of the whole Arab world . . . In Cairo, Germans drank with the Arab friends in cafés. In Baghdad and Damascus they joined hands in treaties committing them to ousting the British oppressors along with the Jewish conspirators.

As the clouds of war gathered, the Yishuv knew it had only one weapon . . . the Haganah. Its membership had grown to over thirty thousand men, women and children. This was an army unlike any other. Except for a handful of paid full-time officers, it was made up of civilians molded into one of the most efficient striking forces ever. In a large and real sense, the Yishuv was the army.

Within the Haganah there was a superior intelligence organization. The British knew it . . . and Haj Amim knew it. Every kibbutz and moshav was a part of the network. One encoded signal was sufficient for a thousand men, women and children to hide their arms caches within moments. Scarcely a decade old, the efficiency of the Haganah was enough to make the British envious, and increasingly worried.

Seeing Britain's growing inability to play the Jews and Arabs against each other and thereby control both, Haj Amim made his own move for control of Palestine.

Encouraged by him, in the spring of 1936 a new series of riots erupted. It began with the repeated charge, "The Jews are stealing our lands, desecrating our holy places, with the British lackeys' consent." The carnage began in Jaffa, it then spread from city to city as the customarily defenseless old orthodox Jews of the holy cities became victimized.

AS the atrocities continued to increase, the head of the Haganah, Binya Yariv, called Reuven into his office. His face was grim as he sat at his desk and looked across at Reuven. "Haj Amim intends to stop at nothing. His people are coming into Palestine from Lebanon. I want you to take command of a unit and start a kibbutz." He took out his map, and his pointer fell on Tel Amal.

Reuven took a unit to establish a new addition to traditional kibbutzim—tower and stockade. The first stockade was built of double wooden shelves filled with pebbles, surrounded by a court of 35-by-35 meters containing four cabins that became the observation posts at the four corners. At a distance from the wall, barbed wire was laid in the middle of the court. An observation tower with a searchlight was put up. A small generator in the tower provided the energy, and water was stored on top of the tower to supply the camp.

In the morning hours, after the tower had been erected, the camp was ready to confront the Arabs. Reuven had dispatched twenty-two boys to stand watch during the night, their weapons fourteen grenade rifles and a small number of hand grenades.

On the fourth night the attack came. A thousand Arab riflemen flanked with machine guns poured fire into the stockade. For the first time the Arabs used mortar fire. Reuven's unit lay low and waited for the Arabs to begin their assault.

As the Arabs now came, belly-to-the-ground, knives between their teeth, a half dozen searchlights darted out from the stockade to sweep the field, partially blinding the Arabs. Reuven's people then sent out their counterfire—killing some ninety Arabs in the first burst. Reuven then led half his force out of cover of the stockade. Dead and wounded Arabs littered the hills of battle. Those who survived fled back to high ground.

Despite murderous counterattacks, the armed kibbutz became a permanent fixture, and Reuven was largely responsible.

As he sat in his tent now, contemplating his next maneuver, the flap of his tent opened and, to his amazement when he looked up, he saw Pnina, dressed in the uniform of the Haganah. After the past weeks, seeing her was wonderful as it was surprising. "Pnina, I can't believe you're here—" and then he reminded himself that he wasn't . . . or shouldn't be . . . so happy she was in Tel Amal. The danger was too great. "What are you doing here? This isn't a place you can just walk into—"

"Do I really need an invitation to visit my favorite cousin?"

"Yes, if it's here. No, if it's Tel Aviv."

"I wish we were in Tel Aviv," she said, and her voice was the voice of a woman, no longer a little girl . . . In the year he hadn't seen her she had grown into an extraordinarily voluptuous young woman.

She walked over to him now. "Well, don't I at least deserve a kiss for making your life worthwhile?"

He got up uncertainly, held her at near-arm's length and gave her a cousinly kiss on the cheek.

"Is *that* the best you can do?" She pulled him nearer.

"Pnina, please . . . be a good girl and move into one of the women's tents, I have a lot of work to do—"

"Am I being dismissed by my C.O.?"

"You catch on quick. Now, I really mean it, I have to—"

She kissed him quiet and left quickly before he could call her a "girl" again. She'd show him . . .

The next day Binya Yariv was also a visitor of Reuven. Smiling—something Yariv rarely did—he said, "You did quite a job, Reuven. I think it's time we move out, leave a token unit here and move on to Hanita, where we'll set up the same operation."

Yariv also noted the deep fatigue in Reuven's face. "Tell you what, Reuven, suppose you take a few days off. Swim in the surf, lay on the beach, soak up a little sun."

Reuven thought about it. He also thought about Pnina.

Next morning after breakfast he took Pnina aside. "I'm taking off a few days. Just a short holiday. Want to hitch a ride to Tel Aviv?"

"I wouldn't mind, *sir* . . ."

"Okay, forget the sarcasm and get your gear together. Be ready in twenty minutes. That's an order."

And one she was more than pleased to carry out . . .

IN Tel Aviv, Reuven registered, and took two rooms on two different floors. Then he took Pnina, out of uniform and now in a lovely frock, to dinner, and afterward they danced until two in the morning.

Next day, at the crack of dawn, Reuven's phone rang. "Damn that Yariv," he mumbled, what a thing to do to him . . . call him back into service after only twenty-four hours . . . "Hello—"

"You sound a little out of sorts," Pnina said.

"Oh . . . it's you . . . well, to tell the truth, I am. I sort of hoped this was going to be a holiday when I could get a little sleep for a change—"

"Oh, you can do that any time . . . Now, get out of bed, shower, shave, dress and I'll meet you downstairs in a half hour . . . and *that's* an order. Also, wear your swimming trunks."

And they swam, then lazed on the beach, and whether it was the unwinding, or Pnina's closeness, or both . . . Reuven didn't know . . . he was distinctly uncomfortable . . . Pnina disturbed him, and *that* disturbed him even more . . .

That evening they danced and dined again, then walked along the shore of the Mediterranean, saying little until Reuven took her back to the hotel.

When they arrived at her room she opened the door, took his hand firmly and led him in. He did not resist . . . didn't even try . . . much as he knew he should. Well, shouldn't he?

He sat in a chair. She sat on the edge of the bed.

"Reuven, we have no guarantees for tomorrow. No more games— there's no time for playing games, acting coy, pretending. I happen to be in love with you. I have been for a very long time . . . I can't remember a time when I didn't love you. In case you haven't noticed, I'm proposing to you. Proposing marriage."

Reuven got up, went to the window and looked out at the Mediterranean, its white caps gently caressing the sandy beach. Impossible . . . it was impossible . . . and wrong. Turning around slowly, he told her so.

"Wrong? Only if you don't feel the same about me. Don't you?"

"To be honest . . . and I admit I can be pretty dumb at times . . . I hadn't thought of you . . . well, that way . . . as a woman. At least not until a few days ago. I was wrong . . . you're a woman, all right . . . a magnificent young woman . . . but we have a problem—"

"For whom?"

"For you. You're eighteen and I'm thirty.

"Reuven, darling, that's stupid. For a sabra, age doesn't count."

"We're also first cousins, and marriage means children . . . It really isn't the best idea in the world—"

"My dearest Reuven, I'm not going to get scientific about this, but many first cousins have married and had perfectly beautiful, healthy children. My proposal stands. If you love me the way I love you . . . well, then I want us to be married as soon as possible."

He took her in his arms. "You know, Pnina, you're a lot like my mother. She never gives up on anything, either. Never takes no for an answer—"

"Bravo for Aunt Chavala. May I take it you've *finally* said yes?"

He held her closer, led her to the bed and eliminated any possible doubts he might have had that he would be marrying a *woman* . . .

In the morning the first person they called was Dovid, who not surprisingly was at first shocked, feeling the misgivings Reuven had had in the beginning. But, loving them both as he did, his shock soon gave way to pleasure . . .

The next phone call was to Dvora and Ari. They too were concerned, but gave their blessing . . .

And the next call was overseas. Chavala shared none of the negative thoughts. Uppermost for her was that they were keeping the family within the family. Reuven had no time for honeymoons or family weddings. Two days later they were married, and he proceeded to get on with his mission. . . .

THE trail of murderers and saboteurs led back to Led el Awadin, and so the Haganah ordered Reuven to capture the *mukhtar,* head of the village, dead or alive.

Reuven's plan called for the Haganah men to disguise themselves as British soldiers, complete with uniforms, helmets, English cigarettes and British army bully beef. They drove up to Led el Awadin in army trucks, giving orders in English, and gathered all the men of the village onto the threshing floor. When the unit arrived, Reuven ordered, "Take your positions and surround the house." The two-story house was demolished, and the *mukhtar* was killed.

Haganah was no longer only defensive. It was a force the Arabs would learn to reckon with.

And the British too. British raids were made on the Yishuv at the kibbutzim in search of "illegal" arms, and if any were found the custodian of those arms was immediately thrown into Acre prison. The Yishuv now found itself in perhaps its darkest moment so far. The Yishuv appealed once again to Whitehall, and the reply, not unexpectedly, was that, terribly sorry, nothing could be done.

Jewish militant factions could no longer be restrained. They lashed out in a series of raids, bombing British offices, clubs, attacking Arabs. They demolished British arsenals, ambushed convoys. Leaders of the Yishuv Central and former raiders were thrown into Acre jail.

Still, the plea went out from Ben-Gurion to the Yishuv to once again use its wisdom and restraint against the British. He denounced the terror tactics, and with the help of Binya Yariv, most militant factions in the Haganah were held in check. For the moment . . .

But in Germany there was no moderating force. Even the formerly most self-deluded German Jews knew what their fate would be if they stayed. The British, though, had made it as difficult for German Jews to get into Palestine as it was for Palestinian Jews to leave.

Orders came from the Yishuv Central to Dovid that he must try to get into Germany. The Germans were exploiting the visa market literally for all it was worth . . . the more desperate the Jews became, the higher was the price of their freedom charged by the Reich. Whole foturnes were given for a single visa. They were stolen, forged. Visas meant life. Without them death was certain.

Dovid managed to slip over the Lebanese border and on foot proceeded to Beirut. There, using a forged passport, he caught a boat for Marseilles and, in another week, showed up in Berlin.

Now Dovid was faced with terrible decisions—who received visas and who did not. In fact, he was threatened, offered bribes. He listened to desperate pleas and heard the cries of those he had to refuse . . . the lives of the children had to be saved at any cost.

Next on the essential list were scientists, doctors, professionals. Dovid was able to get many of the children as well as the others out through the underground Aliyah Bet, from where they were eventually accepted in France.

He actually went into negotiations with the Gestapo to try to sell them on the idea of issuing more permits. He argued that since Britain and Germany were competing for Arab favors, it would surely harass the British if German Jews, en masse, were to hit the shores of Palestine. Negotiating with the Gestapo? He'd buy from the Devil himself if it meant getting the visas. And the Devil himself, in the form and shape of one Adolf Eichmann, issued five hundred visas in exchange for thousands of American dollars. Later this same Eichmann would provide a "final solution" for the Jewish problem. Today he would profit from them . . . as long as he couldn't kill them. His time, and theirs, would come. He could afford to wait . . .

Time was running out, and Dovid received his orders to return to Palestine. But first he had to try to help Sheine.

No one had heard from her during these last terrifying months. There was no way for him to know that she lay sick in her bed, terrified more for her son, her Erich, than for herself.

From the day of his birth, Sheine's mother-in-law had taken him in hand, made him her charge. He loved his mother, her quiet sweet gentleness, but he had grown up a German and became active in the Nazi Youth movement. Being a champion soccer player helped make him especially popular in the Hitler Youth. Besides, it was difficult for a young boy not to be carried away with the mood of marching bands, flying banners, stadiums roaring with *sieg heils* to the führer. Erich was a German boy who believed along with all good German boys that Hitler, their führer, was God.

Listening to him glorify Hitler, rail against the Jews, Sheine wanted to die, but she held her tongue . . . as she had on and since the day of his birth. Germans whose records allegedly showed that somewhere back three or four hundred years they had had a Jewish antecedent were taken off, never to reappear. Erich, half-Jewish, was in greater danger than they, Sheine knew . . .

During the dread-filled summer of 1939 Dovid had accomplished a great deal. Now he faced his greatest personal challenge.

He called Gunter Hausman.

Gunter was shocked to see Dovid in Berlin. Well, there was no time for amenities. Dovid quickly told Gunter why he had come to Berlin, that the lives of a handful had been saved but even if it had been only one it would have been worth the effort . . . But now he was on a personal mission . . . "I've asked you here, Gunter, to warn you that your wife, my sister-in-law, is in great danger. Her only hope is to leave at this moment. I will see to it that she and Erich get into Palestine, and when this madness is over . . . well, you can be together again—"

"You, a Palestinian, know more about my country than I do? I thank you very much for your great concern, but you must remember that I am married to *Elsa Beck Hausman,* not Sheine Rabinsky. No one here knows her background. If I thought for one moment that her life were in peril, loving her as I do *and* my son, do you imagine that I would not have suggested her leaving? Believe me, Dovid, Elsa is one of the few who has nothing to fear. These are bad times, I apologize for the behavior of the Third Reich. But the Third Reich is not Germany. It is a temporary government of thugs, hoodlums, addicts. A crazy house-painter sits at its helm. Now, Dovid, will you please get on with your most important mission, and leave Elsa and Erich in my hands?"

Dovid shook his head, but there was nothing more he could say. Gunter meant well, no question about it, but he sadly underestimated the men he'd spoken against. At least Sheine was married to a man who realized the injustice being done to her people, but was that enough . . . ?

The two men shook hands, and in parting Dovid said, "I pray to God, Gunter, that you are right." And to himself . . . Because if you aren't, your wife and son are already dead . . .

Dovid left Germany two days before Hitler invaded Poland, touching off World War II. As he reached the shores of Palestine, and home, in Berlin Jews were being beaten unmercifully by crowds of hoodlums. Windows were smashed, books were being burned. An all-out reign of terror had descended on the Jews. Old bearded men were commanded to fall to their knees. The hairs of their beards were torn out. They were ordered to bark like a dog.

The world had gone mad. That night marked a new beginning for the rise of German barbarism—*Kristallnacht*—the night of the broken glass, a night that gave the signal for the extermination of six million Jews . . .

Gunter sat in his overstuffed chair reading a humorous short story by Guy de Maupassant. Life was so grim these days, he detested even looking at the newspaper. His mind strayed for a moment when he realized that he'd been giving Elsa increasingly larger doses of medication to calm her nerves, but her tensions were so great it seemed the only way to help her function at all.

He tried concentrating again on his reading—the doorbell rang. He glanced at his watch . . . 11:35. An odd hour for a social call. He got up and went to the door. When he opened it, standing in front of him was Klaus Stein, dressed in a long black leather belted coat, his cold blue eyes emphasized by the black felt hat which he'd pulled down to his forehead. Klaus Stein, an officer in the dreaded Gestapo, reporting to Adolf Eichmann.

Gunter swallowed hard, tried a cordial greeting. It was not returned. Stein only said, "You are Herr Doktor Hausman?"

"Yes, and what may I do for you?"

"I believe you have some information of importance to us."

Gunter knew too well why Stein had come. He tried to rally himself, and invited Stein in. Other *Schutzstaffeln* men remained outside while Stein followed Gunter into the living room.

"May I get you brandy, Herr Stein?"

"No. This is not a social call. Tell me about your wife."

"My wife? Well, she's quite beautiful, what every lovely German woman should be—"

"But she's not German, is she?"

Gunther paused, forced a smile. "We've been married for so long, I have difficulty remembering that she's not."

"If you can remember, where does she come from?"

"From Equatorial Africa."

"Tell me how you met."

"Well . . . it was during the First World War. I was stationed in the Middle East. There's really little else to tell."

"How well did you know her during that time?"

"How well? Herr Stein, she was my chief surgical nurse and I had known her for a year, two, I'm not sure—"

"Thank you for your information. Now will you be kind enough to summon Frau Hausman?"

"She really has not been well lately—"

"I've just given you an order. I wish to see Frau Hausman. *Immediately.*"

Gunter went upstairs and found Sheine in a deep sleep. He stood at her bedside, breathing hard . . . dear God, what could he do? No one knew about her, he kept telling himself. Trying to rationalize . . . this was a harsh procedure now followed in the cases of *all* Germans married to foreigners . . . He sat on the edge of her bed, took her hand gently in his, stroked her hair and kissed her gently. Her eyelids fluttered. "How nice, Gunter, what a nice way to awaken me . . ."

Get to it, he told himself. "Darling, I wanted you to rest, but there's a gentleman downstairs that would like to ask you a few questions. Now please don't worry—"

She was now fully awake . . . and she understood. "They've come to take me away, Gunter. I know they've come to take me—"

"*No*, darling. It's just routine questioning of foreign subjects married to Germans."

She got out of bed, dressed, and suddenly, as she looked at herself in the mirror, felt surprisingly calm, almost peaceful. The awful fear that had whipped her all these years was abruptly gone. As she reached in the closet to take her coat, Gunter said quickly, "What are you doing? . . . you don't need your coat."

"I think you're wrong. I have a feeling, Gunter. I won't be returning for a long time . . ."

Slowly she walked down the staircase, Gunter at her side. When she reached the living room she said, "You've asked to see me?"

"Yes, Frau Hausman. If you will be kind enough to accompany me to headquarters."

With Gunter at her side she followed Stein out to his waiting car, and the three were driven to Gestapo headquarters.

When they arrived, Stein seated himself behind his desk, leafing through a large, yellow-paged case history. Gunter and Sheine sat on the opposite side of the desk. Both were thinking about Erich.

Gunter tried to convince himself that when this was over Sheine and he would return home and the reasons that brought them here tonight would be done and over. In his heart he suspected otherwise . . .

The door to the adjacent room opened and, between a complement of two guards, Dr. Ludwig Breslauer was brought in. In front of Stein, on his desk, was Sheine Rabinsky's psychiatric case history, assembled by Breslauer.

Gunter cursed himself for having sent Sheine those many years ago to Breslauer—a Jew. All of his records had now been confiscated. If not for that mistake, Elsa Beck Hausman would not now be here.

The questioning of Sheine and Ludwig Breslauer went on and on until the early hours of the morning, despite that Stein well knew all the answers. His sadism, though, was piqued . . . he dearly loved to see them squirm.

Sheine was taken away without even being able to whisper "I love you," to Gunter.

Beyond grief, he went home to contemplate not so much the fate of Sheine—he now knew its inevitability, and that he was helpless to do anything about it—but to dedicate himself to somehow getting Erich out of the country.

But time had run out for that too. Stormtroopers broke down his door, demanded Erich Dieter Hausman. Gunter thought he would go out of his mind . . . *"He is not here, he is not here—"* He was knocked to the floor by a rifle butt as two of the troopers ran up the stairs, methodically opened each door, until Erich was found.

He followed them, asking, "Why are you doing this to *me?* What have I done? I am a German, a son of the Fatherland—"

A hard slap across his face made him lose his balance, toppled him over.

"Get up, you Jew bastard, son of a Jewish whore. Get up and follow me."

Totally bewildered, he obeyed. On the way out he looked at his father, looked for an explanation that, of course, could not be given.

Gunter listened to the staff car drive away, sat down heavily in his chair, then realized his mother was standing there, brought by the commotion in Erich's room. Now she seemed as bewildered and disbelieving as Erich was about the accusation that he was a Jew. She lashed out at Gunter, "Did you *know* when you married her what she was?"

He nodded.

"You *knew*, and you brought that . . . that Jewish woman to live in *my* home . . . My God . . . how could you have done it, disgraced us, destroyed your own family for . . . *that* . . . ?"

Gunter looked up at his mother. At the moment he wanted to kill her. He ran out of the house, got into his car and drove through the streets of Berlin, then onto the highway until he came on a German convoy. Accelerating, he drove faster and faster and, in one blinding moment of hatred, rammed into the moving vehicle. Both went up in flames. Gunter, a father who could not save his son, a husband who could not save his wife, could no longer justify living. At least he could take a few of their murderers with him. . . .

Sheine and Erich were taken to Auschwitz where, mercifully, Sheine died . . . At least, Erich thought, she had not lived long enough to be tortured the way others were that he lived to see. He prayed for one thing —to stay alive long enough so that he could revenge himself against those who had once made him believe that he was a member of their murderous "superior" race. That day *would* come, and for that, he would survive.

Chapter Thirty-eight

WHEN DOVID RETURNED to Palestine he found that Reuven and Joshua had joined the *British* army. Zvi too. And then he got the explanation. It seemed the charity of Britain was boundless when it became a matter of its own pressing needs. The war was going badly for them. Rommel was very close to Alexandria. Reuven was an important, knowledgeable officer in Syria. And Reuven and the Jews welcomed the opportunity to fight for Palestine *against* the Germans, even in the British army. Ben-Gurion recommended it and the Yishuv listened.

Reuven quickly recruited, trained and led his men into action . . . and along with British and Australians . . . the Australians were wonderfully fierce and courageous fighters . . . put Rommel out of business so far as using Syria as an invasion base for Palestine was concerned.

But Reuven ached for Pnina. He was also bone-tired, and damned lonely . . . .

When he did manage to get to her, when she saw him getting out of his army jeep, she ran to greet him, took him in her arms and just held him quietly, tightly. As though afraid she might lose him if she ever took her arms away.

Finally, taking him by the hand, she ran to the house, where Dvora was baking bread. Hands full of flour, Dvora reached up and kissed him, nearly as excited, and grateful, as Pnina to see him.

That evening they tried to catch up on their lives. Ari said, "You made quite a splash for yourself in Syria . . .."

Reuven laughed. "We didn't do so bad, considering we had foreign units who didn't always get the same signals. But we did accomplish what we set out to do, and let me tell you . . . Zvi did a fine job. You should be proud. He told me to send his love . . . he seems busy with a very pretty blond sabra in Haifa . . . He said you'd understand."

Ari laughed. "After a battle like that, who wouldn't understand . . . Do you think he's serious about her?"

"Well . . . he didn't come back for Aunt Dvora's baked bread. Joshua sends his love too, but he wanted to go into Jerusalem to see our father." . . .

The next week Pnina and Reuven lived an idyll. They hiked the countryside, made love among the eucalyptus. When they worked together in the fields they shared a pleasure in the feel of a plow in their hands instead of a gun.

It was over too soon . . . Reuven was needed in Jerusalem, and Pnina went back to her unit with the Palmach.

During the war the Yishuv had courageously supported the British, as it had in the First World War. Thanks in part to the great efforts of the Yishuv, Rommel never reached Alexandria. No other community, no country had given so much and received so little . . . The British, afraid that if the Jews were too applauded, too appreciated, they might use this against the British when bargaining for a homeland later on. When the British needed spies in the Balkans, they turned to the Jews to train them as parachutists. Thirty were sent behind the enemy lines and not one was found alive.

The Arabs . . . as fickle as the British . . . noted that the winds of war were turning in favor of the British and against the Germans. The Germans were no longer their liberators. Haj Amim el Husseini ran off to Hitler's Germany. The Arabs now declared war on Germany . . . how else to get a vote at the peace conferences, to block the Zionists in Palestine. As for the Zionists, their only vote was the number of their dead. Their only hope . . . to try to prove to the world that they had made a great contribution, that they deserved a long-promised homeland.

But an ill wind began to blow for the Yishuv—its name was Ernest Bevin, the new Labour government's foreign minister. It had been hoped that Britain's Labour party would be sympathetic to the Yishuv's plight, but Bevin was especially ill-suited to deal with the imponderable tangle of Palestine and the remnants of the Nazi Holocaust. When the world was finally compelled to face up to the horrors of the concentration camps, Bevins's comment, in answer to the clamor of the displaced persons to be sent to Palestine, was: "If the Jews for all their suffering want so badly to get to the head of the queue, I believe that it presents a danger of another anti-Semitic reaction through it all. Were the British government to be allowed into Palestine, and resettle even in detention camps for the time being, you understand it would be at the expense of British taxpayers. That, of course, could constitute a minimum of two million pounds. And those are pounds that war-torn Britain can scarcely afford."

Following the bitter disillusionment with the Labour party, in September of 1945, President Harry S. Truman received from Clement Attlee, the new British prime minister, a negative reply to his request to allow the immigration of one hundred thousand Jewish survivors of the Holocaust. A few days later the Labour government ruled that Jewish immigration to Palestine would not exceed eighteen thousand a year. The whole western part of the land of Israel would become a country with an Arab majority. The Jewish Yishuv was to be frozen into a minority of one third. To enforce the White Paper restricting immigration, a flotilla of the British navy month after month prevented Jewish refugees from Europe from reaching the country.

For the Yishuv the White Paper spelled an end to the Zionist adventure. It also spelled an end to the restraint the Haganah had used. It stirred up the already explosive tensions in the more aggressive factions in the country—among which was the Irgun Zvai Leumi, which now came more and more to prominence.

IN April, 1939, three refugee ships full of half-dead Jews who had somehow escaped from Germany and Roumania reached the shores of Palestine, and were turned back by the British. In November two battered tramp steamers, the *Pacific* and the *Milos,* arrived in Haifa with eighteen hundred Jews, and once again the passengers were not allowed to disembark. The British surrounded them, announced that they would be sent to the island of Mauritius for the duration of the war. They were transferred to the British steamer *Patria*. On the day the *Patria* was scheduled to sail there was an explosion aboard and more than two hundred people were blown to bits or drowned within the safe haven of Haifa port while their relatives and much of the population of Haifa watched with horrified eyes . . . among them Joshua Landau, who, standing on Mount Carmel, high above the panorama of Haifa, observed thrashing bodies drowning in the water, dead being dragged into boats by fishhooks.

THE press of such events had brought the two factions of the Yishuv closer—the Haganah and the Irgun. Passiveness was no longer tolerable.

Joshua sat in the meetings and was impressed that, at long last, the Yishuv was beginning to take the initiative. The memory of the *Patria* and those dismembered victims was seared in his brain.

He went to headquarters to see Binya Yariv, Reuven and his father and announced, "I've an idea that I *think* might work."

Dovid thought of Chavala. She, too, usually had a plan.

"So, what's the plan?" Yariv asked.

"Usually the passengers on illegal ships coming out of Europe during the war carried only about two hundred or so people. How about a ship large enough to carry ten thousand people, or more?"

"And where are you going to get such a ship?" Reuven pressed him.

"In America."

"America?" Yariv looked at Dovid.

"Yes . . . you meet a lot of people in Jerusalem. The other evening I just happened to be sitting in a café and, well, who do I meet but a great big bruiser . . . bigger and much fatter than Reuven. But, anyway, it turns out he's a Jew and his name is Harvey Rosen, and can you guess what business he's in?"

"A shipbuilder?" Reuven said.

"Close. He owns ships, and just the kind we need. He's got a tramp steamer, perfect condition, weighs about eleven thousand tons, about five hundred feet long. It can take on about ten thousand, stripped clean except for bunks."

Dovid said, "I always get a little nervous when I hear about things being too perfect. All right . . . *suppose* this ship is everything your friend Harvey Rosen says, how do you expect to get that size ship into any harbor in Palestine with the British on your tail?"

"Got it all worked out. First, of course, before he gets any money

I want to see the merchandise, which of course means going to New Jersey where his docks are—"

"Sounds nice. You get a ship and a vacation at the same time," Reuven said. "But, you didn't answer *abba,* how are you going to get a ship that size into Palestine?"

"I was getting to that. The ship will sail under American colors, owned by an American company, operated by an American crew, carrying some civilians just *dying* to see the Holy Land."

Nobody laughed.

Yariv said, "So far, some of this makes sense, but you have to pick these civilians up going to see the Holy Land at Marseilles. The minute those refugees come aboard, and you hit the high seas, you'll have the British following you all the way, and you'll get stopped the minute you hit Palestinian waters."

"You're a pessimist, Yariv," Joshua said. "Let's take it a day at a time. I know, I know, you've been handling the Haganah for a long time without my help, but now I'd like to try to contribute . . ."

There was silence in the room. Yariv looked at Dovid, a look that seemed to say, When you're young you have dreams, and if you try hard enough, some of them come true . . .

"All right," Yariv said. "Go to America, get your boat, and we'll, as you say, play it a day at a time. . . ."

That same night Joshua met the family at Lydda Airport. He kissed Pnina and Aunt Dvora, shook hands with Ari and Zvi, held his father close, then said, "I'm going to do it, *abba.* "

"I believe you are, Joshua. Now, good luck, and give your mother my love. I'll tell her you're coming when I call her later this evening."

THE next day Joshua's American family greeted him at La Guardia. Chavala, delighted to see him, said, "So, it took a ship to get you to pay your mother a visit?" She smiled when she said it.

"That sounds like I should have a little Jewish guilt, and if you think I should, you're right. But please remember, mama, I couldn't make a visit while *Der Führer* was having his party. So it's really been the first time, mama, that I've had the chance to say hello and that I love you. By the way, I do."

She smiled. "Enough excuses. Now, come home. The whole family will be together. Wait till you see Chia's twins."

The next morning Joshua and Chavala drove out to New Jersey to see Mr. Harvey Rosen. When Joshua took a look at Harvey Rosen's "perfect" ship, he found a stinking hulk rusting and listing to port. *"This is what you were telling me about that night in Jerusalem? . . . my God, this thing wouldn't make it out of New York harbor, past that lady in the bay."*

"You don't know a good ship when you see it. The only thing it needs is a little paint, a few repairs. I tell you what I'll do, give me half down and the rest I get only when I deliver her. And one other thing, remember I happen to be the captain on this little trip . . . if anything happens it's my tail as much as yours. Excuse me, ma'am. But I feel strong about this. She may not be pretty but she's seaworthy, and *that's* a lot more than I can say about some prettier ladies."

Chavala smiled. "He's got a point, Joshua."

"Could be. I haven't had too much time for ladies these days, not even for the beauty right here."

Chavala smiled appropriately. She was very proud of Joshua. The pain of separation was forgotten, seeing the man he'd grown into.

Now the most pressing question of all was asked by Joshua. "How long is it going to take to strip this ship, put in bunks, a mess hall, separate heads for men and women, *and* a dispensary?"

"Six weeks at the latest," Rosen said.

"Make it four and you've got a deal."

Chavala spoke for the first time, "In my business, the diamond business, when a deal is made, two people shake hands and wish one another *mazel* and *broche.*"

Rosen looked at Chavala. "That's sensible, a piece of paper don't mean a thing."

"You're right . . . Tonight I'm giving a party for just you, Mr. Rosen, and my family, that we should live to see the day that the Holocaust is over and may I, please God, find out what happened to my poor sister I haven't gotten a letter back from for years. I'll see you at seven o'clock tonight in the lobby of the Waldorf-Astoria Hotel. It's been a pleasure, Mr. Rosen."

ALTHOUGH she saw a little of Joshua during the month he was in the United States, still, having him with her in his old room . . . she was up every morning, making breakfast for him, fussing over him even more than when he was a little boy. . . .

The month, of course, ended all too soon. And too soon she was again standing and watching a ship take off a loved one . . . the newly renovated *Star of Liberty,* enlisted to save Jewish lives, slowly disappearing beyond the horizon.

AS promised by Harvey Rosen the ship was sound, and in a week she was docking at Marseilles. The crew of the Aliyah Bet directed some ten thousand that came aboard to their quarters. *Liberty* lay at anchor that night, waiting for the tide. Next morning she weighed anchor in a calm sea and headed out beyond the three-mile limit to international waters. But cruising along, she was spotted by a British destroyer. In spite of American colors and the vessel being registered in the United States, with an American crew and captain, the *Liberty* had still picked up ten thousand refugees in Marseilles. Well, this was peacetime and at least she couldn't be waved aside to be boarded . . . all the British could do was wait until she got within the three-mile limit of Palestine. But then they would move . . .

Rosen and Joshua kept an eye on the British ship with their binoculars. "I said we've got to play it a day at a time, and that's what we've done up till now. But in two days we're going to be close to Palestine, so I've got to start thinking about a little more than a day at a time. Now how are we going to get rid of that British bastard behind us?"

"The only way we can land is with a diversion in Haifa," Joshua said. "I'll get a message to my father."

He gave the encoded message to the wireless operator, asking for some action between Haifa and Jaffa, or any other place, so long as it helped them get free to land at Athlit. The landing date was given. Dovid was informed that they were being trailed, and asked to use whatever influence he still had with the British.

Next morning, the British vessel was apparently no longer following them. Dovid had received the message, called on one of his few remaining contacts in the British command, who was really a Zionist agent, and had sent new counterorders to the captain of the destroyer. . . .

Now that they were finally in the Mediterranean, Joshua walked down from the bridge to the deck, stood against the rail . . . someone was close by . . . he turned around . . . and was startled to see a beautiful young woman next to him, her arms on the rail. Her looks were as improbable to encounter on this trip as anything he could imagine . . . in fact, she was, at first glance anyway, too good to be true. To be *there.*

His first words were less than suave. "Oh, hello . . . my God, you're beautiful."

"Thank you."

"How is it I haven't seen you before?"

"Maybe because there are, as I understand it, some ten thousand other people on board."

"Oh . . . yes . . . well, I just feel it's my loss, I mean being on this ship all this time and meeting you only a few days away from Palestine . . ."

"I've noticed you. You've been very busy."

"Well, I'm not so busy now . . . my name is Joshua Landau."

"I know. Most everyone on board does. My name is Simone Blum."

"Simone Blum? That's French. But you speak perfect Hebrew?"

"I learned while I was in the underground. I knew that one day I was going to live in Eretz Yisroel. Somehow I convinced myself I wasn't going to die."

A considerable woman, obviously . . . he pressed her for more . . . She was born a Parisian, as were her mother and father, both doctors, and she was, in fact, in her second year of medical school when Hitler did his obscene jig at the Arc de Triomphe. After that she was secretly rushed off to live in Provence with a Catholic family that gave her love and treated her as though she were one of their own, at the same time encouraging her to continue being the dedicated Zionist she already was.

When the war was over, Simone joined a Zionist organization that had, once again, sprung up in Paris, and there it was that she became a member of the Mossad Aliyah Bet . . . "And that, Captain Landau, is how I happen to be on this cruise."

"And I'm very glad for that . . . when we get to Palestine I'd like to be in touch with you . . ."

Simone Blum nodded, and said that would be fine with her. . . .

The next day was taken up with landing and getting ten thousand people, crew, and members of the Aliyah Bet ashore. For all of Joshua's bravado he knew there were always hitches. Once again he sat in the radio room and sent a coded message, to Reuven this time. The coded message came back quickly: T-H-E B-R-E-A-D I-S B-A-K-E-D A-N-D M-A-M-A'-S W-A-I-T-I-N-G. Watches were synchronized, motors were slowed, the Aliyah Bet were instructed about their passengers, the crew was ready. Rosen and Joshua kept their eyes fixed on their watches.

First diversion: 250 Palmach members raided Athlit with the British in hot pursuit.

Second diversion: Two Haganah units attacked three observation posts of the coastal guard.

Third diversion: Shortly before midnight the station in Giveat Olga was destroyed by explosive charges.

Fourth diversion: The Sidney Ali station was blown up and the garrison stationed there was attacked with automatic fire.

Under cover of all of this, the *Liberty* sailed in, just beyond the shoals of Athlit. Dovid was waiting there, and saw Joshua taking things firmly in hand. The operation was swift, efficient. As soon as people hit the beach they were met by the Palmach, and instantly transformed into Palestinians . . . their clothes were discarded for white shorts and blue tops. They were rushed into waiting trucks that drove them to the kibbutzim. The young people looked like any youth group, and quickly fitted in with the settlers. The men and women were dressed as farmers, and seeing them along the road in trucks, one would naturally assume they were going to their moshav or kibbutz.

The operation was a success—up to the last ten people, among whom was Joshua, two Palmachniks and Rosen. Joshua was furious when he saw the British truck driving up. Still, ten out of ten thousand was not so bad . . . except it wasn't easy to be philosophical.

Especially not when he was arrested and taken off to Jerusalem Prison. The interrogation was long and tough for the prisoners—especially for Captain Joshua Landau.

"You've been a very busy man," said the British interrogation officer Dudley Spencer. "What were you doing at Athlit tonight?"

"Taking the night air, sir."

"Forget the sarcasm, Landau. I repeat, why were you at Athlit tonight?"

"Saving lives, *sir.* Now, I believe I have reservations here, I wouldn't want to lose my room—"

Spencer called two guards to take him away. Tomorrow he'd lose his sense of humor . . .

The next morning Joshua was again led into the interrogation room. Once again he was told to acknowledge his reasons for being at Athlit. And once again he refused. This time he was stripped, his hands were tied, he was suspended from the ceiling and flogged unconscious. Afterward he was dragged back to his cell, thrown on the floor.

The two Palmachniks received the same.

Rosen did better. He was an American, which caused some pause to the captors. He challenged the British to create an international incident.

As he was being released, he suggested that they be so kind as to pay back their war debts to Uncle Sam.

The other six were of different nationalities, German, Polish, Roumanian, and none spoke English. By the time interpreters, except for the Germans, could be found, arrangements were made for them to be taken off to the dreaded internment camp on Cyprus.

WHEN Joshua forced open his swollen eyes he looked across the cell and barely made out a young man, dark hair . . . he had the strangest, most improbable feeling that he knew him. But if so, from where? His muttering seemed to be in German. Maybe he'd seen him during the voyage . . . but the thought persisted that it was more than that . . . that he *knew* this person . . .

Finally he said, in the little German he knew, "Where did you come from?"

The young man's eyes were cold, angry. No answer.

Understandable, Joshua thought. Concentration camps tended to make a person less than sociable. Nonetheless, he persisted, asked the same question in German again.

Almost hissing, the man said, "Don't talk to me in German. I speak English. And don't ask me questions, it's none of your damned business. I don't owe you anything. I hear you are a big hero . . . congratulations, you saved the world—"

"Wait a minute. I'm not the enemy. I'm in here with you, or haven't you noticed?"

Pause. Then: "I remember that you're also not a friend."

"Hold on there. I think I understand how you feel, but let's find out whether I'm your friend, and before I can do that I'd like to know what your name is."

His response was to roll up his sleeve, revealing the tattoo of blue numbers. Shoving it out in front of Joshua's eyes he said, "That's my name."

They didn't speak for the rest of the day. There was no point in it for now, Joshua decided.

DOVID was busy scanning the columns of case histories of those who had recently come into Palestine illegally . . . records that had been given to him by the Aliyah Bet:

FRIEDA (SURNAME UNKNOWN), AGE 9: Born in Auschwitz. Neither parent known. Presumed to be Polish.

DANIEL DUBNIK, AGE 16: Roumanian nationality. Found at Bergen-Belsen by British troops. Boy witnessed death of entire family.

SADIE RABINOWITZ, AGE 14: Nationality unknown. Family survivors unknown. Liberated at Auschwitz.

MICHAEL ROSSINI, AGE 4: Nationality Italian. No survivors. Liberated at Auschwitz.

ERICH DIETER HAUSMAN, AGE 20: Born in Berlin. Liberated at Auschwitz. No family survivors. Mother, a Jew, died in Auschwitz. Father, a Christian-German, dead. Cause and place unknown . . .

Dovid suddenly couldn't catch his breath as he sat there. He put the list down on the desk, his mind barely able to accept what he saw. The irony . . . it was frightening. Sheine's son had been rescued, and was now in the same cell with his cousin Joshua . . . Dovid had seen Erich—though at the time he hadn't known who he was—when he'd wangled permission to see Joshua.

Dovid took out the photograph of Erich that Sheine had sent when he was fifteen. Obviously, after the ordeal that the boy must have been through, he had changed physically, but the eyes *were* Sheine's. Bitter, yes, but they were Sheine's.

Dovid immediately went to pay a call on a very special friend in the British command—one he had helped many years ago as an agent. He had a special favor coming to him, and this was the one time Dovid meant to collect . . .

At four o'clock in the afternoon of the following day, two British soldiers, all spit and polish, stood in front of Dudley Spencer's desk as he squinted down at the orders for Joshua Landau to be transferred to Latrun Prison, which had greater security than the jail in Jerusalem, and for the immigrant known only as Tattoo 4319195 to be removed immediately to the Jaffa Detention Compound, whence he would be sent to Caraolos camp on Cyprus. The orders bore the official stamp of Sir Ian Henry-Grant. Spencer sighed, shrugged. Actually he could think of nothing better than to have the matter of Joshua Landau out of his jurisdiction at the moment. He would have loved to see the uppity Jew hang by his thumbs, but since the success of the *Liberty* had created more than an embarrassment for the British, he'd deal with him at a later, more appropriate time.

The Haganah had seen to it that the *Liberty* story hit the wire services and made news all over the world. This, after all, had been the first time since the British blockade that a ship of *Liberty*'s size, with so many illegal immigrants abroad, had managed to land and elude the British. The *Liberty*'s daring run had seriously compromised the British blockade.

Whitehall had let the high command in Palestine know its displeasure, and demanded an explanation . . .

Without hesitation Spencer had the prisoners brought from their cell. Handcuffed, they were remanded into the custody of waiting British soldiers, whom Joshua was pleased to recognize as English Jews who had joined the Haganah.

The charade was played out . . . Joshua was thrown into one staff car, Erich into another, and the two vehicles sped away from Jerusalem. Just before they reached the gorge of Bab el Wad, they stopped at the side of the road. Joshua and Erich were hurried into the back seat of a waiting car. At the wheel was Reuven, with Zvi beside him.

Reuven wasted no time with amenities as he instructed both his passengers to lie down on the floor, where they were covered with blankets.

Now, for the first time, Erich spoke up. "I demand to know where I am being taken . . ."

"Well, well," Joshua said, "so you can actually speak . . . all right, damn it, lie back and keep very quiet."

Erich froze. At this moment Auschwitz seemed very close.

They were driven high up into the hills of Haifa to an abandoned Arab village that the Haganah had scouted. The car stopped, the back door was opened, the blanket removed. Joshua got out first, Erich reluctantly following.

The door to the mud hut was opened.

Dovid was waiting.

Joshua said, "Never thought I'd be so happy to see you, *abba.* They sure trained you good in the NILI, didn't they?"

"Good enough to get you out, young man . . . now, I suggest that we all sit down and talk about why you're here." Dovid hesitated, looked at Erich. "This will come as something of a surprise—maybe a shock—to you, but I'm your Uncle Dovid, and these are your cousins." He hurried on as he saw Erich's disbelieving reaction. "Joshua, you know. Reuven, you don't, although he drove you here along with Zvi. Now, I have a feeling we all have a lot to talk about."

Joshua, Reuven and Zvi were surprised, of course. Erich was shocked. His mother had told him nothing. Thinking back, he recalled vaguely that she had tried, but there'd been no time. But this must have been the secret she wanted to tell him . . .

Dovid waited, then, understanding Erich's difficulty, said quietly, "Erich, try to believe this . . . the only way you can rid yourself of all the terrible hurts is to talk about them. You have a family now. We love you, and we want you, and we thank God that you've been able to come to us."

Erich's anger was like a reflex. Six years of degradation had nurtured it. "Don't talk to me about thanking God and how much you love me. Don't tell me to talk away six years in ten minutes. I think the world is a sewer. I hate it, it should all have been buried with Hitler in his damn bunker."

"All right, Erich . . . we don't talk about any of this today. You're right, you need time."

That night Erich woke up screaming from the nightmare he lived with . . . drenched in perspiration and thrashing about in the bed. Joshua, who was in the next bed, went to him and held him in his arms. "It's all right. It's all right, Erich. It will be, I promise you . . ."

Erich's breathing slowed to normal as he looked at his cousin. It seemed a thousand years since anyone had treated him like anything but an animal. He lay back, wanting to say thank you, but the words wouldn't come.

THE next days helped Erich believe and accept that these people who called themselves family really were. The men kept up a lively banter about Haganah's exploits and their roles. There were no heroes. Mishaps, errors in judgment were fully aired and even made light of . . . "Many were the times we were caught—sometimes literally—with our pants down," Reuven said.

Gradually Erich found the voice inside him . . . "I didn't think I'd ever talk about this. You see, I'm not the same as you. I was born a German and I grew up thinking Hitler was God and the Reich was the ultimate state. The best of possible worlds. I *believed* in the lie of the Aryan race's superiority. I was raised, trained to give my life for it. I believed *Mein Kampf* was the Bible . . . Do you understand how I felt when I found out they'd lied to me? I *believed* that Jews were the cause of the world's troubles. What was happening to them was what they deserved. Hitler said so, and Hitler could do no wrong . . . Until the night when I was taken away and called a Jew. My mother and I were taken to Auschwitz, and my fine Aryan father didn't lift a finger to help us—"

Dovid interrupted. "I knew your father, Erich, and I think you're wrong about him. He was one of the few Germans that knew the truth, but he too was helpless. I was in Germany just before the war. I spoke to him. He was convinced that nothing could hurt you because no one knew your mother was Jewish. He was wrong, yes, but what he did, he did trying to protect you—"

Erich didn't seem convinced. "I don't have any idea where he's at. I don't want to, but I wonder what he would have thought if he'd seen Auschwitz in 1941 . . . When we got there we saw lawns and flowerbeds around the buildings. You know what those buildings were? Gas chambers. I guess I was lucky. Because of my father's fine *name*, Dr. Hesseman —he'd been a colleague of my father's—knew me, decided to take pity on my Jewish soul and do me the honor of letting me work in the laboratory. I could go on for days and never have enough time to tell you what happened there. Little kids injected with cancer cells. The legs of pregnant women tied so they couldn't give birth. Men castrated. And thanks to Dr. Hesseman's generosity, I was allowed to see my mother. Let me tell you about my mother. They tried to teach me otherwise, but she was an angel, the only human being I'd ever felt close to. I knew that the next morning it was her turn to go to the 'showers.' I couldn't accept that. She was dying from a typhus injection they'd given her. That night I went to my mother. I took hold of her hand and held onto it while she drank the sleeping potion I'd stolen. When she was asleep . . . I . . . put the pillow over her face and I kept it there until . . ."

He forced back the tears that he would not have believed he still was capable of. "It was very quiet, I remember. I took her out of the shed, which had been her home, and not more than ten feet away I found a shallow rut between a clump of pine trees, and there I put her down, covered her with dirt, picked up a twig and drew a Star of David in the earth. I kept telling myself that at least I saved her from being gassed to death."

When he'd finished there was silence, except for the quiet sobbing of Erich Dieter Hausman, the first tears he'd shed in over six years. . . .

Erich slept well that night, at least without the nightmares, and in the morning after breakfast Dovid said, "I think it's time, Erich, that you should meet the rest of your family."

"I'd like that, Uncle Dovid, except understand my name is *not* Erich Dieter Hausman. I am *not* a German. I am a Jew, so I want to be called

Yehudah. And in memory of my mother . . . Rabinsky."

Dovid took the boy to him and held him close. As his own.

WITH all that was going on in Palestine between Haganah, the Irgun Zvai Leumi and the British there were few who paid attention to the Wanted posters for Joshua Landau. The *Liberty* incident was nearly forgotten in the wake of riots and retaliations. So it was considered safe for them to leave the hills of Haifa and go back to Kfar Shalom.

When they arrived, Erich was greeted with such warmth that the past was almost put in the past. Dvora could not get over him being there. For Erich, Pnina expecting her first child in a few days, his cousin Reuven being so friendly . . . it was hard to believe, but he was learning . . . Maybe, just maybe someday there might even be someone for him. For Yehudah Rabinsky . . .

Although Erich's . . . Yehudah's . . . need for love was certainly different than Joshua's, Simone Blum had been steadily in his thoughts ever since they'd met. Until now, though, there had just been no time to do anything about it.

He called her headquarters and found she was off duty for a few days and could be reached in Jerusalem. He phoned, keeping his fingers crossed that she would be home . . . She wasn't. He called every half hour until finally he heard an hello at the other end.

"Hello . . . I've been trying to get you all evening . . . Oh, this is Joshua . . . Landau."

As though she wouldn't recognized that voice. She'd heard it often enough on that trip across the Mediterranean. Anyone else . . . she might have thought it was some *chutzpah* to be calling after all this time, not in Joshua Landau's case. She knew the repercussions when the *Liberty* landed. She'd even felt guilty that she'd been one of the lucky ones to escape and he'd been caught. So she was actually pleased that he hadn't forgotten her. "How are you, Joshua Landau?"

"Lonely."

"So?"

"So, come meet me."

"Where are you?"

"At home . . . Kfar Shalom."

Silence . . . "How would you suggest I get there . . . by plane?"

"I didn't mean here. How about Tiberias? They have a great kib-butz near there where we can swim, and a fine symphony orchestra.

It's a perfect place to get acquainted . . ."

"Well, I think that's pretty far. Why not Jerusalem? You told me it's your favorite place."

"Well, I'm afraid I'm not so popular right now in Jerusalem. Please . . . I'll meet you at the Hotel Ramal in Tiberias at 5:00 this afternoon . . . I'd pick you up, Simone, but the gendarmes might not let me get there."

"I understand," she said quickly. "I'll be there." A wanted man was entitled.

When she walked into the hotel, she was even more beautiful than Joshua's memory of her, standing at the rail of the *Liberty*. She was dressed in a simple silk frock. Her face was radiant, and her deep blue eyes were remarkably blue.

"I am, as they say, at a loss for words," he said with huge unoriginality. "Well, let's get out to the kibbutz."

She hesitated. "If you don't mind, I'm awfully hungry, could we stay here and have dinner?"

He said they could. He'd go or stay anywhere with this lady.

They sat at a window table, looking out at the surf below. Hard to believe, they both were thinking, that there was an angry, murderous world out there. Joshua ordered a bottle of wine and they toasted their meeting. The orchestra struck up, and they danced. When the orchestra stopped it was one in the morning, and Joshua suggested that they stay the night and go to the kibbutz later on in the day.

Simone went along . . . until Joshua asked for only one room. "Joshua, I'm very attracted to you, but I don't go to bed with a man the first time I spend an evening with him. I want you and I to know each other much better."

Joshua might understand but he was hardly pleased. Grumpily, he ordered two separate rooms.

He tossed and turned and hardly slept that night, and at breakfast the next morning he was ready to tell her that they were going back. But confronting that extraordinary face . . . he forgot his pique. Be grateful for small favors, he told himself. After breakfast they changed into their bathing suits and swam in the marvelous soothing waters. After lunch they walked through the hills and Simone picked armfuls of wild flowers. They bought apples from a Druse vendor along the road, sat among the wildflowers and looked down at the panorama of Tiberias—blue, the fields buttercup yellow, the sky pink and white. Joshua was only human . . . he took Simone in his arms and kissed her. "You're the most beautiful woman I've ever seen. Give me the slightest hint of encouragement and I'll probably ask you to marry me. I'm not just impetuous, I have excellent taste and my work does tend to keep me away—"

She released herself from his arms. "Joshua, we've met exactly twice. What do you know about me? Almost nothing. What do I know about you? More, but not enough. I'm not even thinking about marriage now—"

Joshua got up, annoyed in spite of himself.

"Joshua, people need to get to *know* each other very well before they talk about marriage—"

"Well how do you get to *know* anyone when you have separate rooms on different floors?"

"Not too difficult, Joshua." She allowed herself a smile. "You give one of them up. *When* you've gotten to know each other better."

"I only have four days, Simone. Do you think *that's* enough time?"

"I don't know, probably not—"

He grabbed her hand, walked quickly down the hill until they reached the hotel. "We're going back."

"Well, you do give up easily."

Okay, he'd take the challenge, annoyed—or frustrated—as he was. He'd stick it out for the next four days. She wasn't going to defeat him, damn it. And he was going to seem far more indifferent to her than he felt. Some chance.

The first days passed tranquilly enough . . . sun and surf, dancing, moonlight walks. Romantic but not intimate.

On their last night, Joshua had just shut his door when there was a knock. He opened it and was confronted—rewarded—by Simone, dressed in a blue silk peignoir she'd kept hidden from those other members of Aliyah Bet . . . she was French, after all. A Zionist, but definitely a *French* Zionist.

She had to come to him, he stood there like a lump. She closed the door behind her, walked toward him, dropped the robe, kissed him, and said, "I think the time has come when we can be very good friends."

Trying to control the throbbing between his thighs, he took her in his arms, kissed her, and then the urgency each felt took over. The gentle surf was a fitting accompaniment to their lovemaking . . . gentle, powerful and repetitive . . .

IN the morning, Joshua had no doubts about being in love with Simone. Never mind if it was sudden. It was there. His whole life moved quickly. He had no doubts. He watched her lying there for a moment, then kissed her.

"Simone, I want you to marry me. Please don't put me off with how sudden this is and so forth. I *know* what I feel. How about you?"

"Not yet . . . Joshua, I told you I was attracted to you. Last night, God knows, was wonderful. But it's a beginning—"

"You are a damned stubborn woman, Simone, but I'll try to love you anyway." He forced himself to wink and appear to be a good deal more jolly than he felt.

They drove up to Caesarea, wanting the day to last as long as possible, and had lunch, then visited the old Roman aqueduct, the ruins near the old harbor, and went on to the Roman amphitheater. Simone sat on a stone bench in the middle of the huge arena. Joshua stood below on what had once been the stage. From that platform he spoke out and his voice resounded in that ancient theater . . . "To be or not to be, that's the question . . . Marry me, Simone, marry me . . ."

His answer was her applause. Not what he wanted, but at least she didn't say no. Progress? He thought so. Hoped so . . .

With those good thoughts they left and he took her as far into Jerusalem as he felt it was safe for him to go. He kissed her just before she boarded the bus and warned her he'd call her every day.

As he watched it speed away, he held to her promise that it was the beginning, and with this reassurance for himself he turned westward and drove back to the unknown future in Kfar Shalom.

THE house was still, everyone asleep. Dvora sat at her kitchen table wondering how she could find the words to tell Chavala the terrible news. No way, except to tell the truth of it:

> My dearest Chavala:
>
> We've survived many things, you and I. I wish there was a better way . . . a different way for me to tell you what I am about to say.
>
> I'll tell you details later, but through the most extraordinary set of events Sheine's son is with us here at Kfar Shalom. God must have planned it. Erich was one of the refugees that was saved on the ship that Joshua brought to Eretz Yisroel. He is a very upset young man, but with love and understanding he'll recover. Somehow I see a great

deal of you in him. He refused to be denied his birthright.

The tragedy I have to tell you is that Sheine was not saved. She did not suffer, she died in her sleep. She cheated the devil and through her son she defeated and outlived Hitler. He lies buried in the ashes of Berlin, and her son now fights for the freedom of a new land that will one day soon be born . . . the State of Israel.

It pains me, dear Chavala, to be the bearer of such news, but we have shared the best and we will share whatever life has in store for us.

God takes away, but God gives back. Maybe that's what gives meaning to the whole thing.

Being both sisters and grandparents makes us closer than most. Our Pnina and Reuven were blessed with a baby girl. She was named Tikvah, and rightly so, for that is what she is . . . hope for the future.

She is very beautiful, Chavala. Pnina was very brave through it all, and Reuven was at her side.

Joshua has fallen madly in love with a delightful young woman you will more than approve of. She is a French Jewess, Simone Blum. She is a survivor of the Holocaust and a part of Aliyah Bet. Joshua has been very occupied, and if he has not written and told you about this it's not because he doesn't think about you. I'm sure you'll hear from him very soon.

I pray that this good news will at least help ease the loss of our beloved sister. Please take care and give my love to the family as I give mine to you.

Dvora

At another time Chavala's joy about Joshua and the birth of her first grandchild would have offset any sorrow. But nothing seemed to mitigate her grief over Sheine.

For days she lay in bed and brooded. She did not berate God. She did not question why. God wasn't responsible for the evils of man.

AND God was certainly not responsible—though perhaps his opposite, the Devil, was—for the disruptive violence of Haj Amim el Husseini, the mufti, who was running the Arab politics of Palestine from his exile now in Cairo. Thanks to him, the violence between the Arabs and Jews escalated. The British were increasingly unable, it seemed, to control the situation. The Haganah could no longer exercise its restraint. The jails were filled with Jews whose worst crime was to be charged with possessing a weapon, which was against British law.

Out of this turmoil the Irgun emerged into increased prominence. And the British proceeded to retaliate against the Irgun, including raids on the settlers of the kibbutzim—during one of which a sixteen-year-old girl was arrested for carrying a weapon concealed under her petticoat. She was taken to prison in Jerusalem, beaten and died of internal injuries with a British major watching.

Yehudah Rabinsky, formerly Erich Hausman, took it upon himself to avenge this girl's death—his feelings no doubt reinforced by his frustrated need to avenge his mother's end. Acting independently of the Irgun command, Yehudah and four other survivors of the Holocaust waylaid the British major as he parked his car. Next day he was found shot through the head. The Yishuv as well as the British was shocked. But for the British it was about the last straw. They could no longer even pretend to keep order. They had long ago, of course, sown the seeds of their troubles by betraying the Jews, by playing them off against the Arabs, and often favoring the Arabs while presumably being friends of the Jews, who had served them so well through two world wars. Palestine, they decided, was no longer worth the effort.

Chapter Thirty-nine

ON THE AFTERNOON of November 29, 1947, a five-thousand-year-old problem for the Jewish people was placed on the world's agenda. Zionist Chaim Weizmann and now-statesman Dovid Landau assembled in a cavernous gray building in Flushing Meadow, New York. Present were delegates of fifty-six members of the General Assembly of the United Nations. They had been called upon to decide the future of that small strip of land that ran along the eastern rim of the Mediterranean. No debate in the brief history of the United Nations had stirred the passions aroused by the controversy over the piece of land.

Dovid worked quietly behind the scenes. He had been delegated to keep up with the hourly shifts, find any weak spots, reassign his men to meet any unexpected changes and to become the chairman of any committee-room debates.

The Arabs had come to the Assembly confident of victory. The

Moslem bloc comprised eleven votes in the General Assembly. The Yishuv, which had contributed so much to the building of the land and to the Allied cause, had not a single vote.

On that afternoon the delegates from Palestine sat in a downtown hotel room, glued to the radio as the General Assembly of the United Nations was ordered into session.

Chavala sat alone in the gallery. There was a hush in the hall as the gavel came down and the Yishuv awaited its fate. The chairman stood behind the lectern and announced, "This Assembly is now in order and the rollcall for the nations on the partition resolution will begin. Two-thirds majority is needed for passage. Delegates will answer in one of three ways: for, against, or abstain."

Afghanistan was the first to be called on . . . verdict? . . . Against. The vote went on and on, until a shout erupted in that downtown hotel which housed the delegates from Palestine. After all those hours of agonizing waiting they had won their two-thirds majority . . . barely. *Mazel tov* was the word most heard.

Dovid read the tally, then picked up the phone and called the overseas operator and asked for Ben-Gurion's private number in Tel Aviv.

In Tel Aviv, as in every other city, kibbutz and moshav, pandemonium had broken out. In the streets of Tel Aviv there was dancing. Tears of joy rolled down the faces of the revelers. There were no strangers tonight. It was as though the entire Yishuv was one small, united family. Young boys kissed and embraced old ladies with wrinkled faces. There was dancing and singing and clapping and the storekeepers opened their doors . . . tonight everything was free . . . today a miracle had occurred . . . a long-awaited one.

When his phone call was finally acknowledged, Dovid said, "*Mazel tov.* It took a long time but we made it."

Ben-Gurion, the leader of the Yishuv, was not quite so exuberant. He knew the battle was only half-won. "Wait a minute, Dovid. There's so much going on in the street below I can barely hear you. Let me close the windows." He returned, picked up the phone and said, "That's better. Now, what were you saying, Dovid?"

"That we made it."

"Yes . . . but by the skin of our teeth. A long time ago I remember telling you on a leaking boat coming from Odessa that I was a builder, a builder of dreams. But the dream's not realized yet, Dovid. For the miracle to become a solid reality we'll have to fight for the independence of our state, and when we win that battle, then the dream I dreamed so long ago will have been worth the effort. Now, sleep well. And remember we've only just begun. *Shalom,* and come home soon."

Dovid hung up and looked at the silent phone for a long moment. Ben-Gurion's words were sobering. Dovid knew he was right, that only half the battle had been won and that the ultimate victory would no doubt still have to be fought with Jewish blood. Still, for at least a while, he didn't want to think about it. He just wanted to savor what they'd won. And for that he wanted to feel his wife Chavala in his arms. . . .

Together with her now, he poured champagne and toasted, "To the State of Israel."

Chavala then led him to the dining room, where she had prepared a celebratory supper. She told him what she'd seen through her binoculars from the upper gallery. "You should have seen those Arabs faces every time there was a yes vote . . . And what about Russia voting yes? You know how much *they* love the Jews . . . and the same with Poland . . . I loved it that the Catholic countries voted for us. I could have jumped right down from the balcony into the arms of, what was his name?"—she looked at the roster—"here it is, Professor Fabregat of Uruguay. And the delegate from Venezuela . . . I could have kissed them all. Oh, God, Dovid, it was so exciting."

Let Chavala be happy tonight. But like Ben-Gurion, Dovid knew that getting the partition of Palestine was only a prelude to winning independence. That would take much more than a two-thirds majority in the United Nations. "It was exciting," he said, but the tone of his voice was sobering to Chavala. She reached across the table, "What is it, Dovid?"

"What? Nothing . . . really, I'm very happy, I've worked and prayed all my life for this day."

She got up and went over to him, put her head against his shoulder. "Dovid, dearest, I'm so happy for you . . . for all of us, but I wish I'd had more faith. I thought the British would be in Palestine forever, and after that another empire. But you never once doubted. You were right, and I wrong—"

"*No,* Chavala. I think you believed more than you realized. We worked in different ways, but our dreams weren't so different. No matter how many miles separated us, I always felt we were together. I've never stopped feeling that way. I never will."

It was more than she had dared hope for, and she poured out her love for him in the way she knew best. As a woman . . . as a wife.

Chapter Forty

The next major task that lay ahead for the world Zionist groups was to launch a fundraising campaign for the purchase of arms.

That celebratory night in Tel Aviv, David Ben-Gurion turned to Golda Meir and said, "Golda, I think you better get ready to take a little trip."

As she poured the coffee in her kitchen and lit an ever-present cigarette, she said, "Me?" I'm the best you can think of? I haven't even got a new dress. Why don't you send Chaim Weizmann, he's got a beautiful new suit, or call Dovid Landau, he has a good mouth. That one knows how to talk."

"But you've got one thing they don't have. You've got the appeal of a woman, a mother with a heart that could make the Devil cry for mercy. Who could resist you, Golda?"

"Start with a dozen cabinet members."

Ben-Gurion laughed. "Them, I wouldn't worry about. From them you wouldn't get any money anyway."

The next day, with no more than the thin spring dress she wore and the handbag over her arm, she boarded a plane for New York. When she arrived on the evening of the following day, freezing in the bitter cold night, this remarkable woman who had come to New York in search of millions, had all of ten dollars in her purse. When the perplexed customs agent found that was all she had when he went through her belongings, he asked, "How are you going to get along on ten dollars?"

Her reply was, "I have a very big family here."

Two days later, trembling on a podium, Golda Meir found herself facing a distinguished gathering of members of that family. They were leaders of the Council of Jewish Federations who had come from forty-eight states of the Union. For the daughter of a Ukranian carpenter, the task ahead seemed impossible.

Now Golda Meir listened to the toastmaster announcing her name. After that, without a single note, she proceeded to weave her spell . . .

"You must believe me when I say that I have not come to the United States solely to prevent seven hundred thousand Jews from being wiped off the face of the earth. During these last years, the Jewish people have lost six million of their kind, and it would be presumptuous indeed of us to remind the Jews of the world that seven hundred thousand Jews are in danger. That is not the question. If, however, these seven hundred thousand Jews survive, then the Jews of the world will survive with them, and their freedom will be forever assured. If not, then there is little doubt that for centuries there will be no Jewish people, there will be no Jewish nation, and all our hopes will be smashed."

She paused, then went on, "In a few months a Jewish State will exist in Palestine. We shall fight for its birth. That is natural. We shall pay for it with our blood. That is normal. The best among us will fall, that is certain. But what is equally certain is that our morale will not waver no matter how numerous our invaders may be.

"I came here to ask you Jews of America, to plead for an almost impossible sum of money. It will take twenty-five to thirty million dollars to buy the heavy arms needed to face the invaders' inexhaustible arsenals." Again she paused, taking a sip of water. Then her deep, sad eyes looked out over the crowd and she went on.

"My friends, we live in a very brief present. When I tell you we need this money immediately, it does not mean next month, or in two months. It means right now . . .

"It is not for you to decide whether we shall continue our struggle or not. We shall fight. The Jewish community of Palestine will never hang out the white flag before the mufti of Jerusalem . . . but you can decide one thing—whether the victory will be ours or the mufti's."

The hush that had fallen over the audience convinced Golda that she had failed. Then the entire assembly of men and women rose in an overwhelming wave of applause. Immediately, while the echoes still rang through the room, volunteers scrambled to the platform with their pledges. Before dinner was over, Golda had been pledged over a million dollars, to be paid immediately in cash.

When the assembly left, Golda Meir sat alone at the long, empty table as the lights of the banquet hall began to dim. She couldn't quite believe what had taken place this evening. It was as though she hadn't spoken but that God had somehow whispered the words in her ears and she had merely repeated them. Totally spent, she lit a cigarette, picked up her cup of cold coffee and was about to sip from it when she looked up to see Dovid Landau standing in front of her, with an attractive woman alongside.

She recalled how much she had wanted him to do what she had miraculously managed to do this evening. "I'm happy to see you, Dovid, and delighted you stayed after all the others left . . . The response was something . . . I still can't get over it. But, still it's so good to see someone from home, someone you've shared so much with . . ."

"You were magnificent, Golda. No messenger of God or Israel could have equalled you."

Golda looked at him closely. She was not a shy woman, but compliments always embarrassed her. "It wasn't my eloquence that did it. It was the great need that our people have always rallied to."

"Only half true . . . Now, I would very much like you to meet my wife, Chavala."

Golda extended her hand to the attractive woman she'd noticed earlier. "It's my pleasure to meet Dovid's wife."

"And it's my honor," Chavala said, and quickly handed Golda Meir a check made out to the National Jewish Federation fund, in the amount of one million dollars.

Golda looked at it, then at Chavala. "In the name of Israel, I thank you."

Chavala swallowed back the tears. If there had been an Israel, her sister Sheine would not be lying in a shallow grave in a land where even that grave would have been considered a desecration. "This won't be the last . . . I only hope it will help."

Golda Meir answered simply, "It will help."

BACK home, Chavala thought about how once she'd actually hated Palestine. And a million dollars seemed barely a poor gesture in behalf of its rebirth.

Lying next to Dovid in the dark, she said, "When the British leave, there'll be a war, won't there, Dovid?"

"I'm afraid so."

Silence, then: "You know what I've been thinking, Dovid?"

"What? You're always thinking," and he turned to embrace her.

"No . . . Dovid . . . listen . . . I think I need a vacation."

He had to laugh. Chavala, of course, always had a plan. He could almost hear the gears meshing. "Where are you planning to go?"

"Israel, where else? I haven't seen my sons, Sheine's boy, my other nephews, to say nothing of my granddaughter."

"You've gotten pictures—sorry, sorry, a bad joke," he quickly said when she gave him a rap in the ribs. "How long a vacation?"

"I can't say, I'm not going to think about time. Now . . . if you think you could stay until the day after tomorrow, we could fly back together . . ."

He wanted to shout out his pleasure. They were facing a war, God only knew how bad or for how long, but at this moment none of it could intrude on the feeling he had from holding in his arms the woman that meant more to him than life itself.

WHEN they arrived in Israel, Chavala spent the first few days in Jerusalem seeing Raizel, then Dovid drove her to Dvora's where she would stay.

At Dvora's house in Kfar Shalom the pandemonium nearly equalled what had gone on in Tel Aviv the night Israel was voted its partition. Laughter, tears, whoops . . . and a sudden quieting when Chavala met her nephew, Sheine's son, Yehudah Rabinsky. Then once again laughter and exclamations at the sight of her granddaughter Tikvah. The child was almost two-and-a-half, and Pnina was expecting again. She laughed and cried at the sight of her handsome sons, and embraced Simone as though she were her daughter, and because soon she would be her daughter-in-law. And most of all because she had made Joshua so happy.

A week later, at Dvora and Ari's farm, Chavala and Dovid witnessed the marriage of Joshua and Simone. The *chuppah* was white satin, which Chavala sewed, insisting that she had never lost her touch. Everyone agreed she was right.

That morning the bride's coronet was made of white roses from Dvora's garden. The short tulle veil was placed beneath it. Her dress was a simple white embroidered organdy, and around her slim waist was a crushed cummerbund of the violet velvet. Simone carried the only thing she had left from her mother, a small Bible. Between the pages of the Book of Ruth was a white satin streamer to which was attached a spray of violets.

Joshua was dressed in his uniform, and wore a white satin *yarmulke*. Standing on either side of him were Dovid and Chavala. Since Simone had no parents, Dvora and Ari escorted her to Joshua. Reuven and Zvi waited near the *chuppah* even after the bride and groom were alongside each other.

The ceremony took place under the spreading almond tree in Dvora's garden. The rabbi who had married Pnina and Reuven performed the ceremony in front of the community of Kfar Shalom . . . they were all like family. After being pronounced man and wife, the groom kissed the bride, stomped on the glass, and the festivities began.

Cakes and cookies had been baked by the dozen in Dvora's kitchen. Homemade breads and rolls, roasted chickens, turkeys, salads and platters of fresh fruit strained the table's capacity to hold them. But it was a day of days. Even Raizel had consented to leave Mea Shearim and come with her sons, their wives and children. It was a day that would be remembered forever. A day of joy. A day of family.

Israel
1948

Chapter Forty-one

THE BRITISH, AT long last, were leaving.

It was May 14, 1948. British soldiers were leaving the old walled city of Jerusalem. There was a solemnity about them as they marched along the worn cobblestones in formation. At the head and the rear of each column one soldier held a Sten gun crooked in his arm. The sound of bagpipes reverberated inside these ancient stone passageways for the last time.

Along the Street of the Jews from the sculptured stone windows of their synagogues and the mildewed hallways of the sacred houses of learning, bearded old men watched them pass by, watched as their ancestors before them had watched other soldiers march out of Jerusalem—Babylonians, Romans, Crusaders, Turks, and now the last, one prayed, were leaving.

As the last British column moved down the street, it veered left up a twisting cobblestone alley and stopped in front of the Hurva Synagogue. Inside, surrounded by his collection of holy books, Rabbi Mordechai Weingarten, an elder of the Jewish Quarter, hesitated for a moment at the knock on the door of his private study. He got up, put on his black long coat, adjusted the old rimmed spectacles, then his black hat, and stepped out into the courtyard.

In front of the rabbi stood a middle-aged British major wearing the yellow-and-red insignia of the Suffolk regiment. From his right hand dangled a bar of rusted iron. With a solemn gesture he offered it to the elderly rabbi. The old man looked down at the object in his hand and then said, "This is the key to the Zion Gate. From the year of 70 A.D. until this moment a key to the gates of Jerusalem has never been in Jewish hands. This is the first time in eighteen centuries that our people have possessed it."

Extending a trembling hand, Weingarten held the hand of the British major as the British major accepted the gesture, then stood at attention and saluted. "I regret to say that our relations have often been strained, but let us part as friends. Good-bye and good luck."

The Englishman turned and marched his men out of the courtyard as the rabbi intoned, "Blessed art thou, Oh God, who has granted us life and sustenance and permitted us to reach this day."

Scenes elsewhere that day were not quite so benign or touching. As Sir Alan Cunningham, the last British High Commissioner for Palestine, sailed from Haifa he deliberately left behind a chaotic land without police or public services, confident that the Arab superiority of numbers would fill the vacuum.

On that day in another part of the world, London to be exact, Whitehall had been hopeful almost up until the very end that, after the ratification of the partition and with the problems that had fallen on the Jews, the Yishuv would turn to the British for help. But the Yishuv that had stood up to the terror and bloodshed of Haj Amim el Husseini would not ask the British for its help now. . . .

In another part of what was now the State of Israel, five Arab countries were poised like vultures at the borders of Israel, only waiting for the British to evacuate so that they could wage their holy war against the Israelis. . . .

At Israeli General Headquarters, Israel's commanders had been assembled. They listened now to their leader, their Commander-in-Chief, Binya Yariv. Yariv looked at the young faces of his commanding officers and said, "I hardly need tell you that by tomorrow morning we will be at war. It will be an undeclared war. We need no formal declarations, we know who the aggressors are. Now let us get down to it."

Yariv took a sip of water, cleared his throat and looked at a few notes. "The strength of the invading Arab armies has been estimated at twenty-three thousand five hundred. They are equipped with British and French tanks, airplanes, heavy artillery, spare parts and ammunition. We have some three thousand regulars under arms and approximately fourteen thousand inadequately trained recruits, most of which have come from the camps. The others are newly arrived immigrants. They may be raw, but they are on fire with the conviction that we have no alternative except to win. *Never again Masada* is their faith, and ours." Yariv flipped over the sheet of notes and went on. "Now, what we have in the way of arms is only ten thousand rifles with fifty rounds of ammunition each, no tanks, four ancient cannons smuggled in from Mexico, and thirty-six hundred submachine guns . . . and a very unusual piece of hardware called the Davidka."

Yariv smiled. "We can thank God for its inventor, David Leibovitch. It's made up from waterpipes and packed with explosives, nails and bits of scrap metal, and it's about as effective as David's slingshot when it comes to destruction. But it's at least accurate and it makes a hell of a lot of noise, enough, we hope, to make the Arabs run.

"Now, with the British gone, Dovid Landau tells me that those arms that have been stored in Alexandria by him are already en route, and that he's making progress in Czechoslovakia. He told me this last night. This morning when I spoke to him from Paris he had purchased two small one-engine planes. A little obsolete, but they can at least drop hand grenades . . . All right, gentlemen, let's break for lunch and then we'll get on with the campaign."

After a brief luncheon, the men stood around the campaign table and scanned the maps.

Pointing to the sectors, Yariv said, "You, Daniel Avriel, will take command of the Negev . . . Ehud Biton, you will defend the Galilee . . . Dov Laskin, the Huleh . . . Nachman Messer, Tel Aviv up to Haifa. You will all have your instructions shortly." He looked at Reuven. "I don't have to tell you what we're up against, or that the most important of all is Jerusalem . . . anything we gain will be a loss unless Jerusalem holds . . . without Jerusalem there will be no Israel. Reuven Landau will take command. Joshua Landau will be second in command, and Zvi Ben-Levi will act as liaison."

Yariv paused and tried to put out of his mind what these young commanding officers would be facing . . . outnumbered, with a small cache of arms, they would truly have to fight like the lions of Judea . . .

"And you, Yehudah Rabinsky, will be in command of Tiberias, Hebron and Safed . . . Safed is the most vulnerable." And almost in a jocular tone he added, "I suggest to you, Yehudah, that you equip yourself with a Davidka . . . the Arabs are firmly in control of those cities. Now, I wish you God's speed. And more than your share of good luck . . ."

And so the Holy War began. In the south the Egyptian forces jumped off from their advance bases in Sinai and crossed the frontier. Passing through Arab-populated territory, one group moved up the coastal road to Gaza, another landed by ship at Majdal further north while a third drove up from Abu Aweigila northeast to Beersheba, some of its units pressing on to the Arab town of Hebron, where they linked up with Trans-Jordan's Arab legion and took up positions just south of Jerusalem. Their main thrust was aimed at Tel Aviv.

The fighting was fierce, and both sides suffered great losses.

Any loss for the Haganah was devastating. Twenty-seven settlements had been badly hurt. But the loss of Yad Mordechai was the most crushing blow the Haganah could have. That *kibbutz* was special. It had been born out of the Warsaw Ghetto uprising of 1943. It had been named after a twenty-two-year-old man who took command and helped fight off the Nazis for forty-two days and nights with almost no weapons. He died, of course, but in dignity. He had not been led to slaughter like an animal. But that kibbutz was also considered by the Egyptians vital to liquidate if they were to proceed with their drive on Tel Aviv. Yad Mordechai was on the coastal highway between Gaza and Majdal and blocked the link-up of two important Egyptian bases. The fighting was terrible. The defenders were outnumbered, but it took the Egyptians five days of hard fighting to overcome them. But finally Yad Mordechai fell. Its resistance, though, had been crucial to the Haganah cause. It had held up the main Egyptian advance and was able to strengthen the Haganah defenses near Tel Aviv, thereby buying a little time for Jerusalem. . . .

At his headquarters outside of Jerusalem, Reuven spoke to his unit. "I'm sending a small squad into the Old City and up to Mount Scopus. If we can hold and capture that sector, then we'll have a better chance of taking the New City."

When he sent that small squad into old Jerusalem, Reuven had hoped that because within the walls of that city were the remains of Christian and Moslem shrines, the Old City would be left untouched. Which was why he'd sent such a small garrison of men to be used for defense of the Jews only.

But from the top of Mount Scopus fifteen vehicles bringing down doctors, nurses and scientists from Hadassah Hospital were attacked, and the dead bodies were desecrated by the Jordanians. The Haganah within the Old City was doomed by the strength of the overpowering Jordanian army.

On May 29, 1948, after ten weeks of violent fighting following the proclamation of the State of Israel, the Jewish Quarter of the Old City was in flame. Pillars of smoke marked the end of almost two thousand years of Jewish residence in the ancient alleys beside the western wall, the famous Wailing Wall. There were few survivors, civilian or military. . . .

Reuven could not reconcile himself to the loss of Old Jerusalem. He questioned whether he was the right one to be defending Jerusalem. Yariv told him differently. "When a soldier stops feeling, he no longer is a human being, and for you to feel as you do makes you more human."

Still, even after the loss of the Old City of Jerusalem, West Jerusalem remained intact and in possession of the Israelis. But Reuven realized that they were still in desperate straits . . . West Jerusalem hadn't fallen, but its one hundred thousand Jewish citizens were holding out on a starvation food ration. And even worse was the shortage of water. The pipelines bringing water to the city had been ruptured, and Jerusalem had to survive on the water stored in its reservoir and in the cisterns under private homes. The People's Guard, mostly elderly men, took over the distribution of the water.

To break the siege of Jerusalem, Reuven knew, he had to capture Latrun. The first attempt was thrown back by the Arabs. A second and third also failed. Jerusalem was on the edge of starvation.

Reuven hadn't slept for days. His eyes were hollows, his cheeks sunken, and his spirits in no better shape. As he sat at his desk looking for the answer, a soldier delivered a note. Quickly, he tore it open, and his spirits were lifted. Pnina had given birth to a baby son.

Maybe it was the inspiration of his son's birth . . . he didn't know . . . but from whatever source it came he thought he'd hit on a possible way to save Jerusalem.

He summoned his men to headquarters. "Between Jerusalem and the coast there's a link and it's serviceable. There's a rough dirt track, broken by a steep *wadi,* and maybe if we work day and night we can make it fit for vehicles to pass through."

As it was being dug out and smoothed, the men dubbed it the "Burma Road." Before it was finished, within five kilometers of the most difficult terrain still separating the sappers working up from Tel Aviv from those working down from Jerusalem, food began to pass into Jerusalem.

The opening of the Burma Road came just in time. Unknown to the Arabs—and to the Jewish population of Jerusalem itself—the city was down to one day's ration of bread. Now Jerusalem was linked to the coastal plain and soon afterward the piping of water to Jerusalem was resumed. The siege was over. The long, hard battle for Jerusalem was won, but at a great price. Especially for the Landau family.

Joshua Landau was dead. He lay on the bloodstained cobblestones. A sniper who had heard of the truce wanted to give Allah one more sacrifice, and between the turrets at the Old Wall he shot the Jew through the heart.

REUVEN was at his headquarters in West Jerusalem when Zadok Ben-Ami, a member of his unit, came in white-faced and stood at attention in front of his commanding officer. There had never been any formality among the officers and their men, but Zadok now stood ramrod-straight, eyes forward. He saluted. Reuven nodded with some irritation and casually returned the salute. "Yes, Zadok?"

The man seemed unable to speak. "What's the problem, speak up."

"It's . . . Joshua."

Reuven knew immediately, he didn't need to hear the words. But his mind refused to believe, to accept . . . *"What about Joshua?"*

". . . He's been shot, Reuven . . ."

Reuven found himself running into the streets, as though he would find Joshua there and prove this was all a stupid lie.

Zadok Ben-Ami went after him, took his arm and gently led him to where Joshua was.

Reuven dropped to his knees. He turned his brother over, lifted him and held him in his arms, rocking him back and forth like a small child. And in his grief he said, "You were my brother, my responsibility . . . I wasn't there when you needed me . . ."

When the litter came to take Joshua away, Reuven was still on his knees. He looked down at his hands, red with Joshua's blood. Zadok tried to help Reuven up and was pushed away. It was several moments later that Reuven was able to get off his knees and walk slowly back to headquarters, Zadok following.

In his office, the door closed behind him, Reuven sat and thought about all the years he'd spent training his brother to be a soldier. To be brave, never to be afraid . . . He thought back to the night of Joshua's birth, the first time he'd seen him in Dovid's arms. He'd loved Joshua from that very first moment, and now he was gone . . . And Simone, a young bride and now a widow . . . she'd given Joshua so much, but she couldn't give him the days of life to see the child she now carried.

How long he sat there he didn't know, but he did know he didn't want to see his father or his mother, not yet. First he had to see his newborn son. He had to hold him and feel him and know there was something new and *alive* in the old world built on old hates and death . . . Well, his stubborn people would refuse to die. They would *not* die, and they would never give up . . . When would the world believe them?

PNINA tried to comfort him. He only took his child in his arms, and more to himself than to Pnina he said, "We'll change his name from Jonathan to Joshua. They both mean the same. Both died in battle. May this Joshua be more blessed with long life than his namesake . . . ."

When Reuven went to his father, he was almost as tongue-tied as the soldier who'd tried to tell him about Joshua's death.

Dovid immediately went to Chavala. The moment Dovid walked into Dvora's house, Chavala knew . . . knew from the anguish in his eyes that nothing could hide. She knew one of her sons was dead, but which one? "Dovid, I know," she said, "just tell me who."

He held her close, and barely managed to whisper Joshua's name.

She trembled uncontrollably, but at this moment there was not a tear. Only the words . . . "My baby . . . my little boy . . . my Joshua . . . my youngest baby . . . my baby son . . . ."

The Landaus' was not the only grief in Kfar Shalom, nor were they the only family to lose a son. Thirty sons and daughters were buried. It was a village in deep mourning. All throughout Israel there were young widows and grieving parents. The faith of their fathers was put to the extreme test.

Simone was near-unconsolable, and Chavala reached out to her. They seemed to comfort one another. For to Chavala, Simone was like Tikvah . . . her hope. She carried Joshua's child.

ALMOST from the very beginning, when he'd first been brought back into the family circle, Yehudah Rabinsky had felt a special closeness to Simone. She too had lived through the Holocaust. Both were survivors whose parents had died. There were times when they revealed things to each other that were left unsaid to any one else. A special bond existed between them. Simone could understand that Jews had been a "necessary commodity" to the Germans. Simone knew that Jews built the concentration camps by their labor, that Jewish bones had been crushed to be used as fertilizer. Yehudah could talk to her about the gold extracted from the teeth, about warehouses of eyeglasses and storage houses of hair to be used for mattresses. About fat used for soap and skin for lampshades. He and Simone had lived through it all. Maybe her circumstances during those terrible years hadn't quite been his, but she had suffered as he had. They shared the awful memory of each other's private horrors.

Now she was the widow of his dead cousin. He felt an even greater bond with her. He wanted to comfort her, perhaps love her. Privately he hoped that in time she would reach out to him, as the one who could best understand her deep pain. In time she might want, need a father for her child. But most important, he wanted to become a father to Joshua's child . . . he owed Joshua his life. His sanity.

ON June 11, 1948, the United Nations peacekeeping effort brought a ceasefire. Israel had won the War of Independence, and for the moment there was an end to hostilities. For the moment.

THE months passed slowly. On August 22 Simone brought forth a new life. Joshua's baby.

Chavala held her youngest grandchild in her arms. With Dovid at her side, they looked down at this precious little girl, both silently remembering the night Joshua was born.

When the baby was to be named, Simone asked Chavala if she would like to make the choice. Chavala looked at this beautiful young woman who had become like a daughter and understood why Simone had offered her this gift. She was telling her that she too would be a mother to this child, this child who was all she would have in life of her dead son . . .

Chavala nodded and said, *"Eliana . . .* Hebrew is such a rich language . . . that name means so much . . . 'My God answers.' Well, He has. You gave us Joshua's child."

CHAVALA had been in Israel for almost a year now. They'd not spoken of it, but Dovid was sure she'd be getting back soon. Moishe had been calling more frequently from America about urgent business matters. Chavala had, after all, built a small empire and had many obligations . . .

This day, they sat under the almond tree in Dvora's garden, Dovid said, "Well, darling, you came for a 'vacation,' and I hope it never ends . . ." He certainly wouldn't be the one to mention her going home.

She looked down at Eliana, sleeping in her arms. "You know, Dovid, for a long time I never really knew where home was. When I went to America, I wasn't convinced then. But I thought it was a necessity. Now?

With one son gone and the other with two children . . . my Israeli family here and a Jewish State being born . . . well, who knows?"

"What about your business?" He hardly dared hope she was saying what he thought.

"I've thought about that. I don't know . . ."

"You've built a great deal, you did so much, and all on your own."

"No, Dovid. No one builds anything on their own. I had help . . . from God and a few good friends . . . Which gets us back to where home is. You know what I think?"

"No . . ." He could only hope.

"That *you* are home to me, Dovid. And that Israel is where I belong."

He didn't say a word. He was afraid she might change her mind.

"And as for my great business . . . I'm not so needed. Let Moishe take it over. He's very capable and it's about time he stopped depending so much on me. Julie loves the business, and so does Chia, and her husband is a good lawyer. He'll make it into a family corporation. I don't need it any longer. What I need is *you.* I always did, in case it's news to you."

Dovid was six inches off the ground. "Where do you want to live? In the hills of Haifa, in a big house you talked about to Dvora once?"

"No, Dovid, I was mistaken then. It doesn't matter what hill you live on. It's who you live on it with. Do you know what I would love? To buy a nice farm here at Kfar Shalom and build a house with a lot of bedrooms for the grandchildren, a big dining room to use for Passover and simchas. And I'd like a wide porch. The American family can come whenever they want. And someday, when you decide to slow down, you can take hold of a plow again . . . you always loved the land so much, Dovid."

He laughed. "And you always hated farming."

"So, where is it written I have to be a farmer? You farm and I'll cook and I'll have the *naches* of seeing my grandchildren running out of their *bubbe* and *zayde*'s house." She smiled for the first time in a very long time, a truly contented smile.

"You know, Dovid, I love Hebrew, but somehow grandma and grandpa in Yiddish sound better. More like what they really are. That's good. It's time we all faced up to what we really are, and be thankful for it . . .